REGENCY
Gamble

Bronwyn
Scott

MILLS
BOON

D0332776

First Published in Great Britain 2016
By Mills & Boon, an imprint of HarperCollins*Publishers*
1 London Bridge Street, London, SE1 9GF

REGENCY GAMBLE © 2016 Harlequin Books S.A.

A Lady Risks All © 2013 Nikki Poppen
A Lady Dares © 2013 Nikki Poppen

ISBN: 978-0-263-92372-8

52-0916

Our policy is to use papers that are natural, renewable and recyclable products and made from wood grown in sustainable forests. The logging and manufacturing processes conform to the legal environmental regulations of the country of origin.

Printed and bound by
CPI Group (UK) Ltd, Croydon, CR0 4YY

**ROM
Pbk**

A REGENCY

Collection

A Lady Risks All

This one is for my dad who kept asking me
when was that billiards book coming out.
Here it is, finally, with much love.

Bronwyn Scott is a communications instructor at Pierce College in the United States, and is the proud mother of three wonderful children—one boy and two girls. When she's not teaching or writing she enjoys playing the piano, travelling—especially to Florence, Italy—and studying history and foreign languages. Readers can stay in touch on Bronwyn's website, www.bronwynnscott.com, or at her blog, www.bronwynswriting.blogspot.com. She loves to hear from readers.

Chapter One

Brighton—March 1837

There was nothing quite as exhilarating as a man who knew how to handle his stick. Mercedes Lockhart put an eye to the discreet peephole for a second glimpse, separate trills of excitement and anxiety vibrating through her. Rumour was right, he *did* have an amazing crack.

Outside in the billiards hall, that crack would sound like a cannon. But here in the soundproof peeping room, she could only watch and worry about what his presence in her father's club meant.

There's someone I want you to meet. The phrase rang through her head for the hundredth time. When fathers said that to their daughters it usually meant one thing: a suitor. But those fathers weren't billiards great Allen Lockhart. He was more likely to bring home a gem-studded cue than a suitor. Perhaps that was the reason she'd been so surprised by the summons. 'Come down to the club, there's someone I want you to watch,' he'd

said. It had been a long time since he'd needed her in
that way. She didn't dare refuse. So, here she was, ensconced in the 'viewing room', eye riveted to the peephole, taking in the player at table three.

He was a man she'd have noticed even without her
father's regard. Most women would. He was well built;
broad shouldered and lean hipped, an observation made
inescapable by the fact he was playing with his coat off.
At the moment, he was bent at the waist and levelling
his cue for the next shot, a posture that offered her a silhouette of trim waist and tautly curved buttock, framed
by muscled thighs that tensed ever so slightly beneath
the tight fawn of his breeches.

Her eyes roamed upwards to the strong forearms
displayed tan against the rolled back cuffs of his white
shirtsleeves, to the taper of lean fingers forming a
bridge through which his cue stick slid effortlessly,
expertly as he made his shot.

He straightened and turned in her direction, accepting congratulations on the shot. He pushed back
the blond hair that had fallen over his face. Mercedes
caught a glimpse of startling blue eyes; a deep shade
of sapphire she could appreciate even at a distance. He
was confident, not cocky in the way he accepted the
congratulations of others. There was no doubt he handled his cue with ease, his playing strategy sound but
straightforward, his use of the 'break' progressive and
in line with the new style billiards was starting to take.

But Mercedes could see immediately there wasn't
a lot of finesse in it. It was understandable. A player
with his skill likely didn't see the need for finer mach-

inations. That was something that could be improved upon. Mercedes halted her thoughts right there. Why? Why should she improve him? Is that what her father wanted her opinion for? What interest did the legendary Lockhart want with a handsome young billiards player? The anxiety that had plagued her trilled again. Was he a suitor for her? A protégé for her father?

Neither option sat well with her. She had no intentions to marry although she was aware of her father's ambition for her to wed a title. It would be the final feather in his cap of self-made glory—Allen Lockhart's daughter married to a peer of the realm! But she had other goals and neither a suitor nor a protégé was among them.

Mercedes stepped back from the peephole and scribbled a short note to her father, who sat in the main room in plain sight. There was no skulking in private viewing chambers for him, she thought with no small amount of frustration. It hadn't always been like this: spying through peepholes and pretending she didn't exist. It used to be that she had the run of the place. But she'd grown up and it was no longer seemly or prudent, as past events had proven, for her to roam the halls of Lockhart's Billiards Club, no matter how elegant the setting or how skilled the player. The bottom line was that men didn't like to be beaten by a woman. Thus had ended her career of playing in public. For now.

This was why the thought of a protégé met with her disapproval. If there was to be one, it *should* be her. She'd honed her own skill at her father's side. When she'd shown some aptitude for the game, he'd taught her to play as only a professional can. She'd learned his secrets and developed her own until she was on par with the best. Then she'd committed the crime of turning seventeen and her freedoms had been curtailed; in part by society and in part by her own headstrong judgement.

It was something of a curse that the one thing she was good at—no, not merely good at, excellent at—was a talent she did not get to display. These days she practised for herself, alone in the privacy of their home and she waited, forever ready if the chance to prove herself came her way.

Mercedes folded the note and sent it out to her father. She bent her eye to the peephole one last time, a thought occurring to her as she watched the man pot his final ball. Maybe he was her chance. Her earlier excitement started to hum again. She'd been waiting five years for her opportunity, alert for any possibility. In all that time, she'd never thought her chance would come in the form of a handsome Englishman—she'd had her fill of those. But if her father could use him, perhaps she could too.

Slow down, she cautioned herself. A good gambler always assessed the risk and there *was* risk here. If her father intended him to be a protégé and she assisted with that, she could effectively cut herself out of the picture altogether. She would have to go carefully. On the other hand, it would be a chance to show her father what she could do in a situation where he would be unable to deny her talent.

It was a venture that could see her exiled or elevated,

but she was nothing if not her father's daughter; a gambler at heart who knew the risks and rules of any engagement and chose to play anyway.

Gamblers of any successful repute generally acknowledged the secret to luck resided in knowing three things: the rules, the stakes and when to quit. No one knew this better than English billiards legend, Allen Lockhart. He couldn't remember a time when the stakes hadn't been high—they always were when all one had to risk was a reputation. As for quitting—if there was a time to quit, he hadn't discovered it yet, which was why the usual ritual of a brandy with long-time friend and partner, Kendall Carlisle, did not fill him with the usual satisfaction on this dreary March afternoon.

Normally this time of day was his favourite. It was a time when he could sit back in one of the club's deep chairs and savour his domain. *His domain.* Carlisle managed the place, but it had been *his* billiards money that had built this and more.

Across from him, oblivious to his restless observations, Carlisle took a swallow of brandy followed by a contented sigh. 'This is the life, Allen. Not bad for two junior boot boys.'

Allen smiled in response. It was a well-loved reminiscence of his. The two of them had done well over the years kowtowing to the rich gentlemen in the subscription rooms of Bath for shillings. They'd watched and they'd learned, eventually establishing their own small empire. Now *they* were the rich gentlemen. Now *they* ran the subscription rooms, not in Bath, but in more lucrative Brighton. They earned much more than shillings from customers these days. At the age of forty-seven, Allen Lockhart took great pride in having used the rules of billiards to rise above his poor beginnings.

From their grouping of chairs by the fire, Allen could hear the quiet snick of ivory balls on baize, the unmistakable sounds of lazy-afternoon billiard games going on in the room beyond him. Later in the evening, the club would be crowded with officers and gentlemen, the tables loud with the intensity of money games.

Allen felt his hand twitch in anticipation of the games to come. He didn't play in public often anymore, not wanting to tarnish his image by making himself vulnerable to defeat. A legend couldn't be beaten too often without damaging the illusion of being untouchable. But the desire was still there. Billiards was in his blood. He was the legendary Allen Lockhart, after all. He'd built this club on his fame. People came here to play, of course, but also to see him. It wasn't enough to be good at billiards; one also had to be a showman.

He knew the power of a well-placed word here, a timely stroke tip there. It was heady stuff to think people would talk about a single sentence from him for months in London. 'Lockhart says you have to hit the ball from the side' or 'Lockhart recommends African ivory for balls'. But lately, the usual thrill had faded. Such excitement had become *de rigueur*. He was restless.

The resounding crack of a hard break shattered the laconic atmosphere of the room. Allen briefly acknowledged it with a swift glance towards table three where a young officer played before turning back to Kendall. 'I hope you're coming up to the house tomorrow for the party.'

'I wouldn't miss it. I'm looking forward to seeing the new table.' Carlisle raised his glass in a toast. 'I hear Thurston has outdone himself this time.'

Lockhart grinned broadly like a proud first-time father. 'Slate tables with rubber bumpers are the way of the future. They're fast, Kendall.' Another loud break from table three interrupted. This time Lockhart spared the table more than a passing glance. 'Good Lord, that lad's got some power.' He chanced a look in the direction of the secret viewing room and wondered what Mercedes would make of it. Kendall hadn't lied when he'd said the lad could play.

Their chairs were angled to take in the expanse of the elegant club if they chose. Both men fell silent, focusing on the game, looking out into the well-appointed billiards floor. Long windows let in enormous amounts of light for quality shots. Subtle forest-green wallpapering with matching floor-to-ceiling curtains gave the room the air of a sophisticated drawing room. This was no mean gambling hall. This was a place meant to invite a higher class of gentleman to engage in the noble sport of billiards and right now table three was heavily engaged.

The 'lad' in question was not a boy at all, but a blond-haired officer with the broad-shouldered build of a handsomely put-together man. A confident man too, Lockhart noted. Effortless charm and affability poured off him as he potted the third ball and proceeded to run the table. Affable and yet without any feigned humility.

'He reminds me of you back in our salad days,' Carlisle murmured after the officer made a particularly difficult corner shot.

'How old do you think he is?' Kendall would know. Information gathering was Kendall's gift. His own was using it. The combined talent had been invaluable to them both over the years.

'Mid-twenties. He's been in a few times. His name's Barrington. Captain Barrington,' Kendall supplied as Lockhart had known he would.

At that age, he and Kendall had been living on the road, Lockhart thought wistfully. They'd played any money game they could find in just about every assembly hall between Manchester and London. They'd run just about every 'angle' too—plucking peacocks, two friends and a stranger and a hundred more.

'He's bought a subscription,' Kendall volunteered.

'On half-pay?' Any officer in town these days with time for billiards was on half-pay. But on that salary, a subscription to his fine establishment was a luxury unless one had other resources.

Kendall shrugged. 'I cut him a fair deal. He's good for business. People like to play him.'

'For a while.' Lockhart shrugged. Barrington would have to be managed. If he was too good, players would tire of getting beaten and that would be just as bad for business. He didn't want that to happen too quickly.

'With the big championship coming up in July, I thought he might generate some additional interest,' Carlisle began, but Lockhart's mind was already steps ahead. Perhaps the Captain could be taught when to lose, perhaps he could be taught a lot of things. Carlisle was right. The young man could be very useful in the months leading up to the All England Billiards Championship. The old thrill began to course.

'Thinking about taking a protégé?' Kendall joked.

'Maybe.' He was thinking about taking more than a protégé. He was thinking about taking a trip. For what reason, he wasn't sure yet. Perhaps the urge was nothing more than a desire to walk down memory lane one more time and relive the nostalgia of the old days. Perhaps he wanted more? His intuition suggested his restlessness was more than nostalgic desire. There were bigger questions to answer. At forty-seven, did he still have it? Could the legend make a comeback or was the 'new' game beyond him?

'Is that all you're thinking?' He felt Kendall's shrewd gaze on him and kept his own eyes on the game. It would be best not to give too much away, even to his best friend, if this was going to work. A footman approached with a folded note. Ah, Mercedes had announced her verdict.

Lockhart rose, flicking a cursory glance at the simple content of Mercedes's note and made his excuses, careful to school his features. Kendall knew him too well. 'I've got to go and see about some business.' Then he paused as if an inspiration had struck suddenly. 'Invite our young man up to the house tomorrow night. It might be fun for him to see the new table and I want him to meet Mercedes.'

If he was going to try this madcap venture at all, he would need her help. She'd already consented to the first bit by coming down today. The hard part would be convincing her to try it all on. She could be deuced stubborn when she put her mind to it. With any luck, he wouldn't have to do the convincing. He'd leave that to a certain officer's good looks, extraordinary talent with a billiards cue and a little moonlit magic. He knew his daughter. If there was anything Mercedes couldn't resist it was a challenge.

Chapter Two

Captain Greer Barrington of the Eleventh Devonshire had seen enough of the world in his ten years of military service to know when the game was afoot. It was definitely afoot tonight, and it had been ever since Kendall Carlisle had offered him an invitation to the Lockhart party. There seemed little obvious logic in a man of Lockhart's celebrity inviting an anonymous officer to dine.

Greer surveyed the small assemblage with a quick gaze as Allen Lockhart greeted him and drew him into the group of men near the fireplace, a tall elegant affair topped with a mantel of carved walnut. Suspicions confirmed. First, the small size of the gathering meant this was a special, intimate cohort of friends and professional acquaintances. Second, Allen Lockhart lived finely in one of the forty-two large town houses that comprised Brunswick Terrace. Greer had not been wrong in taking the effort to arrive polished to perfection for the evening, and now the buttons on his uniform gleamed appreciably under the light of expensive brass-and-glass chandeliers.

'You know Kendall Carlisle already from the club, of course.' Allen Lockhart made the necessary introductions with the ease of a practised host. 'This is John Thurston, the man behind the manufacture of the new table.' Greer nodded in the man's direction. He knew of Thurston. The man ran a billiards works in London and a billiards hall off St James's.

'John,' Lockhart said with great familiarity, 'this is Captain Greer Barrington.' Lockhart had a fatherly hand at his shoulder and Greer did not miss the reference. Either Lockhart was a quick study of military uniforms or he'd done his research. 'The Captain has a blistering break—sounds like a cannon going off in the club every time. He ran the table on Elias Pole yesterday.'

Ah, Greer thought. So Lockhart *had* been watching. He'd thought he'd sensed the other man's interest in his game. Appreciative murmurs followed with more introductions.

Talk turned to billiards until a young woman materialised at Lockhart's side, stopping all conversation— something she would have done without saying a word. 'Father, dinner will be served shortly.'

This gorgeous creature was Lockhart's daughter? Whatever game was afoot, Greer mused, he'd gladly play it and see where it went if she was involved. There was no arguing her beauty. It was bold and forthright like the flash of a smile she threw his direction.

'Captain, you haven't met my daughter, Mercedes,'

Lockhart said affably. 'Perhaps I could persuade you to take her in to dinner? I believe she's seated you with her at the one end.'

'It would be my pleasure, Miss Lockhart.' Yet another pleasant addition to the evening. This invitation was turning out splendidly. Mercedes Lockhart was a stunning young woman with dark hair and wide grey eyes framed with long lashes. But there was an icy quality to that perfection. Beautiful and cold, Greer noted. Greer was confident he could change that. He smiled one of his charming smiles, the one that usually made women feel as if they'd known him much longer than they had.

She was less than charmed. Her own smile did not move from that of practised politeness, her sharp grey eyes conducting a judicious perusal of their own. Greer stepped back discreetly from the group, drawing her with him until he had space for a conversation of his own.

'Do I pass?' Greer queried, determined to make this haughty beauty accountable for her actions.

'Pass what?'

'Inspection is what we call it in the military.'

She blushed a little at his bluntness and he took the small victory. She looked warmer when she blushed, prettier too if that was possible, the untouchable coldness of her earlier hauteur melting into more feminine features.

'I must admit more than a passing curiosity to see the man who beat Elias Pole. My father talked of nothing else at supper last night.'

There was a fleeting bitterness in her tone, some of her hard elegance returning. Provoked by what? Jealousy? The defeat of her champion? Elias Pole was a man of middle years, not unattractive for his age, but certainly he wasn't the type to capture the attentions of a young woman.

Greer shrugged easily. 'I am flattered I aroused your curiosity. But it was just a game.'

Her eyebrows shot up at that, challenge and mild disbelief evident in her voice. 'Just a game? Not to these men. It would be very dangerous to think otherwise, Captain.'

Ah. Illumination at last, Greer thought with satisfaction. Now he had a better idea of why he was here. This was about billiards.

Dinner was announced and he took the lovely Mercedes into supper, her hand polite and formal on the sleeve of his coat. The dining room was impressive with its long polished table set with china and crystal, surrounded by the accoutrements of a man who lived well and expensively: silver on the matching sideboards and decanter sets no doubt blown in Venice.

Greer recognised the subtle signs of affluence and he knew what they meant. Allen Lockhart aspired to be a gentleman. Of course, Lockhart wasn't. Couldn't be. Lockhart was a billiards player, a famous billiards player. But fame could only advance a man so far.

That was the difference between Lockhart's shiny prosperity and the time-worn elegance of Greer's family estate. Greer's father might not be wealthy by the exorbitant standards of the *ton*, but he'd always be a gentleman and so would his sons. No amount of money could change that. Nevertheless, Greer knew his mother and sisters would be pea-green with envy to see him sitting down to supper in this fine room. He made a mental note to send them a letter describing the evening *sans* its circumstances. His father would be furious to think any son of his had sat down to supper with a gambler, even if the son in question wasn't the heir.

Greer pushed thoughts of family and home out of his mind. Those thoughts would only make him cross. Tonight he wanted to enjoy his surroundings without guilt. He had delicious food on his plate, excellent wine in his goblet, interesting conversation and a beautiful woman in need of wooing beside him. He meant to make the most of it. Life in the military had taught him such pleasures were fleeting and few, so best to savour them to the fullest when they crossed one's path. Life had been hard these past ten years and Greer intended to do a lot of savouring now that he was back in England.

'Where were you stationed, Captain?' A man to his right asked as the fish course was served.

'Corfu, although we moved up and down the peninsula with some regularity,' Greer answered.

Corfu caught John Thurston's attention. 'Then you may have played on the table we made for the mess hall there.'

Greer laughed, struck by the coincidence. 'Yes, indeed I did. That table was for the 42nd Royal Hussars. I wasn't with that regiment, but I did have the good fortune of visiting a few times. The new rubber bumpers made it the fastest game to be had in Greece.'

John Thurston raised his glass good-naturedly. 'What a marvellously modern world we live in. To think I'd actually be sitting down to supper with a man who played on one of my tables a thousand miles away. It's quite miraculous what technology has allowed us to do. To a smaller world, gentlemen.'

'My sentiments exactly.' Greer drank to the toast and applied himself to the fish, content to let the conversation flow around him. One learned a lot of interesting things when one listened and observed. Mercedes Lockhart must think the same thing. She was studying him once more. He could feel her gaze returning to him time and again. He looked in her direction, hoping to make her blush once more.

This time she was ready for him. She met his gaze evenly, giving every indication she'd meant to be caught staring. 'They're wondering if they can take you, you know,' she murmured without preamble. 'There will be games after dinner.'

Was that all they wanted? A game against the man who had beaten Elias Pole? Greer managed a nonchalant lift of his shoulders. 'Elias Pole isn't an extraordinary player.'

'No, but he's a consistent player, never scratches, never makes mistakes,' Mercedes countered.

He raised a brow at the remark as if to say 'is that so?'. The observation was insightful and not the sort of comment the women he knew made. The gently reared English women of his experience were not versed in the nuances of billiards. But Mercedes was right. He knew the type of player she referred to. They played like ice.

Never cracking, just wearing down the opponent, letting the opponent beat himself in a moment of sloppy play. Yesterday that particular strategy hadn't been enough to ensure Pole victory.

'And now they know your measure. Pole has become the stick against which you are now gauged,' she went on softly.

'And you? Do you have my measure now?' Greer gave her a private smile to let her understand he knew her game. 'Is that your job tonight—to vet me for your father?'

'Don't flatter yourself.' She gave him a sharp look over the rim of her goblet. 'The great Allen Lockhart doesn't need an agent to preview half-pay officers with shallow pockets for a money game.'

There was no sense in being hurt. The statement was true enough. There was no advantage *to* fleecing an officer. He had no source of funds *to* fleece. Even his subscription to the club had been bought on skill and a politely offered discount from Kendall Carlisle. Lockhart had to know. Whatever someone at this table managed to win from him would hardly be more than pocket change.

Greer dared a little boldness. 'Then perhaps you're in business for yourself.'

'Again, don't flatter yourself.' Mercedes took another sip of wine. To cover her interest? Most likely. She was not as indifferent to him as she suggested. He knew these discreet signs: the sharp comments meant to push him away in short order; the pulse at the base of her bare neck, quickening when his gaze lingered overlong as it did now.

This room displayed her to perfection. Greer wondered how premeditated this show had been. In the drawing room, she'd merely looked like a lovely woman. In the dining room, she might have been posed for a portrait. Her blue gown was a shade darker than the light blue of the walls. The ivory ribbon trimming her bodice, a complement to the off-white wainscoting and moulding of the room, acted as an ideal foil for the rich hues of her hair, which lay artfully coiled at her neck. Greer's hand twitched with manly curiosity to give the coil a gentle tug and let its length spill down her back.

But he could see the purpose of the demure coil. It drew one's attention to the delicate curve of her jaw, the sensual display of her collarbones and the hint of bare shoulders above the gown's *décolletage*. It was just the work of another skimming glance to sweep lower and appreciate what was *in* the gown's *décolletage*, that being a well-presented, high, firm bosom. Mercedes Lockhart was absolutely enticing in all respects.

She would be stunning regardless of effort, but Greer couldn't shake the feeling that this had all been engineered, right down to the colour of Mercedes's gown for some ulterior purpose he had yet to divine. He understood the basic mechanics of the evening well enough. This dinner party was about business.

Under the bonhomie and casual conversation, there was money to be had. Lockhart, Carlisle and Thurston were in it together. Thurston wanted to sell tables. He'd likely promised Lockhart and Carlisle a commission for the advertising. Each of the other gentlemen at the table owned billiard halls, some in Brighton, a few others from nearby towns. Purchasing a table would be good for their businesses in turn. They understood the favour Lockhart did them by letting them be the first to place orders. It was all very symbiotic. He alone was the anomaly. No one would mistakenly assume he'd be purchasing a table on tonight's venture.

Mercedes took up an unobtrusive spot in the large second-floor billiards room and plied her needle on an intricate embroidery project. She knew she looked domestic and that was the point. Billiards was a man's domain. The men gathered around the new Thurston table would not dream of her joining their game. But as long as she looked utterly feminine and devoted herself to her embroidery, her presence would be acceptable. They would see her as the indulged only child of Allen Lockhart, a daughter so loved, her father could not bear to let her wander the house alone while he entertained close business acquaintances. Under those circumstances, what could really be wrong with her joining them as long as she stayed quietly placed in her corner?

Mercedes pulled her needle through the linen and surreptitiously scanned the men. They had finished talking business. Rubber bumpers, warming pans and all the latest technologies to keep the table fast had been discussed. Now it was time for action, time to see what the table could do. It was time to play, the one thing the men had been yearning to do all night.

Her father passed around ash-wood cues from a rack

hung on the wall. The two men from the other Brighton billiards halls had the honour of the first game. But her eyes were on the young captain, Greer Barrington. Up close, he did not disappoint. He was precisely as she'd seen him from behind the peephole: tall, blond, broad shouldered and possessed of an easy charm that had no limit. Those blue eyes of his were captivating, his flirtations just shy of obvious, but that was part of his charm. He was not one of London's sleek rogues with deceitful agendas, even though he possessed the unmistakable air of a gentleman.

Mercedes watched him laugh with Thurston over a remark. Instinctively, she knew he was genuine. Honest in his regard. Yet many would mistake that quality for naïveté, to their detriment. That could be a most valuable commodity if she could tame it. He was no gullible innocent. He'd spent time in military service. He'd seen men die. He'd probably even killed. He knew what it meant to take a life. He knew what it meant to live in harsh circumstances even as he knew what it meant to be comfortable amid luxury.

The opulence of her father's home had not daunted him. This was where her father was wrong. He saw a young man with no purpose, a half-pay officer at loose ends with few prospects outside the military. Mercedes disagreed.

Greer Barrington was a gentleman's son. She'd lay odds on it any day. He didn't have the beefy build of a country farm-boy, or the speech of a lightly educated man. That could be sticky. Gentlemen's sons didn't take up with billiards players mostly because gentlemen's sons had better prospects: an estate to go home to, or a position in the church. Her father, whatever his intentions were, wasn't counting on that.

Captain Barrington stepped up to the table. The prior game was over and her father was urging him to play one of the men who'd come over from nearby Hove. Carlisle spoke up as the two players chalked their cue tips. 'You're a good player, Howe, but I'll lay fifty pounds on our Captain to take three out of five games from you.'

Mercedes's needle stilled and she sat up a bit straighter. Fifty pounds wasn't a large bet by these men's standards, merely something small and friendly, but big enough to sweeten the pot. But fifty pounds would support a man in Barrington's position for half a year. There was a murmur of interest. To her father's crowd, the only thing better than playing billiards was making money at billiards.

Howe chuckled confidently and drew out his wallet, dropping pound notes on the table. 'I'll take that bet.'

'Captain, would you care to lay a wager on yourself?' her father asked, gathering up the bets.

Barrington shook his head without embarrassment. 'I don't gamble with what I can't afford to lose. I play for much smaller stakes.'

Her father laughed and clapped him on the back. 'I've got a cure for that, Captain. Don't lose.'

But he did lose. Captain Barrington lost the first two games by a narrow margin. He won the third game and the fourth. Then Carlisle upped the wager. 'Double on the last game?'

Howe was all confidence. 'Of course. What else?'

Mercedes wondered. Was this a set-up? Had Carlisle and her father arranged this? Were they that sure of Barrington's skill and Howe's renowned arrogance? If so, it would be beautifully done. Howe wasn't the best player in the room, but he thought he was and that made all the difference. If Barrington beat Howe, the others would be tempted to try, to measure their skill.

Barrington had the lay of the table now. He'd made adjustments for the speed of the slate and the bounce of the rubber bumpers. He won the break and potted three balls to take an early lead. But Howe wouldn't be out-done. He cleared three of his own before missing a shot.

Mercedes leaned forwards in her chair. Barrington's last two shots would be difficult. He stretched his long body out, giving her an unadulterated view of his back-side, the lean curve of buttock and thigh as he bent. The cue slid through the bridge of his fingers with expert ease. The shot was gentle, the cue ball rolling slowly towards its quarry and tapping it with a light snick, just enough to send it to its destination with a satisfying thud in the corner pocket while the cue ball teetered success-fully on the baize without hazarding. Mercedes let out a breath she'd been unaware she held.

'Impossible!' Carlisle exclaimed in delight. 'One shot in a million.'

'Think you can make that shot again?' Howe chal-lenged, not the happiest of losers.

Her father shot her a look over the heads of the guests and she mobilised into action, crossing the room to the table. 'Whether or not he can must wait for another time, gentlemen.' She swept into the crowd around the table and threaded an arm through Captain Barrington's. 'I must steal him away for a while. I promised at dinner to show him our gardens lit up at night.' Whatever her father's reasons, he didn't want Barrington challenged further. As for her, she had suddenly become useful for the moment.

Chapter Three

'So this is what billiards can buy.' Barrington looked suitably impressed as they strolled the lantern-lit paths of the garden, which must have been what her father intended. The gardens behind their home were well kept and exclusive.

'Some of it is.' Mercedes cast a sideways glance up at her companion. He was almost too handsome in his uniform, buttons winking in the lantern light. 'My father invests.'

'Let me guess—he invests in opportunity, like tonight.' His insight pleased her. Barrington was proving to be astute. Would such astuteness fit with her father's plans? 'Tonight's party was about selling tables.'

He'd guessed most of it. Her father *was* selling tables tonight, but he was also attempting to buy the Captain. Perhaps her father meant to use him to drum up business for the All England Billiards Championship.

'That doesn't explain what I'm doing here. I'm not in the market for a table and your father knows it.'

Too astute by far. Mercedes chose to redirect the conversation. 'What *are* you doing here, Captain? Any plans after you leave Brighton? Or do you await orders? We've talked billiards all night, but I haven't learned a thing about you.'

'I thought I'd wait a few months and see if I am recalled to active duty. If the possibilities are slim, I'll sell my commission.'

'You like the military, then?'

Captain Barrington fixed her with a penetrating stare. 'It beats the alternative.'

They'd stopped walking and stood facing each other on the pathway. There was seriousness in his eyes that hadn't been there before and she heard it in his voice.

Her voice was a mere whisper. 'What's the alternative?'

'To go back and run the home farm under my brother's supervision He's the heir, you see. I'm merely the second son.'

She heard the bitterness even as she heard all the implied information. A man who'd experienced leadership and independence in the army would not do well returning to the constant scrutiny of the family fold. A little thrill of victory coursed through her. She'd been right. He was a gentleman's son. But he was staring hard at her, watching her for some reaction.

'Are you satisfied now? Is this what you brought me out here to discover? Had your father hoped I might be a baron's heir, someone he might aspire to win for your hand?' His cynicism was palpably evident.

'No!' Mercedes exclaimed, mortified at his assumptions, although she'd feared as much earlier, too. Her father had tasked her with the job of unearthing Barrington's situation, but hopefully not for that purpose. If not that, then what? An alternative eluded her.

'Are you sure? It seems more than billiards tables are for sale tonight.'

'You should ask yourself the same thing, Captain.' Mercedes bristled. He'd put a fine point on it. She'd stopped analysing her father's motives a long time ago. Mostly because being honest about his intentions hurt too much. She didn't like thinking of herself as another of his tools.

The comment wrung a harsh laugh from the Captain. 'I've been for sale for a long time, Miss Lockhart. I just haven't found the highest bidder.'

'Perhaps your asking price is too high,' Mercedes replied before she could think better of the words rushing out of her mouth. She had not expected the charming captain to possess a streak of cynicism. It forecasted untold depths beneath the charming exterior.

'And your price, Miss Lockhart? Is it too high as well?' It was a low, seductive voice that asked.

'I am not for sale,' she answered resolutely.

'Yes, you are. We all are.' He smiled for a moment, the boyish charm returning. 'Otherwise you wouldn't be out here in the garden, alone, with me.'

They held each other's gaze, blue challenging grey. She hated him in those seconds. Not hated *him* precisely—he was only the messenger. But she hated what he said, what he revealed. He spoke a worldly truth she'd rather not recognise. She suspected he was right. She would do anything for her father's recognition, for the right to take her place at his side as a legitimate billiards player who was as good as any man.

'Are you suggesting you're not a gentleman?' Mercedes replied coolly.

'I'm suggesting we return inside before others make assumptions you and I are unlikely to approve of.'

Which was for the best, Mercedes thought, taking his arm. She wasn't supposed to have brought him out here to quarrel. Of all the things her father had in mind, it wasn't that. Perhaps her father thought they might steal a kiss, that she'd find the Captain charming; the Captain might find her beautiful and her father might find that connection useful. She could become the lovely carrot he dangled to coax Barrington into whatever scheme he had in mind.

The garden had not been successful in that regard. Not that she'd have minded a kiss from the Captain. He certainly looked as if he'd be a fine kisser with those firm lips and mischievous eyes, to say nothing of those strong arms wrapping her close against that hard chest. Truly, his manly accoutrements were enough to keep a girl bothered long into the night.

'Shilling for your thoughts, Miss Lockhart.' His voice was deceptively close to her ear, low and intimate, all trace of cynicism gone. The charmer was back. 'Although I dare say they're worth more than that from the blush on your cheek.'

Oh, dear, she'd utterly given herself away. Mercedes hazarded part of the truth. 'I was thinking how a quarrel is a waste of perfectly good moonlight.'

He'd turned and was looking at her now. 'Then we have discovered something in common at last, Miss Lockhart. I was thinking the same thing.' His blue eyes roamed her face in a manner that suggested she had the full sum of his attentions. His hand cupped her cheek, gently tilting her chin upwards, his mouth descending to claim hers in a languorous kiss.

She was aware only of him, of his other hand resting at the small of her back, intimate and familiar. This was a man used to touching women; such contact came naturally and easily to him. Warmth radiated from his body, bringing with it the clean, citrusy scent of oranges and soap.

It wasn't until the kiss ended that she realised she'd stepped so close to him. What distance there had been between their bodies had disappeared. They stood pressed together, her body fully cognisant of the manly planes of him as surely as he must be of the feminine curves of hers.

'A much better use of moonlight, wouldn't you agree, Miss Lockhart?'

Oh, yes. A much better use.

'Will you help me with him?' It was to her father's credit, Mercedes supposed, that he'd waited until breakfast the following morning before he sprang the question, especially given that breakfast was quite late and the better part of the morning gone. The men had played billiards well into the early hours, long after Captain Barrington had politely departed and she'd gone up to her rooms.

Mercedes pushed her eggs around her plate. 'I think that depends. What do you want him for?' She would not give her word blindly; Barrington's remarks about being for sale were still hot in her ears.

Her father leaned back in his chair, hands folded behind his head. 'I want to make him the face of billiards. He's handsome, he has a good wit, he's affable and he plays like a dream. For all his inherent talents, he needs training, needs finishing. He has to learn when it pays more to lose. He has to learn the nuances of the game and its players. Billiards is more than a straightforward game of good shooting between comrades in the barracks. That's the edge he lacks.'

'Playing in the billiard clubs of Brighton won't give him that edge—they're too refined. That kind of experience can only be acquired...' Mercedes halted, her speech slowing as realisation dawned. 'On the road,' she finished, anger rising, old hurts surfacing no matter how deeply she thought she'd buried them. She set aside her napkin.

'No. I won't help some upstart officer claim what is rightfully mine. If you're taking a protégé on the road, it should be me.' She rose, fairly shaking with rage. Her father's protégés had never done her any good in the past.

'Not this again, Mercedes. You know I can't stakehorse a female. Most clubs won't even let you in, for starters.'

'There are private games in private houses, you know that. There are assembly rooms. There are other places to play besides gentlemen's clubs. You're the great Allen

Lockhart—if you say a woman can play billiards publicly, people will listen.'

'It's not that easy, Mercedes.'

'No, it's not. It will still be hard, but *you* can do it. You just choose not to,' she accused. 'I'm as good as any man and you choose to do nothing about it.'

They stared at each other down the length of the small table, her mind assembling the pieces of her father's plan. He wanted to take Barrington on the road, to promote the upcoming July tournament in Brighton.

'Maybe he's not interested.' Mercedes glared. What would a gentleman like Barrington say to being used thusly? Maybe she could make him 'uninterested'. There were any number of things she could do to dissuade him if she chose. A cold shoulder would be in order after the liberties of last night.

'He'll be interested. That's where you come in. You'll make him interested. What half-pay officer turns down the chance to play billiards for money and have a lovely woman on his arm?' So much for the cold-shoulder option.

'One who has other options. He's a gentleman's son, after all.' Of course it was a wild bluff. She knew how Captain Barrington felt about his 'options'. 'Even if his options are poor, no family of good birth is going to let their son go haring about the country gambling for a living.'

That comment struck home. Her father had always been acutely aware of the chasm between himself and his betters. No amount of money, fame or victory could span that gap. 'We'll see,' he said tightly. 'Men will do all variety of things for love or money. Fortunately, post-war economies do much for motivating the latter.' Mercedes feared he might be right on that account.

'I need you on this, Mercedes,' he pleaded. 'I need you to travel with us, to show him what he needs to know. I'll be busy making arrangements and setting up games. I won't have near enough time to mould him.'

'I'll think about it.' She was too proud to surrender easily, but in her heart she knew it was already done. It was the only offer she was likely to get and she was her father's daughter. She'd be a fool not to invest in this opportunity. On the road, she could show her father how good she really was, how indispensable she was to him. Perhaps they could recapture some of the old times. They could be close again, like they'd been before her tragic misstep had driven a wedge between them. Anything might happen on the road. Even the past might be erased.

'Well, don't think too long. I'm sending a note to Captain Barrington inviting him to dinner. If this proposition succeeds, I want to leave within days.'

Yes, anything might happen, especially with weeks on the road with the attractive Captain and his kisses. Damn his blue eyes. His presence would make the trip interesting once she decided if she should love him or hate him. He was both her golden opportunity *and* the fly in her ointment. He was the man stealing her place beside her father, but, in all fairness, the place hadn't been hers to start with. She didn't possess it outright and hadn't for years. She merely aspired to it, as much as the admission galled her. Then there were his kisses to consider, or not. She had to be careful there. Kisses were dangerous and she wasn't about to fall in love with her father's protégé. She knew from experience such an act would dull her sensibilities, make her blind to the job that needed doing. But perhaps one could just have the kisses. She'd be smarter this time.

All in all, going on the road was an offer she couldn't afford to refuse. Perhaps Barrington would say she'd just found her price.

Greer sat at the small writing desk in his lodgings, sorting through the dismal array of post. At least he had an 'array' of it. He should take comfort that the world had not forgot him even if it had nothing pleasing to send.

He slit open the letter from the War Department. It was his best hope for good news. A friend of his father's with higher rank and influence had enquired about a new posting on his behalf. Greer was eagerly awaiting a response. He scanned the contents of the letter and sighed. Nothing. It was something of an irony that the goal of the military—to maintain peace and order—was the very thing that made the military a finite occupation. In peace, there was no work for all the aspirants like himself.

Greer set aside the letter. It was becoming more evident that his military options were coming to a close. Of course, he could stay on half-pay as long as he liked, but with no re-posting imminent, it seemed a futile occupation.

The second letter was from home and he opened

it with some dread. He could predict the contents already: news of the county from his mother and a directive to return home from his father. As always, a letter from home filled him with guilt. He should *want* to go back. But he didn't. He didn't want to be a farmer, and he didn't want to be a countryman. His father was a viscount, but a poor one. The title had come with only an estate four generations ago, and money had always come hard for the Barringtons. He did not want a life full of expenses he could barely meet and responsibilities he was required to fulfil. His older brother was better suited to that life. To what he himself was suited for, Greer did not yet know.

He reached for the third letter, surprised to see it was from Allen Lockhart. The short contents of the note brought a smile to his face. *Mercedes and I would like to invite you to a private supper this evening to become better acquainted.*

The sentiments of the note might be Lockhart's, but the firm, cursory hand that had penned it was definitely Mercedes's. Greer could see Mercedes penning the note with some agitation, her full lips set in an imperious line, in part because she didn't want to see him again and in part because she did. He was quite cognisant that Mercedes had no idea what to do with him—kiss him, hate him, or something in between if that was possible.

Mercedes.

She'd stopped being Miss Lockhart the moment he'd taken her in his arms. Their kiss had been far too familiar, far too intimate to think of her any longer on a last-name basis. In his arms, she'd been alive, warm and far more passionate than the sum of her cold hauteur had indicated at dinner. It had been the most pleasant surprise in an evening full of surprises. Therein lay the rub.

Had it been a surprise? Greer thumbed the corner of the heavy paper in contemplation. The kiss had seemed completely spontaneous at the time. They'd been quarreling. He'd thought the moment for stealing a kiss had passed and then suddenly the moment had returned.

He'd done the kissing. He distinctly remembered making what might be termed as the 'first move'. But Mercedes had supplied the motivation. She knew very well what she was doing with her reference to moonlight. Was the flirtation contrived? Had it been her last effort to comply with some secret plan of her father's for the evening? Had she realised that quarrelling with a coveted guest was not constructive? The note he held in his hand certainly suggested as much. There had to be a reason for getting 'better acquainted'. And yet the kiss itself did not seem contrived in his memory. Instead, it seemed very much the honest product of curious passion.

And now there was to be a private dinner. Greer was aware there was more to it than a simple dinner, but even so, he was looking forward to it a great deal. There would be good food, good wine and the intriguing Mercedes would be there. That alone was enough to secure his acceptance.

Chapter Four

The atmosphere at dinner was decidedly different than it had been the prior evening—less orchestrated, less of a show—but no less impressive because of it, and Greer found he was enjoying himself immensely.

The three of them dined informally in a small, elegantly appointed room done in subtle shades of gold designed expressly for the purpose of holding more intimate entertainments. Even the mode of eating reflected that intimacy. They dined *en famille* on juicy steaks and baby potatoes, helping themselves to servings from the china bowls in the centre of the round table and pouring their own rich red wine from glass decanters, thus removing the need for hovering footmen.

Greer had lived with the deprivations of military life long enough to fully appreciate the little luxuries of the moment, and man enough to appreciate the woman across from him.

Mercedes Lockhart glowed in the candlelight, dressed in a copper silk trimmed in black velvet, a gown so lovely it would have driven his sisters to violence.

Her hair shone glossy and sleek, the flames picking out the chestnut highlights winking deep within the dark tresses. Tonight, she wore those tresses long, their length furled into one thick curl that lay enticingly over the slope of her breast, a most provocative cascade to be sure and a most distracting one. He nearly missed Lockhart's next question.

'What are you doing in Brighton, Captain?' Lockhart poured wine into his empty glass. 'Our sleepy little resort town must be tame by comparison to the military.'

Greer picked up his newly filled goblet. 'Waiting for the next adventure.' Brighton wasn't all that different in that regard than the military. There'd been plenty of waiting in the army as well. Hurry up and wait; wait to live, wait to die. He was still waiting, only the scenery had changed.

'Will there be one? Another adventure?' Lockhart probed in friendly tones but Greer sensed he was fishing for something, looking for some piece of information. He'd discussed his situation with Mercedes last night but she'd apparently not chosen to pass the details on to her father. He shot Mercedes an amused glance. Why? To prove she wasn't her father's agent as he'd accused?

'Well, that's the question.' Greer saw no reason to dissemble. His life was a fairly open book for those who cared to read it. Open and relatively dull, if the truth was told. 'A family friend is making enquiries on my behalf, but I am not alone in my desire for a posting.'

'I expect not these days,' Lockhart replied with a knowing nod. 'There are a lot of officers looking for work. Half-pay is a hard way to live. It's not enough to support a wife or start a family.' Lockhart offered him a smile that bordered on fatherly. 'No doubt those things are on your mind at your age.'

'Eventually, I suppose, sir.' Greer thought the question a bit too personal on such short acquaintance. Lockhart was still fishing, but this time Greer chose not to bite. Lockhart was not put off by his cool response.

'Sir?' Lockhart laughed good-naturedly. 'The military has trained you well, but there will be none of that here. We are not so formal as that, are we, Mercedes?'

'Of course not, Father. We're very friendly here,' Mercedes said. She spoke to her father, but she was looking at him, something sharp and aware in her eyes as she studied him.

'Call me Allen.' What was going on here? Greer was instantly suspicious. The request was friendly enough, to borrow Mercedes's word, but far too familiar. His father had raised him to be wary against such easily given bonhomie.

'Allen' leaned forwards. 'Have you considered that you don't need the military to provide the next adventure?'

Ah, things were getting interesting now. Very soon, all would be revealed if he played along. 'Forgive my lack of imagination; I'm hard pressed to think of another outlet.' What would a man like Lockhart have in mind? Did he want to make a salesman out of him? Have him sell Thurston's tables? Wouldn't that rankle his father? A viscount's son hawking billiards tables. It might be worth doing just to stir things up.

'Come on the road with me. I need to drum up business for the All England Billiards Championship in July. Why don't you come along? I'll pay all expenses, give you a cut of whatever money we hustle up along the way, and the best part of it is, I am not asking to put your life on the line for a little fun and adventure.' *Unlike the military* came the unspoken jab at his other alternative. And he could bet with surety they wouldn't be sleeping in the mud and the rain or eating bread full of weevils and spoiled beef.

'What would I do?' Greer questioned. He'd have to do *something* to earn his keep; his pride wouldn't let him accept a free ride around England.

Allen shrugged, unconcerned. 'You play billiards. Kendall tells me people like to play you. Your presence will be good for business, help people think about making their way to Brighton when summer comes.'

It sounded simple, simple and decadent—to make money doing something he was so very good at. But something philosophic and intangible niggled at him, likely born of the conservative life-lessons his father had instilled in him. Lockhart was right: he wasn't risking his life. But he might well be risking something more. His very soul, perhaps. 'The offer is generous. I don't know what to say.' This was not the 'gentleman's way'.

Lockhart smiled, seemingly unbothered by his lack of immediate acceptance. 'Then say nothing. Take your time and think about it. I like a man who isn't too hasty about his decisions.' He set down his napkin and rose. 'I must excuse myself. I have some last-minute business to take care of at the club tonight.'

Greer rose, understanding this to be his cue to leave as well, but Lockhart waved away his effort. 'Sit down, stay a while, talk it over with Mercedes.' Lockhart winked at Mercedes. 'Persuade him, my dear,' he chuckled. 'Tell him what a fabulous time we'll have on the road, the three of us bashing around England. We'll hit all the watering holes between here and Bath, catch Bath at the end of their Season, and turn north towards the industrial centres.'

Greer raised a brow in Mercedes's direction. 'The three of us?'

Mercedes gave a small, almost coy smile, her eyes fixed on him knowingly as if she understood her answer would seal his acceptance. 'I'll be going, too.'

She was daring him with those sharp eyes. Was he man enough to go on the road with her? Or had he had enough after last night? Was he brave enough to come back for more? More of what? Greer wondered. Her tart tongue or her sweet kisses? Potent silence dominated the room as they duelled with their eyes, each very aware of the thoughts running through the other's mind.

Allen Lockhart coughed, a thin, near-laughing smile on his lips as he reached into his coat pocket. 'In all the excitement, I almost forgot to give you this.' He handed a thick envelope to Greer. The flap was open, revealing pound notes.

'What is this for?' Greer stared at the money. It would keep him for quite a while in his drab rented room. Perhaps he could even send some home. His father had mentioned the roof needed fixing on the home farm. *Stop*, he cautioned himself. This wasn't his money. Not yet.

Lockhart's smile broadened. He looked like some-one who has taken great pleasure in pleasing another with a most-needed gift. 'It's yours, from last night's winnings.'

Greer shook his head and put the envelope down on the table. 'I didn't wager anything.'

'No, but I did. I bet on you and you worked for me last night. This is your cut for that work, your salary, if you prefer to think of it that way.'

It was so very tempting when Lockhart put it that way. 'I can't take it. You wouldn't have billed me if I'd lost.'

Lockhart nodded in assent. 'I understand. I respect an honest man.' He scooped up the envelope and tossed it to Mercedes who caught it deftly. 'See if you can't find a good use for that, my dear.'

'What shall it be?' Mercedes gathered up the ivory balls from their pockets around the table. 'The losing game? The winning game? Colours? Name your pref-erence.' She'd brought the Captain to the billiards room after her father had left. Another look at Thurston's table wouldn't be amiss. Nothing persuaded like excellence.

'You play?' She could hear Barrington's chalk cube stop its rubbing, a sure indicator she'd stunned him into silence.

Mercedes set the balls on the table and fixed him with a cold smile designed to intimidate. 'Yes, I play. Why? Does that surprise you? It shouldn't. I'm Allen Lockhart's daughter. I've grown up around billiards my whole life.' Mercedes selected a cue from the wall rack, watching the Captain's reaction out of the corner of her eye. To his credit, he didn't follow up his surprise by stammering the usual next line, 'B-b-but you're a woman.'

Captain Barrington merely grinned, blew the excess chalk off his cue and said, 'Well then, let's play.'

They played the 'winning game', potting each other's balls into various 'hazards' for points. Mercedes played carefully, a mix of competence and near-competence designed to draw Barrington out, expose his responses. Would he play hard against a woman? She potted the last ball into the hazard with a hard crack. 'I win.'

She gave him a stern look, suspecting he'd purposely let up towards the end of the second game. 'I shouldn't have. You gave up a point when you missed your third shot.' It had been a skilful miss. An amateur would have noticed nothing. Near-misses happened; tables were full of imperfections that could lead to a miscalculation. But she'd noticed. 'Are you afraid to beat a woman?'

He laughed at that—a deep, sincere chuckle. 'I've already beaten you once tonight. *I* won the first game, if you recall?'

'I do recall, and I suspect you were too much of a gentleman to win the second.' Mercedes was all seriousness.

This was the type of thing her father wanted her to ferret out and destroy. Chivalry was anathema on the road. She supposed his idea of chivalry didn't stop at women, but extended to poor farmers who'd come to town on market day and stopped in to play a game, or to men seemingly down on their luck, or to men, unlike him, who wagered with what they couldn't afford to lose. Such chivalry stemmed from the code of *noblesse oblige* that gentlemen were raised with and it would definitely have to go.

'Such fine sentiments will beggar you, Captain.' Mercedes flirted a bit with her smile, gathering up the balls for another game.

Barrington shrugged, unconcerned. 'Manners beggar me very little when there's no money on the line. We were just playing.'

'Is that so?' Mercedes straightened. *Just playing?* Her father would blanch at the idea of 'just playing'. There was no such thing in his world. She reached for the envelope where she'd laid it on a small table. She tossed it on to the billiards table. 'I want your best game, Captain. Will this buy it?' She'd known precisely what use her father meant for the envelope. She was to buy the Captain with it.

'Are you serious?' His eyes, when they met hers, were hard and contemplative, not the laughing orbs that had not cared she'd accused him of going easy on her.

'I am always serious about money, Captain.'

'So am I.'

She knew it was the truth—the calculation in his eyes confirmed it. This was a chance to rightfully win what her father had offered earlier. He'd desperately wanted that money; she'd seen the delight that had flared in his eyes ever so briefly. Only his honour had prevented him from taking it. 'You're on, Captain. Best two out of three.'

She won the first game by one point, earned when

he barely missed making contact with his ball, legitimately this time.

He took his coat off for the second game and rolled up his sleeves. Was he doing it on purpose to distract her? If so, it wasn't a bad strategy. Without his coat, she could see the bend and flex of him clearly outlined by his dark-fawn trousers, and there was something undeniably attractive about a man only in waistcoat and shirt, especially if the man in question was as well proportioned as the Captain.

He was handsomely turned out tonight in a crisp white shirt and fashionable, shawl-collar waistcoat of burgundy silk, showing off those broad shoulders. His blond hair had fallen forwards, the intensity of their play defeating the parting he wore to one side. Now, all that golden perfection fell forwards, hiding his eyes from her as he concentrated on his next shot.

It was a sexy look, an *intense* look—a crowd would love it, a woman would love it, looking up into that face, that hair, as he moved over her, naked and strong. Mercedes pushed such earthy thoughts away. She had a game to lose. This was no time to be imagining the Captain naked and in the throes of love-making.

Barrington won the second game, just as she'd planned. His honour ensured it. He'd promised her his best game and he could be counted on to keep his word, his honour making him blind to any dishonour in another. It would prevent him from seeing her game as anything other than straightforward and perhaps his bias would, too. No matter what a man said, a man never believed a woman was a real threat until it was too late.

She didn't think the Captain was any different in that regard. It was the nature of men, after all, to believe in their infallible superiority.

'This is it. Winner takes all.' Mercedes set her mouth in a grim line of determination. Whether anyone knew it or not, there was just as much pressure to lose well as there was to win. But Barrington was nearly untouchable in the third game, potting balls without also hazarding his cue ball, and it made her job easier. He was starting to smile, some of the intensity from the second game melting away, overcome by his natural assurance and confidence.

'Look at that,' he crowed good-naturedly after making a particularly difficult shot, 'just like butter on bread.'

Mercedes laughed too. She couldn't help it. His humour was infectious. *This must be why people like to play him*, she thought. Even if you were losing to him, you wanted him to win. His personality drew you in, charmed you. *That* would have to be saved. She added it to the mental list in her head: chivalry, no, personality, yes. She wondered if she could change the one without altering the other? Without altering *him*? Because Greer Barrington was eminently likeable just the way he was. She had not bargained on that. She lined up her last shot and took it with a little extra force to ensure the slip. She would make her shot—he would be suspicious if she didn't— but her cue ball would hazard and that would decide the game in his favour.

Mercedes thumped the butt of her cue on the floor with disgust. 'Devil take it,' she muttered on her breath for good, compelling measure, her face a study of disappointment. 'I had that shot.'

Barrington laughed. 'You're a bad loser.' He said it with a certain amount of shock as if he'd made a surprising discovery. He shifted his position so that he half sat on the edge of the table, his eyes alight with confidence and mischief. But Mercedes already knew what was coming. Part of her wanted him to take the money and be done with it. If he was smart, he'd pocket that envelope, walk out of here and forget all about the Lockharts. His blasted chivalry was about to work against him.

'I'll give you a chance to win it back. One game takes all, I'll wager *my* envelope against '

She interrupted. 'The road. Your envelope against the road. I win, you take my father's offer.' *Don't do it. The wager is too much and you should know it.*

Barrington studied her for a moment. 'I was going to say a kiss.'

'All right, *and* a kiss,' Mercedes replied coolly. But she wasn't nearly as cool as she let on. This wouldn't be like the previous set of games where she'd been entirely in charge of the outcome. She'd decided who'd won and it had been easy to control things simply by losing. She wouldn't have that control here. Her only option this time lay in complete victory.

She chalked her cue and watched Barrington break one of his shattering breaks in the new style becoming popular in the higher-class subscription rooms. She studied the lay of the table and took her shot. On her next shot, Mercedes carefully leaned over the table, displaying her cleavage to advantage where it spilled from the square neckline of her gown. If he could take off his coat, she could make use of her assets, too. She looked up in time to catch Barrington hastily avert his gaze, but not until he'd got an eyeful. She smiled and went back to her shot. 'Like butter on bread,' she said after it fell into a pocket with a quiet plop.

Barrington shot again. 'Like jam on toast.' He raised a challenging eyebrow in her direction. His shot had been an easy one and he had the better lay of the table. None of his remaining shots would require any particular skill or luck. If she didn't do something now, he'd outpace her and win. The shot she was looking for was risky. If she missed, it would assure Barrington's victory and she'd have some explaining to do to her father. But if she didn't try she would likely end up losing anyway.

She bent, eyeing the table. Unhappy with the angle, she moved, bent, sighted the ball and moved again. Finally pleased, she aimed her cue. 'I find jam a bit sticky.' She shot, the cue ball splitting the pair she'd sighted perfectly, each one rolling smoothly to their respective pockets.

The Captain favoured her with a sharp look. 'Impressive. I think you may have been holding out on me.'

Mercedes lifted a shoulder in a shrug. 'A lady must have her secrets, after all.'

Two shots later she claimed victory. Her risky shot had paid off.

Barrington settled his cue on the table, a not entirely happy look on his face. 'You win. The road it is.'

Mercedes came around the table and stood beside him, guilt threatening to swamp her. She'd goaded him into this. She'd directed the evening towards this very outcome. Perhaps it hadn't been fair. 'You'll like it. You can play billiards all day, all night, and my father will introduce you to a lot of people. You'll have opportunities.' She pressed the envelope into his hands. 'And you'll have your money. You won't have to take up the home farm for a while.' She tried for a laugh, but it fell flat.

'I lost.'

'I don't recall asking for the envelope if I won.' Mercedes smiled up into his face. She hoped he saw that smile as one of friendship. She'd been hard on him tonight, whether he knew it or not. But they were in this together now. He was her chance. His successes would be her successes, at least for a while, at least until she decided he'd served his purpose as he had tonight.

She boldly took the envelope from his hands and put it inside his waistcoat. His body was warm through his shirt where her hand made contact with his chest. She tucked the envelope securely into an inside pocket.

'You don't mind the road all that much, do you? I was fairly sure last night you didn't have any plans.' Mercedes was gripped by another bout of conscience. She hoped she hadn't ruined anything for him.

'No. I'm looking forward to it, actually.' Barrington gave a fleeting smile, perhaps designed to appease her guilt. 'I was merely wondering what my father would make of all this.' Ah, the sainted Viscount with his empty coffers.

'Sometimes fathers don't always know best,' Mercedes answered softly. 'Especially if what they want for us is holding us back. Our paths can't always be theirs.'

He gave her a look that held her eyes and searched her soul. Before he could ask some difficult, probing and personal question, she stretched up on her tiptoes, put her arms about his neck and kissed him hard on the mouth.

He answered it; the evening had been too intense not to use the outlet the kiss offered, a place to spend the energy. His tongue found hers, duelled with it as their eyes had duelled over dinner, sending a trail of goosebumps down her arms. He unnerved her, excited her. It wasn't that she'd never been kissed, never been physically courted by a man before. She was not one of the *ton*'s innocent débutantes. It was the sheer strength of him.

He pulled her close, that strength apparent where his hand rested at her waist, a reminder that this man exuded strength everywhere—physical strength, mental strength. He was a veritable font of it: strength, honour, and self-control. A lesser man would have devoured her mouth by now, swept away with his own base lust. Not Captain Barrington.

He released her, unwilling to make her a party to his baser urges right there on John Thurston's billiards table. Not because he didn't have them, but because it was what a gentleman did. That was a bit disappointing. Captain Barrington unleashed would be a sight to behold. 'What was that for?' It was not said unkindly.

Mercedes stepped back, smoothing her skirts, in

charge of her emotions once more. 'It's your consolation prize. Go home and pack your things, Captain. We leave Thursday.'

Chapter Five

Thursday morning found Greer sitting opposite Mercedes in an elegant black travelling coach complete with all the modern conveniences: squabs of Italian leather, under-the-seat storage for hampers and valises, a pistol compartment, large glass-paned windows with curtains for privacy when passengers tired of the scenery outside. Even his proud father would feel some envy at the sparkling new coach.

That didn't mean his father would approve. Coveting did *not* equate with approval where his father was concerned. A gentleman might quietly desire his neighbour's fine coach, but a gentleman would never lower himself to acquire it by working for it. A gentleman had standards, after all. Standards, Greer was acutely aware, he had violated to the extreme on several occasions in the last week.

'Your father certainly knows how to travel in style,' Greer commented appreciatively, trying to make conversation, anything to push speculations of his father's reaction to his latest undertaking out of mind.

Mercedes shrugged, unconcerned with the wealth and luxury surrounding her, or perhaps just less impressed. 'He likes the best.' That was all she said for a long while. Mercedes proceeded to pull out a book and bury herself in it, leaving him to the very thoughts he was trying to avoid.

It was just the two of them at the moment. Lockhart had chosen to ride outside along with the groom overseeing Greer's own mount, another circumstance with which his father would take umbrage—an unmarried woman alone in a carriage with a man. Or, in this case, an eligible bachelor alone in a carriage with entirely the wrong sort of woman, the sort who might take advantage of said bachelor in the hopes of marrying up.

Very dangerous indeed! Greer fought back a wry smile. It was laughable, really. He was an officer in his Majesty's army. He could handle one enticing female. If Lockhart had intended anything to happen, such a ploy was obvious in the extreme.

Greer gave in to the smile, imagining all nature of wild scenarios. If Mercedes was to compromise him, how would she do it? Would she leap across the seat, provoked by the slightest rut in the road, and tear his shirt off? Would she be more subtle? Maybe she'd stretch, raise those arms over her head in a way that thrust those breasts forwards and exclaim over how hot she was.

His thoughts went on this way for a good two miles. It was a stimulating exercise to say the least. He had her halfway undressed and fanning herself before he had to stop. A gentleman had to draw the line somewhere.

If Mercedes knew what he was envisioning, she might have chosen to engage him in conversation instead.

But since she didn't and since he'd taken his thoughts as far as he ought in one direction, Greer spent the better part of the morning taking them in the other, most of which involved contemplating how it was that he'd packed up his trunk and his horse, the only two items of any worldly worth in his possession, and left town all for the sake of a beautiful woman.

It was definitely one of the more rash things he'd done in a long while. The military was not a place where unwarranted gambles were rewarded. An officer must always balance risk against caution and he was no stranger to the charms of beautiful women: the lovely *señora* in Spain, the mysterious widow in Crete. But looking at Mercedes Lockhart engrossed in her book, their loveliness paled for the simple reason that Mercedes's beauty was not found in the sum of her features: her exotic eyes with their slight uptilt, the high cheekbones and the full sensuous lips that seduced every time she smiled. Nor was it that she knew how to enhance those physical qualities with the styling of her hair and expensive gowns.

No, the core of Mercedes's beauty lay in something more—in her very being, the way she carried herself, all confidence and seduction. She wasn't afraid of her power or her ability to wield it. Mercedes Lockhart was no blushing, *ton*nish virgin or even a woman who affected false modesty in the hopes of appearing virtuous. His father would not approve of Mercedes Lockhart any more than he'd approve of the reasons Greer was in the coach. Both were scandalous adventures for a man of Greer's birth and station.

However, his father would be wrong, Greer thought, if all he saw in Mercedes was a woman of loose scruples. Woe to the man who mistook her for no more than that. What she was was potent and alluring and quite possibly deadly to the man who fell for her. The French had a term for women like Mercedes. *Femme fatale.*

Well, he'd faced worse in battle than one beautiful woman. Greer settled deep into his seat and smiled, deciding to play another secret little game with himself, one that left her better clothed than the previous. How long could he stare at her before she looked up at him? Thirty seconds? One minute? Longer?

At thirty seconds she started to fidget ever so slightly, trying desperately to ignore him.

At forty-five seconds, she was taking an inordinately long time to finish reading the page.

At one minute she gave up and fixed him with a stare. Greer grinned. His *femme fatale* was human, after all.

'*What* are you looking at?' Mercedes set aside her book.

'You,' Greer replied. 'We're to be together for an indefinite period of time and it has occurred to me as I sit here in *silence*, watching the morning speed by…'

'Watching *me*,' Mercedes corrected.

'All right, watching *you*,' Greer conceded. 'As I was saying, it has occurred to me that I've set out on a journey with two strangers I hardly know even though my immediate future is now tied to theirs.'

Mercedes favoured him with one of her knowing smiles. 'Perhaps you're more of a gambler than you thought, Captain.'

Greer considered this for a moment. 'I suppose I am. Although we don't have to remain strangers.'

'What do you propose?'

'A little Q and A, as we call it in the military.' Greer stretched his legs, settling in to enjoy himself. 'Question and answer.'

'Or a consequence,' Mercedes supplied with a smug little smile. 'I know this game, Captain. You're not so terribly original.'

'No. No consequence,' he explained, watching Mercedes's smug smile fade. 'There is no choice to *not* answer. Question asked, answer given. There is no option to refuse.' Greer folded his hands behind his head. 'Ladies first. Ask me anything you'd like.'

'All right then.' Mercedes thought for a moment. 'Have you always wanted to be a soldier?'

'I was raised to it, ever since I can remember,' Greer replied honestly, although he was cognisant of the omissions that answer contained. 'How about you? Were you always good at billiards? Born with a cue in your hand?'

The beauty of the game was that it allowed the participants to ask directly what they'd never dare give voice to in polite conversation over dinners and tea trays. They traded questions and answers over the dwindling hours of the morning, his knowledge growing with each answer.

Greer learned she'd travelled with her father until she was eleven and he'd sent her off to boarding school.

After that she'd come home on holidays and wandered the subscription room, watching and studying the game around which their lives were centred.

He learned her mother had died from birthing complications, that her name was Spanish for mercies—although in Latin it meant pity—quite apropos for a baby girl left to the tender sympathies of a single father, a gambler by trade, who could have just as easily have abandoned her to distant relatives and never looked back. But Lockhart hadn't. He'd taken her, cradle and all, on the road and continued to build his fame and his empire until his baby girl was surrounded by all the luxuries his ill-gotten gains could buy.

Those were the facts and when Greer had accumulated enough of them, he did the thing that made him so valuable to the military: he took those singular facts and coalesced them into a larger whole. In doing so, he saw quite well all the fires that had forged Mercedes Lockhart, that were still forging her—this incredible woman of refinement and education and emotional steel.

Was she doing the same to him? Her questions, too, had dealt only in basic, general curiosities—did he have a large family? What were his parents like? What did he like to read? To do in his spare time? Was she taking all those pieces and digging to the core of him? It was an unnerving prospect to think she might see more than he wanted to reveal. But that was the risk of the game—how much of oneself would one end up exposing?

As the game deepened, the questions moved subtly away from generally curious enquiries about each other's family and history and towards the private and personal. 'Who is the first girl you ever kissed?' Mercedes flashed him a mischievous smile as she added, 'And how old were you?'

'Oh, it's multiple questions in a single shot now, is it?' Greer quipped good-naturedly. He didn't mind. The question was harmless enough.

'A first kiss is only a good question if age is attached. It adds perspective,' Mercedes replied, willing to defend her ground in good fun.

'Well, it was Catherine Dennington,' Greer recalled with a fond smile. 'I was fourteen and she was fifteen. Her father was the village baker and she was plump in all the right places.' He feigned a sigh. 'Alas, she's married now to the butcher's son and has two children.' Greer winked at Mercedes. 'How's that for perspective?' He studied her with the exaggerated air of an Oxford professor. 'Speaking of perspective, Miss Lockhart,' he said in his best mock-academic voice, 'It's only fair, if you want to talk about kisses, that you tell me about your first intimate encounter.'

He'd asked mostly out of spirited mischief. She couldn't stoke the fire and then run away. Even with the intended and obvious humour behind the question, Greer had half expected her to scold him for such impertinence and he'd let her wiggle out of her obligation to answer. He'd not expected her to answer it.

She narrowed her catlike eyes and returned his studied stare, making sure she had the whole of his attention. 'Dismal. It was a wet, messy foray into adolescent curiosity. He was in and out and done before it really began for me. And yours, Captain? Better or worse?'

The fun disappeared, replaced by something far more serious. They weren't talking about kisses any more. But Greer matched her with a succinct answer of his own. 'Better, much better.' But it was more than an answer. It was an invitation, one no sensible gentleman would have issued and they both knew it.

'Well played, Captain.' Mercedes leaned back against her seat, impressed. He hadn't been frightened off. Instead of being embarrassed for her, he'd gone on the offensive with a self-assured disclosure of his own. She could choose to take him down a notch with a sharp comment about the natural arrogance of men when it came to estimating their sexual prowess. But such a rejoinder merely led down a tired road of well-worn repartee.

'Now we know each other's secrets,' Greer said quietly in a manner that fit their newfound solemnity, 'what's next?'

Mercedes peered out the window, buying some time to put together an appropriate answer. The coach began to slow and she couldn't resist a smile. Perfect. 'Lunch. That's what's next.' She couldn't have timed it better herself. The stop would bring their game to a close and with it an end to any awkward probes into her past. The things in her past were best left there. She'd made mistakes, trusted too freely. She didn't want to create the impression such a thing would happen again. It wouldn't do to have Captain Barrington entertaining any untoward notions.

She knew what those notions would be: to get her

into bed, have a dalliance and leave her when the differences in their stations became too obvious to go un-
remarked. Sons of viscounts could offer her no more
than a bit a fun. It was not that she'd mind an affair with
the Captain. He'd already demonstrated a promising
propensity for bedsport and he was certainly built for
it. But such a venture would have to be on her terms
from beginning to end. Mercedes fanned herself with
her hand. Was it just her or was it getting hot in here?

It felt good to get out of the carriage and stretch her
legs. The morning mist had cleared, giving way to a
rare, sunny April day. The spot her father had found
was delightful: a place not far off the road, and populated by wildflowers and a towering oak with a stream
nearby for watering the horses.

Mercedes took herself off for a few moments of privacy, letting the coachman and the groom have time
to take care of the horses before she began setting out
the food. But when she came back, she saw she was too
late. Someone had taken charge and set up 'camp' without her. A blanket was spread beneath the oak tree. The
hamper was unpacked and the man most likely responsible for all this activity stood to one side of the blanket,
his blond hair falling forwards in his face as he worked
the cork free on a bottle of wine with a gentleman's dexterity, a skill acquired only from long practice.

It was yet another reminder of the differences in their
stations. Her father had never quite mastered the art of
uncorking champagne on his own. He always laughed,
saying, 'Why bother when I have footmen paid to do
it?' Her father had come late to the luxuries of a life-

style where champagne was considered a commonplace experience. Not so with Greer. He could talk all he wanted about the hardships of the military and the lack of wealth in his family. The indelible mark of a gentleman was still there in the opportunities that surrounded him. Boot boys from Bath hadn't the same experiences.

Greer looked up and smiled when he saw her, the cork coming out with a soft pop. He poured her a glass and handed it to her. 'It's still chilled.'

The wine, with its light, fruity tang, was deliciously cold sliding down her dry throat. At the moment, Mercedes couldn't recall anything tasting better. It wasn't until Greer had poured his own glass and had gestured for her to sit down that she realised they were completely alone—the servants off at a discreet distance, her father peculiarly absent. 'Where's my father?'

'He decided to ride on ahead. Apparently there's a spring fair in the village an hour or so up the road.' Greer began fixing a plate from the bread, cold meats and cheese spread out on the blanket. 'He wants to make sure we have rooms at the inn.'

Likely, he wanted more than that. He wanted to see the billiards situation, what kind of people were in town, which inn had a table, who was the big player in the area. He'd have the lay of the land and a new 'best friend' by the time they arrived.

Mercedes glanced overhead at the sky. It was noon. They'd be in the village by two o'clock at the latest. There would still be plenty of time to stroll around the fair and enjoy the treat. They could have all gone together. An hour wouldn't have cost her father anything.

But he'd wanted to go alone. There was a reason for that. She'd have to be cautious and not acknowledge him unless he wanted her to. Perhaps he wanted them to appear to be strangers. He and Kendall had done that sort of the thing in the old days.

'Mercedes, your plate.' Greer had finished assembling the food and, to her surprise, the plate he'd been concocting had been for *her*. Of course it was. It was what a gentleman did and Greer did those things as effortlessly as he uncorked wine. She wondered how he would respond to the kinds of confidence games her father liked to play? The kind of games where the limits of honesty were grey areas?

'Thank you.' She settled the plate on her lap and watched him put together his own plate, long, tapered fingers selecting meats and cheese with purpose.

'I was thinking you might like to ride this afternoon since the weather turned out to be nice,' Greer offered. 'I noticed both you and your father brought horses.'

It would be perfect. The afternoon was far too fair to be cooped up in the carriage. It was the ideal conversational offering as well.

They spent lunch talking about riding and horses, something she didn't know half as well as she knew billiards. She liked listening to Greer talk about his stallion, Rufus, and other horses he'd owned. He had a face that came alive when he spoke, and an easy manner that was fully engaged now. She'd caught glimpses of it before; when they'd played billiards and this morning in the carriage, but always somewhat tempered by the side of him that never forgot he was an officer and a viscount's son.

This afternoon, sitting under the oak, he was quite simply *himself.* And she had been quite simply herself, not Allen Lockhart's daughter, not always planning the next calculated move. It was nice to forget and she *did* forget right up until the flags of the fair came into view and it was time to remember what they were there for.

'Should we find your father?' Greer asked, looking for a place to leave the horses until the carriage and servants caught up to them.

Mercedes smiled and dismounted. 'I think we'll let him find us. Meanwhile, you and I shall enjoy the fair.'

Chapter Six

This was pure recklessness, Mercedes privately acknowledged as they tethered the horses on the outskirts of the fairground. She was inviting all sorts of trouble being alone with the Captain. Not the usual kind of trouble. She was too old to need a chaperon and the Captain wasn't likely to take advantage of her. Her danger lay in mixing business with pleasure. She was on this trip to groom him, introduce him to the world of professional billiards. She was *not* here to picnic under trees, or walk fairgrounds, or to play parlour games in coaches with him.

Those all led to perilous places where business became confused with emotions. But she was not ready to let go of the afternoon. That would happen soon enough. Her father would have plans for the evening that would demand it. But not yet. For now, the afternoon was still hers.

They browsed at the booths, smelling milled soaps from France and laughing when a few of the little cakes were reminiscent of cloying old ladies. They admired the bolts of fabric at the cloth merchant's, the vendor mistaking her for Greer's wife as he tried to convince her to buy some chintz for recovering seat cushions in her sitting room.

She had blushed furiously over the mistake, but seen no way to rectify it. Greer had politely steered them on to the next booth, taking the remark in his stride. The booth contained various blades and he soon became engrossed with the owner in a discussion of blades and hilts. Mercedes moved on to a display of ribbons. She'd been debating the merits of the green or the blue ribbon with the vendor, a woman of middle years, when Greer stepped up behind her. 'She'll take them both,' he said with a laugh, passing over the shillings. 'They're too pretty to choose just one.'

'You have a good husband, ma'am.' The woman smiled, pocketing Greer's coins with a wink in his direction. 'Knows how to spoil his wife properly. You'll have a long marriage, I think.'

'You shouldn't have done that,' Mercedes hissed once they'd moved away from the booth.

'Why not?' Greer teased. 'Don't you like people thinking we're together? Am I too ugly for you?'

She shook her head with a laugh. It was impossible to stay angry with him. 'You know you're not. That woman was rather disappointed you were so devoted to your "wife."'

'Aye, she was likely hoping I might be devoted to her later this evening. But alas, my heart is claimed elsewhere.'

'Stop it,' Mercedes insisted with little vigour. 'You're being ridiculous.' But she was laughing too.

They'd reached the perimeter of the fairground. Their horses weren't far off and the crowd had thinned, leaving them alone. Greer took out the blue ribbon from his coat pocket. 'Will you permit me?' He didn't wait for an answer. He moved behind her, but instead of putting the ribbon in her hair, he slid it about her neck and when she looked down, a tiny silver charm in the shape of a star dangled from the ribbon. She recognised it immediately. She'd stared at it overlong at the jeweller's booth. It had been of surprisingly good worksmanship and Greer had noticed. It had not been cheap either.

'You shouldn't have,' Mercedes began quietly, settling her hair.

'Shouldn't have what? Shouldn't have commemorated this glorious day?' Greer argued in equally soft tones. He turned her to face him. 'I haven't had many nice days like this for a while. As you can imagine, there aren't picnics and fairs in the military. And for once, I don't have anything pressing to worry about. There's no one shooting at me, there are no worms in my food. Life has definitely improved since I've met you.'

She felt guilty. She wanted to tell him she wasn't worth it, that she'd been brought along to tame him, to turn him into something that could make her father money. But she let him have the moment. He'd been a soldier, he'd faced death and delivered it too. He worried for his family and over their finances, and finally he'd had a day where there was fair weather overhead, money in his pocket that bills couldn't claim, and a pretty woman by his side. She could not bring herself to steal that from him. Taking that from him meant taking that from her, too, and she couldn't do it.

Mercedes gave up the fight and said simply, 'Thank you, Greer.' Her hand closed over the charm where it rested against her skin. She would treasure it always, as a reminder of the day a gentleman had treated her like a lady. She stepped closer, her head tilted up in encouragement. Perhaps he'd like to seal the day with a kiss. And he might have if he'd got the chance.

'There you two are!'

Her father approached, his spirits high. Mercedes stepped back, putting more space between herself and Greer. If her father was in a good mood, things must have gone well in town. 'We thought you'd find us when you were ready,' Mercedes offered as an explanation for their truancy.

'You thought right, my smart girl.' He chucked her under the chin playfully. 'I've got rooms at the Millstream Inn, but the billiards table is at the Golden Rooster.' He rubbed his hands together. 'Two inns! Not bad for a sleepy little place. We'll have some fun tonight. Everyone hereabouts is in town with money to spend after a long winter. Are you ready to play, Captain?'

Her father inserted himself between the two of them as they walked back towards town, horses in tow. Behind her father's back, Greer caught her eye and gave her a grin. Mercedes smiled, swallowing her disappointment. The afternoon was officially over.

* * *

Bosham was a pretty fishing village at the east end of Chichester Harbour. A Saxon stone church sat neatly on the High Street not far from their rooms at the Millstream Inn, and Greer would have liked time to tour the town with Mercedes. She'd been a game sightseer at the fair and he would have enjoyed exploring the town's countless legends about King Harold and Canute with her.

There would be no time for such an indulgence. Lockhart had not only found them rooms at the comfortable inn, he had already bespoke a private parlour for dinner and was eager to get down to the business of playing billiards.

'We'll go over to the Golden Rooster,' Lockhart said between bites of an excellent seafood stew. 'I want to see what you can do, what your natural inclinations are, how badly you want to win.' Lockhart winked and handed him some funds. 'That should get you started.' Lockhart rubbed his hands together, the gleam of excitement in his eye. 'There's money to be had in this little town tonight. People are happy, they've made money today, they've been drinking and thinking they've got a bit extra in their pockets.'

Greer cringed inwardly at Lockhart's implication. A single walk through the streets had shown him these were simple people: merchants, farmers and fishermen, some of whom depended on seasonal fairs to last them through the year. The thought of taking their money sat poorly with him, souring the rich stew in his stomach.

Mercedes was watching him. He must have reflected

his distaste for the venture in some small way. Quickly, Greer tore off a chunk of bread and dipped it into his bowl, looking busy with eating to mask any other telltale signs of reluctance. Her eyes slid away towards her father.

'I'll be there too.'

'No, I think you should stay here,' Lockhart corrected. 'Relax, spend the night by the fire, enjoy some needlepoint.' He smiled kindly at his daughter, but Greer didn't think Mercedes would fall for the expansive gesture.

She saw right through it. 'I'll come,' she said with the same brand of feigned politeness her father had used. 'I'm not tired. It will take only a moment to change. Shall I wear the maroon gown?' Greer's lips twitched, suppressing a smile as he watched the two of them play with one another. Would Lockhart be so easily managed?

Lockhart rose and held Mercedes's arm. His voice was low and firm, more fatherly when he spoke this time. Greer recognised it as the tone his own father took when he was younger and he and his brother had pushed the limits of their father's patience with a jest or prank. 'I prefer you remain here. The Golden Rooster is no gentleman's club. With the fair in town, who knows what kind of element will find its way out tonight?'

Mercedes's eyes narrowed. 'I cannot help him if I cannot watch him. By the time we get to the big towns it will be too late to coach him. If he has a flaw, we need to fix it while we're in the villages.'

Greer raised his eyebrows. 'I am still here.' He didn't

like being talked about as if he were a thing to be studied and fixed. Mercedes spared him the briefest of glances before turning back to her father.

Lockhart shook his head, his tone softening. 'Please, Mercedes, a tavern is no place for you. When there are subscription rooms or private billiards parlours, you'll be able to join us then. Please, besides, your clothes will give us away. Your gowns are much too fine for the Golden Rooster.' He swallowed and dropped his gaze, arguing softly, 'I would not have you treated less than you deserve, my dear. You know what the men there will think.'

That was the end of it. The last argument seemed to carry some weight. Mercedes acquiesced to her father's better sense with moderately good grace and what could pass as a warning. 'Just for tonight. But don't think I'll sit idly by again. We'll have to find a way to make my presence acceptable long before we get to Bath.'

'Fair enough.' Lockhart kissed his daughter's cheek and turned to Greer. 'Are you ready, then?'

The Golden Rooster was at the other end of town, closer to the fairground than the quay like the Millstream Inn, and the fair crowd had definitely gathered there. At the back of the room was the billiards table. Greer and Lockhart parted ways, Lockhart heading for the bar and Greer for the table with Lockhart's advice in his ear: watch first, then play slow and easy, nothing fancy.

Watching helped settle his nerves and misgivings. These were regular men, not all that different from those he played in the army. They seemed cognisant of what they were doing and the attenuate risks. For a while, players came and went, the winner of a match earning the right to stay at the table and play the next challenger and the atmosphere was congenial. Then, a cocky braggart of a man stepped up and won a few games. He was not a kind winner and Greer felt his blood starting to rise. He wanted to beat this man. When the chance came to play, he took it, hefting the ash cue in his hand with grim determination.

He didn't stay grim for long. It felt good to play and in spite of the worn condition of the table, the balls rolled predictably. He played the braggart again and again, defeat egging the man on until he had to withdraw, his ego and coins spent. The crowd around Greer had grown with a rising raucousness, spurred on by Greer's victories against a disliked opponent. He caught a glimpse of Lockhart shouldering his way into the crowd.

'Who else will play?' Greer called out in friendly tones. Now that the braggart had been routed, they could get back to the business of fun. The crowd parted and a young man, younger than he, emerged. He was tall and sturdily built. His face was tanned, his eyes merry, shoulders broad and thick from hauling nets. A fisherman, a local. A few men clapped the young man on the shoulder and Greer surmised from the comments that the young man was something of a town favourite, newly married with a baby on the way. His name was Leander and he blushed ever so slightly and proudly when the men teased him about Ellie. 'Finally let you out of the house, has she?' they joked.

Leander brushed off the comments. 'Never mind them,' he said good-naturedly to Greer. 'They're just jealous I'm married to the prettiest girl in town.' Most definitely a town favourite, Greer thought as the men laughed.

And a decent player too, Greer amended a few games later. They'd played four games, each winning two and money exchanging hands on an equal basis. Lockhart was frowning in the crowd. Greer would have to step up his game. It would be too much for Leander. If Leander was smart, he'd recognise the superior skill and walk away. At this point, Leander wasn't out any serious money and he could stop whenever he wanted.

Conscience subdued momentarily, Greer took the next three games. Leander was getting frustrated. Greer hoped the young man would stop and call it a night. Instead Leander said, 'Double or nothing on the next game.' There were a few cautious murmurings from the men beside him, warning him to reconsider.

'You played well, Leander, let it be,' one man suggested with an arm about his shoulders, hoping to lead him away. But Leander was young and typically hotheaded where his pride was concerned.

'Think about Ellie and the baby,' another said. 'You'll need that money for the doctor later.'

If it had been up to him, Greer would have put down the cue and walked away, claiming tiredness, but it wasn't up to him. Lockhart was standing there, wanting him to go on and Leander would not back down. Between them, they'd taken away one choice, leaving Greer with only one other avenue of recourse. Three shots in, he scratched, potting the cue ball along with his own and forfeited the game, followed by what he hoped was a sincere show of disbelief.

Greer put down the cue and handed the money over to a beaming Leander. 'Go home to your wife,' he said in low tones, and he was sure the men present would make that happen. Some of them clapped him on the back, as he made his way to the front. Others offered to buy him a drink, but he refused. Lockhart had gone on ahead and would be waiting outside. He wouldn't be pleased and Greer needed to face him.

'You had him,' Lockhart began as they walked back to the Millstream. 'You were doing brilliantly. You ousted the braggart, showed yourself worthy of playing the local best, got the local favourite to come out and play, worked him up to where he offered double or nothing and then you let him go. What were you thinking?'

'I was thinking he didn't have the money to lose.' Greer didn't back down from his choice. 'He's a fisherman with a pregnant wife at home.'

'Maybe.' Lockhart shrugged in the darkness. 'Perhaps they're all in it together and that's the story they tell outsiders.'

Greer grimaced. He hadn't thought of that, probably because it seemed a bit ludicrous. 'I doubt it.'

'Still, no one put a gun to his head,' Lockhart argued.

Greer passed him the original sum Lockhart had

given him earlier that night. 'What do you care? Your stake is intact and a little more. You didn't lose anything tonight. My choice cost you nothing.'

'Not yet.' Lockhart sent him a dubious sidelong glance. 'Lord save me from do-gooders.' He took the money and tossed Greer a half-sovereign when they reached the entrance to the Millstream. 'There's your take of the winnings tonight: ten whole shillings, barely the price of a bottle of Holland's Geneva.' Lockhart gave a derisive chuckle. Greer understood the insult. Holland's Geneva was a popular, but not high-quality, drink, definitely not the drink of a gentleman used to a superior claret or brandy.

'Certainly not enough to keep a woman like Mercedes in trinkets and silks,' Lockhart added astutely as they stepped inside.

'I'm not looking to keep a woman like Mercedes or any other. I believe I've mentioned as much before,' Greer growled.

'Really? You could have fooled me today.' Lockhart chuckled. 'Well, no matter. She's in the parlour, remaking a dress if I am any judge of character.' Lockhart nodded towards the private room they'd used for dinner where a light still burned. 'I'm for bed. We'll head out in the morning and try again tomorrow.'

Chapter Seven

Gentlemen were the very devil with their principles and codes! Lockhart stretched out on his bed, hands behind his head and stared at the ceiling, his mind assessing the events of the day. The Captain had lived up to his suspicions, or down to them depending on how one looked at it. Barrington had gone soft at the critical moment.

It wasn't the money he minded losing. These stakes had been small. But what if they hadn't been? What if Barrington chose his conscience over him when real money was on the line? Mercedes would have to be the one to fix that particular flaw. Barrington had not been receptive to his own words of wisdom on that point tonight. Perhaps Mercedes would have more luck.

There was no 'perhaps' about it. He'd seen the way the Captain had looked at Mercedes from the start. Mercedes would be his insurance on this. What the Captain wouldn't do for him, the man would do for Mercedes. When it came to charms, he simply couldn't compete with his daughter where the Captain was concerned. That was one area Mercedes had an advantage on him.

He did wonder how reciprocal those charms were. To what degree did Mercedes return the Captain's attentions? He'd seen the two of them at the fair, strolling the booths arm in arm and that telling moment by the horses at the end. If he'd interrupted a little later there would have actually been something to interrupt. And that bauble. Sheer genius on the Captain's part.

Oh, *that* had been nicely played, although in all probability the Captain had likely meant whatever sentiments went with it. Men like him usually did. Lockhart chuckled in the dark. A gentleman's principles might be sticky wickets when it came to billiards, but they could be useful things indeed when it came to a lady's honour. There were worse people who could court his daughter. He'd seen them and not one of them was good enough for Mercedes with her hot temper and passions.

Mercedes would have to be careful. It would be too easy to fall for a man like the Captain, all handsome manners and good breeding, the very best of English manhood. But she would never fit into Barrington's world and he would make her unhappy in the end. In the interim, it wouldn't do to have Mercedes pick the Captain over him. There could be no running off with the Captain on the grounds of false promises the Captain had no intention of keeping. Of course, she could marry the Captain. He wouldn't stand in the way of that, but he would tolerate nothing less.

Mercedes could be managed. He'd saved her from the consequences of her impetuous nature once before and that deserved her loyalty. He would remind her of that if need be. Still, he wasn't worried. Mercedes had been down that road before. She'd be wary about trusting the Captain outright.

Lockhart laughed out loud. If he and Mercedes played their cards right, he'd come out of this with a protégé and a son-in-law. He'd give anything to be a fly on the wall in that parlour right now. If Mercedes was smart, she'd give the Captain a piece of her mind and then a piece of her heart.

Mercedes knew something had gone wrong the moment Greer stepped into the parlour. 'What happened?' She could guess what it was, though. Her father's competitive streak had run into Greer's principles. Nonetheless, she tucked her needle into the fabric and stilled her hands, giving Greer all her attention.

'This is not what I signed on for—fleecing locals.' Greer fairly spat the words at her in his frustration.

'You were warned,' she said evenly. 'The night we played for the road, you said you were always serious about money. I thought you understood what that meant.' In moments like this, she was convinced men were just overgrown boys, squabbling over principles instead of toy boats. A woman was a far more practical creature. A woman had to be.

Greer pushed a hand through his hair. 'Since when has "come bash around England and generate interest in the billiards tournament" been synonymous with taking money off unsuspecting local players who don't have any idea who they're up against?'

Mercedes set down her sewing and rose. 'Listen to me. If you'd come down off your moral high horse, you'd see the wisdom of it. *You* need to practise. You can't simply walk into an elite subscription room in Bath, or a gentleman's private home, and expect to be perfect without practice. A real player knows "practice" means more than shooting balls around the baize. It means knowing how to work the room to maximum advantage. Places like Bosham are where we practise that skill *before* we try it out for real in places that count, places that don't give you a second chance.'

Greer glared at her. 'What an absolute delight you are. You really know how to cut a man down.'

'Because you came looking for sympathy and I gave you truth?' Mercedes stood her ground. His words hurt, especially after the fun of the afternoon and the flirting in the carriage that morning. But she had a job to do, for her father and for herself. Neither job involved making friends with Greer Barrington, no matter how enticing that option appeared on occasion.

'Lesson one, Captain, is to separate your feelings from your pocket. A good gambler is not emotional about money.'

'I'm not,' he snapped. 'You know very well I don't wager what I cannot afford.'

'Your money *or* theirs,' Mercedes amended. 'Emotions go both ways. Your problem is that you get emotional about *their* money.' She paused, letting the words sink in. 'And maybe you should,' she added.

'Maybe I should what?' Greer challenged.

'Maybe you should play with what you can't afford

to lose. You might try harder to win.' Mercedes held his gaze, refusing to back down. He had to learn this most primary of lessons before they could move on. A player who could not set himself apart from the money would never reach his potential. She'd seen it happen too many times.

Greer blew out a breath and she had the sense she'd pushed him too far. 'I can't believe you're siding with him.'

The words sliced her as surely as any blade. If he only knew! She wasn't on her father's side. She wasn't on Greer's side. She was simply on *her* side, trying to make a place in a world that insisted there wasn't one for a female. Her own anger began to spill. 'I'm not siding with him. I'm trying to save you from yourself. Or maybe you don't care. Not all of us have the home farm waiting for us if this doesn't work out.'

Damn him and his high-road principles. She didn't want to need him, but the reality behind all her bravado about emotional detachment was stark and simple. *He* was her chance. Her success was tied to his although she dare not tell him that.

'I must apologise.' Greer clicked his heels together and executed a stiff bow, his tone just as rigid. 'I've taken my frustration out on you. You are merely the messenger of unpleasant news.' He reached out and covered the star charm where it lay against her neck. His hand was warm on her skin, the gesture intimate, his fingers achingly near her breast. He smiled. 'We're in this together.'

Until it's time not to be. Mercedes masked the self-serving thought with a smile. She needed to exit the room. The atmosphere between them was charged with a new emotion more reminiscent of their unfinished business from the fairground.

'We're not meant to be at each other's throats,' she offered by way of acknowledging his apology. If she didn't leave soon, this conversation would veer into territory best left unexplored for the moment until she could make her mind up about the handsome officer— was he to be more than a protégé to her? But her feet stayed rooted to the ground.

'Oh, I don't know about that.' He raised a hand to the back of her head, trapping her, drawing her closer, a secret smile on his lips. 'Being at each other's throats isn't all bad.' He took her mouth in a hard kiss, letting his lips wander along her jaw and down the length of her throat, teasing her with a flick of his tongue here, a nip of his teeth there, until he captured her mouth again, challenging her to a heated duel of tongues.

'Or being in them,' she managed between kisses. This was new territory indeed! Usually *she* was the aggressor. It was what she preferred. It reduced the opportunity to be taken by surprise. More importantly, it let her drive the encounter. But it was very apparent that Greer was driving this one.

Her hands anchored roughly in the thick depths of his hair. This was not a gentle exchange and she roused to it, revelling in the feel of his hands at her hips, hard and strong as they held her, the thrill of his lips pressed to her neck, to her mouth.

She sucked at his ear, her teeth taking sensual bites

of his lobe until Greer gave a fierce growl of pleasure, but she couldn't completely shake the thought that had taken up residence in the back of her mind. She'd use Greer, use this chemistry between them until he and it had served their purpose. Then she'd cut him free. She'd *have* to.

Such an assumption had always been an underlying tenet of her plan. She was turning out too much like her father. She'd not meant to be. It was a rather sobering revelation and one she was definitely not proud of.

Chapter Eight

'What are the rules to a good hustle?' Mercedes all but barked across the table in yet another small inn in yet another middling, nameless town. Good Lord, the woman was driving him crazy on all levels.

Greer gave her a steely look across the billiards table. If she asked him how to hustle one more time he was going to walk out of this room. Every morning in the carriage it was the same drill: 'Tell me the best place to aim a slice, the proper way to split a pair, what are the best defensive shots.' Every afternoon, it was practice, practice, practice until he could execute the strategies in his sleep. At least he could when he wasn't dreaming of her.

Since Bosham she'd managed to torture him by day as well as night; the temptress that had sucked his ear lobe to near climax in the Millstream parlour had taken up residence in his dreams, leaving him waking aching and hard. But that temptress became a termagant in the morning.

'Well? What are the rules to a good hustle?' Mercedes prompted when he met her questions with silence. 'Aren't you going to answer?'

Greer put down the cue stick and folded his arms across his chest. 'No, as a matter of fact, I am not.' Then he did as he'd promised himself. He walked past Mercedes and out the front door of the inn into the glorious spring afternoon.

'Greer Barrington, come back here. I have asked you a question.'

Oh, that did it. He was *not* going to acquiesce, not before he gave her a piece of his mind. He didn't stop until he'd reached the town green though he was aware of her behind him every step of the way, her anger palpable as it chased him across the street. Greer turned and faced her, fixing her with a hard stare. 'Can you leave me the hell alone for once? What is it you want? "How do you shoot a slice, how do you split a pair, how do you compensate for angles?" It never stops!'

His voice was too loud, but he didn't care. It felt good to let out the frustrations, sexual and otherwise, that he'd carried for days.

Mercedes answered him evenly, unfazed by his harsh words. 'I like the best, Captain. That's what I want. And if you want what I want, you'd better be the best because I don't have time for anything less.' Nothing got to her. Just once he'd like to see something get under her skin.

'You did in Bosham. You had time for a picnic, time to stroll around the fair.' Greer made a wide gesture to indicate the park around them. 'Spring is passing you by while you're penned up in a dark inn shooting slices and teaching hustles.'

Something shifted in her grey eyes and her gaze lost its hardness. Her anger was fading. For a fleeting moment he thought he saw something akin to sadness in them, then it was gone, replaced by something more stoic, more like the Mercedes he'd come to know. 'If I am, it will be worth it. I can enjoy next spring. Chances don't come my way very often, Captain. I have to take them when they do, spring notwithstanding.'

'Greer, please. No more "Captain." You only call me "Captain" when you're angry.' Greer gave up the last of his anger, intrigue overriding his frustration. 'What opportunity is that, Mercedes?'

'To be on the road with my father,' she said simply but tersely, and Greer sensed this was not a direction she'd willingly take the conversation. Her relationship with Lockhart was a touchy subject and, quite frankly, the relationship seemed a bit odd to him. It was nothing like the relationship his sisters had with his father. Mercedes and Lockhart were more like partners than a father and daughter.

It was strange, too, to think the indomitable Mercedes would yearn for time with her parent like any other child. He'd spent his childhood lapping up any crumb of attention from his father's table, treasuring those rare moments when his father came out of his office to take him riding. Even now, he knew he still craved his father's approval. He'd wanted to make his father proud of his military career.

Greer gave Mercedes a considering glance as they

walked; she was so beautiful and proud it was hard to imagine she harboured the same wants as the rest of them. But she'd no more admit to it than he would, if asked. The conversational angle was played out. She would let him go no further with it. All he could do was tuck her arm through his and change the topic.

'Have I ever mentioned how much you remind me of my superior officer, Colonel Donald Franklin? We had a secret nickname for him.'

Mercedes favoured him with a tolerant smile, the kind reserved for belligerent six-year-olds. 'And what was that name? I'm sure you're going to tell me whether I want you to or not.'

'Drill book Donny or sometimes Old Prissy Pants.'

'I'm sure you want to tell me what he'd done to earn such lovely monikers.'

'He never relented. Buttons, boots, hilts—he'd have as big a fit over them not being polished to perfection as he would over something important like messing up manoeuvres.'

'Little things matter,' Mercedes said defiantly, taking the Colonel's part. He'd known she would even if it was just to be stubborn. He understood that. It was better to be stubborn than vulnerable. 'Besides, he brought you back alive didn't he? His lessons couldn't have been that useless.'

He didn't miss the subtle analogy. *She* could bring him back to life, give him the spark his life was missing if he'd just listen to her. Still, for the sake of argument, he had to respond. 'Buttons and boots can't get you killed.'

'I disagree. Buttons, boots, manoeuvres—they're all part of acquiring discipline. In fact, it was one of the first things I noticed about you: your well kept uniform. It spoke volumes about the kind of man you were.'

'What kind of man is that?' He was enjoying this now. They were good together this way—walking and talking, sharing insights the polite people of the *ton* would consider too bold between a man and a woman.

'A man who can be relied on to follow the rules.' She tossed him a coy smile. 'There was no Colonel Franklin to insist on polished buttons that night in Brighton and yet they were. No matter how much you may rail against his rules, you will follow them.'

Greer gave a growl of dissatisfaction. He wasn't sure the analysis was all that complimentary. 'You make me sound like a milksop, as if I can't think for myself.'

'Not at all. I've never once thought you were weak. Following rules makes you a man of discipline. It makes you reliable. I find that a very attractive quality.' She smiled again, a smile made for bedrooms and the dark, not public parks in the brightness of the afternoon.

She was flirting overtly with him now, the first time since Bosham. Greer felt himself go hard. Did she have any idea what sort of fuse she was lighting? She was by far the most intriguing woman he'd ever encountered. She called to him body and mind. The very physicality of her sensuality beckoned in wicked invitation while her mind fascinated him with its insights on human nature. To truly know her would be a heady prize, one he doubted any man had yet to capture. But one, he was sure, many men had failed in the attempting.

'Circe,' he said softly, letting the air charge between them and the afternoon be damned. If she wanted to play this game, who was he to deny her? He was confident enough in his abilities. Perhaps he'd be the one to claim the prize.

'I beg your pardon?'

'You,' Greer drawled. 'You're Circe, the siren from Homer's *Odyssey*.'

She tossed her head, tiny diamond studs in her ears catching the light, an entirely seductive movement that drew the eye to her face. 'Tell me, did Circe play billiards?'

Greer laughed. 'No, she was, and I quote directly from Homer, "the loveliest of all immortals." She enticed men, but when they failed to win her, she turned them into animals.'

Mercedes cocked her head to one side, giving him a smouldering stare of consideration. 'Do you think I'm in the habit of reducing men to their baser natures? I think men do that quite well on their own without any help from me.'

'I think, Mercedes, you know exactly how you affect a man.' They'd come to an old, wide oak that hid them from the view of others in the park. It would be the most privacy they'd have. The game was getting dangerous now. How far did he dare take it? How far would Mercedes allow him to take it?

'And Circe? Did she know or was it the type of curse where she was doomed to attract men? I must confess, I wasn't all that good with the classics at school.'

He could imagine that. Mercedes was the practical

sort; the classics wouldn't hold any appeal for her unless they held the secrets to turning metal into gold. 'What were you good at?'

Mischief flickered in her eyes. 'Palm reading. Would you like me to read yours?' She took his hand and turned it palm up between them.

'They taught palmistry at your school?' This must have been an interesting school indeed.

'No,' Mercedes said without looking up, all her attention riveted on his palm. 'The gypsies did and they camped near the school every spring.'

'And you ran off to visit them?' At least he hoped her gaze didn't drop any lower. There was an impressive show going on in his ever-tightening trousers. He'd have to get it under control before they started walking again.

'Of course.' She did look up briefly, then, her eyes dancing. 'And no, my father doesn't know.'

He should have known. Greer chuckled. 'Well, go on, tell me what you see.' *Besides a full-blown erection just inches from your skirts.* He was going to have to start wearing his darker trousers. A man couldn't hide anything in fawn. Inexpressibles. Hardly. They were more like *expressibles*.

'For starters, you have an air hand. That means you have long fingers and a squarish palm.' She traced the outline of his hand with a slow finger. 'I noticed your long fingers right away that first night.'

'An air hand? Is that good or bad?' He didn't really care, he just liked the feel of her fingers tracing the lines of his palms.

'Neither. It simply describes characteristics. You

like intellectual challenges. You are easily bored. That would explain your enjoyment of the military and your eagerness to avoid the home farm, don't you think?'

Once more they skirted a truly personal issue. This time it was he who shied away from it. He caught her looking up at him from beneath her dark lashes. He chose to play the cynic. 'It would if I hadn't already told you that. How do I know you're not just putting pieces of fact together and making this up to suit?'

'You have to trust me.' She spread his fingers and studied them each in turn. 'Look at that.' Mercedes licked her lips, looking entirely wanton and very much like a gypsy. He was positively rigid now. Her next words just about did him in. She caressed the flat of his palm. 'You are a sexual creature who excels in the intimate arts.'

'Be careful, Mercedes,' Greer warned in low tones. He was about to 'excel' right there.

'Or what? I'll find my skirts up and my legs wrapped around your waist? Is that a promise?' Mercedes gave a throaty laugh. The image she painted was a potent one but this was not the time or place for such a demonstration.

Greer grabbed her wrist none too gently. 'That's enough.' She needed to be taught a lesson about toying with a gentleman's sensibilities. 'I will not play the animal to your Circe in the middle of a public park.'

She shot him a hard look and yanked her wrist away from the shackle of his grip. 'Of course you won't. In the end, you'll always abide by the rules.'

It was said mockingly. She was daring him and he

was almost tempted to prove her wrong, that he *would* break those rules and take her right there. Goodness knew it was what his body wanted.

'Is that what you want?' Greer asked tersely. 'Do you want me to take you here in this most uncouth fashion?' He could feel the closeness between them evaporating.

'What I want is for you to concentrate on tonight,' Mercedes snapped. Just like that the termagant was back. For a few moments they'd been something more than travelling partners. The lines that defined their association had blurred ever so briefly. He was coming to recognise Mercedes was very good at such blurring, especially when it helped her get something she wanted.

Damn her.

It all became crystal clear: *the best target is someone whose ego is greater than their skill. Give up a bit early, let them think they've got the upper hand, then raise the stakes and win the game. Always quit while you're ahead.* Greer blew out a breath and had the good grace to laugh. 'Are you hustling me, Mercedes?'

She smiled, wicked and knowing, a finger trailing lightly down his shirt front. 'I don't know, Greer. Tell me again, what are the rules to a good hustle?'

Chapter Nine

'There he is. That's your mark,' Mercedes whispered at his ear a few hours later. The quiet inn had been transformed into a noisy crowd of people. It was a Friday and wages had been paid out. Men jostled at the bar for tankards of ale and the activity was brisk around the billiards table. Even a few women were present, although none were as stunning as Mercedes.

Tonight she wore a tight-fitted gown of deep-blue satin, trimmed in black lace and cut shockingly low, shoulders bared, the star pendant hanging from a black satin ribbon at her neck. Looking as she did, Greer was almost ready to forgive her for hustling him that afternoon. Almost.

He kept a hand at her back, ushering her through the crowd to an empty space near the billiards table where they could watch the games. 'Him?' Greer nodded towards a tall man in his early thirties playing at the table. The man in question had been winning.

Mercedes nodded, but he noticed her gaze kept moving about the room, always landing on one man in particular, a handsome auburn-haired fellow who boldly returned her attention. 'Greer, why don't you get me a glass of wine, if they have any?' she said absently.

Greer questioned the wisdom of leaving her. Every man in the room had noticed her by now, Mr Auburn-haired included. When he hesitated, she laughed up at him and he had no choice but to go in search of wine. 'I'll be fine. But it is sweet of you to worry.' He was going to end up fighting someone over her tonight, he just knew it.

By the time he had returned, hard-won glass of wine in hand, he could see his suspicions weren't far off. The auburn-haired man had moved to her side in his absence and men hovered around Mercedes. Worst of all, that little minx was encouraging it.

'Your wine, my dear.' Greer elbowed Auburn Hair at her side with a little more force than necessary.

She took the glass from him with a smile and a laugh. 'There you are, I thought you'd got lost.' Then she addressed the group around them. 'This is Captain Barrington. He's a fair billiards player, too, like your Jonas Bride there.' Impressive, Greer thought. She had the name of the mark already.

She batted her eyelashes at Auburn Hair. 'Do you think my Captain can take him, Mr Reed?' Her hand idly fiddled with the star charm where it lay against her bare neckline. Every man's eyes were riveted on that bare expanse of skin, especially Mr Reed's. Mr Reed's eye might be a bit darker for it too.

Mr Reed shot him a cocky glance men everywhere

have understood for centuries. *I can take her from you.*
To Mercedes he said, 'Shall we see?'

Mercedes reached into her cleavage and pulled out
pound notes with a graceful gesture while half the room
sucked in their breath. Good Lord, she was putting on a
show. Even knowing that, Greer couldn't help but feel
the first stirrings of desire. Then Greer understood.
The mark wasn't Jonas Bride, not really, not unless he
chose to make the man his personal mark. The real mark
was Mr Reed and she'd been drawing him to her since
she'd walked in the room. *Find someone who likes to
bet beyond their ego.*

Reed called over to Jonas Bride and a game was
quickly established. Mercedes blew him a kiss, the signal to lose. *Give up a bit, build the opponent's confidence.* This would be for both of them should he choose
to engage Jonas Bride. It was what Mercedes was waiting for, his test for the evening. Would he personally
engage in a hustle? Would he be able to win when he
needed to, unlike in Bosham?

'Bride, care for a wager between us?' Greer offered,
the affront to his own pride goading him into it. He'd
show Mercedes he could play this as well as she could.

Greer lost the first game good-naturedly. Mercedes
passed her pound notes to Reed and tossed her dark
head. 'Shall we go again?' she said coyly, drawing more
money from her bosom. Reed practically salivated. She
blew him another kiss. And another.

Reed was standing too close to her, staring too much
by the time she gave the signal to win. Greer doubled

his own wager with Mr Bride, who gladly took it, seeing it as a chance for easy money. He'd just won three straight games.

Greer broke and won, careful to win just barely. There was no sense in making Bride look foolish. Reed bent over Mercedes's hand and kissed it lavishly before he surrendered the funds, his eyes lingering on her breasts.

It's just a game, Greer reminded himself, watching money pass back and forth between them. She's playing with Mr Reed, working him out of his money. It's you she likes. It's you whose ear she sucked into oblivion; it's you who she kissed in the parlour at Bosham, *really* kissed. You kissed her first and she kissed you back.

But it was hard to remember that when Reed had his hands on her, his mouth possessively close to her ear as if he had any right to Mercedes. And that cocky stare of his! He positively gloated every time he caught Greer looking at them.

Looking at them was proving costly. Reed slid a hand along Mercedes's leg and Greer shot a poorly aimed slice that nearly caused him to scratch. Mercedes laughed and slid a hand inside Reed's waistcoat. Greer clenched his jaw and tried to focus on the game. He should split the pair and make the table difficult for Bride. It was what Mercedes would recommend.

'Don't miss, Captain,' Reed called out. 'I'd hate to have to console your lady if you lost again.'

Greer looked up. Lucifer's balls, Mercedes was in his lap, her mouth at Reed's ear. That was it. No defence, no strategy. He was going to clear this table, take his winnings and his woman and get the hell out.

Greer aimed and aimed again, the shots coming in rapid fire. He saw only the table, only the balls until he'd potted them all.

'I think that might have been the fastest game ever played,' a man breathed somewhere in the crowd. Greer didn't care.

'I'll take my money, Bride.'

'And give me no chance to win it back?' Bride was disappointed.

'No,' Greer said tersely although he could see the answer was not popular with the crowd. Bride had lost a considerable sum. Greer stuffed the money in his pocket. 'Mercedes, we're leaving.'

Mercedes shot him a disapproving look, but he was done. He wasn't going to stand by and watch her flirt with another, especially when he didn't know exactly where he stood with her. It was time to stake that claim.

'Maybe she doesn't want to go, *Captain*,' Reed sneered, deep in his cups by now.

'The lady is with me.' Greer planted his feet shoulder width apart and flexed his hand.

'Is she?' Reed drew Mercedes to him, but she was too quick. A small blade flashed in her hand, coming up against Reed's neck.

'I am.' Mercedes's eyes glinted with the thrill of the hunt.

Reed released her. She moved backwards to his side and Greer felt a profuse sense of relief to have her with him. Ale had made Reed slow, but his sluggish brain was starting to work it all out. 'Hey, that's not fair. You made me believe—'

He couldn't complete the thought before Mercedes interrupted. 'You're right. I made you believe and you fell for it.' She slipped the blade into the hidden sheath in her bodice and gave Reed a wink. 'The last rule of a hustle is to quit while you're ahead. Adieu.'

Greer grimaced. He wished she hadn't said that. Reed wasn't drunk enough to ignore the slight, but he *was* drunk enough to fight. It didn't take a genius to know who he'd be swinging at. It wasn't going to be Mercedes.

Reed lunged. Greer was ready for him. His arm came up, blocking the punch while his other fist found Reed's jaw, laying him out in one staggering blow. Cries of injustice were rising. This was going to get ugly. He and Mercedes were woefully outnumbered. It was past time to get out.

Greer shoved a bench or two in the way to slow down pursuers and pushed Mercedes ahead of him with one word of advice. 'Run!'

But the patrons were unfortunately bored or game or both. And they were happy to give chase. At the door he needed his fists to secure an exit and still they followed them into the streets. He had Mercedes by the hand as they ran through dark streets, winding through alleys until the mob gave up the pursuit.

'Alone at last!' Mercedes gasped, half panting, half laughing as she bent over to catch her breath. Her hair had come down and her face was flushed. Greer thought he'd never seen anything lovelier. Until he remembered. He was supposed to be angry with her.

'You almost got us killed back there!' he panted.

'Beaten up, maybe.' Mercedes laughed, dismissing his concern.

'Easy for you to say. You weren't the one they were going to punch.' Greer felt his anger slipping away. It was deuced hard to stay mad at her. But he could stay mad at Reed.

Mercedes leaned against the brick wall of a building, her breathing slowing. 'You're looking at me strangely.' She raised a hand to her face. 'Do I have dirt on my cheek? What is it?'

'This.' Greer braced his arm over her and bent his mouth to hers, adrenaline surging through them both, the kiss hard and bruising, its unspoken message was clear. 'You are mine.'

This was a dangerous kiss. All of his kisses were. But that didn't help her resist. Mercedes fell into the kiss, the thrill of the chase finding a new outlet in this physical release. They had kissed before, just as hard and just as furiously. Tonight, it wasn't enough. In the moments of escape, she wanted more and so did Greer. Desire and adrenaline fairly rolled off his body. His hips pressed into her and she could feel the extent of his want, pulsing and hard as his mouth devoured her. Why shouldn't they have more? Why shouldn't they celebrate this moment? Why did it have to mean anything beyond now?

Mercedes reached for him, finding his hard length through the fabric of his trousers. She stroked it, firm and insistent, moulding the cloth about its rigid form until she felt the tiniest bit of dampness seep through. Greer groaned, sinking his teeth into her throat, his bite an intense mix of pain and pleasure against her skin. His hand too, was not idle. He cupped her breast, thumbing her nipple into erectness beneath the satin of her gown, creating an exquisite friction against her skin. A moan escaped her, swallowed up by his mouth. He was branding her with his kisses, with his touch. She ought not to let him. She belonged to no man. And there could be no future in belonging to this one, only disappointment. But, her body chimed in, not until after great pleasure. Greer would be a matchless lover, their passion unequalled.

Her skirts were up, the evening air cool on the heated skin of her body, her leg hitched around the lean curve of his hip, the decadence of their position fuelling their ardour. They were in a public place. Technically, anyone could come along at any time. It was a naughtily delicious thought to imagine being caught with this man. Even she had not dared so much in such a place before. Greer's hand slipped inside her undergarments and found her cleft, stroking, teasing her into unquenchable flames, his own breathing coming ragged and fast.

Mercedes fumbled in haste with the fastenings of his trousers. 'Come on, get that out here to play.' Her own voice was hoarse with want as her fingers groped for access to that most male part of him. Almost! She almost had it. That was when she heard it: the sound of horse harness and carriage wheels. They were about to be discovered by, 'My father!'

Mercedes tugged at her skirts, giving Greer a shove into action and pushing him away from her just as the Lockhart coach stopped in front of the alley entrance, travelling lanterns lit. A dark figure jumped nimbly down from the coach box. 'I heard there was a little commotion at the inn and thought you might be looking for a ride.' Her father strode forwards looking at ease.

They *did* need a ride, but damn the man, he was showing up at the worst times. First at the fair, now this. How in the world was she ever going to get Greer into bed at this rate? After tonight, that was precisely where she wanted him and the consequences be hanged.

She could feel Greer at her side, his hand warm at her back, his body emanating unsatisfied heat. 'This is not over,' he growled for her ears alone.

'It certainly isn't,' Mercedes replied *sotto voce*. No one passed up a lover of this calibre no matter what the circumstances.

'Am I interrupting anything?' Her father grinned. 'Celebrations, perhaps? I heard someone cleaned out a particular Mr Reed tonight and a Mr Bride. I am assuming it was you two?' He elbowed Mercedes good-naturedly. 'Everyone is talking about the woman in the blue dress. Good job, my dear.'

Normally, she would have basked in his praise, but tonight her mind was too full of Greer to spend more than a passing moment on the acknowledgement. At the carriage, Greer handed her up and followed her in, her father choosing to ride up on the box with the coachman and take in the mild evening. But the damage had been done. There would be no resuming of the alleyway. The recklessness of the moment had passed, but it would come again.

She and Greer were headed towards consummation. It was only a matter of time. Still, a foregone conclusion was not without its own delicious torture. A waiting game had been invoked tonight. When would it come? Where and how? Would it be fast and hard and decadent like the alleyway? Would it be a dilettante's pleasure—a slow fire building towards a raging inferno by degrees? He would be capable of both.

Mercedes studied Greer in the lantern light, the blue eyes and the strong set of his jaw. He'd fought for her tonight, kissed the living daylights out of her in an alley. Of course they were headed to bed.

But what then? How long could she keep such a hero? Well, she wouldn't think about that tonight. There were other more pleasant things to ponder, such as how Greer might take her. And less pleasant things, too, such as how she was going to convince her father to let her play. They were nearing Bath where her father wanted to make a considerable stand and she was no closer to earning his public approval than she had been before they left Brighton.

Greer reached below the seat and pulled out the blankets kept there. He handed her one with a smile. 'Go to sleep, Lady in Blue.'

She took the blanket. 'You were jealous tonight.'

Greer nodded, not shying away from the truth. 'I was. I didn't like seeing Reed's hands all over you.'

Mercedes smiled softly as she spread out her blanket. 'Well, try not to punch anyone else. I'd hate for you to ruin your hands before the tournament. It is just a game, Greer.' She settled her head against the cushioned walls of the carriage.

'My shoulder might be more comfortable,' came Greer's low tones. He didn't wait for a response. Perhaps he sensed forcing a direct answer from her would be too much of a commitment.

Greer slid over to her seat and wrapped an arm about her, drawing her close. She could smell the sandalwood of his soap mingled with the sweat of the evening and clean linen, a comforting, masculine smell of a man who knew how to take care of himself and of others. She was used to hard kisses and fast-spent passions in her associations with men. She was not used to this: the sense of being protected and cherished. She'd not been prepared for the Captain to turn out to be a man who was strong and passionate with a capacity for tenderness. Before she drifted off to sleep she thought she heard the whispered words, 'You're not a game, Mercedes, not to me.' Her heart cried out one last futile warning. Here was a man who could ruin her.

Here was a woman who could ruin him. Greer stayed awake long after Mercedes had fallen asleep against him. In the moonlight and lanterns she looked harmless enough, a peaceful sleeping beauty to the unsuspecting connoisseur. But he knew better, far better than she knew. He was living on borrowed time and every mile they drew closer to Bath, more sand drained from the hour glass.

Bath would be full of people, *his* kind of people—

barons and viscounts who were there before moving on to London or back to their estates for summer. It was unlikely hc'd escape detection. There'd be someone there who would know his brother or his father and word would get home. When that happened, there'd be hell to pay.

It wasn't just his father's disapproval he was risking—he'd risked that often enough in the past. His father's disapproval was a private matter kept in the family. There would be no hiding this. Society would know what he'd done and that would bring shame to the entire family. He, a captain in the military, second son of a viscount, had taken up with a billiards hustler and his daughter. Never mind that Lockhart was a celebrity. Playing billiards for a living was patently unacceptable. Flaunting Mercedes in the face of decent society was a direct slap in the face to all the eligible young girls looking for husbands. Mercedes could be his mistress and be kept discreetly out of sight, but nothing more. To be seen with her publicly at the gatherings of 'decent folk' was inappropriate.

It would send his mother swooning and his father might actually disown him this time for good. Mercedes was wrong when she'd accused him of having nothing to risk in this venture. He had everything to risk. What would happen if he lost the security of knowing the home farm waited for him? It was not a destiny he wanted, but it was there like a safe harbour should all else fail.

He'd joined the military to make his own way in the world. But that choice hadn't come at the cost of his family. Never before had 'making his own way' come with a price. His family had issues, but they were his family, the only one he'd ever get. If it came down to his own independence or them, would he give them up? He would need to decide soon. Even if he escaped Bath unscathed by recognition, it would be good to know where he stood. He couldn't plan a future without knowing.

Sleep started to settle on him. Mercedes shifted against him and he tightened his grip about her. Maybe she wasn't the only reason he'd got in the carriage in Brighton. Maybe he'd known this choice would push him to make the decision he'd put off for so long. It was time to face his future head on: home-farm manager, professional billiards player, half-pay officer waiting for a post, or something else altogether. Greer sighed. He wondered if there was a choice that could include Mercedes. That was the problem with options. They made one have to choose.

Chapter Ten

'It's time to work on your defence.' Mercedes tossed Greer an ash cue. They'd picked up the London-Bath Road and were in Beckhampton at an inn on the turnpike where her father knew the owner. At this pace, they'd be in Bath the day after tomorrow at the latest and the true work would begin—real games, real promotion of the tournament in Brighton. These early stops had been meant to be the warm-up for the real campaign; time to turn Greer's instinctive talent for the game into a more sharply honed skill, a calculated tool of intention without drawing attention to him until they were ready.

Mercedes arranged the balls in strategic clusters around the baize. 'We'll start with the group to the right.'

Greer grinned disarmingly. 'That's hardly fair. There's no direct line between my ball and the shot.'

Mercedes smiled back with feigned sweetness. 'That's why we have to work on your defence. So far we've been playing opponents who play like you do.

They make great offensive shots. But what happens when someone *doesn't* play the table straight on you? Those men are waiting for you in Bath. You'll need to do more than pot balls; you'll have to know how to set up the table as well as setting up your shots if you want to impress them.'

Greer had a natural aptitude for the strategies. But she knew the real challenge would be whether or not he could pull each strategy out of his repertoire and use it at relevant points in a game.

They ran drills for an hour before her father came over to watch their progress, the perfect opportunity if she chose to seize it. If she didn't do something today, it would be too late. She didn't want to make Greer her whipping boy, but time was running out and so were her choices. She could only hope he'd understand.

Across the table, Greer raised an eyebrow, questioning her hesitation. 'Are you going to rack them?'

She answered with a non-committal shrug. If she did this, Greer was going to hate her for it. A small part of her was going to hate herself too. She drew a deep breath. 'All right, if you think you're ready, Greer, let's play.' It was now or never.

That should have been his first clue something was amiss. Mercedes had opted out of lessons and drills far earlier than usual. His second should have been the way she'd chalked her cue. She held his gaze while she blew the excess chalk off the tip, a most seductive look that made a man think with a whole different set of balls than the ones of the table. 'I'll break.'

'Fine.' Greer was pretty sure most men would agree to anything with those eyes looking over a cue at them and those lips suggesting chalk wasn't the only thing they'd be good for bl—*that* was not worthy of him. But he was also pretty sure Mercedes knew exactly what she was doing. She'd done it with Mr Reed. Now she was doing it with him. Why?

Something sensual and wicked flaring between them was not new. Innuendo always lay just slightly below the surface with them. Why would she push this now when he needed to concentrate on the game on the table instead of the one in his head? His brain knew better; he just had to send that same message to his body and quell the early stirrings of his arousal.

Lockhart was watching intently and Greer knew Mercedes wasn't going to go easy on him. There was no need to. He was up to any challenge Mercedes might present. Greer bent to survey the table at cue level. No straight shot presented itself, Mercedes would be happy about that. He would be forced to select a skill from their lesson right from the start. Greer aimed his cue to hit the ball slightly off centre, using a slicing shot to send it to the pocket while sending the cue ball on ahead to safety, away from the hazard.

'No, wait.' Mercedes interrupted his concentration. 'You're still aiming too low. A slice shot is to be off-centre, not high or low. The shot you want to take will put your cue ball in the pocket too.'

'It's fine,' Greer said with a tight smile, not wanting

to be taken to task in front of Lockhart. He was a man, for heaven's sake, not a sixteen-year-old schoolboy. He knew what he was doing.

Mercedes shrugged and let him take the shot, raising her eyebrows in an 'I told you so' gesture when his ball followed the other into the pocket. He blew out his breath. She briskly gathered up the two balls and set them back on the table. 'Try again. This time, let me show you.'

She stood close, wrapping her hands over his, positioning the cue. He was not unaware of her body pressed to his, the light floral scent of her soap or the womanly curve of her where her hips cradled his buttocks. The arousal that had sparked earlier was in danger of being fully achieved. This time the shot went in. She put the balls back into place one more time. 'Now, try it again on your own.' Greer lined the shot up carefully, thinking there might be something else he'd be trying alone if she kept this up. This time he sank the shot and the game was fully engaged.

By the second round, Greer was certain there was more than one game being played out. Mercedes was shooting out of her head. He'd never seen anyone make the shots she made, and he'd most definitely not seen *her* display this level of skill, which was saying something.

He'd thought her formidable before. Now, there wasn't even a word in his vocabulary to adequately describe her talent. Phenomenal, stupendous—easy word choices, but inadequate. What did she think she was doing? But there was no time to contemplate hidden agendas. Greer played harder, his shirt sleeves rolled up, his jacket off. The intensity increased. He plied his skill tirelessly with slices, stop shots that careened on the lip of the pocket, bank shots that circumvented barriers to direct shots, but nothing would stop Mercedes.

Greer lost all three games, honourably and by mere inches to be sure, but in the end he'd simply been outplayed. When the last ball fell, Mercedes threw a triumphant smile in her father's direction. Greer expected to see Lockhart grinning at his daughter's success—perhaps he even expected a little scolding directed his way over having lost. But the scold that came was for Mercedes and it was not what Greer had expected at all.

Lockhart rose, fury on his face. He strode towards Mercedes and yanked the cue stick from her hand. 'What the hell do you think you're doing? Parading yourself like that? No man wants a woman who plays better than himself or even a woman who plays, for that matter, let alone one who has any skill at it. Act like a lady.'

Mercedes had a fury of her own. 'Act like a lady? What happened to "you've always understood the game"? You were happy enough to have me act any way I pleased as long as you could use it.'

Greer felt like an interloper. This was private, family business being aired in the midst of an inn. His family would not have dared to display their conflicts so openly. Then again, his family preferred to keep those sorts of things tucked away and ignored, pretending they didn't exist, like their financial deficiencies.

'You are not playing in Bath. That's final.' Lockhart's voice was terse, a tic jumping in his cheek.

'I'm better than any man,' Mercedes replied. 'Why are you so afraid?'

'It's not seemly. You've been raised to be a lady in bearing, if not in name. Is this how you repay me? Is this what your fancy dresses and fine education are to come to?'

Mercedes would not back down. 'You did that for yourself. *You* wanted that for me. You never once asked what I wanted. Why show me billiards at all if you never expected me to excel?' Mercedes's eyes glittered with wet, as of yet unspilled, emotion. Greer's heart went out to her in that moment. How brave she was. He'd been taught a man bore the decisions of the world stoically and without complaint. Never mind that he'd thought many of the same things Mercedes gave voice to now.

'That is enough, Mercedes.' Lockhart had gone rigid 'If you don't like my decision, you are welcome to go home and await our return there.'

Mercedes shot him a look full of blazing discontent and stormed out of the inn, the door slamming behind her. She was nothing if not magnificent in her anger. Lockhart turned to Greer, his hands held out in a gesture of reconciliation. 'I am sorry, Barrington.' He sighed. 'She's emotional in spite of her pretensions to the opposite.' Lockhart gave a quiet chuckle. 'She's a woman, no? What can we expect? You have sisters. You know how it is.'

'Yes, two of them,' Greer said tightly. He didn't want to be corralled into taking sides against Mercedes, but neither did he want to offend Lockhart. Lockhart could send him packing as easily as he could Mercedes, and the ride had really just begun with the first big test looming in Bath if he embraced it.

'Two sisters—then you're used to their high-strung tendencies.' Lockhart made a shooing gesture with his hand. 'Go and talk to her. I don't like her on the streets alone, but I'm the last person she'll want to see. Maybe she'll listen to you.' He gave a fatherly sigh of defeat. 'The world is what it is; she can't change that, no matter how much she rails against it.'

Greer was more than glad to go after Mercedes. He didn't doubt she was safe, armed as she was with the knife in her bodice and her temper. No man with any intelligence would fail to read the signs of an angry woman. He could do with some air himself, some time to sort through what had just happened.

The more he thought about it, the more he couldn't help feeling that Lockhart, the consummate showman, had turned even a personal quarrel with his daughter to his advantage. If he was willing to do that with an issue of a private nature, what else would he stoop to use or who? Was there any sacred line in the sand?

That didn't make Mercedes the innocent party here by any stretch. It did occur to him as he walked down the street, replaying the quarrel in his mind, that she might have been using him to make her father angry, that he was a tool for flaunting her own independence in all ways. The realisation took the bubble off the wine. He didn't want their kisses, their passion, to be part of some other game she played. He didn't want to be another 'Mr Reed' to her, someone she used for other ends. It was time to confront her on that issue.

Mercedes saw Greer approaching out of the corner of her eye. She flipped open the little watch she carried. 'Ten minutes. Very good. I win,' she said without turning from the window.

'I'm sorry, did we wager on something?' Greer said coolly. He had his own issues to settle with her. She'd used him in there.

'I wagered with myself that my father would send you after me within ten minutes. He wouldn't dare come himself. He did send you, didn't he?'

'I was concerned for you.' Greer's answer was evasive. But it confirmed her suspicions.

'If you've come to espouse his cause, forget it. Do yourself a favour and don't play his messenger. I'd like to think you were a better man than that.' She was being cruel on purpose, hoping to drive Greer away. She didn't trust herself at present. If he touched her, if he said anything kind, she might just go to pieces and she didn't want to. She wanted to be strong. Anger kept her strong.

'All right,' Greer said calmly, unbothered. 'I'll just stand here and admire the window with you.' Greer joined her in staring at the goods on display. There wasn't much to look at: a gaudy hat complete with bright purple ribbon and green feather and a few bolts of printed muslin. Beckhampton might be on a major road, but the town was still small.

'Maybe I'll just ask the questions. What was going on there? I don't mean the fight, I mean *all* of it; the blowing on the chalk, the bedroom eyes over the cue, the "let me show you how to line the shot up"? It was quite a show. Was it for my benefit or his?'

'Maybe it was for neither of you,' Mercedes replied succinctly. 'Maybe it was for *me*. Did you think of that? Or perhaps you've put too much construction on what it meant at all.' She tossed him a sharp, short glance.

'I could say the same about you. Did you roll up your sleeves and take off your coat as part of some grand flirtation?'

'Of course not,' Greer answered hastily. 'That's ridiculous. It's easier to play without my coat.'

'My point exactly.'

'Be fair, Mercedes, it's *not* the same thing. It's not like you were taking your *lips* off because they confined your play.'

Mercedes had to work hard to stifle a laugh. But it wasn't time to laugh yet. 'I'm sorry you were distracted—perhaps you should work on that. It seemed to be a problem the other night as well.' She turned to go, but Greer grabbed her arm, a *frisson* of warning and heat running through her body as she realised what she'd done. She could push the well-trained aristocrat in him only so far before she encountered the man in him too.

'You used me back there. I won't stand for that. Don't play with me, Mercedes. I think we've done that enough on this trip. We've been playing games since that night in the garden and most of those games you've started.'

'You haven't minded,' she shot back. 'It was *your*

tongue in my throat in Bosham as I recall, your hips against mine in the alley.'

'You're right, I haven't minded.' Greer held her gaze, letting his own drop briefly to her lips. She licked them. 'I just want to know why. Are these kisses for business or pleasure?'

Mercedes gave a hard laugh. 'If I was using you for sex, Captain, you'd have known it by now.' But she thought her words might be a lie. There was no arguing he was in her blood.

Greer smiled dangerously. 'Likewise. And if you're going to stand there contemplating how best to seduce me, call me Greer.'

'How do you know I'm thinking *that*?'

'Because we have unfinished business. Seduction between us is inevitable—I think the alley affirmed that. Don't you? It's just a matter of who will seduce whom.' He leaned close and whispered at her ear. 'If you're the betting sort, I'd put your money on me.'

Mercedes whispered back, 'If men's cocks were as big as their egos, I might take that bet, *Greer*.' The look on his face was priceless, part shock and part admiration. Now it was time to laugh.

Chapter Eleven

It was a subdued group that pulled into Bath. He had no one to blame for that but himself, Lockhart mused. He shot a look at Barrington, who rode beside him. It was quite telling that the Captain had chosen to ride instead of his usual routine of sitting with Mercedes inside the carriage.

Clearly, words had been said between them when Barrington had gone after her. From the tension at dinner last night, Lockhart didn't think the words had solely been about the billiards game. There'd been a certain spark between Mercedes and the Captain from the start. Travel and close proximity had encouraged it just as he'd hoped. For that matter, *Mercedes* had encouraged it to their benefit. The Captain's 'affections' for Mercedes, whatever their basis, had indeed kept him loyal. If this was a mere flirtation for her, a means to an end, fine. But if she actually developed true feelings for Barrington, there would be trouble ahead should either of them choose to rebel.

Mercedes's rebellion was of immediate concern. She'd been upset by his decision to not let her play in Bath. An upset Mercedes would need to be appeased before she did something reckless which could be disastrous for them all. Bath should go a great way in appeasing her once they got settled. He had a lovely house rented and he'd turn over the social calendar to her. She'd cultivate relationships for him that would be good for the tournament and she'd feel useful. She'd have gowns to wear and the handsome Captain at her side to act as an escort to balls and other entertainments. She'd forget she was angry.

As for Barrington, the Captain would be in his element, among people like him. And he was looking forward to making the most of Barrington's entrée. Bath would be most lucrative for him riding in on the Captain's coat-tails. He and the Captain would make a splendid duo in the clubs. He could feel the cue in his hand already. Between the two of them, they'd be unbeatable. Everything was working out splendidly and Mercedes would come around. He'd see to it with plenty of money and entertainments to keep her busy, and a few well-placed compliments.

Lockhart gave the coachman directions to the terraced house. This would not be an overnight stop. He planned for them to spend two, maybe three weeks in Bath, where the season was already under way.

The coach stopped in front of the Bath-stone town house with its neat wrought iron railings and large windows. Lockhart was pleased to note even the Captain was impressed with the lodgings and location—right on the Crescent and within walking distance of all the important places: subscription rooms, the assembly hall, the theatre and the almighty Pump Room, where the heart of Bath beat on a daily basis.

He dismounted and helped Mercedes down himself. She looked up at the house, a small smile on her face. Lockhart would take it as a good sign. 'Can you get us settled? I shall see you at dinner.' He drew her aside to let Barrington and the trunks head into the house.

'You've done splendidly with him.' Lockhart nodded to indicate the Captain as he passed. 'He's come a long way. His play has been refined. He has a sense of strategy now. Well done, Daughter.' He beamed at her. 'You should get some new dresses made up while we're here.'

'I may. I have plenty.' Mercedes didn't thaw any further.

'Well, it's up to you. A pretty dress might go a long way with the Captain. He wants to impress you. Make sure you keep him dangling. That can be a useful tool, a leash to keep him on.'

When Mercedes said nothing, he swung back up on his horse, calling down a promise, 'I'll see about tickets to the theatre while I'm about it.' 'It', of course, was arranging entrance to the subscription rooms where men would play billiards all day long, serious gentlemen like himself.

'How many should I expect for dinner tonight?' Mercedes gave him a half-smile. She knew very well he was plotting already. Good for her.

'None tonight, but the invitations will start rolling

in by tomorrow.' Lockhart winked at the Captain as he came down the steps. 'Tonight will be the last night you're saddled with only my company.' Hopefully the Captain would take the hint. If there were any loose ends between him and Mercedes, Barrington had better tie them up quickly. In Bath the Captain might face competition for Mercedes. Not nearly so highbrow as London, Bath would be more tolerant of Mercedes's antecedents and he needed Mercedes and the Captain together for now. If Mercedes froze him out, he'd have to manage her through the Captain.

Her father would not manage her as if she were a little girl. He was *not* forgiven. He could dazzle and compliment and offer new dresses and theatre tickets all he liked, but he was not forgiven, not this time.

Mercedes stepped into the terraced house, her mind already whirling. Her father wasn't the only one with plans to set in motion. She'd had all morning alone in the carriage to adjust her strategy. Plan A had failed. Her father was not going to allow her to go public with her talent. The quarrel the previous day had shown her that very plainly and there was no longer any reason to hold out false hope things would change in that regard. But there was always Plan B.

She smiled to herself, surveying the luxuriously appointed drawing room, a place ladies would want to come and be entertained. This house was going to be perfect. With its location at the heart of Bath, it was well positioned to become a social centre to rival the Pump Room. She would see to it.

'Does it meet with your approval?' Greer had come up behind her, directing the grooms to take the trunks upstairs.

She turned to face him, hardly able to prevent her features from radiating her excitement. 'Absolutely.' To keep him from suspecting too much, she crossed the room with a brisk stride and pulled open the double doors, leading to the dining room. 'Very elegant,' she commented, running her hand down the length of the polished table. 'We can seat fourteen for dinner. That will do nicely.'

'Do you really plan on doing a lot of entertaining?' Greer queried dubiously. 'Do you know anyone in town?'

She tossed him a coy glance. 'Not yet. But we will, you'll see. We'll have tickets to the theatre by tonight and invitations will fill the salver in the entryway by tomorrow. That was no idle boast my father made. He knows how to play this game.' Mercedes smiled smugly. She knew how to play the game too and she could play it every bit as well her father could.

'You didn't go with him?' Mercedes said as they made their way upstairs to see the private chambers. The downstairs had been perfect. Along with the drawing and dining room, there was a small office, a lady's parlour and, best of all, a room with a billiards table. She suspected the room was normally used as an informal dining parlour or second sitting room. But the table was Thurston's and fit the space admirably, and she would put that table to good use.

'I could tell he wanted to be alone,' Greer offered charitably. 'This is his town, isn't it? He grew up here?'

Mercedes nodded. That was something Greer would only have known from listening to bits and pieces of conversations, further testimony to the fact that he was a good listener, a keen observer. One had to be careful around people like that. 'He and Kendall Carlisle were boot boys in the subscription rooms until a gentleman noticed their interest and took them under his wing. He showed them the game and the rest, as they say, is history.'

They came to a large room done in dark, masculine greens, clearly designated for the master of the house. 'You can put my father's things in here,' Mercedes directed the grooms. She would have to get staff hired this afternoon. She mentally added the task to her list.

Down the hall were two other rooms across the hall from each other, one in pale blues and the other in a deep gold. She stepped inside the latter and surveyed it, taking in the large, heavy four-poster bed and the clothes press. The room was simply done, but not shabby.

'Will it do for you, do you think?' It would be interesting to have Greer so close to her. On the road, most inns hadn't had three separate rooms available. He and her father had shared a room on those occasions. Having him alone and across the hall in a private home was far different. She wondered what he'd do if she were to slip into his room one night? She wondered if she *would* do it?

'Mercedes?' Greer was talking to her, *had* been talking to her.

'Yes?'

He shook his head. 'You haven't heard a single word I've said. What's going on in that head of yours? Your brain's been running a mile a minute since you got out of the carriage.'

Mercedes smiled sweetly and sailed towards him, running a hand up his chest. 'I was wondering what I'd find if I crossed the hall in the middle of the night.'

'You'd find me.'

'Yes, but which you?' Mercedes murmured, head cocked to one side, eyes on him. She watched desire flicker in his eyes as it warred with his sense of decency. 'Would I find the gentleman? The officer? The rogue? The gambler, even? I wonder what would happen to your wager then?'

'You coming to my room doesn't preclude my ability to seduce you first,' Greer countered.

'But it does make the waters murky,' she parried. 'One might argue I won because I opened the door. I started it.'

'You start a lot of things, Mercedes.' Greer's hand covered hers where it lay against his chest, his eyes going quietly blank, all desire pushed back for the time being. 'I thought we'd agreed yesterday it would be foolish to pursue this aspect of our relationship.'

'I recall no such thing.' Of course, it had been there in the subtext of their exchange. *If I was using you for sex, Captain, you'd have known it by now.* And his bold, '*likewise*', with the candour of a rogue. But it was the gentleman she faced today and the gentleman was troubled.

'It could get complicated.' He raised her hand to his lips and kissed it—a gentleman's gesture. Almost. The press of his lips to her hand wasn't quite chaste in the same way her hands on him, helping manage his cue yesterday, hadn't been quite instructional.

'Complicated? How so?' She breathed, dreading his answer. Something had changed for him.

'People may know me here. Associating with me may make things difficult for you.'

That was the most polite way she'd ever heard it phrased before, but the meaning was still the same. 'Difficult for me or for you?' she questioned. 'I'm fine with it. I am proud to associate with you. I'm sorry you don't feel the same.' Tears threatened. She was not going to cry, not for him and *not* over this. This was an eventuality she'd known was coming at some point. Viscounts' sons were made for débutantes, not for the daughters of Bath bootboys.

She let anger come to her rescue. 'I'm good enough for a quick one in the alley, to push up against an oak tree when no one's looking, but heaven forbid people actually know we associate with one another.'

There was more she'd like to have said. She didn't get the chance. 'Stop it, Mercedes. That's not what I meant,' Greer hissed.

'It's exactly what you meant. You're a hard man, Greer Barrington,' she whispered, drawing her hand slowly away from him and stepping backwards towards the door.

'Yes, yes, I am.'

A swift glance south confirmed it. Mercedes smiled coldly. 'Good luck with that. Let me know when you get it all worked out.' Maybe bed wasn't a foregone conclusion after all. Her practical side offered consolation. Not bedding Greer avoided a number of extenuating complications, but her other side, the larger part of her, was extraordinarily disappointed. It was a small consolation to hear Greer's door slam moments later. Apparently he was disappointed, too. At least the issue of status was out in the open now. They were no longer dancing around it and all the ways it would define what could or could not be between them.

Being with Mercedes, or *not* being with Mercedes, was like a bad waltz: one step forwards followed by two steps back and a couple of missteps in between. This latest exchange was a definite misstep. He'd not meant to imply he didn't want to be seen with her, only that there might be people who would make it difficult for her, who might say cruel things because of her association with him, not the other way around.

Men could be fortune hunters and simply be called rogues. Women who did the same were grasping and desperate or considered licentious wantons. The grasping and desperate might be tolerated with pity, but licentious wantons were exiled. Whores had their places, after all. He didn't want that for Mercedes. He wanted her to be acceptable. *So that you can have her without cost.* It would be the easiest solution, or it would have been if he'd phrased his concern better. Now he had to dig himself out of this hole he'd dug. It was a shame. Things had been going well.

Greer wanted to punch the wall. It would serve Mercedes right if he broke his hand. But a broken hand did him no favours so he opted for pacing in the hopes it would subdue his temper and his erection.

He'd thought they'd made progress in their relationship in Beckhampton, building on their exchange in the park in the prior town and their wild run through the streets. They'd moved from flirting and testing the waters of their attraction to suggestive banter. That banter had become a contract. He thought it was fairly clear from their discussion in Beckhampton where they were headed: into a relationship of sorts.

Of sorts. How was *that* clear? His logical mind laughed at him. Was all this about bedding her or having something more with her? Perhaps the whole problem was that they hadn't worked that out. Every time they seemed to make progress, one of them threw a roadblock up—a snapped comment, a shrewd insinuation, or a challenge, and then they withdrew until the next time. No wonder they were frustrated and reading things into conversations that weren't necessarily there. They had to stop overthinking this.

Greer stopped pacing and looked out the window of his room. He'd hurt her feelings today, inadvertently. It was up to him to make the next move and put things back into their proper orbit. It was up to him, too, to decide his future here in Bath, to stop thinking about what others wanted from him and consider instead what he wanted for himself.

Greer smiled. It felt as if a great weight had been lifted. Life had suddenly become simpler. He knew what he wanted: Mercedes. And he was going to get her.

An idea came to him. He went to his trunk and pulled out his uniform, shaking out his scarlet jacket. Perhaps an association with him *could* work in her favour. Perhaps, if the need arose, he could make her acceptable.

Greer laid the jacket aside. One problem solved. Pacing had subdued his temper and given him clarity. There would be a price for this decision, but maybe it was time to pay it. He looked down at himself. There was still his erection to deal with, the problem pacing hadn't resolved. It was a good thing he hadn't punched the wall. He was going to need that hand after all.

Chapter Twelve

By half past six, Mercedes had the house well in hand; a cook, a housekeeper, one maid and two footmen-cum-valets, happy to act as men of all work, were established below stairs having performed their services for the evening with sufficient dexterity. Keeping busy had taken her mind off Greer. But she prepared for an evening at the theatre with a growing sense of trepidation. Either Greer would be downstairs waiting or he would not. Her father would have her neck if Greer had left and she would be vastly disappointed, but not surprised.

She'd not left things on a good note with him that afternoon. Perhaps she should have let him explain. But it had been easier to get angry, *safer*. She'd started that conversation with the intention of taking things further, of acting on the implicit contract they'd established in Beckhampton. But then, at the slightest hint of trouble—those ambiguous words about the consequence of their association—she'd retreated. Not only had she retreated, she'd thrown up a fortress. It would be no wonder if Greer left. Any other man would have. Men didn't like difficult women. Now, as she took a last look in the mirror, she was betting Greer wasn't like any other man.

She'd worn the oyster-coloured summer organdy and pearls and put her hair up in a simple twist. The effect was one of elegance and class. Tonight, she dared any lady to look better. Greer would be proud to have her on his arm if he was downstairs. Mercedes drew a breath to steady herself. There was no more waiting.

At the top of the stairs, that breath was taken away at the sight of Greer. He'd stayed! Relief swamped her, mingled with abject appreciation of his appearance. He leaned casually on the banister, one foot on the bottom step, his head resting on his hand as he looked up at her, his gaze hot and approving as he took her in. He was turned out in the full glory of his dress uniform, much as he had been that first night in Brighton.

'I'm sorry I'm late,' Mercedes said, taking the final step. The comment was *de rigueur*. She wasn't truly late, merely the last one downstairs, and the curtain didn't rise for another half hour.

Greer took the matching mantlet from her and stepped behind her to drape it. 'Beauty in any form is always worth waiting for.' His hands skimmed her shoulders, his voice low for her alone. 'I'm sorry about this afternoon.'

'I thought you might have left.' She drank in the scent of him, all citrus and sandalwood. His hands were warm where they lingered at her shoulders.

'Don't worry, Mercedes. I never leave until I get what I came for.'

'You mean me.'

'I mean you.' He offered her his arm. 'Shall we? Your father is waiting outside. He has rented a small victoria for the evening.'

'Greer?'

'Yes?'

She smiled mischievously. 'Nice buttons.'

The ride to the theatre was uneventful unless one counted the butterflies fluttering in her stomach. Greer had stayed *for her*. The realisation played in her mind like a litany. It didn't mean all their problems were magically solved, but it did mean they could move forwards to wherever they wanted to go.

The carriage stopped to let them disembark in front of the tri-arched Theatre Royale. Brighton had its culture, to be sure, but there was something distinctly exciting to be attending the theatre in Bath. The press of people and the buzz of a hundred conversations only made it more so. She put her hand in Greer's and he squeezed it as he helped her down, a shared look passing between them as if he knew what she was thinking and perhaps shared the feeling.

Inside, her father had secured prime seats in the box of his newest 'best friend', a Sir Richard Sutton, his wife, Olivia, and his daughter, Elise. Introductions were made, Sir Richard and her father acting like old friends instead of acquaintances who'd met only hours earlier. Seats were taken and the lights dimmed as Greer slid into the space beside her. She had not missed the fact that for the first time since their association, her father had introduced Greer as Lord Captain Barrington. Sir Richard had been impressed. If the reference had bothered Greer, he'd made no show of it.

The play was a rendition of Shakespeare's comedy *As You Like It*, and the cast was good. There was champagne at the intermission, their box filled with the Suttons' acquaintances. It turned out Sir Richard was a prominent yacht builder with connections to the royal family and those in the exclusive royal set. As a result, he was quite popular with the titled families that had come to Bath before heading to London.

Mercedes smiled to herself. It was becoming clear why her father had ingratiated himself with this particular individual. But she liked Elise and thought Lady Sutton would serve her own purposes quite nicely. By the time the Lockharts and Suttons parted ways for the evening, Mercedes had an invitation to join them in the Pump Room tomorrow. They would have an invitation from her the day next for cards and afternoon tea, only they didn't know that yet.

Plan B was going swimmingly.

The next day set the pattern for the days to come. Mercedes slept late, dressed carefully for a promenade with Greer in the Pump Room, during which she'd meet with her newly accumulated friends: Elise Sutton and her mother, and by extension of that, Lady Fairchild, Mrs Ogilvy, Lady Dasher, whom all her friends called

Dash, red-headed and vibrant Mrs Trues and her friend Lady Evelyn.

After the gossip of the Pump Room, where Mercedes made an enormous effort to listen to everything that was being said and about whom, there were the afternoon activities. Most of these were organised or prompted by her. She talked Mrs Trues into arranging an 'historical tour' of the Roman ruins. She convinced Lady Evelyn, who loved painting in the countryside, to put together an 'artist's picnic' for the ladies. The event was such a success the ladies decided to do it once a week, weather permitting. There were the weekly card parties Mercedes hosted herself in the elegant drawing room of the rented terraced house.

Then it was on to the evening entertainments, the balls at the assembly rooms, nights at the theatres and private entertainments. Greer always escorted her and put in a lengthy appearance beside her before disappearing with her father to the elegant subscription rooms and gentlemen's clubs.

Greer proved to be a most able dance partner and by far her favourite time of day was in the evening when she could spend it on the dance floor in his arms. He was a popular partner with all the ladies, never letting any wallflower go unattended. On more than one occasion she'd been discreetly approached by the young ladies of Bath inquiring about her 'situation' with the Captain. To which she merely responded, 'He is a friend of my father's.'

'You should have told them we have an "understanding.'" Greer gave a mock grimace as he swung her through a turn at the top of the ballroom one night.

She smiled up at him, flirting a little with her eyes. 'Do we? I wonder what that might be?' He'd made no obvious overtures since they'd reconciled after their quarrel and yet he'd not been inattentive. Just the opposite, in fact. He'd been her unfailing escort in the mornings to the Pump Room, to some of the afternoon activities to which she'd invited gentlemen, and every evening. Surely a man who invested that kind of time and energy in a woman wasn't unmoved?

'That pleasure awaits us when the time is right.'

'Pleasure, is that what it would be?' she challenged coyly.

He bent his mouth close to her ear. 'It's not always dismal, Mercedes.'

'For the man you mean,' she rejoined, but there was heat in her belly, conjured there by his words, breathed so seductively in her ear she thought she might collapse right there on the ballroom floor. They were not the words of a gentleman.

The dance ended and in the press of people leaving the floor, his next words were lost. But she thought his lips had formed the phrase, 'care to find out', before they broke into a most tempting smile.

Maybe she would. The time would be right just as soon as she got phase two of her plan underway.

Mercedes was up to something. It was a marvel Lockhart didn't notice it, Greer thought, leaning against his billiards cue in the subscription room. But Lockhart was too busy revelling in his fame. The billiards champ had been well received in Bath, everyone eager to hear his opinions on Thurston's tables. Everyone was eager to see him play, too, and to learn about the championship coming up in Brighton.

Lockhart was undeniably in his element and it was, admittedly, an exciting place to be. Lockhart introduced Greer to players who shared his seriousness about the game and to others who might be able to advance a second son's ambitions in other ways. The evenings were full of entertainments and then the gentlemen adjourned to the subscription rooms for games much like MPs would adjourn from dinner to a late-night session of Parliament. And with about the same level of gravity.

Lockhart had been right. In Bath there were serious games to be had and Greer was grateful for the hard work Mercedes had put him through in preparation for them. But since their arrival, Mercedes had backed away from billiards. True, she played him on occasion at home. But it appeared she'd meekly accepted Lockhart's verdict in Beckhampton and Greer didn't believe it for a minute. She'd become the epicentre of Bath with her circle of friends and whirlwind activities. For the record, he didn't believe that either.

Greer lined up a difficult shot and made it, using a gentle slice stroke. Lockhart nodded his approval. They were playing as a team against two other gentlemen, industrial princes from the north. But Mercedes was claiming a lot of his concentration. She was up to something, but what?

Chapter Thirteen

'I think the arrangement will be to your liking.' Mercedes fixed the woman across from her with a confident stare over the rim of her teacup. The woman in question was none other than Mrs Booth, proprietress of Mrs Booth's Discreet Club for Gentlemen, located just off Royal Victoria Park.

The attractive businesswoman smiled back. 'Twenty per cent of whatever you make?' she clarified the terms.

'Twenty per cent.' Mercedes nodded. There were only so many places in a town where a girl could make money, 'discreet gentlemen's clubs' being one of them.

'I have to ask: why here?' Lucia Booth took a bite of lemon cake.

'I like your clientele,' Mercedes said easily. She'd done her research in the last week. Mrs Booth's was a familiar destination for many of the husbands of her newfound friends. It would provide her a little leverage should she need it. Mercedes leaned forwards, giving the impression she was about to impart a juicier answer.

She lowered her voice to complete the impression. 'I'm going to play in the All England Billiards Championship, if I can raise the entrance fee.' It was true, too. She'd made up her mind ages ago when the tournament was first announced, but she still had to raise the entry fee. There was no way to raise that money in Brighton where everyone knew her.

Mrs Booth arched her dark brows. 'That would be something, to see a woman play.'

Mercedes caught the approval in the woman's voice. She set down her teacup and rose, wanting to end the interview on a positive note. 'I'll start tonight. I'll come in the back around nine o'clock.'

Mrs Booth rose with her. 'I'll be happy to have you. The men need a new distraction, but I want to be sure you understand.' She paused for a moment. 'You do know this is not your usual gentlemen's club?'

Mercedes knew very well what she meant. Mrs Booth's wasn't a club like White's or Boodles or even the subscription rooms. Mercedes smiled. She'd have to have been blind not to notice this club's main attraction was its women. It was not so much a club as it was a brothel. Classy and elegant, it catered to rich gentlemen with discerning tastes. 'I know very well what this place is.'

'All right then, because I won't be tolerating any trouble from an angry husband, father, or brother, who comes looking for you.'

Mercedes thought of the wig and gorgeously provocative gown she had stashed in her wardrobe, acquired from a 'discreet' modiste in town who probably catered to the employees of the 'discreet gentlemen's club'. 'It will be as if I'm hardly here,' she promised with the glimmer of a mischievous smile.

Mrs Booth smiled back and extended her hand. 'Call me Lucia. I think we shall get along just fine.'

Indeed, one would have been hard pressed to recognise Mercedes when she arrived at Mrs Booth's that night in a deep-red gown trimmed in jet beads and cut shockingly low. The gown was expensively done and Mercedes felt decidedly wicked in it. The wig, purchased from the theatre company, was a soft brown, much lighter than her usual dark tresses. It was styled with braided loops to give the impression that her hair was pinned up. Together, the wig and the gown created a most tantalising image of a proper lady behaving badly, a juxtaposition that was certain to distract the gentlemen, if not drive them a little mad.

And it did. The gentlemen flocked to the table, eager to play at first out of novelty, then, seeing her true skill, out of desire to prove themselves. They vied for her attentions, they bought her glasses of champagne, from which she sipped delicately, careful not to overindulge. As the night wore on, she recognised a great many of them as the spouses of her friends, who'd come to the charms of Mrs Booth's establishment after having done their duty with their wives.

She'd known the nature of those society marriages, but encountering it first-hand was more difficult, especially when Lord Fairchild, well in his cups, made an inappropriate overture after losing a large sum to her at the table. Louisa would just die if she knew her husband had propositioned the billiards girl at Mrs Booth's. Mercedes fended him off with a smile and turned her attention to the next game.

The first three nights had been easy. She was trading on novelty. But by the fourth night, word had got around about the 'new feature' at Mrs Booth's and curiosity over the unknown had blossomed into interest. Everyone wanted to know who she was. She had a ready fiction to hand, of course, prepared for such an eventuality. She was Susannah Mason, a gambler's widow from Shropshire, whose husband had met his death in a duel over cards.

'Really?' Mr Ogilvy, who'd become a shockingly regular customer and loser at her table, shook his head one night and studied her sharply. 'I could have sworn you looked familiar.'

Mercedes placed a light hand on his arm and gave a throaty laugh. 'Some people believe we all have a twin somewhere in the world. Perhaps you've met mine?' The court gathered around the table laughed along with her.

'Who is next, gentlemen?' Mercedes called out, eager to play. Her nest egg for the entrance fee was coming along nicely. In a few more days she'd have it, which was well enough since her father didn't plan to stay in Bath much longer. She won the break and began to play, bending low over the table, letting the gown do its job.

But Ogilvy was persistent, not nearly as distracted by her bosom as he usually was. 'It's the wrong-coloured hair, of course—the person I'm thinking of has dark hair. She's a friend of my wife's. I've met her a few times on outings,' he mused out loud. His musings chilled her. When he didn't stop, Mercedes fixed him with one of her hard stares. She needed him to stop before he figured out her secret.

'Does your wife know you're here, Mr Ogilvy?' she asked pleasantly, taking time to chalk her cue.

He chuckled, as did the men around him. 'She knows I'm at my club.'

'Does she know what goes on here? Or does she think we sit around and talk politics all night?' Mercedes blew chalk from the tip, deliberately seductive, a fleeting thought about Greer's comments flitting through her mind.

The men laughed heartily. 'No, she doesn't know. That's the best part.' Ogilvy laughed loudly.

Mercedes silenced him with a look. 'Then you'd better hope you're mistaken about the resemblance, sir. I'd hate to tell her what you've been up to with her money.' Helen Ogilvy had let it drop in a private moment on a picnic that Ogilvy had married her for her money to save his ailing estate. He was in line to inherit his uncle's baronetcy later, but while he waited he hadn't a feather to fly with.

Ogilvy looked properly chastised and there was no further comment about her appearance.

The evening had ended well. Mercedes had paid Mrs Booth her fee, put her wig and gown away at the club and headed home, tired but pleased. Plan B was working splendidly. She let herself into the house and stifled a scream as a large hand covered her mouth and an arm dragged her against the rock-solid wall of a man's chest.

'Where have you been?' a voice growled in her ear. Then she could smell him, the familiar scent of oranges. Greer.

He dropped his hand.

'Not in my bed, as you very well know. Been checking my room, have you?'

'I was worried. I came home and you were gone.'

'So you thought you'd scare me half to death. Fine idea,' she scolded in a loud whisper before going on the offensive. 'What are you doing home in the first place? Aren't you supposed to be playing?' She'd thought her father had arranged a private party at one of the subscription rooms tonight.

He wagged a finger at her in the darkness. 'Unh, unh, unh. No questions from you just yet. *You* were supposed to be with Elise Sutton at Mrs Pomfrey's musicale.'

'I was.' *For a while.* Until she'd claimed a headache and left for more lucrative climes. Musicales were not one of the places a girl could make money.

Greer danced her backwards towards a chair, both hands gripped her forearms. 'What's going on?' He pressed her down into the chair and took the one across from it, pulling the chair up close.

'Nothing is going on.' Mercedes tried to sound outraged at the accusation. 'Is my father home?'

Greer shook his head. 'No, he decided to stay on with some old friends who've just arrived in town. Now, don't try to change the subject. I know you're up to something. Tell me what it is.'

Mercedes crossed her arms. 'What makes you think I'm up to anything? I had a headache and came home. Later, I decided to go for a walk. I thought the fresh air might clear my head.'

Greer laughed, leaned forwards and took a deep breath. 'Mercedes, you smell.'

She probably did smell of Mrs Booth's. Mercedes seized the lapels of his evening wear and drew him close. 'Nobody likes a nosy parker, Greer,' she whispered low and throaty before she slanted her mouth over his. She'd meant to distract him, a game only. But it had been ages since she'd kissed him and it was like coming home. He tasted of brandy and wine, and his body was strong against her when she slid from her chair onto his lap. She kissed him slowly, tasting, drinking him. She was hungry for this man who was so handsome and good, a definite departure from the groping hands and crass innuendo of the supposed gentlemen at Mrs Booth's. Surely he wouldn't become like those other men, forsaking their wives for the momentary charms of expensive whores.

Her hands moved to his cravat, exquisitely tied as always. She yanked, rumpling all that perfection in a single pull. She tugged his shirt from his waistband, aware that her own skirts were high on her thighs, provocative and inviting as if she rode astride. She slid her hands under his shirt, moving up beneath the fabric to caress him, to trace the muscled contours of him. His hands tightened where they gripped her thighs, a groan escaping him.

'Mercedes, be careful,' came the hoarse warning,

uttered with great effort. She was sure he was as uninterested in caution at the moment as she was.

'Are you afraid?' She reached a hand between them and cupped him through his trousers. God, he'd be magnificent. She would have slid to her knees and parted his thighs right then if he had not restrained her, his hands tight over hers in a halting gesture that kept her on his lap.

'Damn right I'm afraid, Mercedes. If you had any sense, you'd be afraid too.' He drew a ragged breath, one hand pushing back a strand of her hair that had come loose. His fingers skimmed her cheek. 'What is this, my dear? Just when I think I have you figured out, have "us" figured out, and I've resigned myself to understanding this is a just a game to you, you go and make it feel real.' He shook his head, his eyes holding hers. 'I can't be a game to you, Mercedes. And I don't think it can be a game to you either, whether you know it or not.'

She rose from his lap and shook down her skirts. She turned away and focused her gaze out the window, gathering her thoughts. She wanted to shout at him, but what was there to accuse him of? The truth? Her hand closed over the star charm she wore at her neck. She hardly ever took it off. It was a way of keeping Greer close. He was right, he should be a game. But one could only imagine what would happen if she took anything with Greer seriously. A game was the only way she could have him and still protect herself.

She could feel him behind her, warm and near right before his hands closed gently over her shoulders. 'Don't mistake me, Mercedes. I would welcome you.

I have only one rule: when you come to me, you need to mean it.'

'Is that how a gentleman issues a proposition?' Mercedes snapped, shaking off his hands. She was suddenly tired and irritable. She was not used to having her advances foiled. Most men fell at her feet for the merest tokens of affections and there'd been nothing 'mere' about what she'd been ready to offer Greer.

'No, it's how I tell you I'm perfectly aware you were using the sparks between us to distract me from the true purpose of our conversation.'

Good Lord, he was like a dog with a bone. She huffed and said nothing, but Greer moved away. She could hear his footsteps at the door, halting before he passed into the hall. 'One more thing, Mercedes, your defence could use a little work.'

Her defence? Having her own words thrown back at her sat poorly. Mercedes stood at the window a while longer, staring at the empty street and letting his comment settle. He was right. She'd had only the dandies and the young, bright-eyed officers of Brighton to practise on for so long. She had to remember she was dealing with a man now and a suspicious one at that; possibly the very last thing she needed when she was so close to her goal. Well, he'd have to work fast if he meant to catch her. Two nights more, and Susannah Mason would disappear from Mrs Booth's for good.

Greer lifted his champagne glass in yet another toast. The private room Lockhart had procured for the night was filled to bursting with gentlemen who'd come for one last party, one last chance to hobnob with the former billiards champion. It was time to go. The Bath Season would officially close in little less than a month, sending its society to the country for the summer or, for those who could afford it, on to London where they could join that season under full sail. Already, Greer could feel the social whirl slowing down in anticipation of that shift.

'You'll be in Brighton for the tournament, of course?' Mr Ogilvy asked at his elbow.

'Absolutely.' Greer nodded. The tournament was on his mind a great deal more these days. The sojourn in Bath had been illuminating. For the first time he was starting to see the possibilities. If he could manage to win…he could what? Open his own billiards parlour? His family would cringe at the thought. But it would be a lucrative business, something he could support himself with, something he'd made from his own talent. He didn't believe this would occur without risk. His family might very well shun him, but perhaps that would be their problem, not his.

'It'll be deuce quiet around here with you and Lockhart gone,' Ogilvy said into his drink, looking mournful at the prospect.

Greer shrugged. 'It'll be quiet anyway. The Season's closing down.' But he knew Lockhart's parties would be missed. They'd been lavish, male-only affairs that had promoted jovial camaraderie amongst men who'd been bored beyond words at the predictable social rounds of Bath, a predictable whirl that went on for eight months, October to June. Lockhart had chosen just the right time to show up. Greer wasn't surprised. His arrival had been purposely calculated to draw maximum attention.

'How about a game, one final opportunity for you to beat me?' Greer gestured towards the table where the cues laid crossed like swords and waiting. Ogilvy was always up for a game.

Ogilvy shook his head. 'No, I'm afraid not. I'm cleaned out.'

Greer raised an eyebrow in disbelief. Ogilvy was a fair player, the kind Lockhart hoped to see in Brighton. 'Really? You were up a few games when you left here last night.'

Ogilvy shook his head again. 'I went on to Mrs Booth's, you know, the ole balls and stick.'

Greer laughed and clapped Ogilvy on the back good-naturedly. 'You're a fine billiards player, Mr O., but cards are not your thing. When are you going to learn?' Not much of a card player himself, Greer had watched Ogilvy lose large sums on more than a few evenings.

'Wasn't at cards,' Ogilvy mumbled, hastily taking a drink.

Greer elbowed him. 'Do tell, Ogilvy. It sounds like there's a great story there.' They edged away from the crowd towards a potted palm decorating the room's perimeter.

'Well, it's that billiards girl Mrs Booth's got. Susannah Mason? Haven't you heard of her yet? She's only been there about three weeks.' Ogilvy tossed a look towards the group beyond them. 'Lots of the men have lost to her. Most are too embarrassed to mention it.'

'That explains why I haven't heard about her.' Greer

grinned. It was a good thing Mercedes didn't know about her. Mercedes would be over at Mrs Booth's with a challenge within minutes—another good reason he and the Lockharts were leaving. If Mercedes knew there was a woman playing somewhere, *anywhere*, she'd be impossible for Lockhart to manage. Greer could imagine the scene that would ensue.

'I can't figure out if it's her skill or her gowns that make her so difficult to beat.' Ogilvy was going on about Susannah Mason. 'There's something familiar about her, but I can't place it. She's a card player's widow from Shropshire, said her husband was killed in a duel. It's all very dramatic.' Ogilvy gave a wave of his hand in dismissal, but Greer could see the man was quite taken with Susannah Mason.

Ogilvy put a hand on his sleeve. 'Say, why you don't come with me tonight? You can win my money back. I dare say you won't be as distracted by her charms. Not when you've got Miss Lockhart's attentions.'

It was on his lips to deny that he had Miss Lockhart's attentions, but Ogilvy was already back to his favourite subject of Susannah Mason. 'Then again, the way she blows chalk off her cue tip does all kinds of things to a man's insides, if you know what I mean.'

'Yes, I do believe I know.' Greer said slowly. His earlier thought returned. *If Mercedes knew a woman was playing.* There was no other woman, Greer would bet on it. It was her.

All the little oddities of the last weeks came together: Mercedes's apparent acceptance that she should turn her efforts to more feminine pursuits, her absence last night which might have been one of many. Who really knew what she got up to after he and Lockhart left her in the care of the lovely but sharp-minded Elise Sutton? Elise and Mercedes were thick as thieves these days.

'Shall we?' Ogilvy said.

'Yes,' Greer said grimly. 'Let's go and win your money back.'

Chapter Fourteen

'Double or nothing, then?' Mercedes laughed up at the young heir to an earldom. He was so *very* rich, but he was going to be a few pounds lighter when he left. She ran a light hand down his chest. The poor boy blushed, obviously revelling in being treated like the man he thought he was by a very beautiful woman who'd seemed to have stepped straight from his fantasies. Mercedes moved closer to him and flashed him a come-hither smile. 'Be warned, good sir, I can make that shot all night long.'

'It's true, she can. Your money is safer in your pocket.'

The all-too-familiar voice made her freeze. Good Lord, Greer was here! Mercedes turned from the young earl and faced him, her stomach plunging to her toes when she saw Ogilvy too. Had Ogilvy just happened to bring a friend? Or was something more malicious afoot? Had Ogilvy sold her out after all? He'd be very sorry when Helen heard about it. There was nothing for it but to brazen it out and hope for the latter while believing the former. Greer's comment left her very little room to pretend he didn't know it was her.

Mercedes smiled sweetly and sailed around the table. 'Mr Ogilvy, have you brought a friend?' She linked her arm through Ogilvy's and stared up at Greer, giving him an assessing once-over.

'This is Lord Captain Barrington of the Eleventh Devonshire.'

'Enchantée.' Mercedes unlinked her arm from Ogilvy's and performed a delicate curtsy, the gesture and the French compliments of Mrs Bouchard's Academy for Girls.

Greer took her hand and raised it, pressing his lips to her knuckles, conjuring up memories of the last time he'd done that. *'Mon plaisir*, Madam Mason.' He made her name sound deliciously sophisticated, drawing out the Mason to Ma-sown. *'Est-ce que vous jouez?'* She retrieved her hand and shot him a narrowed-eye look. He knew very well her French was limited to about ten useful phrases and *that*—whatever it was he'd said—wasn't one of them. She hadn't exactly excelled at French. She regretted telling him that during one of their long mornings in the carriage.

'I believe Bonaparte lost the war, Captain. We speak English at Mrs Booth's.' That brought a round of laughter from her court.

Greer wasn't daunted. He selected a cue and began to chalk up. 'Mr Ogilvy tells me you play a good game.' He glanced around the room, smiling broadly. 'Good enough to beat most of the gentlemen present on more than one occasion. He has compelled me to come and defend men everywhere.' He gave the chalk on his cue tip an efficient blow, looking entirely likeable.

'Hear, hear,' came a few cries from the back of the room.

The dratted man was going to steal her crowd if she wasn't careful. Usually she admired Greer's ease, how people *wanted* to cheer for him. She wasn't admiring that trait at the moment. Beneath his aura of bonhomie, he was primed, a veritable powder keg and the fuse was lit. He was going to ignite this room and she'd get caught in the explosion.

He didn't wait for an answer. Greer gathered up the balls and stepped back. 'Your table, Mrs Mason. You may break.'

'Your heart or your balls, Captain?' came a voice from the crowd. Mercedes smiled at the crass comment, privately reassured. She hadn't lost the room yet. And she wouldn't. She'd beat Greer and give these boys a show they wouldn't soon forget. After tonight there would be no coming back. Susannah Mason would go out in glory.

Mercedes met Greer's gaze down the length of the table, eyes wide with secret laughter, her mouth a perfect, discreetly rouged 'O.' A gentleman or two sighed when she chalked up and raised the cue to her lips in her trademark gesture and blew, knowing Greer would get the unspoken message: *game on.*

She bent low over the table, wriggling her shoulders to advantage; she sashayed up and down the table with a sway of her hips; she flashed coy smiles and sipped provocatively from champagne flutes until most men in the room were worked to a frenzy. All but one. Greer remained most disappointingly unaffected. Unaffected or not, it didn't mean he won. He lost the first game and the third, and was on the verge of losing the fifth if she potted her next shot. He seemed unbothered by the circumstance. He matched her mad flirtation with his dry humour. The room was enchanted by the pair of them goading each other to greater heights.

Every eye in the establishment was fixed on them. Money changed hands. Mrs Booth came to stand beside her, watching her sink a shot with the cue behind her back to general applause.

The proprietress applauded, too, but when Mercedes stepped from the table, she pressed a wad of pound notes into Mercedes's hand and whispered fiercely, 'End it with your next shot. I don't care if you win or lose, just do it quickly. Your little duel with the Captain isn't doing business any good. The girls haven't been upstairs with a customer for an hour.'

Greer made his next shot, which would prolong the game. If he'd missed, she'd have had a clear path to victory in one shot. But now they were even and a ball of his blocked her play. Mercedes had no choice but to scratch. She recited the old gambler's mantra in her head: sometimes we win by losing. The wad of notes in her hand proved it. But pride made it deuced hard to swallow that reality. She didn't *want* to lose here or now or to Greer, who had somehow ferreted out her little gambit and had come to ruin her fun.

But she did it, hitting her cue ball too hard and letting it follow its target into the pocket. The crowd groaned.

She groaned, too, but pasted on a smile as if it were a trifling thing and called for champagne all around. This got the girls circulating again, moving in and out of the press with trays of bubbling champagne, turning the gentlemen's attentions elsewhere.

Mrs Booth appeared at her side once more, ushering her and Greer into the hall. She was eager to be rid of them. 'Why don't the two of you settle up privately? Susannah, you can use Lisette's room at the top of the stairs.' Lisette had left yesterday for a more private arrangement with a well-to-do gentleman.

Mercedes understood it wasn't a request: it was a command. But she didn't relish facing Greer behind a closed door, especially if he had the upper hand. She made her choice in an instant. She was *not* going to let him take the offensive and berate her. No doubt he would view this latest behaviour as being entirely beyond the pale. A lady playing billiards in a brothel was almost inconceivable to one of his lofty birth. What he needed to understand was that she was as angry with him as he was with her. He could have jeopardised everything. The moment the door shut behind them, she faced him, hands on hips, and fired her salvo. 'What the hell do you think you're doing?'

'Isn't that supposed to be my line?' Greer crossed his arms. Her verbal offensive had caught him by surprise. He'd anticipated having the first words in this conversation. And the last. But he should have known she wouldn't play by the rules.

'Let's be clear, Mercedes, *you* are the one in trouble here, not me.'

'Me? I'm not the one poking his nose into someone else's business. You could have ruined everything to-night!' She flung an arm in a careless gesture that nearly knocked a pitcher off a delicate table. Greer reached out and righted the teetering vessel, taking a moment to get a grip on his vacillating emotions. He should be furious over *her* taking him to task in the middle of a French whore's boudoir, yet all he wanted to do was kiss her or spank her. At the moment, it was hard to decide which. Both held some appeal.

'Me? *I'm* not the one playing billiards in a brothel, dressed in disguise—' Greer ticked off her sins on his fingers '—and using a false name while emptying the pockets of your friends' husbands.' Lockhart would be furious if he knew she'd been stealing money he saw as rightfully his to win or if being beaten by a woman had scared the men away from the Brighton tourna-ment altogether.

'It serves them right. They shouldn't be here to start with. They should be home with their wives. If they were, none of this would have happened.' Mer-cedes reached up her arms in a motion that brought her breasts into tight relief against the bodice of her gown and began to remove the wig. Definitely spank-ing, Greer thought.

Greer laughed. 'Only you would be able to turn *your* transgression into a moral judgement on your fellow mankind. You make it sound like you've been serving up matrimonial justice instead of simply fleecing them.'

She shook out her hair, a sensual gesture that put kissing back in the lead, but her lips tightened. Her eyes narrowed to blue slits. 'My transgression? I made money the only way I knew how.'

'By flirting with them? I saw what you were doing to that poor lad in there. He didn't know up from down with your hand on his chest. You knew very well you'd have him at a disadvantage,' Greer accused. He knew he played the hypocrite here. He'd been as riveted as the next red-blooded male. She'd been intoxicating to watch. She'd commanded every man's full attention, giving them their fantasies in the flesh. There wasn't an Englishman in the room who wouldn't go home and dream about her tonight.

Greer's groin tightened at the memory of her leaning over the table, the naughty fire in her eyes indicating she knew precisely what he was thinking as she let the cue slide through the bridge of her fingers in erotic reference to other sticks that slid and sheathed themselves in other warmer, wetter portals.

Mercedes circled him, her coy half-smile flitting on her lips, one hand trailing idly over the shepherds and Staffordshire dogs littering the surfaces of the room. Apparently Lisette had packed in a hurry. Must have been a good offer, Greer thought wryly. Mercedes drew a long finger down the back of a pointer, causing him to repress a most male shudder. He could feel that finger on him, caressing, teasing, drawing its manicured nail ever so lightly down something much more worthy than a china dog. At least he thought he had suppressed it. Her next words confirmed he might not have been so successful.

'Jealous, were you?'

It was an obvious gambit and she knew very well what she was doing with her dog-tracing act just as she'd known the effect she'd had all night. He really should spank her. She was in desperate need of a lesson. She was trying to provoke him.

'Jealous? Of middle-aged men and boys without beards? Hardly.' For a moment he entertained the notion that he should resist. Then he thought better of it. No. She would expect resistance. She was planning to lay siege to *him*. Not tonight. If there was any mastering to be done, it would be by him.

Greer picked up her trail, tracking her around the room. He wanted her to know he was coming, wanted her to anticipate the moment he would catch her. He reached for her arm and spun her around to face him, drawing her to him. 'You should play with a real man, Mercedes.'

Her breath hitched, her pupils dilated with excitement. 'I suppose you think that's you?'

'Damn straight it's me,' Greer growled right before he bore her back to the wall.

Mercedes stifled a gasp. She barely had time to wrap her arms about his neck before she found herself pressed deliciously against the pink-and-cream-striped wall, Greer's lips hard at her mouth, his hips grinding against hers in provocative invitation, his desire in rampant evidence where their bodies met. Her breath came uneven and excited as she let the thrill of excitement course through her. He wasn't the only one burning with need. He'd stoked fires of his own tonight.

Her hands made short work of his waistcoat and turned their attentions to the tails of his shirt, pulling them loose from his trousers in frantic jerks valued more for speed than efficiency. She wanted him naked—fast. He seemed to share her thoughts. In all her concentration on his clothes, her own gown had found its way to the floor in an ignoble heap. She hitched a leg about his hip, her petticoat falling back to reveal a long expanse of leg. Greer's hand took the invitation, sliding up its length to cup her bottom beneath the fabric.

The act put her in intense proximity with the most male parts of him. She could feel the intimate swell of him at the juncture of her thighs. She nipped at his ear none too gently to convey her growing urgency. 'Magnificent' might not do it justice. 'Greer, these trousers have to go. Now.' She didn't wait for an answer. She pulled them down herself, swallowing hard when her hand met with the coveted length of his flesh, hot and rigid in her palm.

Greer wouldn't tolerate any play when she made to explore. 'Later,' came the gruff response. But he was right. They were both too far gone to enjoy any foreplay. What they wanted would be explosive and fast and it would happen against this wall.

He lifted her other leg and she wrapped them both about him, finding purchase between his strength and the unyielding wall. He took her then, in a fierce thrust that went straight to her core and wrenched a wicked scream from her throat. This was decadence and pleasure at its finest. She dug her hands into the thick depths of his hair and tightened her grip, holding him deep inside her as she moved her hips to his rhythm. She gloried in the intimate friction of his body inside hers. He shifted slightly, adjusting his position and thrust.

A gasp slipped her lips. She'd not been ready for the unexpected sensation it invoked. Her mind registered only one thought: more. And yet more of such an exquisite glimpse of pleasure would surely drive her mad. But Mercedes was no coward; she'd risk it. 'Again!' she managed, her voice nothing more than a wispy tremble before that singular glimpse transformed into a wave of sensations that threatened to overwhelm her.

She rode that wave, bucking hard against Greer, vaguely aware that he was there with her too in this frenzied roil of rough desires. His hands were hard where they dug into her buttocks, his body heated with exertion as its very life pulsed against her, his voice hoarse with inarticulate need as they crested one final time and the wave broke, spilling them into a sweat-slicked oblivion of sated need.

Mercedes was boneless, useless in the dénouement that followed. It was Greer who brought them to the pink haven of the bed, seeing her settled before he gave in to his own, no doubt considerable, exhaustion. Mercedes felt the bed take his weight as he lay down beside her on the satin sheets. She snuggled into him, her head fitted to the curve of his shoulder, feeling the welcome strength of his arm gather her to him.

Within moments his breathing took on the soft pattern of one asleep. For a while she thought she'd sleep too. She was tired enough. But her mind would not comply. It was still too riotous, sorting through the images of what had transpired. Most of it she understood in an objective sense. Weeks on the road suppressing desires had come to a head, goaded in no small part by the circumstances of the evening and the reality that they'd been attracted to one another from the start. She'd seen it coming, and no doubt Greer had too for all his talk of honour. It had just been a matter of when. She could explain the 'when' and the 'why'. She couldn't explain the 'what' or the 'how'.

The 'what' that had passed between them had no comparison in her previous experience. She'd known such satisfaction was possible for the man, although perhaps not on such a grand scale as Greer's. But the same for a woman? She'd not known, not *imagined* there was anything more beyond the short-lived gratification of simply being physically close to another human being.

She laughed softly to herself, recalling Greer's words so long ago: *'Mine was better, much better.'* She might have to concede that it hadn't been mere male braggadocio speaking that day in the carriage.

The other unknown was the 'how'. How did one go forwards with any normality after such an encounter? She would forever look at him over the dinner table or down the length of a billiards table and see not just Captain Greer Barrington of the fine manners but her *lover*, a man who had brought her unparalleled pleasure. The issue of pleasure raised another question altogether—

how would she be satisfied with just the once? Pleasure like that should be tasted over and over.

She knew without being told it would become an addiction, one she'd have to find a way to live without when this tour was done and Greer Barrington went his own way. She was not fool enough to think such pleasure could be repeated with any man. Empirically, she knew it could not, which made what had happened all that more unique for its rarity.

Mercedes sighed, trailing a finger down his breastbone.

It was no wonder he'd said it couldn't be a game. She agreed whole-heartedly now, when it was too late and she was fully engaged. If the damage was already done, she might as well enjoy sweeping up. Mercedes moved her hand lower.

He awoke to her gentle cupping. She smiled up at him, pleased that his phallus stirred so easily to her touch even after a hearty bout of love-making. She'd feared he'd be spent. She should have known better. There was nothing weak about Greer Barrington. Mercedes reached behind his phallus and squeezed his balls, feeling them tighten. 'You're ready, Captain.' She looked at him from beneath coy eyelashes. 'Unless you need a bit more encouragement?'

Greer rolled to his side. 'I think that depends on what you have in mind.'

'A little equality.' Mercedes slid from the bed with a grin and stood before him, her arms crossed over her breasts in a provocatively modest display, her hands resting on the shoulders of her chemise. She slipped her thumbs under the thin fabric and pulled the garment ever so slowly over her head, letting it tease her nipples as it passed over her chest.

'Naked equality. I like it,' Greer managed hoarsely after the chemise had been discarded.

'Seductive equality,' Mercedes corrected, pulling the drawstring of her petticoat in a quick, decisive tug that rendered the item loose. She stepped out of it, aware of his eyes roaming her nude body with hot appreciation.

She came to bed and straddled him, letting him look his fill. '*I* mean to have *you* this time, Captain.' It was a wicked, selfish experiment she had in mind. Could the pleasure be repeated? Or had it existed because he'd been in charge? Did he control the pleasure or could she snare it for herself?

He raised his hands and filled them with her breasts, kneading in slow, delicious motions that stirred her fires. She could feel her control slipping away already. The effect he had on her was intoxicating, quite literally like drinking too much champagne, the world turning to a lovely place with blurred edges.

'You are more beautiful than I dreamed,' Greer murmured, raising himself up to kiss her, one hand leaving a breast to take up residence at the nape of her neck beneath her loose hair. The ingenuousness of his words was nearly her undoing. She'd been called beautiful before, but never with such sincerity.

'And you, sir, are a paragon of manhood.' She let the laughter dance in her eyes, as she raised herself up over his hips and then lowered, taking him inside as he'd taken her. 'It seems we are well suited.' A seductive smile played across of her lips.

'It seems we are.' Greer's eyes were dark with passion, his body tense beneath her as she began to ride. Slowly, up and down, she tightened her inner muscles as she slid the length of him, feeling him strain against her. Then she began to rock, back and forth, and the magic ignited.

Greer surged into her, arching in his need, his body and mind wild at the sight of her atop him, her hands cupping her own breasts. She revelled in the thrill of Greer Barrington unleashed, unbound by his gentleman's code of conduct in these unguarded moments, but the madness was taking her too. The harder she rode him, the more intense his response until they were on that wave once more, cresting and crashing and the amazing thing was happening again, sweeping her away, her wicked experiment in shambles. Now she knew and that knowledge cast a shadow over the future. To achieve this pleasure, she needed him.

Chapter Fifteen

He needed her. That much was clear and nothing else. Greer would bet she was feeling something of the same. It was as good an explanation as any as to why Mercedes had elected to ride inside the carriage, *alone*, on a splendid morning as they pulled out of Bath. Lockhart had thought nothing of her decision. He'd dismissed the choice as female foibles. 'She wants to collect herself after saying farewell to all of her friends.'

To be sure, there'd been tearful goodbyes on the steps of the terrace house this morning. A large group of women had turned out to see Mercedes off. Mercedes had energised Bath. Her presence would be missed. Elise Sutton had hugged Mercedes tightly, whispered something in her ear and promised to see her in Brighton later in the summer. But Greer doubted such farewells had moved Mercedes as much as they had moved the women who gave them. *They* hadn't spent the night in a brothel 'settling things', to use Mrs Booth's phrase.

Settling wasn't the word Greer would use to describe

what had happened in that room either. Unsettling was more apt. Bedding Mercedes had been an extraordinary moment out of time. If he could just leave it at that—an experience fomented by circumstance—things would be fine. But he couldn't leave it as a singular event and simply forget it. He'd had a few moments like that in his past, enough to know this wasn't one of them. Many officers did. Alone and far from home, he'd sought a night or two of temporary company from women whose names and faces had long since ceased to feature in his memory.

Such behaviour wasn't his usual habit, though, and he normally regretted it afterwards. Unlike many of his acquaintances, he'd never made a practice of treating sex as a mere physical exercise. He preferred more meaningful, long-term *affaires*. Although he'd had lovers over the years, he did not take just anyone to his bed for the sheer sake of a partner, which was why the incident with Mercedes last night had been so unsettling.

Those were poor choices of words. *Incident?* What had happened could not be classified as a mere instance. *Had been?* Still was. Once they'd returned home, he'd slept restlessly for the remainder of the night. From the dark shadows under Mercedes's eyes this morning, she had too. All of which proved that last night had meant far more to them than either had intended. It wasn't the culmination of a month's worth of flirtation. It was the beginning of something new.

Lockhart brought his horse up alongside, cheerful and oblivious to the dilemmas running through Greer's head. 'We're about three days out of Birmingham.' He was already planning the next stage. 'It's not a pretty city, but it's an interesting one. We'll only stay a few days, long enough to spread word about the tournament and whet a few appetites. There are adventurers in Birmingham—our kind of people, Captain.'

Greer cringed at the reference to 'our kind of people'. Lockhart was an intriguing man, to be sure, and there was much to admire about his journey in life. But it wasn't Greer's life and it wasn't Greer's journey. They had billiards in common and this brief interlude was a fascinating departure from Greer's regular patterns. But beyond that? The more he knew about Allen Lockhart, the harder it was to respect him. He and Lockhart operated by very different codes of ethics.

He'd watched Lockhart work the men in Bath, dining out on his celebrity status, entertaining in lavish style. It was a fascinating study in human nature. Lockhart had made those men believe they possessed a potential they didn't truly have and Lockhart *knew* it. Greer didn't want to be that sort of a man, a confidence man, a hustler.

'Do you think many of the gentlemen in Bath will come to Brighton?' Greer voiced his thoughts out loud.

Lockhart nodded. 'Yes. A few of them will play in the tournament. Perhaps Ogilvy will play. But most of them will come to watch, which is exactly what we want. The presence of peers will lend a certain cachet to the event and they'll bring money to town.'

He gave Greer a shrewd look. 'Money is good for everyone. All the businesses will prosper. There won't be an empty inn within five miles of Brighton. People need food and drink and subsidiary entertainment. *And*...' he paused here, drawing out the word for emphasis, 'those gentlemen might not play in the tournament, but they *will* play their own informal games in the subscription rooms around town. Everyone will benefit,' he repeated with a smile.

Lockhart lowered his voice although there was no one around on the empty road. 'Remember this— when the time comes, there's often more money to be made outside the venue than in. The tournament is just the draw, just the lure to bring in the money. The real money will be made elsewhere.' Lockhart laughed. 'I can see I've stunned you. It's not what you expected?'

Frankly, it wasn't. He'd taken this tour far too literally. He'd thought Lockhart had been looking for players when, in reality, Lockhart had been looking for spectators. Lockhart hadn't solely been out drumming up games when he went on ahead. He'd been drumming up business too. He'd probably been making arrangements for ale and food to be brought in. He'd buy it cheap from country vendors who had no way to get their goods beyond the local markets of their villages and then sell it high in Brighton, a simple case of supply and demand.

Lockhart laughed. 'Why would I need players, Captain, when I have you? You're my man. I'd back you against anyone in England, and in July I will.' He favoured Greer with a warm smile. 'You're one of the finest natural players of the game I've ever seen, Captain. You remind me of myself when I was younger, only you've got something I never had, something intangible that I can't name. But all the same, I know you've got it.'

It was elaborate flattery and Greer knew he should be wary of it, but it was nice to hear anyway, a type of reinforcement that he could make his own way if he chose. Lockhart was going on about Birmingham, the canals and the pioneering spirit of the city. Greer let him. Lockhart was good at one-sided conversation. He had other things to think about, like what to say to Mercedes when they stopped for lunch. There'd been no time to speak that morning amid the bustle of last-minute packing but they needed to talk, the sooner the better. A man didn't make love to a woman and then pretend it hadn't happened.

The northern roads towards Birmingham were well populated with villages and it was no trouble to find a promising inn for lunch. The inn Lockhart chose had plank tables set up outside for guests to enjoy the weather and pretty flower boxes spilling with spring blooms, hanging from its windows.

Mercedes was reserved during lunch. Lockhart tried to draw her out with talk of her new friends. 'Elise Sutton's father has a new design for a yacht. I'm thinking of investing. He means to race the prototype next year. If it works out, everyone will want his plans.'

Mercedes smiled at her father's effort. 'Elise works very closely with him.' Greer could hear the carefully veiled barb.

Lockhart reached across the table and tapped Mercedes on the nose in a fatherly gesture. 'That gives us something else in common with them, my dear. It's a smart man who knows the value of a daughter. I knew I liked them. I'll definitely invest then, for the principle of the matter if nothing else.'

The look Mercedes shot her father was icily polite before she turned her attentions back to nibbling at the delicious meat pies. His own was nearly gone. It did amaze Greer that Lockhart with his commendable people skills could be so continually obtuse when it came to his own daughter. Mercedes had not forgiven him for Bath. But then again, people often missed what was right under their own noses.

Greer had just taken a healthy gulp of ale when Lockhart spoke again. 'I was so very proud of you in Bath, Mercedes.'

The man's daughter had been playing billiards in a brothel. Greer choked and Lockhart had to hit him on the back. All those outings and card parties had been a giant smokescreen for her clever little gambit. But for what? He still hadn't worked that part out. There'd been a table in their home. She could have played privately as much as she wanted. What had she needed that required such a venue as Mrs Booth's?

Across the table, Mercedes smiled, apparently finding the same ironic humour in Lockhart's comment as he did. 'I enjoyed Bath a great deal,' was all she said, but her eyes found his and he read a good deal into her simple statement, punctuated with the caress of a foot against his leg beneath the table.

'I enjoyed Bath greatly too.' Greer held her gaze for a moment, sending an unspoken message of his own. It was definitely time to get Mercedes alone. He rose before Lockhart could launch into a discussion of Birmingham. There would be days to talk about that. Right now, he just wanted to talk to Mercedes. 'I noticed some decent-looking shops when we entered town. Would you like to take a stroll before we depart?' He directed the offer at Mercedes, knowing Lockhart would be busy overseeing the horses.

They walked the short distance to the shops in silence, Greer rapidly assessing and discarding conversational openers: 'About last night…' No, too clichéd. 'We need to talk…' No. That sounded too dire. He didn't want her to panic. Good Lord, how hard could it be? He was an officer, for heaven's sake. He'd given more than one inspirational speech to his troops, encouraging men to make impossible stands on battlefields. Surely he could talk to one woman? It wasn't as if he hadn't talked to women before or even about things as delicate as the 'day after'.

But this was Mercedes he was talking to. She was bold and brash. She didn't need him to gingerly and correctly address the subject. She'd want him to be witty, perhaps even to attack the subject with a certain amount of insouciance regardless of the real, deeper feelings provoked by their night.

Greer smiled. He knew how to start. They stopped to study the items in what passed for this little town's idea of an 'emporium'.

'It doesn't have to be a dismal, messy foray into cu-

riosity.' *I enjoyed the pleasure we found with one another last night.*

'No, it certainly doesn't.' *I enjoyed it too.* They were
getting quite skilled at this gambit of staring into store
windows and delivering oblique words about important
things. The word was not the thing. The subtext was.

'Experiences like that are not commonplace.' *I do
not make a habit of one-night encounters. What happened between us was explosive and powerful and not
to be taken for granted. Should we risk repeating it?
Not just the sex, but what it implies—that there is a relationship of note between us?*

Mercedes turned from the window. It was her indicator that the gambit was over. 'I don't know how to
answer,' she said softly. The admission was so entirely
out of character for her that Greer was stunned. Mercedes *always* knew what to say, what to do. She was
always so utterly in charge of herself and her situation. She knew how to use the lightest of touches, the
smallest of smiles to her advantage. But he'd managed
to render her guileless.

'I don't believe it. The great Mercedes Lockhart is
at a loss,' he cajoled, trying to fight back his own rising panic. What would he do if she said there could be
nothing more? 'Is that good or bad?'

Mercedes shook her head. 'I don't honestly know.'
She tugged at his arm and they continued their walk
down the street to the end of the shops where the village
gave into the countryside. 'What shall we do, Greer?
Shall we become lovers? Is that what you want?' She
was cool now that the empty countryside permitted

free speaking. Maybe he'd been wrong to open with concealed wit. Maybe he should have cut straight to the chase: *I want you.*

'I don't think it's up to me alone to decide.' Greer matched her coolness. 'What do *you* want?' He thought about her foot under the table. It *seemed* obvious.

'I know what I *don't* want. I don't want an impulsive decision leading to a disastrous conclusion.' That sounded more like the Mercedes he had come to know: collected and in control. Her sudden lapse had passed. 'The fact is, Greer, we don't know where this *affaire* will lead and we have a lot riding on this trip. Perhaps it's not in our best interest to pursue a romantic attachment at this time. Perhaps we should wait until the tournament is over and assess our feelings then.' Then two steps back.

Greer stared at her in astonishment. She made it sound like a business contract. As for waiting until the tournament was over, that was almost a month away. He'd go mad by then. 'Do you doubt me?'

He could manage that. He could prove to her his feelings were genuine. Another more sobering thought occurred to him. 'Or is it that you doubt *your* feelings?' His anger was starting to rise. He sensed yet another of her exquisitely constructed smokescreens hiding true motives. 'Because if that's the case, I've got to tell you, your feelings were pretty clear last night.' He'd thought last night had been special to her too. Had he been that wrong? All this time he'd been thinking she was worrying over how to face him, how to delicately let him know what last night had meant to her. That hadn't been it at all.

'Is this what you've been sitting in the carriage all morning thinking about? How to put me off without endangering your father's little tournament? How to deter me without your father losing me?' In Bath, it had been her biggest fear—that he'd leave. He should have remembered. Instead, he'd given her womanly sensibilities too much credit. They'd come to a large spreading chestnut. He leaned against the trunk, arms crossed, daring her to admit to it.

'No, that's not it at all.' Something akin to genuine hurt flashed in her grey eyes. 'I was thinking of *your* best interests.' Her voice was sharp and low. She stood just inches from him, her colour high. His desire for her stirred. A woman shouldn't look so beautiful when she was rejecting a man. They'd have been better off standing in front of the store window with their masked conversation. This plain speaking exposed too much. No wonder society didn't recommend it.

'Listen to me, Greer. Last night was supposed to have been wild, a moment out of time fuelled by emotions.' She mirrored his earlier sentiments exactly. He supposed it was reassuring to know they'd started that spiral into passion with the same intentions. But what she said next transfixed him. 'Then it became...' she glanced down at her hands '...*more*.' She looked up at him, her soul evident in her grey eyes as she uttered the next, 'It wasn't supposed to, but it did.' *And if it keeps happening, we might both end up with far more than we sought.*

That's when the truth hit him. She hadn't known. He'd been the first to show her true pleasure, something beyond the physical.

'There *can* be more, Mercedes.' Relief was swamping him. She wasn't rejecting him. She was just nervous, on unfamiliar ground, which he suspected happened very rarely to Mercedes Lockhart. He wanted to kiss her, to reassure her they could manage this. He reached for her but Mercedes warded him off with a nearly imperceptible shake of her head. 'Wait. You have to promise me one thing, Greer.'

'What? Anything.' She could have asked for a hair off the head of the Emperor of China. He would have promised anything, too, in those moments. Desire was riding him hard. But not so hard that he'd forgot the lesson of last night. Mercedes didn't play by the rules.

'That you won't fall in love with me.'

He wanted to laugh at the request but something in her gaze held him back. 'Would it be so terrible if I did?'

'Disastrous. Promise me?' She was in deadly earnest.

'All right. I promise.' But his fingers were crossed, thank goodness, because he suspected he already had.

What had she done? Mercedes was still wondering that very same thing as she dressed for dinner that night. She'd allowed herself to commit to a relationship with Greer Barrington, something she'd vowed not to do when this crazy adventure of her father's had begun. It had not been her intention when she'd started that conversation after lunch. She'd spent all morning in the carriage rehearsing and reasoning.

She'd had her night; the mystique of him had been resolved. She had her entry fee. She needed to focus on the tournament, not a relationship that was bound to be short-lived. It wouldn't last past Brighton. If she faced him in the tournament, she'd have to beat him and he would hate her for it. Until then, though, he might love her, for a little while. It was hard to convince herself it wouldn't be worth it.

Mercedes dug through her jewellery case until she found a pair of small pearl earrings. She laughed at herself as she put them on. It was ridiculous, really, pearl earrings to dine at an inn, albeit an upscale one. It was a sign of how far she'd fallen. Being with Greer was either the bravest or dumbest thing she'd ever done.

In either case, it was definitely selfish. She'd wanted him, had wanted him from that first night in the garden. Even then the risks had been obvious to her, and then, like now, she'd given them no regard. She'd brazened ahead, taking what she wanted and now here she was dressing for dinner at an inn as if it were a lord's manor.

Mercedes gave her hair a final look in the small mirror and smoothed the skirts of her pale peach gown—a perfect affair for early summer in light layers of chiffon, one of the Season's preferred fabrics according to the magazines out of London. She stared at her reflection a moment longer and took the opportunity to give herself a strong reminder. *Be careful.* This was how it had started the last time she'd got into trouble over a man. Luce Talmadge had been debonair and ultimately very persuasive to a young girl's heart. He, too, had been a special favourite of her father's and she'd ended up... well, she'd ended up in a very bad position with him. Enough said.

A knock on the door ended that bout of self-talk. Mercedes answered the door and smiled. Greer stood there, ready to take her down to supper in the private parlour. He, too, had taken care with his appearance, changing out of his travelling clothes into a jacket of blue superfine that did dazzling things to his eyes, buff trousers and a gold-on-gold paisley-patterned waistcoat with the popular shawl collar.

'I like the waistcoat,' Mercedes complimented appreciatively, linking her arm through his. 'Is it new?' She couldn't recall him having worn it before.

'I had it ordered in Bath. Tonight seemed like a good night to break it in.' Greer covered her hand with his where it lay on his arm. The gesture sent a shot of heat to her belly and a gambler's deadliest mantra to her head: *This time it will be different.* If gamblers didn't believe that, a whole lot more of them would walk away from the table a whole lot sooner and richer.

But Greer wasn't anything like Luce Talmadge. Besides, Greer had *promised* not to fall in love with her and a gentleman never broke his word. It was flimsy reassurance at best when he was looking at her with those hot eyes as if he would not only devour her right there on the stairs but would protect her from anyone else who tried to do the same.

Dinner was a festive affair with an excellent roasted beef, fresh vegetables from the local market and newly baked bread, accompanied by a good bottle or two of red wine. Luxurious by country standards, the meal was simple enough to be a welcome departure from the richer meals they'd eaten in Bath.

The three of them had the night off, her father declared with a flourish, pouring a second bottle of wine. There was no billiards table at this particular establishment, although her father had heard there was one in the assembly rooms down the street. He thought he might take a stroll in that direction but Greer needn't come.

'That is if you two are all right on your own?' her father asked solicitously. 'I could stay in and we could all play cards.'

'We'll be fine,' Mercedes assured him. Under the table, she kicked off a slipper and ran a foot up Greer's leg, attempting to finish what she'd started at lunch. 'Maybe we'll take a walk before the light fades.' It wouldn't be a very long walk. She knew exactly what she wanted to do with Greer and it did not involve walking or playing cards.

She found a sensitive spot on the back of his calf with her toe and watched him stiffen in response. She hid her laughter in her wine glass. Dinner finished quickly after that. Her father was eager to get to the assembly room and she was eager to get…well, frankly, to her room and do some assembling of her own, or dissembling as the case might be.

'You're a very naughty girl, Mercedes,' Greer said once her father had departed.

'It's not my fault you're ticklish behind your knee.'

'Truly, Mercedes, at the table? In front of your

father?' He finished the last of his wine and set his glass down.

Mercedes could hear the evidence of humour in his voice. 'It wasn't in front of him. Technically. Besides, I'm twenty-three years old, far too old to be daddy's little girl.' *He'd want me to have you, anyway. It would be good for him*, came the unbidden thought. It was a most uncharitable idea and one she hadn't had for quite some time, at least not since their arrival in Bath.

On the heels of her quarrel with her father in Beckhampton, she'd been far too focused on raising her own stake for the tournament to give much thought to manipulating Greer. In Bath, she'd hardly seen him in a billiards context. Her contact with him, while extensive, had been limited to the social, and her needs had taken precedence. Now that her place in the tournament was secured and the whirl of Bath was behind them, the old thoughts had nothing to hold them back. It was a most unsettling realisation following the commitment she'd made today to Greer and a reminder that there was more than one way she could hurt him in all this. He would be devastated if he ever believed the passion between them had been nothing more than a means to an end. There were two things she hoped he would never find out about her. That was one of them.

'What are you thinking, Mercedes? You've gone quiet.' Greer's own foot was starting to caress a trail up her leg.

'I'm thinking we should take that walk. Then, when my father asks in the morning what we've been up to, we can tell him the truth.'

Greer laughed at that and pushed back his chair, feet games forgot. 'Ah, verisimilitude at its finest, the impression of truth. Perhaps we'll note a few minor landmarks on the way to add more credence to our claim.'

The evening was fair and other couples were out strolling the High Street of the small town. A warm tremor of satisfaction rippled through her at the notion; they were a couple. For a little while, she was Greer's. She should enjoy the moment and not worry so much how it would end. After all, she already knew it would and that was half the battle. It meant no unpleasant surprises.

'People are staring,' Mercedes noted as they made another pass down the street.

Greer seemed unbothered by it. He put his mouth close to her ear so as not to be overheard. 'Of course they are, that's the purpose of all this, isn't it? This is their version of society. They'll go home and talk about who was with whom and what they wore and it will keep them busy until tomorrow night when they do it all over again. It's no different than London or Bath, just a smaller scale.'

'Much smaller.' Mercedes laughed.

'Italy has a similar custom,' Greer said, helping her over a muddy spot in the street. 'It's called *passeggiata*. Literally, it means a slow walk. Every night, people come out into the piazzas and stroll for hours, talking and showing off new clothes.'

'Showing off new loves too, I should think.' Mercedes said the first thing that came to mind. 'It would be the perfect way for a woman to say "stay away, he's mine now."'

Greer chuckled. 'My, my, my, what a calculating little mind you have, Miss Lockhart. Can't it just be for fun?'

She immediately felt guilty. It would be nice to have part of her mind reserved to see things as 'just for fun'. 'It sounds lovely,' she said, trying to make up for her callous comment. 'I have to admit, most of my social experiences have been overlaid with a heavy dose of calculation: the right dress, the right information about a guest used at just the right time to flatter him.' She shrugged an apology.

'Like the night I came to dinner?' Greer asked softly, though there was an underlying edge to the question. They'd come to an intersection and Greer pulled her aside into a quiet street of closed shops. 'I was supposed to meet you that night despite your protests to the contrary. I remember exactly what you said: "My father doesn't need me to vet half-pay officers."'

He paused and searched her face. 'You wore a blue dress a shade darker than the dining room. You looked like you'd been posed for a portrait, so beautiful, so perfect. How much of that was for me?'

'I would have dressed well for the party regardless. My father wanted to sell tables that night.'

'Mercedes, tell me the truth.' His voice held the sharpness of steel in the gathering dusk. She hadn't come out here to fight. 'Your father knew I wouldn't be buying any tables and yet *you*, arguably your father's finest, most persuasive weapon, sat next to me.' A dangerous realisation lit his eyes and Mercedes opted for honesty. Greer would not tolerate a lie. Why did he have to ask these questions now?

Her chin went up. 'I watched you play at the club through a peephole. My father wanted my opinion of your skill.'

'And when I passed inspection, I was invited to dinner to meet you personally.' Greer finished for her. He gave a wry half-smile. 'You've been coaching me from the start, since that very first dinner.' He waved a hand in vague gesture. 'Is that why you don't want me to love you? You're afraid I'll discover I've been nothing but another Lockhart pawn?' Greer drew a deep breath. 'And when you wagered the road against the envelope?'

This was decidedly uncomfortable territory. She feared Greer was slipping away from her already, convinced she was in some conspiracy with her father, that she had used him, maybe was still using him. She had to act fast or her own little *passeggiata* was going to come to a screeching, disastrous halt. 'Your own chivalry worked against you. I didn't ask you to bet the envelope.'

'But you threw the second game, knowing I'd feel badly about beating you twice.'

'Your tendencies are not my fault,' Mercedes argued, thinking how much he'd changed since then. He was far less vulnerable to that strategy, thanks to her. That was one lesson he'd learned well.

Greer gave a self-deprecating laugh. 'I was a fool.'

'Why?' Mercedes slid her hands up the lapels of his jacket. 'Do you regret what has happened? This has been a fabulous opportunity for you and you've done well. I'm hard-pressed to say you've been "used." You've made money, you have new waistcoats to wear.' She smiled at her try for levity. It worked a bit. 'You've been travelling, meeting people and doing something you love.' She shot him a look from beneath her lashes. 'I don't think working the home farm would have provided the same. But perhaps I'm wrong?' she said with an innocent air.

Greer shook his head with a smile. 'Lucifer's balls, Mercedes, I swear you could sell milk to a cow.'

She smiled back; inside she sang a song of relief. She wasn't going to lose him tonight. It scared her just how glad that made her feel. 'Don't overthink things, Captain. Some things we should accept at face value.'

He gave a genuine laugh, loud enough to attract a few more stares their direction. 'Oh, that's rich, coming from the woman who has turned *passeggiata* into a calculated marriage mart.'

She looked up at him, her hands still twined in his lapels. 'It's not all calculation,' she whispered. 'This isn't.' She reached up and dared a soft kiss on his mouth. 'And this isn't.' She blew against his ear, '*Nothing* that has happened between us has been planned, Greer. That's why it's been so very difficult.' If he believed anything he had to believe this. 'I didn't bargain on falling for you.'

Then he nipped at her ear and said the words she so desperately needed to hear. 'I know.'

She ran a hand between them for a discreet caress. 'Let's go back to the room and do something just for fun.'

Chapter Sixteen

Fun turned out to involve the rest of the wine and a bowl of strawberries with cream the innkeeper had put out for dessert. Greer grabbed up the bowl and wine and climbed the stairs behind Mercedes, watching the sway of her hips and acknowledging that he was staking a lot of assumptions on the sincerity of her climax last night.

At the moment, a large part of his body didn't care, but he knew later an even larger part would—the part made up of his honour, his intelligence and self-respect, the core components of a man's pride. He would not stand for being duped, not even for a beautiful woman. In the military, one learned quickly to keep one's wits about them or end up dead. Beautiful women were as dangerous as anyone else, just more distracting, which required double diligence.

At the top of the stairs, Mercedes slipped the key into the lock and turned to him with a secret smile. 'Won't you come in?'

He set the bowl and wine on a small table, taking

in the room. It was bigger than his and far better appointed. A massive oak bed stood in the centre of the room covered in a cheery blue-and-yellow quilt, and a maid had been in to lay an evening fire. There was a dressing screen behind which the private essentials were delicately hidden from view. In all, the room was homey and inviting. Mercedes stood before the fire, pushing down the puffed sleeve of her gown.

'No.' Greer strode forwards, taking her hand gently away from the sleeve. 'Tonight, let me undress you.' Last night had been a hurried joint affair. 'I want to enjoy you, inch by inch.' Last night had been frantic, physical sex. *Fabulous* physical sex, but tonight would be different. It would be a slow feast of love-making or at least as close as one could get to such a thing without breaking his promise, or exposing himself unduly to heartbreak.

He removed her dress first, his hands skimming the soft skin of her shoulders and following the gown down over corseted breasts and slim hips, tracing the erotic silhouette of her, thankful the gown hadn't required a petticoat. He took off the stays next, luxuriating in the feel of her breasts falling free into his hands, their dusky nipples pressing against the thin cloth of the chemise. He stroked them with his thumbs, his own arousal straining and thick in the confines of his trousers. But it was not time for that yet.

'Sit for me.' He pressed her into the chair and bent to her feet, removing her slippers and sliding his hands up one leg and then the other, searching for the hem of her silk stockings. His fingers brushed the damp triangle between her thighs, his erection surging at the evidence she was absolutely ready for him, but he would prolong this if he could, turn it into the most exquisite of personal pleasures for her.

He knelt between her thighs, his face even with hers. Her pulse raced at the base of her neck, further assurance she was enjoying this. He gave a wicked grin. His hands covered hers where they rested on the chair arms. His mouth bent to the top ridge of her chemise, tugging with his teeth at the pale blue ribbon securing it, and pulled it through its eyelet casings. Greer rocked back on his haunches, extracted a knife from his boot and severed the ribbon into two lengths.

'What are you doing?' Her voice was the merest of breathy whispers She was riveted.

'You'll see.' He tied her wrists loosely to the chair and her grey eyes went gratifyingly granite-dark with desire. He'd not guessed wrong about his Mercedes; those who spend their lives in control sometimes like to lose it. His body didn't argue. Instead, it was encouraging him to take his own advice. *Not yet.*

Kneeling, he spread her legs wide and pushed her chemise back until she was exposed to him. It was a provocative sight: a woman revealed. More than that it was Mercedes revealed, her hair loose over one shoulder, eyes dark with knowledge of what was coming. Her wrists were tied, but she was not helpless. She understood the power she had by her very being to stir him His blood began to boil.

He bent to her, his mouth at her core, tasting and teasing, suckling and surprising. He felt her buck and tense where his hands pressed back her legs high on her thighs, the delicious frustration of not being able to use her hands, to bury them in his hair, mounting. She would come for him soon and then they could slake their mutual pleasure together. With a last stroke, he wrenched a cry from her that spoke of utter ecstasy achieved. Her body went slack, her breathing coming hard and fast.

Greer slipped her ribboned bonds from her wrists and swept her into his arms. 'You're in no condition to walk,' he said when she would have protested.

'True. I guess it's a good thing we took our walk earlier.'

He laughed and deposited her on the bed, settling the bowl of strawberries beside her. He dipped one in cream and held it to her mouth. 'You're not worn out already, are you?'

'Never.' She took a bite. 'Get undressed and I'll show you who's worn out.'

Greer undressed quickly. The time for play had passed and his body was eager to join with hers. But she cried foul play at the speed at which his clothes fell to the floor. 'Unfair! Don't I get to look?'

Greer shook his head. 'Another night.'

Mercedes made a pretty moue with her mouth, more seduction than pout. 'You are going to pay for this.'

'With pleasure.' Greer stared down at her, marvelling at her boldness.

'Absolutely with pleasure.' Mercedes licked the cream off her strawberry with a provocative swirl of her tongue, looking entirely wicked. 'Is there any other way?' She pulled him down to her, her hand closing about his engorged length. 'Now, let's take care of this.'

Femme fatale. If they kept this up, she'd definitely be the death of him. And a happy death it would be. There were far worse ways to go.

They took their leisure heading into Birmingham for which Mercedes was grateful, grateful for the nights it afforded her in Greer's arms and for the days it offered her to figure out her feelings. Some of those feelings were easy enough. Greer excited her. His bold passions matched her own and in that regard the blossoming relationship was fairly straightforward. If it had only been about sex, all would have been well. But it would also have been missing a large part of what attracted her to Greer in the first place.

She peered at him over the top of her book. He'd gone back to riding in the carriage with her in the mornings. Sometimes they talked, sometimes they read. Sometimes they even read aloud to one another when they came across interesting passages. Today they were reading silently. As usual, he looked fresh. He shaved every morning and took great care with his *toilette* after he left her bed. She never got to watch that particular domestic intimacy. He always returned to his room for it, but in her mind's eye she had an enticing image of him bare-chested in front of a mirror and basin, running a razor down his cheek.

'Yes? You're staring.' Greer put down his book.

'I was just thinking sometimes a half-naked man is sexier than a completely naked one.'

'Perhaps we can put that hypothesis to the test later tonight.'

'We'll see.' She wondered if part of the attraction to this affair was the clandestine nature of it. There was no guarantee there'd be room arrangements conducive to a nightly visit. There was no guarantee her father would be out playing, although they'd been lucky that he had these last few nights. The unknown added a certain spice to their encounters, never allowing them to take for granted that the encounter would be one of many.

Outside, the scenery started to change. The bucolic countryside gave way to the more organised signs of civilisation Birmingham-style. Canals cropped up, full of the flatbed barges hauling cargo. In the distance, the smoke of factories loomed in a hazy grey sky. Mercedes dropped the curtain with a frown of distaste.

'Birmingham not to your liking?' Greer quipped.

'It's not one of my favourite cities. It's dirty.' There were other more personal reasons she didn't like Birmingham. A distasteful part of her past was here in this city too. It was where she'd first met Luce Talmadge.

'Your father thinks we'll find players here.'

Mercedes shrugged. 'I don't care what he finds here as long as we don't stay too long.' She could handle about two days in Birmingham.

Greer prodded her foot with his toe. 'Then it's the turn for home.'

She nodded. They would not head any further north. They'd turn east and take in Coventry and then south past Cambridge and London before making it to Brighton at the end of June with two weeks to spare before the tournament. The last part of the journey would go quickly. Her father would be eager to spend time in London now that the Season was underway. He'd spare little attention for the small villages and hamlets between Coventry and London. It was the end of May. He would feel time pressing. But that wasn't what Greer had meant with his comment. There were three weeks left of this magical journey with him where everything existed time out of mind. She tried not to think about it.

'London will be nice. You will see many of your acquaintances, no doubt. Will you want to stay at your own quarters there?' Since Bath they'd not addressed the status issue again. It didn't matter that they were together in these nouveau industrial towns full of men with new money. Towns like Birmingham and Coventry thrived because of men like her father, self-made men who had parlayed skills and opportunities into fortunes. 'I do understand, Greer, London isn't Bath. I won't be acceptable there,' she said softly.

She couldn't say she hadn't been warned. She'd known this from the start.

Greer shook his head. 'It's not you. It's what I've been doing.'

Mercedes nodded, but in her mind she made a check on her mental calendar. He would leave her in London. The divide between their two worlds would be painfully obvious. There would be no buffer of the isolation of the road to obscure it. Well, now she knew how it would end. London would be good. It would mean the split wouldn't happen in Brighton over the tournament.

'Perhaps there will be word of a posting.' Mercedes changed the subject. It was the one topic he remained markedly closed on.

'I hope not.'

'Really?' It was the most insightful comment he'd made to date. But he offered nothing more and they returned to their books.

Although Mercedes hated Birmingham, she was glad it was a short day in the carriage. It was not a companionable silence that had sprung up between them. The coach pulled up to a new but elegant hotel in the city centre shortly after noon, and Mercedes was happy to have her feet touch the ground.

'A nice change from rural country inns, don't you think?' Her father took her arm and led her inside, pleased at his choice of accommodations. Luxury always pleased him. She could see why. The lobby sported a large crystal chandelier and twin spiralling staircases on either side of the spacious room leading to the floors above. To one side, Mercedes caught the clink of silverware on china, denoting the hotel restaurant. The clientele milling about were well dressed in the latest fashions. This was a place important people stayed and, above all else, her father liked to be important.

Upstairs, the rooms bore out the signs of luxury evident below. Her bed was wide and her window overlooked the street. She could catch a glimpse of the Birmingham shopping arcade just a few streets over.

A knock on her door distracted her from the view. Perhaps it was Greer, coming to apologise. But for what? London would be difficult. He didn't have to be sorry for the truth. Maybe for speaking it, she thought uncharitably. No one liked to be told they were second rate. Still, unspoken truths didn't make them less true, less existent.

It wasn't Greer at the door and her heart sank a little at the sight of her father. 'Is your room fine?' he asked. His room and Greer's room were right across the hall.

'Yes, it's lovely.' Mercedes put on a smile, but her father was too astute to be fooled.

'What's on your mind? Don't tell me you're thinking about things that don't bear mentioning?' He chucked her under the chin. 'What happened was a long time ago. You're free from all that. Luce Talmadge can't hurt you anymore.'

What if it's happening again? The words nearly burst out. What if she was falling in love with Greer? She couldn't tell him. Her father would either say, 'Well done, it will keep him where we need him', or he'd do something utterly stupid like march them off to a church. After all, it was the kind of marriage he'd always wanted for her.

Her father loved her, but he didn't necessarily understand her, although he thought he did. It was at times like this that she wished she had a mother. Perhaps a mother would know what to say. It was a foolish notion. She was twenty-three, far too old to need a mother. Perhaps a friend would do? She missed Elise Sutton very much in those moments. They'd grown close in Bath and had discovered they had a lot in common with the way they'd grown up as their fathers' favoured children.

'I know.' She nodded, knowing her response would make her father happy.

'Good.' He drew out the thick wallet of pound notes he carried in his inside pocket and withdrew several. 'The arcade is nice. Take the afternoon and go shopping. I'm sure the Captain will accompany you. I don't want you out alone in a strange town. Then, around five o'clock, I want you to meet me at the billiards lounge on this card. It's a subscription room, but you'll be admitted. Tell the Captain to pay the temporary fee.' He winked and she knew precisely what he wanted.

'You've been playing a lot since Bath.' The part of her that wasn't entirely distracted by Greer had noticed. Her father played privately at home, of course. But he seldom played in his own subscription room. He'd played nightly in Bath and he'd gone out since then even on the nights he'd given Greer off.

Her father merely smiled. 'I'm not so old as all that, Mercedes. A man has to have his pleasures. Who says I can't play when I want? I have to keep my game in shape.'

True enough. Her father was a handsome man in his late forties with dark hair lightly streaked with silver, and sharp grey eyes. Moderate in height and slender in build, he still cut an imposing figure at the billiards table. No one could doubt his acumen with a cue. Well dressed and well mannered, his presence was sometimes even considered daunting if one crossed him. Why shouldn't he be out playing? But it *was* out of character for him, and Mercedes couldn't help the suspicion that something else was going on. Perhaps she wasn't the only one living a double life, lately.

'Have fun. Shall I tell the Captain to meet you downstairs in half an hour?' He shut the door behind him and Mercedes set about changing her dress, something that would be appropriate for an afternoon of shopping and for pulling her father's little gambit later, maybe even something that might keep the attentions of *Lord* Captain Barrington, who worried London would be embarrassing.

Lord, that woman could wear a dress! Greer watched Mercedes descend the spiral staircase. Today it was a gown of figured-pewter silk with a fitted bodice and pristine white-lace trim at the neckline. The only adornment was a modest bow offset at her waist. The gown was meant to be lovely in a discreet fashion, but on Mercedes's curves it was an invitation to absolute and complete sin. He was already imagining how to get her out of it before he remembered she was angry with him. Well, maybe not too angry. He noted she'd strung his star-charm on a thin strand of grey ribbon and wore it around her neck.

Still, Greer wished he'd held his tongue about the London comment. She'd been far more sensitive about it than he'd thought. He was so used to her thumbing her nose at the world and its conventions; he'd not anticipated she'd take it so personally or even care. Her silence had spoken volumes.

He moved to the stairs and took her hand. 'You look lovely, but you always do.' He was proud to walk through the lobby with her. He was not oblivious to the subtle glances thrown their way by both men and women. He wondered, not for the first time, what his family would make of her. His sisters would adore her. He could already see them pestering her for fashion advice. His brother would be reserved, but she would win him over. Andrew never could resist a pretty face for long. His father? His mother? Hard to guess. His mother would be a polite hostess and not say anything outwardly offensive, as that was her way. His father would simply be dismayed.

At the doors to the lobby he surprised her with a waiting landau. She shot him a look of question as he handed her in to the open-air carriage. 'I thought it would be easier to drive than to walk, especially if you bought a lot of things.' He hopped in and took the seat across from her.

'Easier for you,' she teased. 'If we walked, you'd be the one who has to carry all the packages.'

The carriage lurched into motion, slowly merging with the traffic. Greer leaned forwards, encouraged by the teasing. 'Am I forgiven, then? We'll manage London somehow.'

She smiled at him and gave him the absolution of a single word. 'Yes.'

'Do you want to know a secret?' Her eyes danced like little silver flames. Of course he wanted to know. How could he not when she looked at him like that?

'I don't want to go shopping. Let's go to the botanical gardens instead.' A light breeze toyed with her hat and she reached a hand up to steady it, looking charming as she made the gesture.

The detour was a short one. The gardens were only a mile from their hotel and the weather, although overcast, was proving to be mild. Much to his delight, however, the overcast nature of the day had kept people from the gardens and the place was nearly deserted, all the better for having Mercedes to himself.

The manicured lawn leading to the four glasshouses containing different varieties of plants spread before them in verdant welcome, a most relaxing departure from the industrial bustle of the city. 'It's hard to believe a place like this is so near the centre of the city.' Greer held open the door to the subtropical glasshouse for her, catching a delicate whiff of her floral scent as she passed, her skirts brushing his leg.

Mercedes looked about her, the expression on her face one of enrapt wonder, and Greer felt an unexpected surge of pride that he'd been the one to bring her here, even though it had been her idea. He often forgot that for all her worldliness she hadn't been past England's shores. Not that it mattered these days: England's empire was bringing the world here.

Mercedes bent to take in a particularly vibrant red flower with a large stem sticking straight out of its centre, inducing all nature of phallic thought which did not elude Mercedes. 'Oh my, this is certainly original,' she exclaimed with a naughty smile. 'I wonder what it's called. Too bad there aren't any placards.'

'I think my brief foray into botany is about to become useful.' Greer chuckled. 'My tutor would be gloating if he were here. This is an anthurium. It's in the bromeliad family.' He leaned close to her ear although there was no one to hear. 'It's also known as the "boy flower."'

She gave a throaty laugh. 'No further explanation needed. It's a very wicked-looking flower indeed.'

It was on the tip of his tongue to flirt a bit and say 'you've some experience with wicked things, do you?' but after this morning's misstep, he thought better of it. Mercedes clearly had some intimate experience beyond himself but she'd never brought it up beyond the game of questions they'd played, a certain indication the situation was as prickly as the long stamen rising from the anthurium.

They finished in the subtropical glasshouse and moved on to the other features. There were acres of lawn and shrubbery to explore and they conjured up images of home. He found himself telling her about his mother's gardens and all the time his tutor spent wandering him through them, teaching him all the names.

'English and Latin? I'm impressed.' Mercedes laughed up at him.

'Not that much of it stuck, though.' He laughed with her. 'At the time I didn't appreciate how inventive my tutor was. He could have had me read it all out of a book instead of letting me enjoy the outdoors.'

'Your mother's gardens sound beautiful. Our garden back in Brighton was already landscaped when we moved in. It's gorgeous, of course, but it doesn't have the thought or the scholarship of your mother's design.'

Her astute comment was disarming. Such a comment

would charm his mother, Greer realised. Few people understood the aesthetic difference between a hand-planned garden and the generic but expensive urban garden like ones behind the terraced houses in Brighton.

'I wish you could see it. It will be in full bloom about now,' Greer ventured cautiously. He didn't want to stir up more dissension between them.

'Well, you know what they say about wishes.'

Mercedes smiled ruefully and he didn't pursue the argument. Instead he said, 'There's a teahouse up ahead. Why don't we stop? I think there's enough time before we have to meet your father.' But the thought of Mercedes meeting his family, which had taken root in the lobby of the hotel, was starting to blossom into a tangible fantasy, one that his overactive mind was starting to play with on a more frequent basis. There were other fantasies that were coming to life as he watched her pour out the tea at their little table, her gestures graceful and confident. His mother would say she could pass for a lady, but he didn't want that. He didn't want Mercedes to ever pass for something she wasn't. He wanted her just the way she was: bold and passionate, insightful and intelligent.

Today had proven to him his attraction to her went far beyond the passion. He'd suspected it had long before now, but he wouldn't be the first man blinded by the power of sex. Today, she'd listened to his stories about home, about his mother's garden and she *under stood* what that garden meant on a fundamental level that had transcended the conversation. How would he ever give her up when the time came? Therein lay the burgeoning fantasy: maybe he wouldn't have to.

'Greer, I asked if you wanted the last scone?' Mercedes poked him with her finger, a most unladylike gesture.

'Let's share it.' Greer picked it up and broke the pastry. The scone crumbled into unfair halves and they laughed together. His heart soared from the simple joy of it. Never had it felt like this, *never*. *This* was good and he'd have to find a way to fight for it. He'd fought for England—surely he could fight for Mercedes.

Chapter Seventeen

The subscription room was sophisticated and avant-garde, allowing women to sit on the sidelines and watch the men play. It was a novel experiment and not necessarily one that was succeeding.

The women, Mercedes noted, were well dressed, but with a tinge of that inherent gaucheness often attached to those who are newly come to money. Their clothes bordered on garish, their jewels on gaudy. These women were not the fine ladies of Bath with their understated elegance and fifth-generation pedigrees.

The men were no better with their brightly striped waistcoats and colourful jackets. Expensive to be sure, but tasteful? One look at the room's population and Mercedes knew exactly what her father wanted to do. He wanted to run 'plucking peacocks', his favourite gambit.

'Are you ready?' she asked Greer quietly, taking up residence at the brass railing that separated the tables from the viewing section.

He rolled his eyes and consented before moving

off to the bar to fetch them champagne. They'd done smaller variations of 'plucking peacocks' before. She knew he disliked it. He thought it was dishonest. She had laughed the first time, arguing that it wasn't their fault people were stupid. A smart man would *never* take the bet. It certainly wasn't her fault there were so few smart men in the world.

'Remember, Greer,' she prompted, taking her glass from him. 'We aren't making anyone do anything against their will. If they bite, they bite.'

They settled in to watch. Her father was playing very well. She'd not seen him play any of the newer versions of the game before where there was no longer any alternating of turns. Instead, players put together runs and shot until they missed, making it possible for a player to clear the table without the other getting a single turn.

Her father potted the last ball to a smattering of applause. She tossed Greer a quick glance. That was their cue. A little way into the next game, she leaned over and blew in Greer's ear. The public display drew a few looks their direction. Now it was Greer's turn. He started to heckle. 'Good shot, old man. I'm surprised you can see the ball well enough to hit it, let alone sink it.'

Mercedes laughed and kissed his cheek, earning them a few censorious looks. But her father had chosen this crowd well. It was before dinner, so 'crowd' was a relative term. The population in the club wasn't nearly as large as it would be later in the evening and these men weren't gentlemen, merely apeing them. A little action wouldn't be terribly amiss to them. It would be exciting.

Her father shot them a withering look and went back to his game, making a difficult shot. Greer gave a mocking round of applause. 'Bravo. I'd like to see you make that shot again.' His sarcasm was evident. He made an aside to Mercedes loud enough to be overheard. 'He's a lucky old bastard. I bet he couldn't do that again. It's one shot in twenty.' They laughed and then she kissed him full on the mouth, becoming very distracting for everyone in the room.

'We're trying to play over here,' her father's opponent called over, pointedly gesturing to the money stacked on the table to indicate the game was serious.

Greer grinned and rose. 'Oh, there's money on this?' He took in the pile of pound notes. He withdrew a wallet from his pocket and pulled out some bills. 'You want to make some real money? I'll bet Grandpapa here misses the next shot.'

Her father's opponent leaned on his cue and gave Greer a look of disbelief. 'Are you joking? My opponent's had the devil's own luck this afternoon and the next shot is easy.' It was, too, Mercedes noted, just a soft straight shot into the side pocket. But she already knew just how her father would play it. It wasn't all that different from the shot she'd missed the evening she'd played Greer.

'Exactly. I'm betting his luck just ran out.' The room had gone silent, everyone watching Greer make his offer.

'Double it, darling,' Mercedes called out in sultry tones.

Greer gave a cocky grin. 'Seems my lady wants me to sweeten the pot.' He tossed down another stack of notes.

That did the trick. The man fairly drooled at the sight of easy money. 'Well, all right, mister. If you're aiming to give it away, I might as well take it.'

Her father chalked his cue and gave a fair imitation of feeling the pressure. He even tried to talk the man out of the wager for good measure. Then he aimed, a soft rolling shot positioned a little too high up on the ball. It hit the edge of the pocket and slid away to the amazed groans of the room, no one more amazed than her father himself. His opponent paid up, begrudgingly, and not without a few deprecating words for Greer, who tucked the pound notes away and simply smiled before looping an arm around Mercedes and walking out. Only Mercedes sensed the tension simmering in the muscles beneath his coat. She didn't have to be a mind reader to know a storm was coming.

'I'm not doing it again,' Greer announced as soon as they sat for dinner in the hotel dining room.

Ah, the storm was breaking. Mercedes settled her napkin in her lap and looked steadily at her lobster. Her eyes drifted covertly between her father and Greer.

'You were absolutely brilliant.' Her father ignored Greer's comment by overriding it with a compliment. He turned to Mercedes, seeking to draw her in as a neutral buffer. 'And you, my dear, were a genius. "Double it, darling."' He chuckled. 'Brilliant. Couldn't have done it better myself.'

'It's not right,' Greer said again with more insistence. 'That man had no idea.'

Her father set his fork down. 'Of course he didn't.

However, such is the nature of any gamble a person takes in any aspect of his life. No one made him take the offer. He considered his options and decided he would.'

'But his options were an illusion.' Greer laid down his fork as well. Eyes clashed across the table. 'There was *never* a chance to win.'

'You listen here, Barrington...' Lockhart took the challenge.

Mercedes drew a sharp breath. How many conversations had begun that way over the years? But Greer was a man and an officer. He could not be handled like a recalcitrant child. It was doubtful he could be handled at all.

'There was *nothing* illegal in what we did.'

'That doesn't make it right.'

The men were halfway out of their seats and Mercedes cast about for a way to divert the impending scene, anything...

'Why, Allen Lockhart! I thought that was you.' The masculine depths of the intruding baritone froze Mercedes in her seat. Anything but that, not *him*. It was what she'd feared in coming to Birmingham, although her father had assured her that in a city of thousands the odds were in her favour. She schooled her features and looked up into the chiselled features of Luce Talmadge. His arrival may have squelched the quarrel brewing between Greer and her father, but in the future she'd be more careful about what she wished for.

'Ah, Mercedes.' Luce grinned, flashing straight teeth. He took a lot of pride in those teeth. They were quite the luxury when one grew up in the rougher neighbourhoods of Birmingham. 'You're as lovely as ever. Lovelier even.' He pulled up a chair without being invited, audacious as always and just as tenacious. It was hard to believe she'd once found those traits attractive.

Luce sat and then half rose when it became apparent no one was going to introduce him to Greer. 'I'm Luce Talmadge.' He leaned over the table and offered his hand, but to her great satisfaction Greer merely inclined his head and offered nothing more than a glacial stare.

'Shall I order champagne for everyone? We should celebrate running into one another.' Luce pushed forwards, undaunted by Greer's snub. 'It's been ages since we've all been together, but I still recall how much you liked champagne, Mercedes.' He tossed her a wink that made her stomach curdle. How had she ever found him appealing? He was a boor, even if he was good looking. Greer would never have put a lady in such an untenable position, would never have insinuated himself into a conversation where he was not welcome, let alone someone else's dinner table.

'I hear there's a tournament in Brighton, an All England Championship. It's your doing, I suppose?' It was Luce's usual strategy—how it all came flooding back to her. He'd just keep talking, a rapid chatter filled with bonhomie until people just gave in and tolerated his presence or forgot they hadn't invited him.

Her father broke in and she could have kissed him. 'You're not welcome here, Talmadge. I must ask you to please leave.' Greer was tense beside her, ready to second her father's request, even though moments before Luce's arrival he'd nearly been at her father's throat.

'Surely, Lockhart, you're not going to let the past keep us from friendship. That was nothing more than the foolishness of youth.' Luce waved a hand dismissively. 'Hardly worth carrying a grudge over. We've grown up and moved on.'

When her father didn't budge, Luce's smile turned mean as his attention focused on Greer. 'I was once sitting where you are. It's the good life, isn't it? Doing Lockhart's bidding? I think of all I learned on the road with him: how to win, how to lose, how to hustle, how to live the high life, which wine to order, which fork to use. Those were good years and they made me into the gentleman I am today.' He held out his arms to indicate the expensive suit he wore.

Mercedes gave a snort of disbelief. The suit was garish and he looked more like the peacocks at the subscription room than a subtly dressed gentleman. Greer would look like a gentleman dressed in a potato sack.

Luce glared at her and rose, finally understanding his welcome wasn't going to get any warmer. He was leaving. She started to breathe easier, thinking she might get out of this encounter unscathed. But Luce wasn't done yet. 'I think of those days with nostalgia, Mercedes. However, I see things have turned out for the best.'

He nodded in her father's direction. 'Best of luck with your new protégé and, Mercedes…' his dark eyes rested on her with the devil's own intentions, '…best of luck with your—what shall we call him? Your new lover? Your *husband*? Well, maybe not a husband. After all, I am fairly hard to replace and you aren't into long-term arrangements.'

How dare he! White fury gripped her. Mercedes seized her water glass and threw the contents straight into his face seconds before Greer's fist found Luce's jaw with a blow that made casualties of the dishes lying between them. The blow took Luce and most of dinner to the floor. Well, she hadn't had much of an appetite for the lobster anyway.

The bastard! Greer's blood was pounding by the time he was straddling Talmadge, the lapels of his gaudy green-checked coat in his hands. Some vague part of him was aware that his hand throbbed. He shoved the pain aside. Greer dragged Talmadge to his feet. Talmadge protested the brutality, looking entirely aggrieved as if he were the wronged party. 'We are both gentlemen here,' he sputtered, trying to simultaneously clutch his jaw and swipe at the water running down his face.

'One of us isn't. You work out who that is,' Greer snarled. He caught Mercedes's eye. She was pale and her hand shook where it clutched the stem of her empty water glass. 'Excuse me for a moment, my dear, I have to take out the rubbish.'

Greer roughly escorted Talmadge to the door, pointedly ignoring curious looks from the serving staff and the other diners. So much for discretion, but he'd be damned before he let a man treat a woman as poorly as Talmadge had treated Mercedes.

'You can have her, you know.' Talmadge tried to jerk free. 'She and that meddling father of hers will never mean anything but trouble to any man. They're users, both of them.'

Greer's answer to that was a hard shove that set Talmadge staggering into the lobby. He watched Talmadge disappear into the street still reeling and off balance.

Certain the bastard was gone, Greer gripped the door frame, finally letting Talmadge's comments sink in. He was reeling too, albeit in a far different way. Mercedes had been married and apparently divorced to the likes of Luce Talmadge, a bounder on all accounts. Impossible.

Greer fought the urge to race back to the table and demand the truth in the hopes that Talmadge had been lying. But that was a slim hope indeed. The pallor on her face at the sight of him was proof enough. For a woman of Mercedes's remarkable steel such a reaction was telling in the extreme.

Racing back to the table would solve nothing if his emotions weren't under control. He needed to face Mercedes with a cool head. He'd punched Talmadge mostly for Mercedes's sake but also in part for himself. He was *not* Lockhart's protégé. He was nothing like that man, had no intentions of being like that man. But it did raise the question of guilt by association and it was high time he grappled with that particular dilemma. This evening in the subscription room, he'd glimpsed just how far he'd fallen and he hadn't even realised it.

By the time Greer returned to the table, Mercedes had gone. While he'd been marshalling his emotional troops, she'd been marshalling hers. It was just as well. Anxious as he was for answers, this was a conversation best held in private. As for the fantasies he'd harboured about showing her his mother's gardens, they'd just become a little more complicated.

Escorting her around London was the least of his worries. Now she wasn't merely the daughter of a celebrity billiards champion, she was also a divorced woman. Of course, she'd been that from the start. She just hadn't told him. He had to wonder what else she hadn't told him? What else was there to discover? What other reasons were being hidden behind the promise that he not fall in love with her? More importantly, did those reasons change how he felt about her? Her absence made it clear she thought they would.

Chapter Eighteen

Greer had found clarity by the time he reached the door of her room. The walk upstairs had given him time to collect his thoughts even if it hadn't provided him any answers, at least not answers he liked. Common sense would recommend he walk away right now. It is what his mother would advise. He could hear her voice in his head: there was a reason the classes didn't mix. Their values and lifestyles were too different.

But his heart was far too engaged with Mercedes to simply walk away because she wasn't a nobleman's daughter. Before he walked, there were things he needed to know. Hastily made decisions weren't always the wisest. He raised his hand to knock and heard permission to enter. The door was unlocked. She'd been expecting him.

'You hit him in my defence and now you've come for your answers, is that it?' Mercedes turned from the window, letting the curtain fall across the wide pane. Distress was evident on her pale features.

'I came to see how you are,' Greer amended. 'I won't lie and say I care nothing about answers, but neither did I come solely out of my own selfish need. I wanted to make sure you were all right.' He paused. 'Are you?' He flexed his right hand. It was starting to hurt now that his adrenaline had ebbed.

Mercedes noticed. 'Maybe I should be asking you the same thing. We need to get ice on this. I'll have the staff send some up.' She took his hand, feeling and flexing each of his fingers in turn. 'Father won't forgive me if you've ruined your hand on my behalf.'

'Stop fussing, Mercedes. My hand will be fine in a couple of days.' Greer covered her hands with his free one, but Mercedes would not be thwarted.

When the ice arrived she packed it around his hand. He insisted it was not necessary, but the colour had returned to her face by the time he was settled to her satisfaction on the little sofa in her sitting room, his hand in ice. The unintended distraction had worked, creating a sense of normality between them, elusive as it might be.

There was nothing left to do but return to the reason for his visit. 'Would you like to tell me about him?' Then he hastily added, 'Not because I am entitled to anything, but because you want to? Ghosts only have power when they aren't exorcised.'

He'd been wrong on the stairs. It wasn't the question of whether or not Talmadge's comments were true that mattered. It was this, right here. If she couldn't tell him, it would be between them always and there was no future in that. He held his breath. Everything hinged on this.

'I was young and foolish,' she began, sitting down on the sofa beside him. Greer began to breathe again. There was hope yet.

'I was seventeen and my head was easily turned by the attentions of a good-looking man.' Her throat worked and it was clear it was hard for her to say the words. 'I was stupid, so headstrong when it came to Luce Talmadge.' She gave a short, deprecating laugh. 'Forgive my hesitation. Saying it out loud makes my mistake much more real.'

'Everyone makes mistakes,' Greer offered. He meant for it to be encouraging, but the words sounded empty even to him.

She raised a dark brow. 'Mistakes aren't usually of this magnitude. My father was already a renowned champion in our circles when Luce took up with us. If I'd been smarter, I'd have seen that Luce was using me as access to my father. Luce was, and is, a consummate user of people, only he's not very subtle at it, which makes falling for him that much worse.'

She shook her head and traced a pattern on the sofa cushion, unable to look at him. 'I mistook his lack of subtlety for boldness and tenacity. When we're seventeen, I suppose we don't make those distinctions. My father tried to warn me, but I was too stubborn to listen. Anyway, my father took Luce on a short tour to advertise the Brighton room. He was good at billiards and even better at separating people from their money.

I went with them and it was heady stuff for a girl fresh out of boarding school.'

Much the same as it was now. The comparison between the two situations was not lost on him. It was the second time in as many hours he'd been cast in the role of Lockhart's protégé, and the label did not sit well with him. He was about to protest that this time was different, but Mercedes read his mind. 'Now that I've started, you have to let me finish.' She put a soft finger to his lips.

'Luce convinced me he was in love and that he wanted to marry me. He painted a compelling picture. We'd be the most dazzling couple in Brighton and I was not immune to the images he conjured. They were exciting and I entirely overlooked the reality that all of Luce's dreams were built on my father's subscription room. He'd assumed I would inherit the club. It was only one of many assumptions Luce made about my connection to my father's wealth.

'We married three days before we returned to Brighton, a secret wedding in the morning in a church in a tiny sea-coast village. Luce told me I was the most beautiful thing he'd ever seen. He wooed me with kisses and a solid gold ring. He'd even been a bit misty-eyed when he slipped it on my finger.'

Mercedes shrugged. 'In truth, I was having misgivings before we married, but in my stubbornness I shoved them away, blaming it on my father. I wouldn't let myself be influenced by him. I was going to make this decision on my own.'

Greer wanted to punch the man again. He knew men

like Luce Talmadge, who preyed on the susceptibilities of young girls. Fortune hunters existed at all levels of society. It just proved that 'susceptibilities' came in all forms; her own inherent stubbornness had been as lethal to Mercedes as a weaker woman's belief in false flattery. But he could well imagine an obstinate Mercedes, a formidable force even at seventeen. Words would not have stopped her once she'd set her mind.

'We didn't tell my father until we got back. He was furious. He said a real man would ask permission, a real man wouldn't slink off behind his back and marry a man's daughter. We were in my father's study and I remember very clearly how my father looked at me and said, "He's only after your money, Mercedes."'

Greer's gut clenched in anticipation of what would come next: a deal of the kind Lockhart loved to make, the kind where no man was forced to do anything other than what his nature motivated him to do, like the greedy man in the club tonight. The only difference was that tonight, the man had been his own victim. In this scheme, it had been Mercedes.

'Of course, Luce made all the requisite noises about being offended by my father's brash assumptions. Then my father stood up and went to his safe. He pulled out a stack of pound notes and a document. He set them on his desk. He opened the document and showed it to Luce. It was his will, in which he left the subscription room to Kendall Carlisle. In the event that Carlisle preceded him in death, it comes to me in the form of a trust to be overseen by my father's solicitor. It's never mine directly.'

'Let me guess—Talmadge didn't like that arrangement?'

Mercedes gave a sad laugh. 'At the time, I thought he was going to faint. It's rather funny now, at a distance. But I assure you, it was not humourous then to look the man you thought you loved in the face and see quite clearly that your love was a one-way thing.'

Promise me you won't fall in love with me. Was that because she didn't feel the same way? Had she extracted that promise in order to protect him? 'What did your father do next?'

'He tapped the pounds notes with his hand and said, "There are a thousand pounds in this stack and I'll write you a personal cheque on my account in London for nine thousand more if you take the money, declare the marriage false and walk out this door today with the promise that you will make no further claim on Mercedes." I don't think it took Luce even a minute to make up his mind. I had not seen him in six years until this evening.'

Tears threatened. Greer could see them swim in her grey eyes. She swiped them away with a dash of her hand. But they weren't tears for Talmadge. 'It's embarrassing beyond words to know you were sold for ten thousand pounds. In my girlish dreams, I'd thought forever would cost a bit more.' She shrugged and tried for a smile.

'I think you have it backwards.' Greer said thoughtfully, his eyes on her. 'You weren't sold. Your freedom was bought.' Whatever he might think of Lockhart, the man had done this one good deed.

She nodded. 'I'll always owe my father for that. He'd warned me. I didn't listen and yet he was still there, in his own way, to pick me up.'

It was one of the ways in which Lockhart had a nobility of his own. Greer saw that. But he also saw the prison it created for Mercedes and he liked that even less. Lockhart was not above using people, even his own daughter. Greer had seen him do it on two occasions. Lockhart knew precisely what he was owed by others, Mercedes included.

Greer pulled his hand out of the ice and flexed it experimentally, slowly. 'I'm glad I hit him.' He knit his brow. 'Is this the reason you didn't want me to fall in love with you? You didn't want me to find out about Luce?' He hoped it was as superficial as that and not his earlier supposition.

'Something like that.' Her answer was not reassuring.

'But not quite? Talmadge and I are not the same. I'm not using you, not looking to trap you. You've said you're not using me.' He could not make it any plainer without breaking his promise to her. He *would* break it, but not yet. An inspiration struck him.

'Why did you come on this trip?' Based on what she'd revealed, coming made very little sense, especially if she saw too many similarities between these circumstances and the previous ones.

He could see this question bothered her more than anything she'd told him about Luce. She rose and paced the room, going back to her curtain at the window and looking out. So he couldn't see her face when she lied to him? He didn't want to believe that.

'Well, Mercedes?' he prodded. 'What is it you wanted badly enough to put yourself through this?' The pieces were coming fast and furious to him now. This trip was a proving ground for her, a chance to claim... something... The fight in Beckhampton... The madness of the Bath brothel. Yes. He had it.

'You...' Greer began, grappling with the reality that flooded him. 'You wanted to be the protégée.' She had coveted what he would throw away, what he felt distaste for. He had unwittingly stolen something from her that she cherished.

She turned back from the window, her face fierce. 'Yes, I wanted to be the protégée. I wanted to show him I could not only train you, but beat you. I did and it still made no difference.'

Because she owed Lockhart. Perhaps he'd been too hasty in suggesting Lockhart had bought her freedom. He'd merely transferred it from one gaoler to another. This was the side of Lockhart that Greer could not countenance. Everyone had a purpose. Greer wondered what his was. He was not naïve enough to think he would be the one singular individual to escape Lockhart's machinations. He wondered, too, if he could free her. Would she ever leave her father? Tonight was not the time to put the question to her.

'I should go.' Greer stood. He needed time to think, time to sort this all out and his place in it as well.

She came to him and ran a finger down his shirt-front. 'I think you should stay.'

Greer trapped her finger with his good hand. 'Not tonight. We both have too much on our minds. I don't think there would be room in bed for all of it.' Not when she was vulnerable, not when she might be tempted to use sex as a way to bind him to her. He kissed her lightly on the forehead. 'Goodnight, Mercedes. I'll see you in the morning.'

But he couldn't help wondering as the door closed behind him if things would ever be the same between them. His mind was far too restless for sleep. A walk would do his body good and the gaslights of the city centre made Birmingham safe enough if a man was careful.

The irony of what occupied his mind, however, was that his thoughts were not on Luce Talmadge and the brief, ridiculous marriage. *He'd* been the first to show her true pleasures. In his more fantastical moments he hoped to be the last and only man to do so some way, somehow.

Knowing about Talmadge made it far easier to understand Mercedes and her reticence to admit this relationship between them was anything more than sex. But that would also be the easy answer. Did she return his feelings or was she using him? Was he still merely a tool to get what she wanted from her father? Was she so determined to wrest it from her father that she was willing to sleep with the enemy? Did she still hate him for being the protégé?

The real issue that occupied his mind as he walked Birmingham was what to do about Lockhart. The longer he thought about it, the more convinced he became that Lockhart was the villain of the piece and he wanted no more part of it—no more inns, no more days on the road, no more nights watching Lockhart trade on his celebrity in big towns or adopting false aliases in small towns in order to 'pluck peacocks' or some other game. Lockhart liked toying with people, determine their price.

Greer felt shame that he'd let Lockhart toy with him for so long. Lockhart had been in his element in Bath, introducing him as Lord Captain Barrington. And Greer had let him, convinced that such a use of his title could buy Mercedes acceptability. In part, he'd begun to believe in his own mystique, charmed by his own growing celebrity as he won game after game, as he danced with Mercedes in his arms, distracted by beauty, lust, and money.

It had been a glorious life for a few weeks. He wanted to be angry at Lockhart for leading him into such iniquity, but there was no one to be angry with but himself. Lockhart had simply dangled the carrot—something the man was very good at doing. No one had made him take it. No one could make him stay.

Birmingham had a direct train route to London. He should be on it first thing in the morning. But truly, he didn't want to go to London. He wanted to go home, to the rich fields of Devonshire, fields he hadn't seen in three years. There would be sense in Devonshire, equilibrium, even if there was a reckoning to go with it. But he couldn't go, not without Mercedes. If he left her now, he would not get her back. If there was one thing he didn't regret about this madcap trip, it was her. Could she say the same for him? Would she come? There was only one reason to come and many reasons to stay. Would she refuse because of Luce?

Only the densest of people would fail to see the parallels there in his request. Or would she refuse because it meant choosing another man over her father, who had rescued her once before and to whom she felt indebted? Or would she refuse because she'd been using him all along? If he was gone, she could be the protégée just as she had planned.

He did not figure well in either scenario. But maybe would she choose him for the simple reason that she was Mercedes Lockhart, a woman possessed of a boldness unequalled? Greer turned back to the hotel. He wouldn't know unless he asked.

Chapter Nineteen

Mercedes could muster no enthusiasm for the sausages and eggs piled on her plate for breakfast the next morning. She'd decided around three that sleeping alone was not conducive to a good night's rest. Around four, she'd concluded neither was a restless mind. Both of which had resulted in having very little appetite for breakfast. A pity, really, when the breakfast looked quite fine. She was certain it looked better than she did. She didn't need a mirror to show her what she already knew. Her appearance was drawn, and dark shadows created purple circles beneath her eyes. She could practically feel the bags.

She was not alone in that regard. Greer, who always looked fresh, looked haggard in spite of his impeccable clothes and polished boots. He must have sent them out after he came back from his walk—his very long walk. She knew. She'd seen him leave the hotel from her window and she'd stood sentinel until she'd seen him come back, safe and unharmed, although the exercise had not resulted in a restful night.

She caught the faintest whiff of the sandalwood soap he preferred as he sat down. But all the grooming in the world couldn't hide the tiredness in his eyes and she felt a twinge of guilt over having been the one to put it there.

'How's your hand?' she asked quietly before her father reached them. He was across the dining room, finishing assembling his plate from the buffet.

'Much better.' He smiled and flexed the hand to show her. 'We need to talk.' He spoke in low, urgent tones, aware that their time alone was limited. 'I've made some decisions.' Ah, so that was what he'd been doing on his walk. Thinking. Deciding. Weighing all things in the balance. There was no time to hear more.

'Good morning, everyone.' Her father smiled broadly and took a seat, effectively interrupting. 'Did we sleep well?' Mercedes gave him a critical stare. He wasn't fooling her. For all his apparent zest, he had not slept particularly well either, but it hadn't diminished his appetite.

'I've decided we should have a slight change of venue,' he said between bites of egg. 'The new railway line runs up to Manchester. I think we should go. We couldn't have hoped to reach Manchester and get back to Brighton in time by coach, but a railway makes it possible. We can take the railway straight to London from Manchester and then—' he snapped his fingers '—we're home from there in plenty of time, just like that. What do you think? I can get us tickets on the eleven o'clock. The coachman can drive the team back to Brighton.'

It wasn't really a question. She knew her father too

well. He'd already decided. They were going to Manchester.

Greer pushed back from the table and set his napkin aside, his eyes serious as they darted her direction in a quick glance she couldn't quite interpret. 'I will not be coming. I told you last night that I was done and I meant it.'

Beneath the table, Mercedes's fingers clenched around her napkin. Greer was leaving. He'd finally had enough of the manipulating Lockharts. This was the decision he'd alluded to. She'd known it would end. But she'd thought she'd have until London. Just yesterday they'd been walking in the botanical gardens, dreaming impossible dreams, and now it was over. Her heart sank with the sudden realisation she'd never wanted anything as much as she wanted Greer Barrington.

Her father took the news with his famous equanimity. If he was upset over this announcement, he didn't show it. He took out his wallet and began counting out pound notes. 'We can meet in London. You can take the coach to Coventry and carry on with the tour.'

'No, thank you, though the offer is generous.' Greer was all courteous politeness, but there was firmness as well. Whatever came next, her father wasn't going to like it. 'I will be ending my tour here. All of it.' Translation—he was ending his association with them. 'I think it is time for me to move on. I thank you for the experience. It has been illuminating.'

She shifted her gaze to her father. What would he make of that? He smiled and dug into his proverbial bag of tricks. 'Is it more money you're wanting? You've been playing well and you're not an unschooled apprentice any longer. How does twenty per cent of the take sound, and a slice of the profits in Brighton? You've earned it.' It was a generous offer. Her father must be desperate to keep him.

'I must decline,' Greer said solemnly. She knew it must be killing him to refuse the money.

Her father's eyes narrowed at the last refusal. 'Is my money not good enough? You think you can simply walk away whenever you want? After all I've done for you? After all Mercedes has done for you? Don't think I don't know what the two of you have been up to.'

Mercedes blanched, embarrassed. Of course her father would make her private business his own if he thought he could use it. But Greer was not cowed and Mercedes silently applauded him. When it came to knowing his own mind, no one knew it better than Greer Barrington. Watching a man be true to his principles was a gratifying experience. So much of her life had been lived around chasing the money, convictions be damned if they got in the way. Principles were easily trampled by pounds.

Greer dropped his voice to a dangerously low tone. 'After all you've done for *me*? I think the accounts are settled. I have earned my keep, sir, and then some. You've done very well with me by your side. You've used my skill and you've used my name to great advantage. Whatever I've owed you has been well and truly paid and you know it.'

Greer rose and offered his hand to her father. There would be no further negotiation. She'd never seen her father so utterly silenced. 'Will we see you in Brighton?' her father asked with a hint of his earlier Lockhart smile.

'If *you* do, it will be as my own man, not as your protégé,' Greer replied. There was an odd emphasis in the sentence. He had said 'you' in contrast to her father's 'we', and it had a singular tone to it. She was still puzzling out his intent when she felt his gaze on her, his hand outstretched.

'Mercedes, will you come with me? My train leaves slightly earlier than your father's.' It was not a choice she wanted to make and certainly not in such a bold fashion. She would have railed at him if she hadn't been so keenly cognisant that he was giving her a choice. He hadn't assumed she'd follow him. He was letting her decide. He wanted her still.

The enormity of his question and all it denoted, all it stood for, overwhelmed her. She fought to master the sensation in the seconds she had to make her choice. She forced her mind to dissect her options with a gambler's assessment of risk. Greer knew her most scandalous secret and he'd chosen her anyway. Because he loved her, although she'd asked him not to? Or because he didn't intend to keep her long enough for it to matter? *He's not Luce, and he's not your father. He doesn't think like that. What he feels for you is genuine.*

Would it be enough? Did it matter? She wanted Greer Barrington and Mercedes Lockhart took what she wanted. She set aside her napkin and stood. She put her hand in his and felt the strength of his grip close around her, warm and reassuring.

'Mercedes, think!' Her father rose, disbelief etched on his face. 'Don't do anything rash. You know how it worked out the last time.' It wasn't a plea, but an accusation, a thinly wrapped threat.

She focused on the feel of Greer's arm at her waist, ushering her towards the door. He was already gesturing for a runner to fetch her trunk and get it to the station.

'Mercedes, stop and listen!' Her father was at her other side, refusing to let them leave without saying his piece. 'This is madness. What do you think will happen? He'll use you like Talmadge did and then he'll throw you away. You don't think he actually loves you, do you? He could never marry you and eventually you'll come crawling back to me, begging me to bail you out. He's a lord, Mercedes, and you're the daughter of a bootboy.'

Hearing her worst fears spoken so blatantly did nothing for her nerves. She had notoriously bad luck in love. For all her bravado, she'd never stood on her own. She thought of the stake money she'd won in Bath, neatly hidden in her trunk. She'd earned money once—she could do it again if need be. 'This is not about Greer. This is about me.'

'Taking her home, are you?' Her father turned to Greer, ignoring her outburst altogether. 'Devonshire, is it? That will be lovely.' His gaze swung back to Mercedes, his features calm as if this was a usual conversation. 'Home to meet the Viscount? Really, Mercedes? How do you think that will go? I know how it will go, but if you need to find out for yourself, so be it. I give it two weeks and you'll be begging me to save you.'

He shuffled through a pile of cards he'd taken from his coat pocket until he found the one he wanted. 'Here it is. There's a gentleman from Bath who's from that area. He invited me to come for a visit. I think I'll change my travel plans and do just that. I'll be there until the twentieth of June.' His eyes softened. 'You can come to me and all will be forgiven.'

'I won't.' She met his eyes evenly. He was calling her bluff. But he didn't understand all the potential that waited for her if she would just embrace it. This time she finally understood no one was going to give her a chance unless she gave one to herself. This time, he would lose.

'I'm going with Greer,' she said firmly.

It was a final declaration of independence. She turned, stepped out the entrance into the bright morning light with Greer beside her, and walked into the busy streets of Birmingham, into her future.

They spoke little on the drive to the station. Her mind was still reeling with what she'd done, acknowledging what she'd done. This time it *was* different. Walking out with Greer was about taking charge of her life, of deciding she wasn't going to be one of her father's pawns any longer. She wasn't going to hide away in his Brighton mansion playing hostess, ignoring her talent and hoping to be noticed some day for what she was. When she'd accepted the offer to come on the road, she'd seen Greer as her chance. She'd not imagined in what way that chance would come. But here it was and she was going to seize it.

* * *

Greer settled into the plush seat across from Mercedes. He'd paid extra for the private accommodation. It would be worth it. There were things that needed settling and there was no time to wait. He'd seen their trunks boarded and they'd had time to settle their turbulent emotions. Now, with the sliding door shutting out the aisle, they needed to talk. The morning had not been without its share of drama.

'I hope your decision is a little bit about me.' He crossed his legs at the ankles and folded his arms over his head in a casual pose. She'd come. He told himself not to get greedy. Last night his goal had been to free her. He'd done that. He'd made the opportunity available and Mercedes had taken it.

'Of course it is. You know it is.' She gave him a small smile that assuaged his male ego.

He understood. She didn't want him to feel any pressure, to feel any sense that she was under his protection now. She was, though. She would protest if he ever said it out loud. But he would protect her, care for her, as long as she would let him. He would have to be subtle about it. She wouldn't tolerate any blatant chivalry.

He also understood that for Mercedes, getting on the train wasn't entirely about him, although for him, asking had been entirely about her. He'd have to change her mind, but for now it was a start. She was still smiling at him, the colour returning to her face as the train pulled out of the station. 'So, we're on the train. Where exactly are we going?'

He laughed the first real laugh he'd had in a while.

'Shame on you for getting on a train with a strange man without even knowing where it goes.' But it was exactly the kind of thing she would do, the kind of thing that made her Mercedes Lockhart, the woman he loved.

'That's nothing.' She gave a wide smile, her eyes lighting up. He shifted his position slightly to accommodate the beginnings of an arousal. He'd have to address that in short order. 'I once heard of a man who went on the road with a woman he didn't know simply because he lost a billiards bet.'

'Probably the best adventure he ever had.' Greer grinned and reached for her. She came willingly, straddling his lap.

She reached up and flipped down the curtain that covered the small window of their sliding door. 'It's about to get better.'

It most certainly was. Her mouth was on his, her hand between their bodies, stroking his cock through his trousers. He groaned, his nascent arousal growing in full force. 'I see great minds think alike,' she murmured against his mouth.

She slid down to the floor and worked the fastenings of his trousers, pushing them down past his hips. 'I believe it's my turn?' They'd not done *this* yet and Greer's breath caught in anticipation.

'I hope that's a rhetorical question.' Real thought, real response beyond the physical was becoming an increasing impossibility. Greer gave a soft moan as she touched her lips to his phallus, kissing, licking, building him to a frenzy with each wicked stroke of her tongue, until she took him in his entirety into her mouth.

Her hand found his balls, and she squeezed ever so gently, just enough to increase his pleasure to nearly unendurable limits. Greer moaned and arched against her, his hands tangled in the silky expanse of her hair. He'd never been touched so sensually before, never experienced such depths of eroticism as the ones summoned up by her hands, her mouth, caressing him in tandem. And yet, when he arched against her, spilling himself in the achievement of his pleasure, the core of him knew that it wasn't the eroticism of the moment alone that had conjured such ecstasy.

She looked up at him, a veritable Delilah with her hair falling over her shoulders, looking for all the world like a very happy cat who'd licked the cream, which of course she had.

Chapter Twenty

Pride was all well and good, but it couldn't feed you, which was why Greer found himself at a billiards table an hour after getting off the train. Still, he wouldn't have taken Lockhart's money for anything. He was going to do this ethically and on his own.

Greer studied the lay of the table. He'd need to use a bank shot to get around the mess of balls blocking his access to the pocket. He bent, lined up his shot and halted in mid-strike, distracted by movement in the open doorway—a glimpse of a coral-coloured gown, of long dark hair curled into a single thick length, the sound of a sultry voice full of unwavering confidence.

'Good evening, gentlemen. Care for a game?' *Mercedes*. It was hardly worth the effort to ask what she was doing here. He knew what she wanted before she began to move from the doorway. She wanted to play. Her eyes met his ever so briefly before sliding away. She was wondering what he'd do. It was something of a shock to realise she wasn't certain of his response—would he support her bid for acceptance or would he usher her straight back to the inn with a scold?

This would be the first test of their togetherness. If he did the latter, he'd prove himself no better than her father and that would be anathema to their relationship. Mercedes didn't want a man who would chain her to rules. Even for her own good.

Greer stood, gauging the reactions of the other men in the room. They were slack-jawed in amazement, as well they should be. Mercedes was stunning. Like many of her dresses, this one wasn't given to excessive trims and bows, relying instead on the curves of her figure for its adornment. The faintest hint of lip-colour highlighted her lush mouth and drew one's gaze upwards towards her eyes as a subtle reminder of where a gentleman *should* be looking when he addressed her. Most of the men in the room were having difficulty remembering that rule.

She strode towards the table, surveying the game. Greer followed her with his eyes, wary and waiting for her to signal what she was up to. This was a test for her, too. He'd been clear that he wouldn't run any of her father's crooked gambits. He would play fairly and without artifice. He needed Mercedes to accept that as much as Mercedes needed him to accept her right to play.

'Is it your shot?' She looked at him for the first time since she entered the room. 'You'll need to use a bank shot to get around that mess.'

Greer smiled in hopes of easing the tension that had sprung up. The men didn't know what to make of a female presence in their male-dominated milieu. He could

help them there and he could help Mercedes. He nodded
and held out his cue to her. 'An excellent assessment.
Perhaps you'd like to take the shot for me?'

A few of the men snickered, thinking he asked out
of sarcasm. He quelled them with a look. Mercedes
was not daunted. She took the cue, bent to the table and
made the complicated shot with practised ease. Appreciative murmurs hummed around the table.

'Would you like to join our game?' Greer offered.
The invitation had to come from him. No one else would
dare go that far. They had to live here after tonight
with wives and mothers who would never let them forget their one lapse in solid country judgement. But he
could tell they were impressed.

'I would love to.' Mercedes chalked the cue and blew
the lingering dust lightly over the tip in his direction. A
few of the men sidled away to join card games in other
rooms, but most remained, intrigued by the woman in
the coral dress who would be gone in the morning, leaving them with a night they'd long remember.

'Were you surprised to see me?' Mercedes asked
as they made the short walk back to the inn well after
midnight.

'No. You wouldn't have got on the train this morning
if you'd meant to hide away in inn rooms.'

'You're very astute for a man,' she teased.

'That's quite a compliment, coming from you.' Greer
laughed into the mild summer darkness. In moments
like this, laughing with her, walking with her, he felt
alive as if he needed nothing more than Mercedes and

enough money in his pocket to make it to the next town. Those were *not* thoughts worthy of a man raised to be a viscount's son, but they were his thoughts and he'd been thinking them more and more often—one of his many fantasies when it came to Mercedes. She provoked the impossible in him.

'You really weren't surprised?' she pressed. 'I wore this dress just for you.'

'Nothing you do surprises me, Mercedes.' He drew her close and stole a kiss, and then another, a slow spark beginning to ignite. Why not? There was no one out that late to see.

'*Nothing?* We'll have to work on that,' she whispered between kisses.

What happened next would always remain blissfully fuzzy in his memory. He was fairly sure it was Mercedes who danced them back into a shallow alley off the main thoroughfare and hitched her leg about his hip. But it was him who rucked up her coral skirts and took her wildly against the brick wall of a building just like he'd wanted to on a prior occasion, both of them aroused beyond good sense by the eroticism of the encounter and the exhilaration of the night. Climax came fast, a blessed, thundering release.

'*Nothing?*' Mercedes sucked at his ear lobe. 'Really?'

'All right,' Greer panted, exhausted. 'Maybe that.'

'*Maybe that?*' Mercedes echoed softly. 'I'll try harder tomorrow.'

Greer caught his breath and arranged his trousers with a laugh. Good Lord, if she tried any harder, he'd be worn to a stub before they reached Devonshire, which might not be an unpleasant experiment.

Mercedes hoped Devonshire would not prove to be an experiment in unpleasantness. Devonshire was close to nothing, least of all Birmingham. It had taken a week's worth of travel to reach this south-west corner of England. The week itself had been extraordinary, made up of billiards games and trains, and coaches, when the rails ran out. Every night was spent in Greer's bed. Every day was spent believing this could work. They could be together—weren't they proving it?

But now that they were here, Mercedes's stomach was an inconveniently tight ball of nerves. By the time Greer's home came into view down a long winding drive lined with ancient oaks, her rampant thoughts had coalesced into one singular concern: what had she done? She was miles from anywhere with a viscount's son, about to meet a family that couldn't possibly welcome her, but who could quite possibly throw her out of their home.

The sprawling estate loomed over a horseshoe-shaped drive, an overpowering sandstone testament to good breeding that dwarfed the Brighton terraced homes and she *knew*. She'd overstepped herself this time, reached too high. On the road it had become easy to forget all that Greer had been born to. There would be no forgetting here, for her or for him. Greer reached over and squeezed her hand, reading her thoughts with alarming accuracy. 'You'll do fine.' He pulled the gig they'd rented in the village to a halt and he moved around to help her down, his hands resting at her waist. 'I would say "they're going to love you..."' he murmured.

'But they're not.' She gave him a smile. They were here for Greer. He needed to make decisions and put ghosts to rest and that could only happen here where they could be confronted.

Do you love me? She hated herself for the traitorous thought. She'd asked him not to love her and now she found that was the very thing she craved. *You don't need him*, her mind rallied. Didn't need Greer? What a lie. She didn't want to need him, but she did. When he'd held out his cue to her, when he'd punched Luce Talmadge, the countless times he'd made her laugh, or divined her thoughts before she'd voiced them—all proved it.

Worst of all, she suspected she more than needed him. She *loved* him. What else could explain why she'd risked coming here where there wasn't only his family to face? There was also the possibility Greer might never leave. He might take a look around and decide to stay. There was no guarantee he'd go on to Brighton. But she would. She had to. Her ghosts had to be exorcised there.

'Don't borrow trouble, Mercedes.' Greer squeezed her hand reassuringly. 'It's just my family, not the Spanish Inquisition.' He led her up the curved stairs to a front door which opened before he could knock, a footman bowing with a gracious, 'Milord, welcome home.' For a second it was all very formal, then chaos broke loose.

'Greer!' Two blonde girls rushed at him from the

wide staircase in the foyer, and more people materialised from doorways. There were hugs and handshakes for Greer. It was not a moment for intrusion. Mercedes stood back, giving Greer the moment to drink in his family. After the initial onslaught of familial affection had ebbed, Greer drew her forward.

'Everyone, this is Miss Mercedes Lockhart. Mercedes, these are my sisters, Clara and Emily.' They were charming, blue-eyed and blonde. Clara was perhaps fifteen, Emily seventeen and on the brink of womanhood. She'd be going to London soon and breaking hearts with a smile that looked so much like Greer's there was no doubting the resemblance.

'This is my brother, Andrew.' The heir, the brother who wanted Greer to take over the home farm. He had Greer's looks, but not Greer's graceful build. He was solid, sturdier, not unattractive, but lacking Greer's magnetism. He was a practical man, a reliable man who'd probably never entertained a risky thought in his life. It was no wonder he couldn't understand Greer's reticence to embrace the home farm.

'This is my mother, Lady Tiverton.' *Viscountess Tiverton*, Mercedes thought. She had a kind smile for Mercedes but Mercedes was reluctant to trust it. Such a smile wouldn't last, not when she discovered the type of woman her son had been fraternising with. It wasn't self-pity or a sense of inadequacy that led to the thought, just honesty. She'd lived in Brighton, after all. She'd seen plenty of nobility and she knew where the lines were drawn. Rich billiards players and their daughters were fine when it was all fun and games. They became *de trop* when blood was on the line.

'And this is my father, Viscount Tiverton.' Greer completed the introductions. The Viscount was tall, having passed on his lean physique to Greer, and his more reserved personality to his older son. Mercedes thought Greer had got the better portion of the genetic deal.

Lady Tiverton ushered them all in to the drawing room and rang for tea, giving the staff time to recover from the surprise of Greer's arrival. Tea would give Lady Tiverton time to arrange for rooms to be prepared. Mercedes had used the ploy more than once when her father had brought home unexpected visitors. For the first time since she'd left her father, Mercedes felt a twinge of loss. She'd had a week to let her anger cool and in the absence of that anger, she missed him.

Tea was a polite interlude. There was nothing more than small talk exchanged. If there was to be an interrogation, it would occur in private. Well, there was no 'if'. Mercedes knew there *would* be an interrogation. She was aware of Andrew's eyes on her, studious and discerning. The next time she caught him watching her she looked him straight in the eye and smiled. He looked away hastily, nearly spilling his teacup and earning a short scold of caution from Lady Tiverton.

Greer nudged her covertly with the toe of his boot as if to say, *play nice*. She'd try, but she'd decided after the second cup of tea she could be nothing other than she was and Mercedes Lockhart didn't tolerate insolence in any form, not even from viscounts' heirs.

When rooms were ready, Mercedes found Emily and Clara at her side, insisting on accompanying her upstairs. They chattered the whole while, pointing out aspects of the house as they passed hallways and closed doors.

'What's down there?' Mercedes gestured to one corridor the girls didn't mention.

'That's all storage. It's where we keep the nice things for special visits.' Clara shrugged as if such an area was commonplace. Mercedes didn't comment, but the corridor intrigued her. It might be worth a visit. She'd noticed a change in the house as they'd moved up the stairs. The public rooms had been exquisitely done up, but the private areas lacked that same veneer.

The runners on the hall floors were clean but worn, having seen generations of Barringtons. The long curtains at the hall windows were faded from years in the sun. Tables that should have been cluttered with knick-knacks were bare.

The room she was given was lovely, done up in light yellows and pinks with a view of the south lawn and gardens, but by no means sophisticated. The old, solid oak furnishings would have suited a well-to-do farm house. Her rooms in Brighton far outclassed them.

The girls made themselves comfortable on the wide window seat, watching in wide-eyed amazement as she unpacked her trunk.

'Don't you have a maid?' Emily asked.

'No. We've been travelling and it's been faster not to be burdened with one.' Mercedes shook out the blue dinner gown she'd worn the first night she'd met Greer.

She hoped he wasn't being interrogated downstairs. She'd felt awkward leaving him after a week solely in his presence. Since Birmingham it had just been the two of them. That would all change. Now there were others vying for his time. She'd have to learn to share him.

Emily's eyes widened further. She was old enough to take in the implications of such a statement. 'You travelled *alone* with my brother?' Mercedes wished she'd worded it more carefully.

'He'll have to marry you!' Clara chimed in with a worthy amount of adolescent fervour over the scandal.

'No, he doesn't.' Mercedes turned away, putting a chemise in a bureau drawer scented with sweet lavender. Would *she* marry *him* if he asked? It was an academic question only. They'd never talked of any future beyond Brighton and even that future had become uncertain lately. Would they go on to Brighton? Or would only she go on? Greer had not mentioned the tournament since leaving Birmingham and it was highly possible, once he saw the benefits of home, he'd simply stop here. He didn't need Brighton, not like she did.

'How did you meet my brother?' Emily asked. 'Was it at a ball? Did he sweep you off your feet? Greer's a great dancer.' Of course, she would think they met at a ball. Where else did nice girls of Emily's background meet nice young men? It was another reminder of how far apart their two worlds were.

The girl would have to be redirected before the questions became more awkward. She wouldn't lie to Greer's sister, but the truth might see her expedited from the house. His parents wouldn't like her telling impres sionable Emily that she'd been travelling the country-side playing billiards with men and masquerading in brothels.

'I met him in Brighton. He had business with my father.' It was true, but it wouldn't hold up for long. It was time to redirect. 'Have you been to Brighton?' She didn't expect they had. Young girls didn't travel further than the distance between the schoolroom and the dining room. 'The Prince's pavilion is a sight to behold. I've danced there once.'

She went on to describe the oriental palace with its spirals and domes, the seaside and the bathing machines that took people out into the ocean. The girls were enrapt and soon questions about their brother were forgotten.

'You have lovely clothes.' Emily looked longingly at the oyster organdy. 'I wonder if Mama would let me wear something like this? She only lets me wear white. She'd never let me have a colour like *that*.' She gestured at the coral gown hanging in the wardrobe. 'But oyster, maybe. It's almost like white, only creamier. White makes me look so pale.'

Mercedes picked up the gown and held it against the girl. 'Yes, oyster becomes you—see how it gives you a little glow?' Emily beamed. Mercedes felt encouraged. She could use a friend in these environs. *Pick someone who is open to your advances.* She pushed the hustling rule aside. She was *not* hustling Greer's family into accepting her. She was merely cajoling them.

'White can be helped along with ribbons.' Mercedes dug through her personal items and pulled out a handful. She sorted through them until she found the one she wanted. It was a gentle aquamarine, not too bright. Lady Tiverton couldn't complain. It would look light but fresh against a white dress. 'Why don't you try this? I think you'll like how it looks.'

'Really? I can keep it?' Emily was thrilled at the impromptu gift.

'If it's all right with your mother.' Mercedes smiled. It wouldn't do to alienate Lady Tiverton. 'Now, how about you, Miss Clara? What kinds of colours do you like to wear?' She would conquer the Barringtons one by one and hope it would be enough. Tea with the family had set a nice tone, but Mercedes was not fool enough to believe that meant her worries were over. The other shoe was going to fall. It was a given.

Chapter Twenty-One

The other shoe was, in fact, falling in the gardens right then. When an unsuitable woman showed up on one's doorstep, action must be taken immediately before word spread. Still, for Andrew such speed was most impressive, Greer thought uncharitably. Mercedes had barely been whisked upstairs before Andrew had asked for this interview on the premise of wanting to show him new plans for a fountain.

Greer eyed a much-folded sheet of paper Andrew withdrew from his inner coat pocket and rethought his analysis. He might be wrong about the speed. His brother might have had a week or two to compose his words. Not even the army moved as slowly as his brother.

'Miss Lockhart is a most improper lady.' Andrew handed him the folded sheet. 'My friend, Mister Ogilvy, wrote to me from Bath. Would you care to read it?'

'I take it we're not going to discuss the fountain?' Greer could feel his temper rising. He didn't like hearing Mercedes maligned so casually. He'd come home to sort through his thoughts and regain his perspective. He'd thought he'd have a little more time before he had to defend his choices. Apparently he was only going to get an hour.

'It's going over by the roses. There. We've talked about the fountain,' Andrew said tersely.

'I haven't been home in three years and the first thing you can think to do is berate me for my companion.'

'We're all glad you're home. We're glad you weren't killed in some meaningless action. But...' Andrew gestured with the letter in his hand, urging Greer to take it '...you've been home for some months. Instead of coming here where you belong you've elected to cool your heels in Brighton and head off to Bath with a billiards champion and his daughter.' He looked at Greer sceptically. 'Half-pay officers must make considerably more than I thought. I know an expensive woman when I see one.'

Greer's fist tightened at his side. 'I should hit you for that. You don't know a thing about her.'

'I know she's got you spinning so fast you can't see straight. Ogilvy says the pair of you were inseparable in Bath and that you had rooms in her home.'

'Her father's home.' Greer corrected. Andrew made it sound as if they'd been living in sin. Greer yanked the letter from Andrew's hand and scanned the page. He'd known something of this nature was bound to happen. England wasn't that big and the peerage even smaller. Everyone was connected in some way and news travelled. Still, *Ogilvy and his brother*? It seemed an unlikely connection. Ogilvy was so gregarious and his brother was, well, *not*.

'How the hell do you know him, anyway?' Greer asked, passing the letter back. It hadn't been nearly as damning as it could have been.

Andrew shrugged and put the paper back in his coat. 'I've only met him a couple of times in London. We are both members of an agricultural society and have exchanged letters about crop rotations over the years.' And now they were exchanging letters about him. Great.

'Ogilvy wasn't even sure you and I were related,' Andrew added. Too bad he'd decided to mention it at all, Greer thought. In all fairness, though, if it hadn't been Ogilvy, it would have been someone else. He couldn't have kept the last two months of his life a secret forever.

'We're getting away from the subject at hand.' Andrew stopped on the garden path and faced him squarely, arms crossed. 'I must ask what your intentions are in bringing Miss Lockhart here. Good Lord, she's upstairs right now with our sisters. Who knows what she's teaching them?'

Probably how to blow chalk off a cue. It would almost be worth it to voice the irreverent thought out loud. Andrew looked so serious, as if the fate of the world rested on this. Greer supposed it did. Andrew's world was considerably smaller than his. 'Father put you up to this. You sound just like him.'

Andrew didn't bother denying it. 'Yes. He thought you'd take it better from me. You and he haven't always been close. He thought you might think he was being heavy handed, as always.' Andrew softened, reminding Greer of the brother he'd grown up with. 'Besides, I volunteered to do it willingly. I'm worried about you. I don't expect you to be excited about the Devonshire life, not after all you've seen. But it's a good life, Greer.'

'It's not the life I want,' Greer answered simply. If he'd learned anything on the road with Lockhart, it was that he'd not be happy isolated in the country doing the same thing every day. There was a tedium to country life that had never quite suited him even when he'd been young. Greer shook his head. His plans were starting to take on a new importance. They had to succeed or it would be the home farm for him.

'What do you mean to do?' Andrew asked when there was no response from him. 'Have you received a new posting?'

'No. I'm thinking about selling my commission.' His family would not like it, but he knew with absolute clarity what he'd do. 'We mean to go on to Brighton. There's a billiards tournament I'm going to play in and then I'm going to open a subscription room. People in Brighton are always looking for entertainment.'

'We? You mean with her?' Andrew was more agitated about Mercedes than the subscription room.

'Yes. If she'll have me. We haven't talked about specifics yet.' He couldn't imagine returning to Brighton without Mercedes, couldn't begin to contemplate launching this new enterprise without her. They'd have to contend with Lockhart, of course, but he might be more amenable to reconciliation once his anger cooled.

'If she'll have you? I'm sure there's no question of

it. You're a good catch for a girl like that.' Andrew's tone bordered on derisive, the moment of softness gone.

'A girl like what?' Greer went on the defensive.

'Well, just look at her. She's the kind of woman who makes a man think with his wrong head.' Implying, of course, that Greer was doing just that.

'Will you accept her?' Greer asked point-blank. He was really asking if the family would accept her.

'Your mistress is your own business, you don't need the family's approval on that. But a mistress isn't to be flaunted in your family's face. You knew better than to bring her here.'

'No.' Greer cut him off before Andrew could begin a sanctimonious tirade about a gentleman's ethics. 'Will you accept her as *my wife*?' It was an admittedly mad-cap idea, marrying Mercedes. He wasn't even sure she was up for it after her *débâcle* with Luce. But once the idea had taken up residence in his brain it wouldn't be evicted. *Lady Mercedes Barrington.*

Andrew shook his head. 'You need to think this through. This could be a scandal for all of us and with Emily's Season next year it's an enormous risk.'

'I don't think the risk is all that great,' Greer countered. 'She's a celebrity's daughter and I'm a second son. I doubt the scandal would last long enough to do Emily any damage.'

'Then there's Father to consider. He won't forgive this, Greer. You will have crossed him for the last time. Think of all you'll be giving up.'

He tried not to think of that. Grandmother's inheritance, left specifically to him. Twenty thousand pounds to be his upon his marriage to a suitable bride.

Andrew dropped his voice. 'That twenty thousand would go so far here. We wouldn't have to live like we do. You know what I mean.'

He did know what his brother meant: keeping up appearances. 'There's money for a new fountain.'

'We're entertaining this autumn. We had to do something.' Andrew sighed. Yes, Greer thought, something to distract the eyes from what was really around them—a tired, worn-out estate.

'With your twenty thousand, we could invest and draw on returns. We could fix the roof.'

'You mean *you* could,' Greer broke in coldly. 'You've been dreaming of the inheritance, haven't you?' He was starting to see where this was all headed. Andrew lacked the sophistication of Allen Lockhart when it came to manipulation, but the end game was the same. He saw his brother's plan. Give Greer the home farm to run, find him a nice baron's daughter to marry and keep him and his twenty thousand here.

'No,' Greer said firmly. 'I will not be emotionally blackmailed into this or threatened into it.'

Andrew's face turned red. 'You'll never see a penny of it if you marry her.'

'Not unless you use your influence with Father to convince him to release the funds.' Greer smiled coldly. He didn't relish what he was going to say next, but it had to be done if he wanted to know Andrew's true colours. 'What if I promise you half of the money if you can get it released?'

The anger left Andrew's face almost immediately, replaced by a calculating glint in his eyes. 'Well, that would be something to consider. Ten thousand would certainly help.' His words were slow as he thought out loud, already imagining how to spend the funds.

Greer wanted to hit him. 'You bastard. This isn't about money.' At least it shouldn't be about money.

'Of course it is, Greer. It's always been about money.' Andrew sneered. 'Don't be naïve.'

'You disgust me.' Greer turned on his heel and headed back to the house. It was something of a setback to discover he'd traded Allen Lockhart's shenanigans for his brother's, and that the two weren't all that different. This visit might turn out to be shorter than planned, but he couldn't leave it, as much as he wanted to. He wanted to spend time with his sisters, to show Mercedes his home and he needed to talk with his father, even if the outcome of that discussion seemed obvious and futile.

Five days in, Mercedes could sense things were going poorly. Not that anyone was going out of their way to be cruel. She almost wished they were. Then she could meet trouble head on. In fact the opposite was true. Dinners had been unfailingly polite, as had the game of cards afterwards. The girls and Greer's mother had shown her around the gardens the next morning. They'd spent a companionable afternoon on the back verandah enjoying the sun and their individual arts. Emily worked with her watercolours while Clara read aloud from a novel while she and Lady Tiverton stitched.

On the surface, it all looked perfect. Like the public rooms downstairs. But underneath there was a very rotten core. She noticed it in the way no one asked her anything personal. There was no attempt to get to know her in any meaningful way. She was included enough to make it clear she was excluded.

Today she was left to her own devices, another reminder of her ultimate exclusion. The girls and Lady Tiverton had gone to the village for a meeting at the church. She'd notably not been invited. It would have required public acknowledgement. Greer was nowhere to be found, as he had been for the better part of the visit.

She saw very little of Greer and they were never alone when she did. Out of respect for the home and his parents, there was no question of a clandestine visit to his rooms or hers. She sorely missed his presence in her bed.

It was the perfect strategy: divide and conquer. She wondered if Greer saw it, this attempt to keep them apart while reminding him of all he had, of who he was, maybe even of what he stood to lose if he defied them. All the while the clock was ticking. She had to think about getting to Brighton.

Mercedes wandered into the storage corridor. Today was a perfect day to check it out. It was intriguing enough to have a storage corridor. Most people used attics. What in the world did they keep in here? She gave the first door a tentative try. It gave and she pushed it open. The room was the size of a bedroom and full of boxes.

Mercedes studied the labels: linens, tablecloths, bed sheets. Curious, Mercedes pulled down one box and opened it. The scent of cedar and lavender wafted from it. She dug her hands into depths past layers of tissue paper. Whatever was in here had been stored with the utmost care. Her hands made contact with the softest of linen and she pulled out a pristine set of white sheets trimmed in expensive lace and exquisitely embroidered. She held them to her nose and inhaled. It brought a little smile to her lips.

'Now you know our dirty little secret.' A voice behind her made her jump. She felt terribly vulnerable. She'd been caught red-handed at snooping.

'Andrew, you startled me.' Mercedes replaced the sheets and rose, brushing dust off her skirts. 'I thought everyone was out.'

'Obviously.' His blue eyes were cold, lacking any of the mischief and warmth she found so often in Greer's. He moved into the room, crowding her between the boxes and his body. 'What do you think of us now? We keep our best things packed carefully away, bringing them out only on special occasions like state visits.'

One look at the sheets and she'd guessed as much. 'It doesn't matter one way or the other to me,' Mercedes offered, stepping past him into the hall.

He grabbed her arm. 'It matters to me. We need him to marry well. He can do much better than you and he should.'

Mercedes jerked her arm free, tempted to go for the knife in her bodice. 'If you'll excuse me, I think I'll see if Greer's returned.'

* * *

But she didn't see Greer until that night at dinner, another polite affair even though the bubble was officially off the wine after her unpleasant encounter with Andrew. She knew where the family stood. Did Greer? He looked immaculate in evening wear appropriate for the country, his blond hair momentarily tamed back from his face. He was tanned from riding and radiated strength and health. Her heart nearly cracked in two at the sight of him. Did he understand he'd have to choose between her and his family? How could she force him to make that choice?

Dinner dragged on interminably. Emily talked about the watercolour she'd painted today. Everyone laughed when Clara told a funny story about the new kittens in the barns. But there were subtle tones of tension that underlay the table tonight. Greer's father was more taciturn than the norm and Andrew was not trying at all to disguise his dislike of her. She wished desperately for some form of escape. She was just about to fabricate an illness when Greer rose right before dessert was served.

'If you would all excuse us, I need to steal Mercedes away. I promised her on the way here that I'd show her the gardens, but I've been remiss so far in carrying out my word.'

'Thank you,' Mercedes breathed once they were outdoors. The gardens were cool and dark in the summer night. They weren't lit like her garden in Brighton. The only brightness was the light thrown haphazardly from the house. 'I didn't think I could stand another moment.'

There was so much they needed to discuss. 'We need to talk, Greer.'

'Hush. We'll talk in a while. For now, just enjoy. Look at the stars. There aren't stars in town like this.' Greer tipped his head back to the sky and she did the same, gasping a bit at the brilliance overhead. The stars had come out in multitudes, diamonds against the black silk of the sky.

'Stunning,' Mercedes offered.

'Like you.' Greer traced a finger along the curve of her upturned jaw. 'You're like the sky tonight, all those *brillantes* in your hair, your gown like a moonbeam. I think I like you in silver best. You're my very own star fairy.' He placed a kiss at the base of her neck and she shivered.

'I must apologise for leaving you alone so long. I had hoped some time with my father might help us resolve some of our differences.' He shrugged to indicate that he'd not been successful in that regard.

So this was it. He *did* know he'd have to choose. How many more times would he touch her like this? They'd resumed walking the open pathways through the knot gardens. The heat of him radiated through his coat, warming her.

'Your brother doesn't approve of me,' Mercedes began.

'Maybe you'll grow on him.' Greer tried to dismiss the concern with humour. 'It might take a while though. Andrew is a slow learner.'

'Do you think there will be time for that?' she ventured, veering carefully towards the conversation they needed to have. Would he stay or would he come to Brighton?

Greer stopped and turned towards her, his eyes taking on a serious cast. 'I certainly hope so.' Something in his demeanour put her on alert. Her hands were in his, flat against his chest. He held her with those deep blue eyes and she waited, unable to form the questions pelting through her mind.

'There is much I need to talk to you about, Mercedes, but I felt I couldn't until I was sure of things. I had arrangements I needed to make, conversations I needed to have. Now all is settled and I can come to you.'

Her heart began to race. She'd understood the first part. There was much to talk about and she could imagine most of it. It was time to say goodbye. But the rest made no sense. Arrangements he needed to make...? A pit formed in her stomach, the roasted fowl threatening to come up. He wanted her to be his mistress. For him it would be the perfect compromise. He could have her without separating from his family.

No, oh, please not that. To have him, but not have him, would be worse than not having him altogether. It would cheapen everything they'd shared. Was that all he'd seen her as? Even if it was all she could expect from a nobleman's son, she wouldn't take half measures. It wasn't the offer that turned her stomach so much as the realisation that she'd thought he'd known her better than to ask.

She tugged, trying to free her hands. Greer held tight. She lashed out with cold words. 'I will never be any man's mistress, Captain Barrington. Not even yours.'

He gave a slight shake of his head. 'Not that.' Then he laughed. 'This is not going quite as I had planned.'

She realised her mistake with a dawning fear that replaced the horror over being his mistress. A man like Greer didn't bring a mistress to the family seat. A man like Greer would only bring home a woman he meant to… Mercedes felt her legs go weak. Oh Lord, Greer meant to propose.

Chapter Twenty-Two

Greer sank to one knee on the stone pavers in front of her and she wished she could do the same. Her hands were still tightly gripped in his. She let their warmth and strength sustain her through this terrible, beautiful moment. She was cognisant of it all—how carefully he must have planned even if it had gone awry; this lovely, private setting, his family home on display at its summer finest with the moon and stars overhead, the faint call of the night birds in the distance.

'Mercedes, will you do me the honour of marriage?' There was no great speech, no listing of her attributes and the fixing of his affections, no protestations of undying love. Yet it was all there in the single line, in the touch of his hands, the dark mirrors of his eyes. 'You would make me the happiest of men.'

That galvanised her into action. 'I would make you the most miserable of men,' she said softly. She didn't want to be cruel. Clearly, this moment meant much to him. It meant much to *her*. Any girl would be flattered

to receive such a proposal from such a man. Men like
Greer didn't grow on trees for the picking. 'Why now,
Greer?'

The romance of the moment passed. Greer sighed
and rose. He sat down on a stone bench, arms balanced
on his knees, head down. She regretted her practical
questions. She'd bungled this. What had he said to her
once? *You really know how to cut a man down to size.*
She'd done that tonight most assuredly. *This moment
will pass and I'll be glad I saved him from this griev-
ous mistake.*

'Why now? Isn't it apparent?'

'Not really,' she answered truthfully. 'Unless it is a
strategy of yours to keep me here with you instead of
going on to Brighton.'

He shot her a cold look. 'A strategy? Is that how you
saw this? Is it how you see everything?' His tone was
not kind. This is it, she thought. *This is where I lose
him.* After all, this was where her father had lost him.
It had been the games, the manoeuvres, and the strategies that Greer could not tolerate about him.

'This was an honourable proposal of marriage, given,
I think, with the sincerest of emotions,' Greer ground
out. 'Brighton is our watershed. We can't keep piece-
mealing our relationship together. We need to decide
what we shall mean to each other. I have decided, but
apparently you haven't.'

Her mind had latched on to one word. 'What do you
mean "Brighton is our watershed?"'

'We're going back, aren't we? Back to where this
all started and for the reason it started. We're going to

play in that tournament and, after one of us wins, we need a plan.'

This nearly reduced her to tears as the proposal had not. *We.* 'How did you know I meant to play?' she whispered.

Greer laughed, his anger dissipating a little. He wasn't gone from her just yet. 'You haven't cornered the market on deductive powers yet. There was only one reason you went to Mrs Booth's. You needed money and there was only one reason you needed it. Then, when you confessed in Birmingham the reasons you'd come on the road, I knew my assumption wasn't wrong. You meant to play. Besides, you got on the train with me and I knew at the time, you didn't get on the train for me. Not solely, anyway.'

Mercedes blushed. 'It was more about you than you think.' How could she tell him she lived in fear of losing him? That she wanted nothing more than to accept his proposal. 'But I don't see how it's going to work.'

'I'll sell my commission. We'll have a little money to start. One of us could win the tournament. The purse will definitely help.'

Mercedes put a finger to his lips. 'Just like a man.' She laughed softly. 'We can survive on our own. Didn't we prove it on the road? That's not what I'm worried about. There are more important considerations than money.' She made a gesture to encompass the grounds. 'There's your family and all of this. You have everything to lose and I have nothing.' *Except my heart.*

'They will accept you, Mercedes, given enough time.'

'You don't know that and you have no reason to believe it. I will not have you throw away your family. No matter what you think of them, they're the only family you've got.' She paused. 'I know what you'll be throwing away, Greer. I miss my father.' She had to make him see reason, see all the things he might be jeopardising.

He kissed the column of her neck, his voice low against her throat. 'Stop thinking of questions, Mercedes, and start thinking of answers. How do we go to Brighton?' She understood—separately as Mercedes Lockhart and Lord Captain Greer Barrington, occasional and unconventional lovers, or did they go as Lord and Lady Barrington, bound together forever by the bonds of matrimony?

Mercedes swallowed. Did she dare reach out and claim her heart's desire, to be with Greer always? The road would not be easy no matter how certain he was of his plans.

'Please, Greer, give me time to think.' The gambler's motto came to mind: know the rules, know the stakes, know when to quit. She'd broken the rules; they were of no help to her now. She knew the stakes, her heart against the odds. As for quitting, was this the time? She simply didn't know.

He kissed her one more time, a slow lingering kiss meant to last. 'While you're thinking, think about this. I love you, Mercedes Lockhart.'

She reached up and twined her arms about his neck. 'I know. That's why I have to think for both of us.'

Predictably, she couldn't sleep. She wondered if Greer had managed to sleep. He'd taken her request with equanimity, if not disappointment. She didn't doubt Greer cared for her. But would such a sacrifice be worth it for him? Would there come a day when he'd regret his choice? When he'd wish he'd married a pale virginal beauty of the *ton*? When he'd wish he hadn't resigned his commission or that he had stayed in Tiverton?

Mercedes got out of bed and put on a simple dress. It would be morning soon enough. Even now, grey light pierced the darkness. Perhaps some exercise would be enough to clear her thoughts. Not surprisingly, her feet found their way to the billiards room. The Barrington table was well worn in the style of the house but solid. Perhaps she might shoot just a few balls to relax.

No. There was light coming from the room. Drawing closer, she could hear the very quiet snick of balls against one another. Someone was playing. She almost turned back and then laughed at her foolishness. Who else would be up besides Greer?

She stepped into the room, realizing too late the blond hair and form bent over the table wasn't Greer, but Andrew. He looked up, pinning her with his gaze like an insect in a display gaze. She felt about as small, too, not that she'd give him the satisfaction that he might be able to intimidate her just a teeny bit. Mercedes met his gaze.

'My brother has proposed. Have you accepted?' Andrew made an angry shot. He was adequate, but not especially good.

'That's none of your business.' Mercedes picked up a cue stick. 'Shall I play you for him? Will that make you feel better? I win, I get him.'

'Do you really think you can beat me?' He was all smug disbelief over the idea of a woman playing.

'Let's find out.' Mercedes racked the balls and they chalked up in taciturn silence, each of them consumed by their thoughts. She played hard, her concentration absolute. Mercedes lowered her cue, catching the ball slightly below the centre, and executed a neat split, putting one ball in a pocket and the other effectively in Andrew's way.

'I wish my father had never taught him to play,' Andrew said, forcefully potting a ball. 'It's been nothing but trouble.'

'It's a gentleman's game. He was honour-bound to learn.' Mercedes struck back with a slice.

'Is it?' he said meanly, missing his next shot. 'You seem to suggest otherwise.'

Mercedes ignored the gibe. 'Greer will never truly be happy here. He has a great gift.'

Andrew leaned on his stick, surveying the table. She'd made it hard on him and he didn't know where his next shot was coming from. 'A gift? And he should use that gift to be a billiards sharp in some club with you?' He gave her full scrutiny. 'Why do you want him? You're not pregnant, are you?' He took a poor shot.

'No, not that it's any of your business,' she answered sharply, making her own. Greer had been careful, but she'd taken precautions too. A child at this point would complicate things even further. Mercedes made her last shot. 'I win.'

'But at what price?' Andrew laid his cue on the table. She could see he wasn't finished with her yet. 'Do you understand? He's got nothing of his own. You were going through the boxes, you know how we live. It's all smoke and mirrors around here and what there is will come to me.'

'I understand perfectly,' Mercedes replied.

Andrew shook his head. 'You must be fabulous in bed, absolutely fabulous. It's the only answer I can come up with. Do you do it all? You must, for twenty thousand. I almost wish I could have a taste of it so I could better comprehend how my brother could give up so much.'

Mercedes's temper surged. 'You're a very crass man, and I haven't any idea what you're referring to.'

Andrew gave a malevolent smile. 'You don't know? Our grandmother left him twenty thousand, available to him upon his marriage to a suitable young lady. He marries you and he won't see a penny of it. And yet he seems determined to pursue that course.' His eyes raked her in an uncomfortable perusal. 'Again, I do wonder.'

Mercedes did not dignify his remark with a response. All she could think of was getting out of the room. He made her feel unclean.

Once up in her room, the guilt came. How many times had she taunted Greer about risking nothing? How he always had the security of the home farm waiting? In truth, he'd risked scandal, both private and public. Now, he risked his future. Twenty thousand would see him set for life if he lived within his comfortable means. But Greer had said nothing about it and was apparently ready to throw it away for her.

She wouldn't let him. Her answer was clear now. She had to refuse him for his own good. Her heart started to rebel. *But you love him.* No, don't think, just do. She would pack and be gone before he rose. She'd leave a note. She wouldn't survive facing him.

Mercedes had packed in record time, fearing to stop for a moment lest she start thinking about what she was doing. At last the note was scribbled, the room clear. A carriage stood waiting at the front door for her. It had been no problem to summon one even at this early hour. The footman had asked no questions when he'd come for her trunk. Apparently if Miss Lockhart wished to leave, everyone was to comply. At the last, she reached up and took off her star necklace and set it on top of the note in the salver in the front hall. Greer would understand this was for the best. And eventually she would too.

Mercedes climbed into the coach.

'Where to, Miss Lockhart?' the coachman asked.

Her throat was tight as she handed him a worn card. 'My father.'

Andrew Barrington watched the carriage pull away into the dawn from the front room window, the note clutched in his hand. Good riddance—the bitch was gone. Greer's twenty thousand was safe. He had every confidence his brother would forget the brazen hussy soon enough. There was a nice baron's daughter a few miles from here who would turn his head. Very soon this dalliance with the fiery Mercedes Lockhart would be nothing more than a bachelor's last fling.

Andrew scanned the note. The hussy claimed to have loved Greer. Too bad. If she hadn't told him already, it was too late. He crumpled the note and threw it into the grate. 'Molly,' he called to the early-morning maid in the hall, 'set a fire in here. There's a bit of chill in the air.'

Chapter Twenty-Three

A chill ran through Greer as he came down the stairs, full of nervous energy. A slice of silver gleamed in the front-hall salver, further compounding his feeling that something was wrong. He'd gone to Mercedes's room that morning wanting to talk, decency be damned, only to find it extraordinarily neat the way a room is after someone has left it. Of course she hadn't left, he'd told himself. It was nine o'clock in the morning. No one went anywhere until noon.

His reassurance slid away as he approached the salver, his worst suspicions confirmed. His hand closed over the necklace. His stomach clenched with confirmation. She was gone. Greer rummaged through the salver, looking for a note. Surely she wouldn't have left without any word? Questions bombarded his mind as he tried to make sense of it. Was this her idea of 'time to think'? Or was this outright rejection? Perhaps something else altogether? Had someone said something to her that had scared her off? She was acutely sensitive about their differences in station and after the proposal she'd feel any jab about her status keenly.

All he knew was that he hurt, physically hurt, at the thought that she was gone. She'd left *him* and he wanted answers.

Muffled voices from the estate office drew his attention. Ah, his father and Andrew were up early. Perhaps they knew something, or, came the sinister thought, had done something to drive her off. It felt good to have his hurt transform into anger he could use. He let it propel him into the office.

'Where is she?' Greer burst in, the necklace dangling in accusation from his fist.

'Ah…' Andrew gave a sad smile at the sight of the charm. 'Miss Lockhart has left us, so I was informed. She called for a carriage early this morning.'

Greer's anger ratcheted up a notch. 'And you let her go without question? A woman calls for a carriage at dawn and you, who just happen to be up, oddly enough, let her drive away?'

'She's not my woman,' Andrew sneered. 'She left you, not me.'

'You knew how I felt. You knew my hopes.' Exactly. Andrew knew and Andrew hadn't approved. Andrew had been awake far earlier than usual. He'd never wanted to do violence to his brother as he did this very moment.

Greer gave in to the base urge. He grabbed Andrew by the lapels, hauling him against the wall. 'What did you do to her? What did you say?'

'It has to be me?' Andrew struggled to free himself,

but Greer held fast. 'Can't you accept the fact that she's had her fun and now she's done? She decided she didn't want you. I caught her yesterday going through our storage room. She knows you haven't a feather to fly with. She's decided she doesn't want to be poor Lady Barrington after all.' Andrew's face was turning red.

'I don't accept lies,' Greer growled. 'Again, what did you do?'

'Boys, that is enough!' His father rose from behind his desk and Greer let Andrew go. 'Miss Lockhart is gone and I say good riddance if she's going to cause this kind of turmoil in our home. It's further proof she's not acceptable.'

Andrew sat down in his chair, smoothing his rumpled jacket. 'Trust me, it's better this way.' He made a conciliatory gesture.

Greer looked from his brother to his father in disbelief. They were simply going to dismiss Mercedes as if she were a bill to settle, and move on. 'Better for you,' he replied. Had he always been a pawn to them? Had it taken all this time away to see the truth? They were not much better than Allen Lockhart, with their schemes and manipulations. He was better off on his own.

Greer exited the room. His direction was clear now. He was halfway up the stairs when his father called up to him.

'If you go after her, you won't see a penny of that money, my son.'

Greer turned on the stairs. 'Neither will you. As for me, I'd rather have her.' It was true, every last word of it, and saying it out loud was a bright spot in a dismal morning. He knew exactly where he'd find her. He was going to Brighton to claim her and to claim his future. He was done here. Devonshire could offer him nothing more.

No distractions! Mercedes chided herself as she bent to the table and lined up a shot. Greer wasn't here. She had to stop seeing him in every blond head that passed. She focused and made the shot. Those gathered around the table applauded.

The tournament began tomorrow and Brighton was bustling with business and tourists. Players and spectators alike crowded the subscription halls, none more so than Lockhart's, to watch potential contestants play. Spectators interested in wagers assessed the odds while players sized one another up.

She'd played every game she could get. Her father hadn't the heart to gainsay her. It was a convenient way for him to bow to the inevitable. In the weeks since leaving Devonshire, billiards was the one activity that took her mind off Greer, off the sinking sensation she felt every time she thought of him and what he'd been willing to give up for her. *Willing.* He'd chosen her and she'd not allowed him that choice. Her current misery was her own fault.

She collected her winnings and racked the balls for another set. There were plenty of men lining up to play Lockhart's daughter for the sheer newness of it, if nothing else. She didn't care what their motives were. She only cared about buying herself a moment's peace from Greer Barrington. If anyone had told her in March she'd

feel this miserable about playing in the tournament she'd
have laughed and wagered against such an outcome.
She'd wanted this opportunity. Now she had it and it
was not enough.

'Are you playing in the tournament, Miss Lockhart?'
someone in the crowd called out.

'Absolutely. Are you?' she called back while the
crowd laughed.

'What happens if you draw your father? Can you beat
him?' someone else chimed in. She'd become something of a celebrity since returning to Brighton. Everyone was interested in what she did and she always
gave them a show.

'We'll cross that bridge when we come to it,' Mercedes said with a saucy smile. The scenario did unnerve
her. She hoped they would avoid each other in the pairings. It had been something of a surprise to discover
her father had entered his own tournament until she'd
sorted through the pieces, the little clues that hadn't
made sense at the time like all the playing he'd done in
Bath and afterwards. He'd used Greer as a smokescreen
for launching his own career. The hard truth was, she
had too. Only she'd fallen in love with her own mark,
something she was willing to admit too late.

'Who's next?' she called out, pasting on a smile. Men
liked to play a pretty woman and any woman was prettier when she smiled.

'I am.' A broad-shouldered man parted the group
from the back. Her breath caught and she had to remind
herself that Greer wasn't here. He wasn't coming. She

had left him and he wasn't going to chase after her once cool-headed logic set in.

'Hello, Mercedes.'

'Hello.' Her heart raced. She gripped the cue for support. Not every man was Greer Barrington, but this one was. He looked a bit tired around the eyes, but it was him.

He smiled. 'Shall we play for dinner? I win, you take me. You win, I take you.'

'Take me where?' She chalked her cue, eyes not leaving him.

'I'll take you wherever you like.' There were some whistles and catcalls to that answer. Her crowd was in a good mood.

'It might be worth losing just to find out.' Mercedes gave the tip of her stick a naughty blow. 'Your break.'

In the end she won, although she suspected Greer's inadequate slice might have had something to do with it. But she was more than willing to live up to her end of the wager. She had questions, and dinner would be the perfect opportunity for answers.

They chose the restaurant at Greer's hotel, a lovely place on the promenade where they could eat outside and watch people as they passed on their evening strolls along the water.

'What brings you to Brighton?' Mercedes asked once they were settled at their table.

Greer gave a short laugh. 'What do you think? The woman I proposed to fled my home in the middle of the night without any word.'

'I left a note,' Mercedes said defensively. Inside, her stomach was doing flip-flops. She wasn't sure how she'd manage to eat anything. *He'd come for her.* Not for the tournament.

His face registered some surprise. 'It did not reach me. But this did.' He pulled out the silver charm. 'I'd like for you to take it back.'

Mercedes took the charm and studied it. It gave her something to look at besides his handsome face. 'I've regretted how we parted, but the reasons I left haven't changed, Greer.' She looked up briefly. 'Your brother told me about the inheritance. I can't let you give that up. Or your family. You will come to hate me. You don't think so now, but you will.'

'Have you missed me, Mercedes? I've missed you and in the weeks it took to raise my own stake for the tournament and come here, I realised that being with you was all that mattered.' He reached for her hands and she let him take them.

'I won't change my mind, Greer.' She hoped he wouldn't call that bluff. Her mind was a malleable pudding at this point. Just seeing him again had reduced her insides to jelly. To have him touch her, to look at her with those eyes, was ambrosia.

'Come with me.' He grabbed up the bottle of champagne from the ice bucket and took her hand.

'What are you doing?' People were starting to look at them.

'Changing your mind. If you won't change it, I'll have to change it for you.' He grinned wickedly as he guided her through the dining room. 'Never say you're afraid?'

'Never.' She smiled back, but she knew this was sheer madness. One more night with Greer would only remind her of all she was giving up because it couldn't be any other way.

Upstairs in the privacy of his room, he stripped for her, seducing her with his movements as he took off trousers and boots, shirt and coat until he stood in front of her, gloriously and unabashedly nude. He would convince her any way he could tonight, with any tool he possessed.

At least she was willing to play along. Mercedes propped herself up on a pillow and licked her lips. 'You certainly know how to give a girl a good show. What do you have in mind for act two?'

She let her skirts fall back and parted her legs ever so provocatively, making her expectations for 'act two' quite clear. He nearly spent himself right there. Act two would be a very short one, leading directly to the main event.

He covered her then. There would be more time for talk later. For now he wanted the desperation of his body to speak for him. His need for her had reached a fever pitch after weeks of enforced celibacy. It had been almost impossible to concentrate on billiards that afternoon. All he could think of was this.

Mercedes drew him down to her, her legs embracing him, urging him, and he took her in a swift claiming thrust that wrung a gasp from her. He thrust again, establishing their rhythm, aware of the feel of Mercedes's long legs locked about him, aware of her body clenching about him, the tight warmth of her sheath as she took his length again and again. Had anything ever felt this good? This right? Then of course, something did. His own release was upon him, pounding and furious, obliterating all else but pleasure in its path until he was spent.

There was champagne then, but not in the usual way. He saw to it even that was an exercise in decadence. He drank champagne from her navel. He licked the juice of strawberries from her lips and her breasts, watching her grey eyes go black with desire, feeling her body arch to him, wanting the pleasure as much as he wanted to give it and he came to her again as a lover complete, until they were too exhausted for more.

It was well after midnight before they found the strength to talk. She lay in his arms, her head against his shoulder, the light floral scent of her hair in his nostrils. 'I'm staying in Brighton, Mercedes, after the tournament.' Greer began laying out the plans he'd formed since leaving Devonshire. 'I am going to sell my commission and open a subscription room. I have a lead on a property not far from here. It's small, but it's a good location. I'm hoping the tournament will help build a clientele for me.'

She laughed softly in the darkness, a throaty sound he'd missed. 'In other words, you hope to finish high enough in the tournament to win both money and attention.'

'Yes. I'd forgotten how good you are at seeing to the

heart of a matter.' Greer ran a hand down her arm, revelling in the feel of having her beside him again. 'My proposal still remains between us. My desire to marry you has not changed. Come run my subscription room with me. You can play. Perhaps you can even have a women's club. Wouldn't that be something? We'd be the only place in Brighton with one.'

'Have you forgotten your family, your inheritance?' Those things remain as well.'

'I will not be their pawn, Mercedes. They can acknowledge me or not. That's their choice, not mine. My choice is you. I wish you would trust that.' He sighed, more than a little frustrated in her obstinate reticence. How else could he show her?

'On one condition, Greer.' She was all business, and his mind quickened at the prospect of one of her challenges.

'Name it'

'Play me for it. Play me for our future.' She rolled out of bed and dressed, while he watched, pondering the request. This was starting to feel like the twelve labours of Hercules.

'Why?' Greer asked.

She came to the bed and kissed his cheek. 'Trust me, Greer. Stay alive in the tournament until you can get to me and you'll see. You have to keep your promise this time.'

'What does that mean?' Greer answered, half humoured and half perplexed. He always kept his word; surely she knew that by now.

'It means you broke your word once before when you promised me something.'

'I don't recall...' Greer hesitated.

'When you told me you wouldn't fall in love with me,' Mercedes prompted.

'Oh, well, then I had my fingers crossed,' Greer argued.

Mercedes shook her head. 'And now? There can be no crossed fingers on this, Greer.'

From anyone else, he would have laughed at the melodramatic nature of the request, but not with her. She was serious and in earnest. He might never get used to the intensity she had for billiards, but he could not doubt her dedication. 'Yes, Mercedes, I promise.'

Mercedes Lockhart took Brighton by storm, as she had fully intended to do. The gown she'd chosen for the tournament was black with a moderately full skirt to facilitate easy movement, but not nearly as full as common fashion dictated and it was most certainly being worn *without* a petticoat—only the gored folds of the skirt kept it from indecency. But nothing kept the bodice from earning such a label, what there was of it. There were no sleeves or neck, only the heart-shaped torso of the bodice, leaving her *décolletage* entirely bare save the single piece of jewellery she wore on a thin black ribbon: Greer's star, shining and silver. Her hair was worn in her customary drape over one shoulder. She smiled at the nearly quieted crowd, only to have it go wild again. Kendall Carlisle, the tournament's designated master of ceremonies, let it. Mercedes Lockhart was good for business. She sailed through the preliminary rounds, her luck and skill holding unchallenged. But in the quarter-finals her luck failed. Her father was still alive and playing spectacularly well.

So be it. Mercedes studied the table, steeling herself for the upcoming match. If she meant to win the tournament, facing her father was inevitable any way. She *did* need to win this game for her plans to advance. Beyond the match with her father lay the semi-final bracket in which she'd face Greer, just as she'd hoped and intended. But first, she needed this game to prove herself to her father once and for all. Mercedes chalked her cue, bent to the table, and broke with a smile. She could do this.

And she did, sweeping the match in three straight games to thunderous applause. If her father had deliberately thrown the match or lost on purpose out of some misguided effort to apologize, she couldn't tell, nor did she want to know. She could no longer feel responsible for his private agendas. She only knew she had what she wanted, a chance to send Greer to the finals and a chance to secure his inheritance in a roundabout way. She couldn't actually claim the trust for him but she could secure the amount he'd given up by coming after her. All he had to do was keep his promise.

Mercedes studied the semi-final brackets on the pairings board. The winner of her semi-final match with Greer would face a flirty rogue of a player from York, Alex Cahill. She'd seen the man play. He was devastating and attractive—an absolute showman. She smiled to herself: Greer would know exactly how to beat him.

Mercedes fingered the large roll of pound notes she'd accumulated and went to place a bet.

Greer met her at the table for the semi-finals, his voice low. 'All right, Mercedes. I stayed alive long enough to face you. Will we survive it?'

She turned and smiled at him. 'We will.' There wasn't time to say more. The games would start very soon. To-night would decide everything. 'Remember what you promised me?'

'I remember. Do you remember what you promised me?'

'Absolutely.' Mercedes picked up her cue and began to chalk with a smile.

She made sure they gave the crowd a show. She was mesmerising and deadly with her splits. Greer was dominating with his slices. She smiled and dazzled, he laughed and charmed, brushing his hair out of his eyes every so often. People would long remember that match. She won the first game. He won the second and when the third game looked like it would somehow end in a dead heat, Mercedes caught Greer's gaze over her cue and bit her lip, sending him the only signal she could. Then she took her decisive shot, deliberately too hard, and the cue ball followed the other into the pocket. The crowd groaned and Greer shot her a thunderous look across the table. There was going to be hell to pay for this.

Kendall Carlisle grabbed Greer's arm and raised it high, declaring him the winner amid applause, but that only delayed the inevitable.

'What the hell do you think you're doing?' Greer seized her none too gently and guided her to a private room the moment they could escape. 'Have you forgotten I've seen that shot before? You forfeited that game.'

'Have you forgotten you promised to trust me?' Mercedes answered. 'You are the one who has to advance.' The words rushed out. 'Please listen, Greer.' She gripped his lapels. She'd known he would be mad, but the reality was far worse than the theory. 'You promised you'd play for me. I am holding you to it. I need you to play for me now.'

Greer paused, his eyes past her in his anger. 'You're the one, Greer, who has the best chance to beat Cahill. I've already secured my reputation by making it this far, but you need that money and you need *your* reputation.' Mercedes held his gaze, willing him to believe her.

'And what do you need?' Greer asked gruffly.

'I need you, Greer.' She kissed him hard on the mouth, then. 'And I need to go pick up my winnings.'

He arched his eyebrows. 'What winnings would those be?'

'The money I placed on you.' She smiled mischievously. 'The odds were more lucrative on you to win.'

Suspicion crossed his face. 'How much did you wager, Mercedes?'

'How much do you think? Enough to make sure you won't miss that inheritance you're giving up,' she said softly. 'I couldn't let you give it all up, Greer. I promised myself I'd make it back for you. But now is not the time to get emotional about money. Lesson number one, remember? Don't get emotional about money. Yours or anyone else's.'

Greer protested, 'At least you should have told me.'

'And risk having you throw the game first?' She shook her head. 'I know you, Greer Barrington, and you would have meddled if you thought for a second it wasn't my best game. Besides, tonight I wasn't betting on you, I was betting on us. Go out there and win this, Greer.'

'You've taken an enormous risk, Mercedes,' he began.

'Of course I have. But you're worth it.' She twined her arms around his neck and drew him down to her. 'For better or for worse, isn't that how it goes?'

'I thought a good gambler knew when it was time to quit?' Greer quizzed sternly.

'If there is such a time, I haven't found it.' She kissed Greer hard. She'd learned her lessons well and knew that sometimes it paid more to lose than it did to win. Just look at what she'd gained when she'd lost her heart.

Three days later, Mercedes Lockhart married the newly crowned All England Billiards Champion at St Peter's Church, the closest thing to a cathedral Brighton had. The church was filled with flowers and friends, and even strangers who'd been caught up in the drama of the tournament. Mercedes had very little attention to spare for those details, though. All of her focus was spent on the man at the altar. Was there ever a more handsome man than the one waiting for her or did every bride think that on her wedding day? No, surely not.

She concentrated on every detail of him: how the filtered sunlight hit his hair, firing it to a platinum sheen; the clean-shaven strength of his jaw and the piercing

quality of his blue eyes as they found her; the square
set of his shoulders in the red coat of his uniform, every
last button and brass polished; his legs long and lean in
the pristine white trousers, a ceremonial sword hanging at his side. It would be one of the last times he wore
it before giving up his commission. But the uniform
had been chosen to send a message, perhaps for her as
much as for the crowd, Mercedes thought. Here stood
a man who knew and did his duty—his honour was not
in question nor should be his choice of bride. She would
have his protection and his devotion all his days and let
no man gainsay him—not his father, not his brother.

He took her hand, giving her father a short bow.
'Thank you, sir.'

She could feel the covert squeeze of his hand as they
turned to face the vicar, a happy round-faced man. He
began the service and she let the words flow around
her, aware that they were nothing more than a pleasant
sound. She was riveted on Greer, on this man who'd
pledged himself to her, who stirred her to a passion so
great she'd defied her father.

Greer bent close to her during a prayer. 'Your father
spoke to me this morning. He has given his blessing.'
Her father had been slow to forgive Greer for deserting
him in Birmingham.

'I know. I played him for it.' She kept her eyes
straight ahead, fixed on the cross above the altar.

Greer chuckled, drawing a moment of censure from
the vicar who shot him a reproving look over the prayer
book. 'Of course you did. You know, you can't settle
everything with a billiards game, Mercedes.'

'Not everything,' she agreed. 'But those things that can be, should be.' She elbowed him. 'Look reverent. It's a prayer, after all.'

'I should have guessed sooner. He said you'd talked to him last night. I couldn't imagine what you might have said.'

Mercedes shot him a quick look as the vicar closed the last prayer. 'I did talk to him. I told him I loved you.'

'Was that before or after you ran the table?'

'After, of course.'

The vicar intoned the closing words of the ceremony, pronouncing them man and wife.

'It just so happens,' Greer whispered, his mouth hovering above her lips ever so briefly, 'that I love you too.' Then he kissed her so as to leave no doubt that all parties approved of this match, no one more heartily than the groom himself, and her heart sang with the knowledge that Greer Barrington loved her even though he'd promised not to.

There was a wedding breakfast hosted at her father's club to accommodate the many guests. By the time they could decently take their leave, Mercedes was exhausted, her mind riddled with names and faces. Who would have guessed weddings could be so tiring?

She was more than eager to slide into the closed carriage that would take them across town to their property. They would live above the subscription room for now. Greer joined her with a firm slam of the door and sank into the seat.

'Alone at last! Are you as hungry or as tired as I am?'

His blue eyes sparkled. 'I never realised how little time the bride and groom have to actually eat at their own wedding breakfast.' He laughed and reached under the seat. 'Fortunately, the cook packed a few extra victuals for us.'

Her stomach rumbled and she smiled. 'Fortunately. We have to keep your strength up, after all.'

Greer uncorked a bottle of champagne, slopping a bit on his trousers when the carriage hit a bump. 'I must apologise—it's not your father's carriage.'

'I don't care.' They were on their own now, wanting to build their life from the ground up. She took the glass, more bubbles than wine in it. She sipped carefully. 'I don't think I've ever drunk champagne in a carriage before.'

Greer gave her a most wicked grin that warmed her to her toes. 'What else haven't you done in a carriage, Lady Barrington?' He slid onto the seat beside her. 'Have you done this?' He blew gently in her ear, nipping the tender flesh of her lobe. 'Or this?' His hand cupped her jaw, turning her face towards him for a soft kiss on the mouth. She sank into it, revelling in his touch. She had missed this!

'How about you, good sir? Have you done this?' Mercedes reached for him, finding him hard and ready. He laughed into her mouth, tasting faintly of champagne, letting her unfasten his trousers.

'You are most shocking, madam. I do not think I've ever been undressed in a carriage before.'

'Ha, and you said nothing I did surprised you.' She shot him a flirtatiously sly look. 'I bet I could "surprise" you a little more.' With that her hand began to move. 'Maybe after this, you could "surprise" me.' But, in truth, he already had.

* * * * *

A Lady Dares

*For Amber and Scott
in commemoration of our great day
sailing Commencement Bay.
And for the Lindsleys
who took me on my first and only sail boat ride.*

Chapter One

Blackwell Docks, Sutton Shipyard,
London—mid-March 1839

She was screwed! Absolutely royally screwed in the literal sense of the word; the word in question being 'royally', of course. Elise Sutton crumpled the letter in her hand and stared blindly at the office wall. Like the other investors, the royal family had finally withdrawn their patronage. And like the other investors, they'd politely waited a 'decent' interval to tell her. They were very sorry to hear of her father's death, but the result was the same. The Sutton Yacht Company was on the brink of bankruptcy, brought to its knees by the sudden and tragic death of its founder, Sir Richard Sutton, six months earlier.

In truth, the idea the company had survived its owner by six months was something of an illusion. It had likely died with her father, only no one had bothered to tell her that. Apparently, courtesy demanded she be allowed to rise at dawn every morning and spend the next sixteen hours a day poring over account books, cataloguing inventory and lobbying investors who had no intentions of staying. She'd worn herself out all for naught and what passed for courtesy let her do it.

Well, courtesy be damned! It wasn't a very ladylike thought, but according to the *ton*, she hadn't been a lady for quite some time. By their exalted standards, ladies didn't work side by side with their fathers in the family business. Ladies didn't design yachts, didn't spend their days adding up columns of numbers and most certainly didn't set aside mourning half a year early to try to save sinking businesses. Ladies meekly accepted the inevitable with hands folded in their laps and backs held rigid.

If that's what ladies did, she most definitely wasn't one. She'd spent the last seven years working with her father. The yacht company was as much hers as it had been his. It was part of her and she would not let it go, not without a fight.

At the moment she had admittedly few tools to fight with. The investors had gone, unconvinced the company could produce a worthy product without her father at the helm. The craftsmen and master builder had gone next. The presence of females had long been anathema in the nautical world and no reassurance on her part could induce them to stay. Even her mother was gone. Playing the devastated widow to the hilt, Olivia Sutton had retreated to the country after the funeral and simply disappeared.

Elise had told enquiring souls that her mother was taking her father's death very poorly. Secretly, Elise thought her mother was managing quite well, too well for her personal tastes. In the months since the funeral, her mother's letters from the country had become increasingly upbeat. There were quiet card parties and dinners to attend and everyone was so kind, now there was no longer an often absent husband to consider.

Her mother had loved Richard Sutton's title; *Sir* Richard Sutton had been knighted two years prior for services to the Royal Thames Yacht Club, but Olivia Sutton hadn't loved the work that had driven and absorbed him, taking him away from her. The marriage had been a convenient arrangement for years. Olivia had been more than happy to leave her daughter and son to manage the business of coping with solicitors, creditors and the other sundry visitors who hovered over a death like vultures.

The pencil in Elise's hand snapped, the fifth one today. The sound drew her brother's attention from the window overlooking the shipyard. 'Is it as bad as all that?'

Elise pushed the pieces into the little pile on the corner of her desk with the remains of their fellow brethren. 'It's worse.' She rose and joined William at the window. The normally bustling shipyard below them was silent and empty, a sight she was still having a hard time adjusting to. 'I've sold anything of value associated with the business.'

There hadn't been that much to sell, but that was only partially true. The shipyard itself was a valuable piece of property for its location on the Thames. She wasn't sure she could face the prospect of giving up the business entirely. This had been her life. What would she do every day if she didn't design yachts? Where would she go if she didn't come here? Giving up the yard would be akin to giving up a piece of her soul. In society's eyes she'd already done that once when she'd chosen to follow her father and not the pathway trod by other gently reared girls with means.

William sighed, pushing a hand through his blond hair, the gesture so much like their father it made her heart ache. At nineteen, William was a taller, lankier version of him, a living memory of the man they'd lost. 'How much are we short?'

'Twelve thousand pounds.' Just saying the words hurt. No one had that kind of money except noblemen. Elise thought of the crumpled letter. She'd been counting on that. Royal patronage would have sustained them.

William whistled. 'That's not exactly pocket change.'

'You could always marry an heiress.' Elise elbowed him and tried for levity. William didn't love the business as she did, but he'd loved Father and he'd been her supporter these past months, taking time away from his beloved studies to visit.

'I could leave my studies.' William said seriously. He was starting his third term at Oxford and thriving in the academic atmosphere. They'd been over this before. She wouldn't hear of it.

'No, Father wanted his son educated,' Elise argued firmly. 'Besides, it wouldn't be enough.' She didn't want to be cruel, she appreciated her brother's offer, but the money would hardly make a difference. Since it didn't, it seemed unfair for William to make a useless sacrifice even if it was a noble offer.

'What about the investors—perhaps they would advance funds?' William suggested. The last time he'd been home, there'd still been a few remaining who had not yet discreetly weaned themselves from the company, still hoping there might be a way yet to continue with the latest project.

Elise shook her head. 'They've all pulled out. No one wants to invest in a company that can't produce a product.' They'd more than pulled out. It was largely the investors' faults she was in such a pickle. Her father had not been debt ridden, but neither had he been wallowing in assets. The investors had withdrawn their support *and* asked for their money returned, unconvinced the latest project they'd financed would see completion.

Said project lay below them in the quiet yard——the half-completed shell of her father's latest design for a racing yacht, planned with new innovations in mind, lay dormant. For the last several weeks, the investors were proven right. Supplies purchased with the investors' money from the outset lined the lonely perimeter, tarp covered and forgotten 'A pity the investors didn't want to be paid in timber and pitch,' Elise muttered. 'I've got plenty of that.'

William's eyes settled on her, brown and thoughtful. 'All the supplies have been purchased?'

'Yes. Father buys—*bought*,' Elise corrected herself, 'everything up front, it makes production faster and we don't have to worry about running out at a crucial point.'

William nodded absently, his mind racing behind his eyes. 'How much would the yacht have brought?'

She smiled wryly. 'Enough. It would have been plenty.' It wouldn't have been just about the yacht. There would have been other orders, too. This yacht was meant to be a prototype. Rich men would have seen it and wanted one for themselves. But it was no use now counting hypothetical pounds.

'You could finish the boat,' William suggested.

Elise furrowed her brow and studied her brother carefully. Was that a joke? Had he been listening to anything she'd said? Her temper snapped. 'I can't finish the boat, William. I don't know the first thing about actually *using* hammer and nails. And in case you haven't noticed, there are no men down there, no master builder.'

She regretted the sarcasm immediately. William looked hurt. It wasn't fair to take her agitation out on him. He was suffering, too. He knew what people had said about him behind their hands at the funeral. 'There's the son, but he's too young to take over the company. If only he was a couple years older, then things might have come out all right.' That was usually followed up by the other unfriendly speculation. 'Too bad the daughter doesn't have a husband. A husband would know what to do.' Husbands solved everything in their little worlds.

'I'm sorry, William.' Elise laid a conciliatory hand on his sleeve. 'It's a nice theory. Even if I had the men, I couldn't finish that yacht. The innovations require the knowledge of a master builder. More than that, I'd need the best.' They would have managed without a master builder if her father had been there to oversee the project, as he so often had been, but no workers were going to take orders from a woman even if she had been instrumental in the boat's design.

She needed a master builder more than anything else to finish that boat. Beyond her father, she didn't have a clue who the best was when it came to ship design. Her own talent notwithstanding, she was female and thus excluded from that circle. It had not bothered her unduly in the past. She'd had her father and he'd given her every opportunity she'd desired to advance her skill even if it was often anonymously. She'd never thought further than that. Why should she have? Her father had been in his late forties, in excellent health and at the top of his game. She'd not appreciated by how slim a thread the privilege to indulge her passion had hung until it had been destroyed in one precarious accident.

'What if I could get you the best?' William persisted in earnest.

Finish the yacht? He was absolutely serious. It was

crazy. The idea started to take hold along with the most dangerous of games, *what if*? *If* she had a master builder, workmen would come. *If* those men came, she could pay them with the proceeds from the sale of the yacht. It could be done. There was less than a month's worth of work to finish. It was March now, the yacht would be ready by the time society came to town for the Season. Elise's mind was whirring. Most of all, if they finished the boat the investors would come back. If that happened, the possibilities were as endless as her imagination.

'I'd say we were back in business,' Elise said slowly, reining her thoughts back to the present. Finishing the boat had suddenly become the gateway to the future, a future where the company was saved, where *she* was saved. But there was still this crucial step to accomplish. Everything hinged on the master builder. 'How soon can we meet?'

William flipped open his pocket watch and studied the face. 'I'd say right about now, but you'd better bring Father's pistol from the safe.'

'His pistol? Whatever for?' Warning bells went off in her head. What sort of master builder had to be met with a gun? The shipyard was relatively protected. The docks were surrounded by high walls with guards posted to discourage intruders. Inside the walls, a person was fairly secure. Outside those fortressed walls was a different story for the unwary, but not for her. The docks were her territory. She'd walked them with her father, much to her mother's complete and regular dismay.

If her brother wanted to be protective, she'd let him. Elise checked the gun to see that it was primed. 'Again, why do I need to bring the gun? I've never needed one before.'

William merely grinned at her objection. 'Well, this time, you might.'

Elise took the pistol more to humour him than out of any genuine belief that she'd actually need it.

She was, however, seriously rethinking that position half an hour later when their carriage pulled up in front of a tavern on Cold Harbour Lane ominously named The Gun. Like most streets in London's East End, this one was crowded and busy, full of the dock and indus·trial workers that generated so much of the city's wealth through the strength of their backs.

The crush and smell of the crowd did not daunt Elise, but what happened next nearly did. They'd barely stepped down from the carriage when the door of The Gun flew open in a violent motion. A man crashed into the street, his careening form barrelling straight into her. She might have fallen entirely if the carriage hadn't been at her back, a rather hard bulwark against the assault. It stopped her from falling, but certainly didn't cushion the blow. As it was, the force of the man's exit bore her against the carriage, his arms braced on either side of her to stop his own flight, his body pressed hard and indecently to hers, his blue eyes taking a moment to register he was quite obviously staring at her bosom as they both struggled to find their equilibrium. He found his first and let out a whoop that nearly shattered her eardrums for its closeness. 'What a day! You're the prettiest pillow I've yet to lay my head on.'

'You'll be laying nothing of the sort,' Elise replied coolly, bringing the pistol up and holding his eyes with an unflinching stare. It was a deep-blue gaze, dark midnight like the sea itself, and the press of his body was not entirely unpleasant. There was muscle and strength beneath his rough clothes and the hint of morning soap mingled with the faint whiff of whisky. All very manly scents when presented in the right proportions. Still, she could not stand there and ponder his masculine aesthetics. Propriety demanded his removal from her person. Immediately.

'Please step away.' Where was her brother? Hadn't he been right beside her?

'That's not who you want to shoot.' Was that laughter she heard in her brother's voice? If he wanted to be protective, he was a bit late.

'Maybe I should shoot *you* instead, William,' Elise said through gritted teeth, tossing him a sideways glance over the man's notably broad shoulder. She shoved at the blue-eyed stranger, who'd made no move to distance himself. Her hands met with the steely resistance of a muscled chest. 'Are you going to get off?'

'Probably at some point. Most women don't like a

man who gets off too early, though, if you know what I mean.' He finally moved away, laughter crinkling his eyes as he studied her. She knew exactly what he meant and she would not give him the satisfaction of blushing over his crass remark. Years on the docks had immured her from taking offence at such colourful references. To be sure, such remarks weren't allowed in her father's shipyard when she was in earshot. Her father had been protective in that way, but the language and innuendo of the docks were hard to escape altogether.

'Elise—' William stepped in '—allow me to make the introductions. This is Dorian Rowland,' he said with a flourish as if the name alone explained it all.

She eyed the man speculatively, taking in the tanned skin, the long tawny hair loosely held back by a strip of leather and streaked from the sun of faraway climes— England never had enough sun to achieve such a look. She was momentarily envious of such artless beauty until the import of her brother's words sunk in. *This* was the man who was supposed to save her business?

The door to the tavern opened again, ejecting three tough-looking men with clubs. Her stranger shot a look over his shoulder. 'Could we finish introductions in your carriage?'

The three men were momentarily dazzled by the sunlight as they searched the area for something. *Someone*, she realised too late. Their eyes lit on her stranger. 'There he is! You're not getting away from us! Halsey wants his money.'

'Come on, Elise, let's go.' William hustled them into the carriage, giving a shout to the driver before the door was shut behind him and they were off, navigating the traffic with as much speed as possible.

'Who are those men?' Elise hazarded a glance out the window, recoiling when a rock hit the carriage as they pulled away. They were going to ruin the paint, yet another expense she could ill afford.

'Suffice it to say, they don't like me very much.' Dorian Rowland, whoever he was, smiled as if he hadn't a care in the world. Then again, it wasn't his carriage being chipped.

She threw an accusing glare at her newly acquired companion. William had clearly made a mistake. 'Well, that makes four of us.'

He laughed, a loud, clear sound that filled the carriage. 'Don't worry, Princess, I'll grow on you.'

Chapter Two

In Dorian Rowland's opinion, the ruckus outside the carriage was entirely unnecessary. Some people were simply unreasonable. Yes, he was late with his payment but he was good for it and Halsey knew it. Another cargo, which he'd been *trying* to negotiate when he'd been so rudely and violently interrupted by Halsey's bullies, would have seen it right within the week.

The carriage hit a mud-filled rut in the street and sent a spray of water up, dousing his pursuers. Dorian could hear their curses outside as they gave up the chase. It served them right. They'd got what they so richly deserved and so had he. *He* was sitting in a plush town coach across from a finely dressed lady and her brother.

He definitely didn't know the woman. He remembered pretty women and he'd have remembered her: all that inky black hair, alert green eyes and a bosom to die for. As for the young man, Dorian didn't quite recall him, although there was something of the familiar about him. He was apparently supposed to know him from somewhere. He racked his brain for the last decent party he'd been to. In these cases of questionable identity, he'd found it worked out well to play along, especially when he sensed he was on the brink of an exciting new opportunity. Halsey could wait.

'So you're the best?' The princess was talking, words forming from those kissable pink lips of hers. What a lovely mouth she had, far too lovely for that tone of voice. The way she said it made it sound like an accusation. The princess struck him as a bit high in the instep.

Dorian grinned and slathered his response in innuendo. He might have even shifted his posture ever so slightly to better display the 'goods', not that he'd admit to such feeble vanity. 'Depends on what you want, Princess.'

Her pretty mouth set in a firm line and he knew a moment's regret. Perhaps he'd pushed things a bit too far.

'Stop the carriage, William,' she said sharply to the young man before turning back to him with a cold politeness that suggested she could rise above the situation. 'I am sorry…Mr Rowland, is it? It seems my brother has made a mistake. I'm glad we could assist your escape from imminent danger, but now it is time to part ways. I'll have our driver put you down at the next corner.'

The brother—what was his name again? She'd just said it. William? Wilson?—intervened patiently. 'Elise, wait. I tell you he is the best. If you would just listen to me.' Ah, so she was definitely *not* in the market for a little blanket hornpipe, because her brother would have absolutely *no* knowledge of his skills in that regard. His wind didn't blow that way.

'Give him a chance to explain himself, please.' The brother waved a hand towards him, tossing him a beseeching look. *Feel free to intervene at any time.* Dorian opened his mouth to assist, but too late.

'He has explained himself,' the haughty princess fired back. 'Just look at him! He's unkempt, he was in a public house in the middle of the day and he was brawling. That's just in the last fifteen minutes. Who knows what else he's been doing?'

It was on the tip of his tongue to say 'the captain's mistress'. But then he thought better of it. A becoming colour was riding her cheeks. The princess had been provoked enough already.

'You would entrust our future to *that*? I don't even want to know how it is that you know him, William.' Too bad. He was counting on her making William explain the connection. Now, he'd just have to keep guessing. But that last comment set him on edge. Pretty princess or not, no one could talk about him as if he weren't in the room, or worse, as if he were an object in the room.

'I hate to interrupt this lovely example of sibling quarrels, but please note, I'm still here.' Dorian stretched out his long legs and crossed them at the ankles. 'I think it would be best if you tell me what you really want and then I'll tell you if I'll do it. I find business is usually much simpler that way.'

The carriage turned on to the docks and stopped before a barred gate. His haughty princess shot him a glare as she leaned out to give a password to the guard. 'You might as well see what I have in mind.'

First pistols, now passwords. This was growing more interesting by the moment. What was a young woman doing down on the docks, throwing around entrance codes like she belonged here? For that matter, what was she doing roaming Cold Harbour Lane in search of *him*? She wasn't his usual type, that type being a bolder, brassier woman, a less-well-dressed sort. Not that she wasn't bold. She had come armed, after all. Hmm. A girl with a gun. Maybe she *was* his type. By the time she led him into the shipyard his curiosity, in all its healthy male parts, was fully engaged.

'There it is,' she announced with a proud wave of her hand, indicating the hull of a racer. 'That's the yacht I need finished.'

She needed a finished yacht? It just so happened he needed one, too. That meant the shipyard was her place. Very impressive. Dorian began a slow tour around the yard, attempting to assimilate the various pieces of information. He made note of the supplies lining the perimeter: the casks of pitch, the piles of timber, the buckets of nails. He peeked under heavy tarps. Everything was new and well organised. These were not supplies that had lain in the weather so long they were rotten or rusted.

He took in, too, the silence and the absence of men.

Whatever had transpired had brought work to a halt, an interesting concept of its own given the scarcity of jobs. Plenty of men were out of work these days. It made one stop and wonder.

'There's no one here. Why is that?' He stopped in front of Miss Elise Sutton, his tone far more serious than it had been in the carriage. This was no longer a laughing matter. 'I think it's time you tell me what you really need and why.'

That got her attention. She stepped back instinctively, but her eyes were as unflinching as they had been outside the tavern. Lord, she was magnificent. 'My father passed away recently and left this boat. I want to finish it and sell it.' It was a succinct tale, but Dorian took nothing at face value. In his world it was best not to if one wanted to live long enough to collect payment.

'Let me guess—the work crew left because there was no one to run the company?' Dorian surmised immediately. Things were becoming clearer: a brother too young to assume responsibility and a woman with too much on her hands. He was starting to remember the lad, too. Sutton. William Sutton. That elusive first name of his was more familiar when paired with the last. There'd been a house party near Oxford last autumn. Perhaps they'd met there during one of his own brief forays into the fringes of society?

'Yes, but I assure you I am more than capable, I—'

Dorian held up a hand and shook his head. 'Enough, Miss Sutton. I am sure you are very capable, but men won't work for you. However, they'll work for me for the simple fact that I am male, although they'll be glad enough to take *your* money. I trust you've thought about how to pay them?' He'd bet his last piece of gold she wanted to sell the yacht because she needed money.

'From the proceeds of the sale,' she said shortly, irritated by his insights.

'I might know some men who'd be willing to work for a future profit.' Dorian shrugged, but his mind was racing. He'd need five men who knew what they were doing and another dozen skilled in carpentry. The promise of delayed payment meant he might have to look harder and in less-savoury places for seventeen adequate workers.

'Would you care to see the plans before you take this any further?' Elise offered coldly. 'This is not just any yacht. It's been designed with several new innovations in mind. It will be important that you understand them.'

Dorian smiled. There wasn't a ship he couldn't build, couldn't sail and couldn't steal, for that matter. 'I can build your yacht, Princess. You can innovate all you like. The bigger question is—why should I?'

Elise put her hands on her hips and a wry smile on her lips. 'Because you need money. The bullies at the tavern intimated as much. Who is it you owe? A Mr Halsey?'

Dorian stifled a laugh. 'Black Jack Halsey hasn't been called "mister" his entire life, Princess. He's been called a lot of other things, but not that.'

'I'll pay you one hundred pounds from the sale to finish the yacht on time.'

'Five hundred,' Dorian countered. A man had to live and pay his debts. If he could make a little extra that was fine, too. It wasn't his fault part of his last cargo had been confiscated for non-payment of port fees. He'd told Halsey they'd not pass inspection and he'd been right.

'Five hundred! That's highway robbery,' Elise retorted, outraged by his exorbitant fee.

'Have much experience with highway robbery, do you?' Dorian chuckled.

Elise chose to ignore his question and stood her ground. 'I'm asking for one month's worth of work, Mr Rowland. You can't earn that much in three years of honest labour.'

'*Honest* being the key word there, Miss Sutton.' He'd make more than that on his next cargo, but he wouldn't attest to those goods all being legal.

'All right, two hundred.' The sharp point of her chin went up a fraction.

'Let me remind you, *you* came looking for me.'

'Two-fifty.'

'Three hundred and I get three meals a day and that shed over there.' He jabbed his thumb at a wide lean-to on the perimeter of the yard.

Her eyes narrowed. 'What do you want with the shed?'

'*That* is none of your business.'

'I won't tolerate anything illegal on these premises.'

'Of course not.'

'Or illicit.'

'Now, you're parsing words, Miss Sutton. Do you want me to build your ship or not?' No doubt they could disagree on the nature of 'illicit' all day.

'We still haven't established why I should let *you*,' she challenged.

'Because I've built boats for the pashas and the Gibraltar smugglers that rival anything your Royal Thames Yacht Club can put on the water. Have you ever heard of the *Queen Maeve*?' He was gratified by the flicker of recognition in her eyes. So the princess wasn't just desperate for money. She knew something about boats, too. 'Fastest racer on the Mediterranean and I built her.'

Built her and lost her, much to his regret. She'd been his dream, but in the end he'd had to let her go. There would be other boats, other dreams. That's what he told himself anyway, although there hadn't been that many opportunities since coming back to England. Not until now. This boat could be his ticket back to Gibraltar, back to the life he'd built there. But that life was based on having a fast ship.

Dorian ran his hand over the smooth, sanded side of the hull where it was finished. The yacht had good lines. The familiar magic started to hum in his veins; the itch to pick up tools and shape something into sleekness thrummed in his hands. Best not let the princess see that longing. It was better they assume she was the only desperate party here.

'You built the *Queen Maeve*?' she queried in sceptical disbelief.

'And others, but she was my favourite.' An understatement.

'I told you, Elise, Rowland is the best,' her brother said, entering the conversation for the first time, apparently happy enough to let his sister handle negotiations. Dorian wished he could remember the young man more clearly.

Miss Sutton studied him. She was weighing hope against desperation. Dorian could see it in her eyes. Could she afford to let him go? She had to know already she could not. Who else would take her deal? She knew the answer to that as well as he did. She'd had a look at reality. Still, caution carried some weight with her. 'You've spent a lot of time in the Mediterranean, an area known more or less for its lawlessness on the seas.'

'Less these days,' Dorian muttered under his breath. If Britain hadn't been so steadfast in taming the seas, he might still be there, but tamed seas were bad for business, his business at least. Tamed seas forced a man to be more creative in his ventures.

She huffed and raised an eyebrow in censure over the interruption. 'I must ask, are you a pirate, Mr Rowland?'

'If I can build your yacht, does it matter?' He winked. 'That's a rhetorical question, Miss Sutton—we both know I'm your last best chance. I'll start tomorrow.' He didn't give her a chance to respond. He strode across the yard to the shed, calling over his shoulder as he opened the door to the lean-to, 'If you need me, I'll be in my office.'

Chapter Three

He was the last thing she needed! And if *he* needed *her*, which would be the more likely case, *she'd* be in her office, a fact Elise demonstrated by loudly stomping up the stairs and slamming the office door, an effect which was ruined by her brother immediately opening the door and quietly shutting behind him when he entered.

'Did you see how he just came in here and tried to take over?' Elise steamed, pacing the square dimensions of the office with rapid steps. 'He's the builder, not the owner. Five hundred pounds, my foot. This is my yard and he'd better remember that.'

'He'll build the yacht, Elise, you'd better remember *that*.'

The firmness of her brother's tone stopped her steps. William had never spoken to her harshly. 'What do you mean?' Elise faced him slowly. He lounged against the wall, casual and elegant, a subtle reminder that he wasn't the adolescent boy she was used to after all these years. The mantle of manhood was starting to settle about him in the sternness of his features. Why hadn't she seen it before?

'I mean, I will be away at university. Mother is gone. There's no one to help you if you lose Rowland. Pay him what he wants, get the boat finished and let's be done with this.'

Elise struggled to keep her mouth from falling open. 'Let's be done with this? What does that mean?' She suspected she knew, but that was not at all what she wanted to hear.

'It means let's clear the debt and start a new life.'

Oh, that was better. She breathed a sigh of relief. 'A new line, yes, of course. I have a lot of ideas about yacht lines and how we can branch out into sailboats. I think racing will fully shift from rivers to open sea in the next few years. We might even think of relocating to Cowes to be closer to the Solent.' She was babbling excitedly now, reaching for a tube containing rolls of her drawings, but a shake of William's head stopped her.

'No, Elise, I don't mean to redefine the company. I mean we should close the book on the company once the debts are paid. There will be a little left over for you until you marry and you can always stay with me. I hope to find a living somewhere or take an associate's post at Oxford.'

It took a moment for William's words to sink in. 'Close the company?' She sat down behind the desk, stunned. Had her brother been thinking this all along?

'Well, what did you think we'd do after the yacht was finished?' William pressed.

'I thought we'd build more boats. You'll see, William. After people view this yacht, there will be other orders. This yacht will relaunch us. It will show everyone we can turn out the same superior product we've always turned out. The investors will come back.' It made so much sense to her. Surely William could see the logic in that?

'How many master builders do you think I know?' William gave a soft laugh.

'I'm not sure how you knew this one,' Elise put in tartly. 'Care to explain?'

William dismissed the question with a wave of his hand. 'It was just a house party put on by the parents of a friend of mine. A few of us went to help balance out numbers and Rowland was there. One night, we started talking and discovered we both had a common interest in yachting.'

Elise wrinkled her brow. 'He hardly strikes me as the Oxford house-party type.' Whatever Dorian Rowland was, she didn't imagine he was the scholarly sort. Tan, blond and hard-bodied, he definitely didn't spend his days poring over books in libraries.

William was growing impatient with her prying. 'Look, I don't know what he was doing there. He said he'd made a delivery, brought something up from London. How I know him is not the point. The point is, I was lucky enough to know this one. He'll finish your boat, but he won't stay. You'll be right back where you started.'

'I'll pay him more,' Elise blurted out, looking for an easy solution. But inside her heart she knew her brother was right: Dorian Rowland wouldn't stay. He'd made it clear he was a man who did what pleased him, when it pleased him. Her proposition suited him for the moment. That was the only reason he'd taken her offer.

'Money won't always be enough for a man like him,' William said with a maturity that surprised her. 'I've bought you time, Elise, to wrap up business and clear the bills, nothing more. Besides, you need to get on with your life, get out to parties and meet people.' By meet people, he meant meet men who would be potential husbands. Elise frowned in disapproval. She'd seen those men and been disappointed *with* them and *by* them.

When she didn't respond he paused awkwardly, his tone softening. 'Not every man is Robert Graves,' William said quietly.

Elise wasn't quite ready to relent. 'Well, thank goodness for that.' Robert Graves, the biggest, worst mistake she'd ever made. She'd thought William might have been young enough to not remember him, or at least to not understand the depths of her mistake.

'Charles Bradford has expressed an interest in you,' William cajoled. Charles was the son of one of her father's former investors. 'He's a very proper fellow.'

'Sometimes too proper,' Elise said briskly. She began looking needlessly through some papers on the desk, wanting to bring this conversation to a close. She wasn't interested in a suitor. She was interested in building a yacht and getting the company back on its feet.

William coughed awkwardly, taking her rather broad hint, once more the younger brother she knew. He made a stammering exit. 'Errm…um…I have some errands to run. I'll see you at home, don't stay too late.'

Elise sank down in the chair behind the desk and blew out a breath. *Welcome to the world of men, you can begin by following our orders and forgetting to think for yourself,* Elise thought uncharitably. In the last months she'd become heartily tired of men.

She was starting to understand all the ways in which her father had shielded her and she'd been unaware. Oh, how she missed him! She thought the missing would get easier with time, not harder. But everywhere she looked, everywhere she went, she was reminded of his absence. Even here, the one place where she'd felt truly at home.

When she'd been with her father at the shipyards no one had questioned her opinions on yacht design; no one had contradicted her numbers in the ledger. People did what she told them to do. Right up until his death, she'd believed they'd done those things because she'd earned their respect with her hard work and intelligence. Then they'd deserted one by one: the workmen, the investors. The message could not be any more concise. *We listened to you because we wanted to please your father so he'd build us fast boats and pay our salaries. Listening to you was just part of the game.* Elise put her head in her hands. It was a cruel blow.

Today had been more of the same, just to make the point in case she'd missed it the first time around. Dorian Rowland had walked in and assumed an attitude of control as if he had a right to this place in his rough shirt and trousers. Her brother had stealthily issued an edict—she was to give up yacht design after this boat and resign her life to one of three unappealing options: marriage, keeping house for her brother or living with her mother. She was to be passed from man to man, father to brother, brother to husband. She'd had fun playing at design, but now it was time to put away her childish things.

She wouldn't do it. Elise squeezed her eyes tight, pressing back tears. Closing the company would be like forgetting her father, as if his life hadn't mattered. This place was his legacy and she would not discard it so easily. There were more selfish reasons, too. She *needed* this. She never felt as alive as when she was designing a model and watching it come to life from her ideas. What would she be without that? The answer frightened her too much to thoroughly contemplate it for long. Well, there was nothing for it; if she wasn't going to contemplate it, she'd simply have to conquer it.

Alone at last! Dorian flashed a lantern up in the direction of the dark office window as he shut the heavy gate to the yard behind him and breathed a relieved sigh. Elise Sutton had finally gone home for the evening and he'd returned successfully from his little foray on to the docks. After the day he'd had, he couldn't ask for much more.

Dorian set down the heavy bag he carried and rubbed his shoulder. When it had become apparent Miss Sutton planned on staying either because she didn't want to go home in a snit or because she didn't want to leave him alone in *her* shipyard, he'd decided to go out and take care of his business in the hopes it would convince her he'd gone home or wherever it was she imagined he went when the sun went down. Whether the princess knew it or not, this was his home now—that nice little shed in the corner of the lot.

He'd gone back to his now-former room, paid the landlady his paltry rent with the few remaining coins he had and gathered up his clothes and tools and made arrangements for his trunk to be delivered in the morning. It was far too heavy and too conspicuous to haul through the streets. No matter, it didn't contain anything he considered absolutely essential. Those items were already packed away in a black-cloth sack. Still, between a single trunk and one black satchel, it was humbling to think they made up the sum of his worldly goods in England, but it had made packing easy.

It also made getting away easy. The last thing he wanted was to be noticed by Halsey's thugs. On the way back, he'd stopped at a few taverns, looking for likely workers. In this case, 'likely' meant whoever would be willing to show up and work for future pay. He just had to get them here. Once they saw the yacht, the project would speak for itself.

Dorian raised the lantern higher to cast the light on the boat. It was showing itself to be an absolute beauty. Longer and leaner than most yachts, it would be fast in the water. He recognised the influence of the American Joshua Humphreys in the design.

He hung the lantern on a nearby peg and reached into his sack for a drawing knife with its two handles and slender blade. The tool felt good in his hands as he slid it against the hull, scraping roughness away from the surface of the wood. There wasn't much to catch—the finished portion of the hull was smooth already—but it felt good to work. Dorian let the rhythm of the drawing motion absorb him. The only thing better was standing at the wheel of a boat feeling the water buck beneath him like a woman finding her pleasure—perhaps a particular black-haired woman with green eyes.

When he'd awakened this morning, he'd never dreamed he'd be building a ship by evening. The arrangement might be a good one. He could hide out from Halsey until he made back his money or until Halsey forgot he owed him. In the meanwhile, he could work a new angle. There was plenty of potential here in the shipyard. Dorian ran a hand over the surface he'd finished scraping. He could make plans for this boat. If the finished yacht was as promising as the shell, he might just find a way to talk Miss Sutton out of selling. It might mean cosying up to the ice princess, but he'd never been above a little sweet talk to get what he wanted. With a boat of his own, he'd be back in business and the possibilities would be limitless.

The possibilities *should* have been limitless, Maxwell Hart mused dispassionately as he listened to young Charles Bradford report his latest news concerning the Sutton shipyard. Elise Sutton had become a thorn in his side instead of bowing to the dictates of the inevitable. Her father was dead, her brother not prepared or interested in taking over the business, investors withdrawn and no obvious funds to continue on her own. All the pieces were in place for her to abdicate quietly, *gracefully*, to those with the means to run the shipyard. Instead, she had not relinquished the property, had not sought out a buyer for the plans to her father's last coveted design. In short, she had done *nothing* as expected. Now there was this latest development.

'There were lights at the shipyard tonight,' young Charles Bradford told the small group of four assembled.

'Do you think it could be vagrants?' Harlan Fox suggested from his chair, looking around for validation. Fox had pockets that went deeper than his intelligence. Those pockets were his primary recommendation for inclusion in this little group of ambitious yachtsmen. 'It's been several months, after all. It's about time for the vultures to settle, eh?'

Maxwell shook his head. 'No, *she's* been going to the office regularly. *She* probably worked late.' He spat the pronouns with distaste. The best thing to do with thorns was to pluck them.

Charles Bradford interrupted uncharacteristically. 'I beg your pardon, sir. It couldn't have been Miss Sutton. She left around five o'clock and she was the last to leave. There were two other men, her brother and a man I didn't recognise. But they'd both gone by then.'

Damien Tyne, the fourth gentleman present, said, 'Any of them could have come back.'

'It wasn't likely to have been her or the brother,' Charles pressed. 'There was no carriage. Whoever returned came back on foot.'

'I still vote for vagrants,' Fox insisted.

But Damien Tyne leaned forwards, curiosity piqued. When Damien was intrigued, Maxwell had learned to pay attention. He and Tyne had made a tidy profit off those instincts and they were unerringly good. 'What are you thinking, Tyne?'

Miss Sutton needed to be prodded in the right direction and in short order. He wanted that shipyard. It held a prime spot on the Thames and he'd coveted it for years. It would be the perfect place to move his own more obscure yacht-building operation and his warehouses. A good location would garner him the notice which to date had eluded him from his current locale in Wapping.

Obtaining the shipyard would just be the start. Hart also wanted to get his hands on the plans to Sutton's last yacht just as badly for the future of his more private, less legitimate side of business with Tyne. Tyne could have the yacht. He wanted the plans. The key to any business venture was the ability to reproduce success.

'I'm thinking,' Damien drawled, his dark eyebrows looking particularly satanic in the coffee house's uneven lighting, 'our Miss Sutton is not going quietly. Nothing she's done in the last months has suggested she is closing up the business as we'd hoped.'

'She has to, there's no money, no workers,' Charles protested. Young and smitten with Miss Sutton, he was also a bit obtuse, a literal fellow who saw only the obvious. 'I should know. My father was a former investor. We were at the funeral.'

Damien smiled patiently at the young cub. 'We know that, but does she? Maybe there's something she knows that we don't, which seems likely.' He nodded towards Maxwell. 'She's held on to the two things that matter most right now: the property and the last yacht. It seems to me that she means to try something before the end.'

'Impossible. The yacht isn't finished,' Charles argued sceptically. 'There's nothing *to* try.'

'Unless she has a builder,' Maxwell put in bitterly. That would drag things out. He had no doubt Miss Sutton would fail in the end, but prolonging that end didn't help his cause. The group had wanted to be in position by the time yachting season opened in May. Back in October when the opportunity had first presented itself, the objective to take over the shipyard had seemed perfectly reasonable. Now, with a month to go, it seemed far more unlikely.

Maxwell pushed a hand through his hair and sighed. 'We have to be certain. Charles, of all of us here, you are closest to the family. Perhaps it's time to pay a friendly visit to see how the daughter of your father's friend is coping with her grief?' He winked at the young man. Everyone in the group knew Elise Sutton had set aside mourning weeks ago, but the subtle sarcasm had flown right over Charles.

Maxwell hoped Charles's decent good looks and refined manners would encourage Miss Sutton to disclose her plans. Even beyond that, he hoped Charles would be able to give Miss Sutton a gentle nudge in the right direction through whatever means of persuasion possible.

Maxwell preferred to accomplish his goals subtly and without any overt force. He was happy to play nice until it was time not to, and that time was rapidly approaching. He and Tyne had money, time and pride wrapped up in this venture the others knew nothing about. He meant to see it succeed. Failure meant he'd lose a lot more than his shirt.

Chapter Four

His shirt was off! It was the first thing Elise noticed when she arrived at the yard late in the morning. For the first time since her father's death, she'd actually slept late. And look what happened. Her master builder was running around without his shirt on. Her mother would have shrieked it wasn't ladylike to notice, but how could she not? The sight was just so riveting.

Elise knew she was staring, but she could hardly look away. His chest was nothing like the average Englishman's. Gone was the pasty skin and skeletal lankiness, replaced by a smooth, *tanned* expanse of torso. It was quite possibly the most perfect chest she'd ever seen. Not that she was a connoisseur of men's chests, but working around the shipyard, she'd caught accidental glimpses on rare occasions.

She might have been able to pull her gaze away if that had been all, but it wasn't simply his chest, There were arms and shoulders to consider, perfectly moulded with muscle, to say nothing of his lean hips where his

culottes hung tantalisingly low on his waist, revealing the secret aspects of male musculature and hinting
at even more. All this masculinity had been pressed
against her yesterday. It was somewhat shocking to see
it on such bold display without the buffer of clothing to
mute the reality. She was still gaping when he sauntered
over, an adze dangling negligently from one hand, that
impertinent grin of his on his face.

'Good day, Miss Sutton. Is everything to your liking?' He motioned towards the yard, the veneer of the
gesture narrowly saving the comment from being outright indecent. She knew very well he'd caught her staring, and 'liking' hadn't only referred to the yard. Elise
looked around for the first time, trying hard to ignore
the distraction beside her.

There were workers! There was the noise of industry.
Not nearly as much as the yard was used to, but it was
better than the silence that had marked the past months.
'Where did you find them?'

Rowland shrugged, thrusting the adze through the
rope belt holding up his culottes. 'Here and there. It
hardly matters as long as they know their job.'

In other words, don't ask, Elise thought. She shouldn't
look a gift horse in the mouth. Men were here, willing
to work on her boat and willing to take future payment. That should be enough. It was more than she'd
had yesterday.

'As you can see, all is well in hand. Is there anything else I can help you with, Miss Sutton?' Rowland

said briskly, impatience evidencing itself in the shift on his stance.

Elise bristled at his tone. He wanted her gone. 'Are you dismissing me from *my* shipyard?' His audacity knew no bounds.

Rowland lowered his voice and jerked his head to indicate the workers beyond them. 'They're starting to look, Miss Sutton. They're wondering what a woman is doing here. You're distracting them.'

Elise was incredulous. '*I* am distracting them? I'm not the one strutting around the yard half-dressed. You might as well be naked the way those trousers are hanging off your hips.'

'You noticed? I'm flattered.' Rowland, damn him, grinned and crossed his arms over his chest. 'And here I was thinking you didn't like me.'

'I *don't* like you,' Elise said in a loud whisper. People were starting to look, but she would not take responsibility for that. She wasn't the one dressed like...like *him*. No wonder society demanded a man wear so many layers over his shirt. No one would get anything done otherwise; they'd be too busy staring.

Rowland laughed. 'Yes, you do, you just don't know what to do about it.' The man was insufferable.

'I want to see what progress you've made.' Elise tried to put the conversation back on a more professional level. It was just her luck her brother had found the best-looking shipbuilder in London. She'd come down here with the express purpose of overseeing the project. She wouldn't leave until she'd done that, half-naked master builder or not.

Rowland had other ideas. He took her arm, drawing her complete attention to the strong tanned hand that cupped her elbow and steered her out of the yard. 'If you want to watch,' he drawled with a grin that made watching sound like a decadent fetish, 'I suggest you adjourn to the office. You, Miss Sutton, are bad for business.'

Elise shot Rowland a hard look. She'd had enough of these games. 'I am their business.' The slightest shake of his head caused her to reassess.

'These men answer to me, Princess. They'll build your boat because I tell them to.'

Elise entrenched, ready for battle. She'd let such reasoning go yesterday. But it would not work twice. 'Is that your mantra? I should accept your decrees simply because you're building my yacht? Do you think that puts paid to any questions I have? This is my shipyard and everything that happens in it is definitely my concern.'

'Upstairs, now,' Dorian growled. It was all the warning she had before a firm hand gripped her arm and propelled her up the stairs to the office. The door slammed behind them. Dorian Rowland's blue eyes blazed with a temper she'd not suspected. His grip on her arm tightened. 'How long do you think these men will work if they think they're working for you? You are the owner's daughter and nothing more as far as they're concerned.'

'You lied to them!' She saw all too clearly what he'd

done. He'd set himself up as the boss, the chief. The man with all the power.

He raised a blond eyebrow in exaggerated query. 'You are not the owner's daughter? Did I misunderstand yesterday?'

'No, but—' She didn't get to finish.

'So you are the owner's daughter. Good, then I've told no lies,' he said as if this were the worst sin he had to worry about.

'I'm more than someone's curious daughter. Did you tell them *that*? Without me there'd be no project.' Elise wrenched her arm free and stepped away. She needed space where her logic wouldn't be distracted by more masculine charms.

'Allow me to be blunt. *With you*, there will be no project if you don't let me do this my way. I am trying to help you. You have nothing without me.'

He advanced and Elise fought a losing battle to retreat. Her back hit the wall. He leaned forwards, one arm bracing himself on the wall over her head. He seemed bigger at close range, not menacingly so, but overwhelmingly potent. Even the smell of him, fresh lumber and salty sweat, was all man—all *nearly naked* man. It was hard to forget that one thing with his bare chest mere inches from her. She'd like to forget it, though. Handsome men had proven to be her weakness in the past.

Elise tried to look anywhere but at him. She could see every intimate detail of his skin: the fine dusting of blond hair, the thin white scar beneath his right breast. Lord, it was hard to concentrate! Even her breathing seemed more erratic.

'Have I made you nervous, Miss Sutton?' He smiled. 'I can't help but notice the inordinate amount of time you've spent staring at my chest.'

Did she imagine it or did he puff that chest of his out intentionally just then?

Elise opened her mouth to respond and then shut it. Had she really just seen his breast jump? Flex? Whatever one wanted to call it. 'Stop that!'

'Stop what?' Pop! There it went again. He was doing it on purpose.

'That thing you're doing with your chest!'

'Oh, this? Flexing my muscles?' He straightened up and treated her to a bawdy show of alternately flexing each side of his chest.

'Yes, *that*.'

He laughed. 'Do you know what your problem is, Princess? You don't know how to have any fun.'

Elise crossed her arms over her chest to make a barrier of sorts between them. How dare he think she was a stick in the mud just because she wore all of her clothes to the office? She knew how to have fun. 'And I suppose you do?'

Another smile split his face. 'Absolutely.'

Elise felt her breath catch. His eyes lingered indecently on her mouth. She was acutely aware of his nearness, that he still bracketed her with his arm leaning against the wall. She licked her lips self-consciously. 'I'll have you know I've had *plenty* of fun.'

'Really?' he drawled, doubt evident. 'Well, maybe you have. I suppose I could be wrong. Let's see, hmmm. Have you kissed a man?'

'I most certainly have,' Elise said indignantly, although why it should matter what he thought was something of a mystery. There'd been a few safe kisses in gardens after dancing, but that had been before society had made her choose between it and the shipyard. It had been before Robert Graves, with whom she'd done far more than kiss.

'Unh-unh.' Dorian wagged a finger. 'Let me finish. Parlour games don't count. Have you kissed a man just for fun in the middle of the afternoon in a public place where you might be caught at any moment?' He was definitely flirting now, the images conjured by his words causing a slow heat to unfurl low in her belly.

She fought it, trying to sound more affronted than aroused. No good could come from letting him see how he affected her with his teasing. 'What, exactly, are you suggesting?' No *gentleman* would imply her virtue was in question.

A slow, wicked smile curved on his lips, his voice low and intimate in the small gap of space between them. 'I'm suggesting you try it. With me.' His mouth took hers then, without waiting for a reply, the press of his lips gently insisting that she give way to his greater experience. His tongue flicked over the seam of her lips and she opened to him, to the heady pleasure rising inside her at the leisurely decadence he invoked: mouth on mouth, tongue to tongue, body to body, cloth to skin. This was a naughty exploration indeed. Of their own volition her hands went to his shoulders, kneading the exposed muscles. He was right; she'd never been kissed, not like this. Those other kisses seemed childish by comparison, nothing more than play, pretend. But this was real, this man was real. And the consequences would be real, too. She'd been down that road before.

That was enough to wake her senses. Elise pulled away. She would not repeat the mistakes of the past; this had to end now. She had scandal enough to worry about without being caught kissing her master builder. 'Mr Rowland!' She hoped her exclamation carried enough chagrin for more words to be unnecessary.

'How about we dispense with the "Mr Rowland" bit?' He made no move to back up and release her. 'You can call me Dorian and I'll call you Princess.'

'My name is Elise,' she snapped, realising she'd been manoeuvred too late.

'Well, Elise it shall be, then, if you insist.' He shoved off the wall. 'Now you can say you've had fun.' He winked. 'If you'll excuse me, I must be back to work if you want your yacht done by the deadline. Have a nice rest of the afternoon, *Elise.*'

She could not stay in that office a moment longer. It took all her patience to wait until *Dorian* was safely engrossed in his work before leaving. She would not give him the satisfaction of knowing he'd succeeded in driving her off her own property.

How dared he? Elise strode through the crowded streets surrounding the docks, burning off her excess energy and anger, if that's what it was. He'd kissed her in broad daylight and for no apparent reason other than the fun of it. One thought overrode even that: he'd been audacious, but *she'd* liked it! Hadn't she learned her lesson with Robert? Handsome men were not to be trusted. They knew they could barter on their looks to take what they wanted unless a woman was careful. Elise was so wrapped in her thoughts, she nearly ran into Charles Bradford before she noticed him.

'Miss Sutton. I was just on my way to see you.' Charles righted her after their near-collision, tucking her hand through his arm. 'Whatever are you doing out here in the street? It's no place for a decent lady.'

'Lunch,' Elise improvised, pulling her skirts to one side to avoid a barrel being rolled to a nearby store.

'Out here?' Charles had to shout to be heard above the street din. 'Might I suggest a quieter venue? My carriage is just the next street over. Perhaps I could escort you?'

There was no gracious way to refuse and perhaps it would be better to be with someone instead of fuming alone over her latest interaction with Dorian Rowland. In no time at all, Elise found herself ensconced in Charles Bradford's open barouche. Of course, it was open. Being alone with a man in a closed carriage was

unheard of for an unmarried woman and Charles was
first and foremost a gentleman. He'd known he was
coming to see her and had planned accordingly. Unlike
certain other males of her recent acquaintance, came
the unbidden comparison. She doubted Dorian Rowland
planned accordingly for anything or even planned at
all. He just did or said the first thing that came to mind.

'I must confess to being surprised to find you
here,' Charles began as the barouche started to move.
'I stopped at your house first and your butler told me
where you were. I didn't think there'd be anything more
to do at the shipyard. If there's still business to take
care of, you should have contacted me. My father and
I would have handled it for you.' There was reproach
in the comment.

The Bradfords had offered as much earlier when
the tragedy had first happened, but she'd insisted on
overseeing it all on her own. She knew what Charles
meant. There wasn't that much to do if she was closing the yard. 'You might be surprised at what a girl
finds to amuse herself with,' Elise answered vaguely,
her thoughts going straight to shirtless men and afternoon kisses. Charles might be all that was proper in a
young man with his well-cut clothes, fashionable hair
and polished manners, but he wouldn't understand her
latest endeavour or the need behind it. If he had understood, he and his father would never have pulled out.

It occurred to her that this might be a prime opportunity to pull them back in. What if they did know what

she was doing? They might re-invest and there would be money again. She wouldn't have to wait until the yacht was finished. That thought only lasted a moment. Charles was looking at her with his calm, brown eyes and she almost blurted it out. But caution held her back. It had only been a day and Dorian Rowland had amply demonstrated he was uncertainty personified. What if he suddenly quit? What if he lacked the skill to finish the yacht? She'd do better to wait and see if her project could be completed before she told a soul. It wouldn't do to be seen as a failure just now. If she was to fail, she wanted to do it in secret.

Charles found them an acceptable tea shop where they could have sandwiches and a quiet table. He was solicitous, asking after her well-being, her brother's plans to return to Oxford and her mother's time in the country. The more solicitous he was, the more the contrast grew. He was nothing like Dorian Rowland. To start with, he wore all of his clothes and he was unlikely to steal a kiss in a public place. Charles was safe. Charles was comfortable. But she couldn't help but wonder— would Charles's chest be as muscled beneath his linen shirt? It certainly wouldn't be as tanned. She blushed a little at the thought. It was most untoward of her to be picturing gentlemen without their clothes on. She could blame that, too, on Dorian.

'Miss Sutton? Are you all right?'

'Oh, yes. Why do you ask?' Elise dragged her thoughts back to the conversation.

'I asked you a question.' Charles smiled indulgently. 'What are you planning to do with the shipyard? My father would be able to help you arrange a sale. I'm sure you'd rather be off to join your mother.'

Actually, that was the last place she wanted to be. How to answer without lying? She opted for part of the truth. 'I'm thinking about keeping the yard, after all,' Elise offered quietly, waiting for his shocked response.

To his credit, Charles kept his shock to a minimum. He didn't disagree with her, but merely voiced his concern. 'Miss Sutton, your fortitude is commendable. But you have no one to run the place. Surely you can't be thinking of doing it on your own?' She knew what he was thinking. To do so was to invite social ostracism for the last time. She'd already skated so near the edge on other occasions. With her father gone, there'd be little pity left for her.

'I have someone.'

'Who?' Charles reached for his tea cup.

'A Mr Dorian Rowland,' Elise said with a confidence she didn't feel.

The tea cup halted in mid-air, never quite making it to his mouth. 'Dorian Rowland? The Scourge of Gibraltar?' The tea cup clattered into its saucer with an undignified clunk. 'My dear Miss Sutton, you must be rid of him immediately.'

She'd hired someone called the Scourge of Gibraltar?

Elise was glad she wasn't holding a tea cup, too, or it might have followed suit. 'Why?' she managed to utter.

The horror in Charles Bradford's eyes was so exaggerated it was almost comical and it would have been, too, if it wasn't aimed at the one man she'd pinned all her hopes on.

'Don't you know, Miss Sutton? He isn't received.'

Chapter Five

'I was not under the impression craftsmen were in the habit of being received at all,' Elise answered coolly, some irrational part of her leaping to Dorian's defence. Perhaps it was simply that she wanted to defend the shipyard and her own judgement, or her brother's judgement for that matter. He'd been the one to recommend Dorian.

Charles smiled indulgently. 'Oh, he's not a craftsman, not by birth anyway.'

'I'm afraid you'll have to explain that.' Elise mustered all the bravado she could. With a label like the *Scourge of Gibraltar* she could guess the reasons without the specifics, though details would be nice.

Charles set his jaw, looking fiercer than she'd ever seen him, a look at odds with his usually calm demeanour. 'Of course you don't know and understandably so. It's hardly a topic of discussion worthy of a lady. I will say only this: he's not fit company for you.'

The fervency in Charles's eyes should have warmed her even if his sentiments did not. She ought to overlook his condescension in light of its motives: he was putting her honour first. He was thinking of her, concerned about who she associated with, even if the tone with which that care was voiced sounded a bit high in the instep. Her father had been a self-made peer, knighted for his efforts, and Charles's own father was a baronet, neither family far removed from the efforts of work that had attained such positions. Yet she could not warm to Charles's efforts with more than polite kindness. Her own body and mind were still engaged in recalling a less-decent gentleman with blunt manners and a blind eye for scandal.

'I appreciate your concern, although it's hardly fair to tell me he's unsuitable and then not tell me why.' As if she needed reasons other than the ones Dorian had already provided this very afternoon with his unorthodox kissing episode. Out of reflex and remembrance, Elise's eyes dropped ever so briefly to Charles's lips. She couldn't imagine Charles behaving so outrageously. The thought was not well done of her. There could be no true comparison between the two. Charles was all a gentleman should be and Dorian Rowland simply was not. Charles would be eminently more preferable. Wouldn't he? He was precisely the sort of man her brother wanted her to find: attractive, steady and financially secure. But even with all these credentials, Elise couldn't help but feel Charles would still come out lacking.

Charles seemed to hold an internal debate with himself, his features suddenly relaxing, decision made. He leaned across the table in confidentiality. 'He is Lord Ashdon's son, second son,' he offered in hushed tones as if that explained it all.

It certainly explained some, like how William might have encountered him at an Oxford house party. Even after William's explanation, she'd been hard pressed to believe William had stumbled across a master ship-builder in the course of his usual social routine. But the one word her brain kept coming back to was *scandal*. It was the very last thing she needed. Her father's death had been sensational, but not scandalous. Dorian Rowland, however, was both. If society had seen him today, one of their own, half-naked and toting tools around the shipyard, shouting orders, it would be out-raged. Then again, it already was. If Charles could be believed, Dorian's transgressions preceded this latest. This venture into the shipyard was just one of many es-capades for him. But she would be the one who suffered.

It was slowly coming to her that Dorian Rowland simply didn't care who he perpetrated this fraud on. He could have told her who he was and he hadn't. He'd let her believe he was a craftsman. And why not? He wasn't received. He had nothing to lose, whereas she had everything to risk.

Her place in society was tenuous. She was the daugh-ter of a dead man who possessed a non-hereditary title. Society had to acknowledge her father. It didn't have to acknowledge her, especially if she put herself beyond the pale. She had only her virtue and reputation to speak for her if she wished to remain in society's milieu. To be honest, her reputation wasn't the best to start with and this latest effort to keep the shipyard open wouldn't help, with or without Dorian Rowland's presence.

Oblivious to the tumult of her thoughts, Charles leaned across the table ready to impart another confidence 'Enough of such unpleasant things. I confess I had other reasons for seeing you. I wanted to ask if you might consider going for a drive some afternoon? I know you're in mourning, but a drive wouldn't be amiss.'

Hardly. Elise thought of her mother's version of mourning in the countryside. A drive was nothing beside her mother's card parties and dinners at the squire's, and Elise had made no secret that she'd set many of the trappings of mourning aside. All right, all of them. She did wear half-mourning, but that was the only concession she continued to make and even that transition had been rushed by society's standards. She returned Charles's smile, but the offer raised little excitement. 'I'd like that.' She really should try harder to like him, to see him as more than a comfortable friend.

They finished lunch in companionable conversation, the subject of Dorian Rowland discarded until Charles dropped her off at the town house. He saw her to the door, his hand light at her elbow. 'It was good to see you, Elise. I'm sorry if the news about Rowland disturbed you. Now that you know, I trust you'll manage the situation appropriately.'

Somehow, Elise thought as the door shut behind her,

she didn't think 'managing appropriately' included afternoons pressed up against the office wall kissing her
foreman with all the abandon of a wanton.

Dorian had abandoned all pretence of being in a good
mood since the previous afternoon. The encounter with
Elise had left him aroused with no hope of immediate
satisfaction save that which he'd had to provide for himself. At the sight of a haphazard nailing job, he ripped
the hammer out of one worker's hand with a snarl. 'Take
it out and do it right.' The others gave him a wide berth.

He didn't blame them. Kissing Elise had put him
out of sorts even though he'd got what he wanted. He
shouldn't have done it. Technically, he knew better but
that had never stopped him before. He took what he
liked and he'd liked her, a princess with her temper up,
her professional reserve down. She'd been furious with
him and it had done fabulous things to her, turning the
green of her eyes to the shade of moss and staining her
cheeks to a becoming pink. In his arms, she'd become
a woman of fire, burning slow and hot, desperate to
prove herself.

That made him chuckle. She'd not wanted him to
think she was entirely inexperienced. Most decent girls
were just the opposite, wanting to prove their virtue.
Even so, there was no question Elise Sutton *was* a lady
in spite of her adventurous streak. Men like him didn't
mess with ladies. Ladies came with expectations while
a man like him came with none.

'Lover girl's here,' one of the men called out, a surly fellow named Adam. He was not the sort Dorian preferred to hire, but choices had been few and he'd been eager to get the project under way.

'Shut up and show some respect,' Dorian growled. He looked up from his work on the hull to see Elise crossing the yard. The princess in her was intact this morning, helped along no doubt by a careful choice of dress. He knew very well that clothes were a woman's armour. Elise was turned out to perfection in a lavender morning dress of figured silk, complemented by the soft grey of her shawl and the matching lace trim of her Victoria bonnet. The ensemble was very demure, very respectful, although not quite up to the standard for a daughter's mourning. He wondered briefly if she'd forgone mourning altogether. Yet the subdued qualities of the outfit did not diminish her. Perhaps that was due to her walk, Dorian mused, watching the sway of her hips and not necessarily her clothes.

She crossed the yard with a purpose, hardly deigning to give any attention to the eyes attracted by her movement. Her superior attitude was for the best. Dorian felt a twinge of guilt over the sort of men he'd hired. These were rough men unaccustomed to ladies. But also he'd not expected her to make herself a daily fixture in the shipyard.

'Clearly my message yesterday eluded you.' Dorian set down the wrung staff he was using to attach planking on the hull.

'Good morning to you, too.' Elise smiled cheerily and ignored the cool greeting. 'I've some things we need to discuss. Do you have a moment?'

The comment elicited a mean chuckle from Adam Bent. 'Are you going to take orders from the little woman? You're not so big now.'

There were other nervous laughs. He had to nip such conjecture in the bud. These men would never respect a man who appeared to be at a woman's beck and call. But he'd dealt with men like Bent before on his ships. With a quick movement, Dorian divested Bent of the racing knife in his hand and pressed it against his throat. 'It's sharp and it will hurt, in case you're wondering,' Dorian said with savage fierceness, leaving no doubt he was not bluffing.

Bent's eyes bulged in fear. Behind him, Dorian heard Elise gasp at the sudden violence. Around them, men stopped their work to stare. Good. Let them. Let them be very sure they knew who was in charge here and what he was willing to do to prove his claim. 'Say you're sorry,' Dorian pressed.

'Really, is that necessary?' Elise stepped forwards, picking a rotten time to intervene.

'It damn well is.' Dorian locked eyes with the frightened Bent. The man was a bully. He would cave. Bullies always did at the first sign of real terror and there was nothing as terrifying as a blade against one's throat. A racing knife, whose purpose was to trace a shape before cutting it out with its thin blade, could leave an especially wicked line. A small bead of red began to show.

'I'm sorry, boss,' Adam stammered.

'Say it won't happen again.'

'It won't happen again.'

Dorian released him with a shove. 'You're right it won't. Now, Miss Sutton, if you'll follow me up to the office?'

Perhaps the office wasn't the best of locations with the memories of yesterday still so recent and hot, but there was no other place to take her.

'Is this how you run your shipyards, Mr Rowland? At knifepoint?' She didn't wait for him to begin the conversation once the door was shut.

'When I must.' Dorian folded his arms. 'I told you yesterday your presence was a disturbance and yet you persist in making appearances.'

'I needed to see you,' she said evenly. Dorian admired her aplomb. There wasn't an ounce of apology in her eyes.

'You could have asked me to call on you at your home. This is no place for a woman.'

'I wasn't sure you'd put your shirt on,' she replied, her implication clear. 'I can't have you scandalising the butler.' She shot him a sideways glance that made him uneasy. 'Although, it's probably too late for that,' she said cryptically. 'I doubt a shirt will make much difference at this point.'

'Shirt on, shirt off, it's all the same to me, Princess,'

Dorian drawled. She hadn't slapped him or any of the other things ladies did when they were too ashamed to admit their passions had been provoked and they enjoyed it. He would take it as progress.

'It *is* all the same to you, isn't it?' She gave him a wry, intelligent smile. 'You're not received. What do you care? You could run around naked if you wanted. Oh, wait, you do.'

So that was the bee in her pretty bonnet this morning. She'd found out who he was. He did wonder how she'd come by that information. It wasn't something a lady would know. 'There are a few homes where I'm welcome,' he offered in his defence.

'Enough to have met my brother.'

'Ah, yes, the house party outside Oxford. It was nothing, just an invite from a friend of a friend I hadn't seen in a while,' he admitted. Meeting William had been a fluke really. Decent society had shut their doors ages ago on him once conjecture of his Mediterranean activities reached them. 'Does it matter? I assure you being received has nothing to do with my ability to build your ship.'

She huffed at the response. 'You seem to think your ability to build my ship excuses all nature of things. I disagree. I think you should have told me you were Lord Rowland, son of the Duke of Ashdon.'

He smiled and leaned his hip against the desk, half-sitting on its edge. 'But then you wouldn't have hired me and we both would have missed out.' His eyes drifted purposely to her mouth, letting her guess on what they would have missed out.

'You've brought scandal to my business simply by being here. If anyone finds out, I'm finished.'

Dorian's smile faded. 'Only if you care about such things.' This was dangerous ground. Had she come here to let him go? The thought sat poorly with him. It had only been two days, but he'd invested effort in this proposition of hers, beating the docks for any worker he could find. He fiddled with her paperweight, a pretty amber piece with an insect inside, giving her a chance to think. 'And do you, Miss Sutton? Do you care?'

He had her there. The look on her face suggested she wasn't sure how to answer. He answered for her, pushing off the desk and pacing the floor like an Oxford professor delivering a lecture. 'That's the thing about scandal, Miss Sutton. It only has teeth if everyone playing agrees to give it power. Frankly, I don't see how you *can* care and pursue this line of work you've put before yourself. Surely you see the dichotomy, too?' He rather worried that she didn't, though. She was the sort whose boldness came from a combination of *naïveté* and ideals, a deadly mixture once society got a hold of them. Somebody was going to have to tell her the truth. This venture of hers simply wasn't going to work. It *couldn't*.

Dorian softened his tone. 'Are you familiar with syllogisms, Miss Sutton? A lady doesn't build ships. Miss Sutton builds ships. Therefore, Miss Sutton isn't a lady.

Indeed, she *can't* be a lady by the very definition of what society says a lady is. Do you see my point?'

Her dark brows were knitted together, a furrow of twin lines forming between her eyes, the look not unattractive. It stirred him to want to do something about it, to erase the consternation. He wasn't used to such chivalrous feelings.

'I understand your meaning quite well and I respectfully disagree.' Her chin went up a fraction in defiance.

'You *will* have to choose,' Dorian insisted. 'My being here or not is the least of your worries if you're thinking about your reputation. Building your blasted yacht is enough to sink you in most circles. No pun intended.' Instinctively, he moved close to her, his hands going to her forearms in a gentle grip to make his point, to make her see reason.

She swallowed nervously, the pulse at the base of her throat leaping in reaction to his nearness. 'Again I disagree,' she said with quiet steel. 'I think this yacht will be the making of me.'

'If it is, it will be the making of a lady most improper.' Dorian gave a soft chuckle, breathing in the tangy lemongrass scent of her just before his mouth caught hers.

Chapter Six

'Rowland's back.' Maxwell made a grimace before taking a swallow of his brandy. He and Damien Tyne had the corner of the coffee house to themselves in the late afternoon. He preferred it that way. The conversation he wanted to have with Tyne might possibly become too dark for the others.

Tyne raised slender dark brows in interest. 'Really? I wonder if his father knows? Gibraltar must have finally got too hot for him. Still, it's gutsy of him to come back here where he's got a number of enemies waiting for him, you and me included. Don't tell me you wouldn't mind a shot at him after what he did?'

Maxwell gave a thin smile. 'We will get our chance. It will be an opportunity to kill two birds with one stone.' He dangled the thought before Damien like bait.

'And how is that? We're rather busy with the Sutton project at the moment. It doesn't seem like the right time to go after Rowland.'

Maxwell's thin smile turned into a grin as he dropped

the news. 'He's working for our Miss Sutton. She told Charles herself over lunch.'

'And he scampered back here like a good boy and told you.' Tyne leaned back in his chair, fingers drumming on the table top beside him. Maxwell could almost see the thoughts running through Tyne's mind.

'You were right,' Maxwell offered, wanting to be included in those usually lucrative thoughts. The fastest way to get Tyne to open up was to compliment him. Tyne was a smart man and a bit of an egomaniac. Tyne liked others to recognise his intelligence. 'Miss Sutton does mean to give it one last gasp. She's hired Rowland to do something.'

'But we have no idea what that is?' Tyne asked.

'She wouldn't tell Charles.'

Tyne snorted. 'She probably didn't get the chance. Charles would have been too busy lecturing her about Rowland's unsuitability. I do hope he told her to fire the reprobate.'

'Charles served his purpose today,' Maxwell reprimanded lightly. Tyne thought Charles was a silly young pup. 'He's our best connection to the inner workings of Miss Sutton's life at the moment without spending money on people to watch her. Charles is happy to do it for free.'

'He's infatuated with her,' Tyne grumbled.

Maxwell idly stroked the short stem of his snifter. 'Yes. If he'd marry her it would be all the better for us, get her out of the business for good. For the record,

Charles did tell her to let Rowland go, but I doubt she'll listen to his advice. She hasn't listened to anyone so far.' Certainly not the investors who'd come to her after the funeral and encouraged her to sell. She could have made this much easier on all of them, herself included.

Tyne's eyes glinted. 'Maybe it's time to make her listen.'

Maxwell leaned forwards with keen interest. He and Tyne had been partners in questionable commerce practices before, but those notorious practices were conducted far from home where their countrymen were less likely to notice what they were up to. Going after someone in London would be different. They'd have to exercise extraordinary caution—something Tyne was not always good at. 'What exactly do you have in mind?'

'I think a nocturnal visit to the shipyard is in order so we can figure out precisely what she's doing behind those walls. It doesn't take a genius to speculate about what she might be doing, but we can't take an appropriate course of action until we know for sure. I know just the men to do it.'

Maxwell nodded his approval. 'I like the way you think. In the meanwhile, I'll tell Charles to continue his courtship.'

'Miss Sutton, there's a gentleman to see you.'

Elise looked up from her reading, more than surprised to see Evans, the butler, in the doorway of the sitting room. It was after seven and she'd given the staff permission to retire for the evening. 'I'm not expecting anyone.' The house was quiet tonight. She'd seen William off earlier in the day and dinner had been a lonely affair, one of many, she supposed. Mourning and the absence of a decent chaperon made attending any social functions out of the question.

'He has a card, Miss Sutton, and he says he has business to discuss.'

Not Charles, then. That had been her first thought. But Charles would never have called on her so late at night, knowing her brother was gone, or have come to discuss something as dirty as business. Unless, of course, he wanted to remind her of the impropriety of a lady living alone. Elise took the card from the silver salver. The paper was a heavy white affair of cardstock with simple black letters in crisp block print. It was of good quality. The name on the card wasn't. Lord Dorian Rowland. Just seeing the name was enough to make her stomach flutter for any number of reasons: a reminder that she'd hired a man who outranked her socially to *work* for her, a reminder that same man kissed liked the very devil whenever the fancy struck him and reduced her insides to jelly.

'Did he say what he wanted specifically?' Elise fought the urge to check her appearance in the little mirror on the wall. She'd obeyed his order not to go to the shipyard today and apparently he'd obeyed hers. Evans didn't look too offended. She could assume Dorian had come with his shirt on.

'No, miss, just business.'

'Then I suppose I shall have to see him.' Elise tried to sound cool. She rose and paced a few steps, trying to gather her thoughts, but to no avail. They continued to run amok. Why had he come? Was something wrong at the shipyard? Had there been an accident? Had something happened to the boat? Surely if something was seriously wrong he wouldn't have come in person and waited patiently in the hall. He would have stayed to oversee the situation and sent a note, or he'd have come barging up the steps, shouting for her. Elise smoothed her skirts in an effort to quiet her nerves.

Footsteps sounded in the corridor. Evans announced the guest. Dorian stepped into the room. Her hands stilled in the folds of her skirts at the sight of him. Dorian had put on far more than a shirt to make this call. Dark breeches were tucked into high black boots; a claret-coloured coat was tailored to show off broad shoulders and the gold-patterned waistcoat and pristine linen beneath. She could almost believe the man standing before her was a lord. Almost.

There were other tells that gave him away. His thick sun-gold hair might be neatly pulled back and tied, but it was still too long for convention. His blue eyes were still too bold when they met hers. A gentleman would never look at a lady in a way that made her mouth go dry.

'Lord Rowland, to what do I owe the pleasure?'

'Dorian, please,' he insisted. 'I've come as I promised to give you an update and because I have questions about the plans.' He held up the long roll of paper in his hand. 'I hope my visit isn't inconvenient? You don't have plans this evening?'

'You know I don't.'

'London's loss, I think.' Dorian smiled and their eyes held in the moment. She felt her face heat. She really shouldn't let him get to her like this. Nothing could come of it and this was absolutely the wrong time to become involved with someone when so much else depended on her attentions.

'Where shall we unroll these?' Dorian looked around the room and gave the plans a little wave, calling her attentions back to the intent of his visit.

'Oh, yes, the plans. There's no place to lay them out in here. Why don't we try the library?' At the last moment she remembered Evans still standing by the door. 'Evans, have a tea tray sent up, please.' She hoped she didn't appear as flustered as she felt. It occurred to her as they headed towards the library that she'd never entertained anyone alone and certainly not a man. Her mother or father had always been with her. The servants were here, of course, but it wasn't the same.

In the library, they busied themselves spreading out the plans on the long reading table and anchoring the corners with paperweights and books to keep the edges from rolling up. Dorian stirred up the fire while she lit lamps. The tea tray came and they found a place for it at the end of the table. The little tasks helped her regain composure. She designed yachts and ran a business, for heaven's sake. It was silly to be daunted by a simple task and one handsome man.

When everything was finally settled to their satisfaction, Dorian pointed to the area in question. 'Here's the problem—I think the centre of the hull is too narrow. It will increase the chance of capsizing. Do you know what your father was thinking when he established these dimensions?'

'These aren't solely my father's plans. We designed this boat together,' Elise said slowly. Even now, no one quite grasped her level of involvement in the shipyard. 'This is my boat, too. I simply don't know how to build it, but in theory it should work.'

Dorian swore softly under his breath and she braced herself for the worst. But it didn't come. He didn't harangue her for the idea that she thought she could build a boat. *'In theory it should work?* Do you have a model? Did you do any kind of trial?'

'No. It will work. I modelled this after Joshua Humphreys's work, only we've used his design with more intensity. This boat is longer, lower and leaner.' She could see he was unconvinced. 'We've installed extra buoyancy bags on the port and starboard sides to compensate for any drastic heeling.' She warmed to her subject now, making her argument with passion as she pointed to the various adaptations they'd made. 'So you see there was no need to test it. Humphreys's design works. We've just modified it.'

Dorian was starting to thaw. 'We'll have to be careful through here and here.' His finger drew invisible circles on the plans. 'But it could work, I guess. It's just that I've never seen it done. Once we get the frame timbered, it will be too late for any alterations. It's almost too late now.'

A little thrill ran through her at the prospect of the fully timbered hull. 'How long?'

'Two days. Then there will be the rigging to discuss.' He gave her a wry grin. 'I don't suppose you designed the rigging, too?'

'Perhaps you'd like to discuss rigging over tea?' Elise smiled, feeling relieved. There'd been a moment when she'd thought he might quit the job.

With tea and biscuits on plates, they settled into the big chairs in front of the fire to discuss the merits of sloop versus ketch and cutter-rigging styles. It was an animated discussion and, for a while, Elise forgot she was entertaining alone, forgot what a scoundrel Dorian was. It felt good to talk about boats and sailing with someone who knew something about it. It had seemed ages since she'd had this sort of discussion. She and her father used to talk boats all the time. They'd talked about yachts the day he'd gone out on the test run. It was the last conversation they'd had.

Dorian broke off in mid-sentence. 'What is it? It looks like a shadow has just crossed your face. Have I offended your sensibilities with my position on ketch rigging?' he joked.

'No.' Elise looked down at her hands, embarrassed over having been caught with her mind wandering. 'This talk of boats reminds me of my father. We had conversations like this all the time. In fact, we'd talked about new ways to increase windage the day he went out.'

'I'm sorry.' Dorian's tan hand covered hers where it lay in her lap. He gave it a warm squeeze. 'You must miss him.'

Elise nodded, not daring to trust her voice. She'd not expected such a tender gesture from the king of insouciance himself. It threatened to undo her. She managed a smile and then a few words to turn the conversation away from herself. 'What about your family? Do they enjoy boats and yachting as much as you?'

Dorian gave a harsh laugh. 'Hardly. My father is a horse man and my brother, too. My father is always quick to remind me that horse racing— the sport of kings, mind you—didn't have such plebian beginnings as yachting. He is also quick to point out that the black sheep of the royal family, Cumberland, was the one who went slumming in the first place.' There was a naughty glimmer of mischief in Dorian's blue eyes. 'To which I say, "My hero".'

She could well believe it. Dorian and the previous Duke of Cumberland likely held many traits in common. The latter had been known in his lifetime as a 'loose fish', a scandalous womaniser who had taken his mistress riding in Hyde Park, and the former was no doubt following down a similar path.

'Your family is not close,' Elise ventured, feeling a little sorry for him even if he didn't feel sorry for himself. He was alone, too. 'Does your father know you're...?' What were the words she was looking for—'working on the docks', 'running questionable cargos for the dockside underworld', 'overseeing a shipyard shirtless', 'threatening workers with knives to their throats'?

He seemed to divine her dilemma and saved her the indelicacy. 'Maybe. He's the Duke of Ashdon, he knows everything he has a desire to know. I stopped caring about what he thought a long time ago.'

Elise could hear the hint of resentment behind the words. She should probably leave it at that, but curiosity propelled her forwards. 'When you became the Scourge of Gibraltar?'

'Something like that.'

'Will you tell me?' The late hour, the fire, the warmth of the tea were all conspiring to create intimacies, pushing her to take chances with the blond stranger who'd fallen into her life a few days ago.

Dorian gave a slight shake of his head, a scold, a warning. 'No, I will not. You're better off not knowing.'

'And the *Queen Maeve*? Will you tell me about your ship one day? She was a legend even up here for those of us who appreciate such things.' Stories of his ship had circulated throughout polite society: how fast it was, how fearless the captain, how the *Queen* had outrun French pirates by manoeuvring them up on to a reef and sheering off in the nick of time to save herself from the same fate.

Elise wondered if she mentioned that tale would it provoke him to reminisce? But she'd left it too late. He rose and set down his tea cup, a prelude to farewell. She felt deflated. She'd pushed too far, pried too much and now he was leaving. Never mind that leaving was the right thing to do. It was late and they were alone. He had no business being here.

Elise rose and helped him roll up the plans. 'I hope my descriptions have been of assistance?' she asked, stacking the books they'd used as corner weights. 'Perhaps it would be best if I came down to the shipyard. I could be there if more questions arose.' She hadn't the foggiest idea what she'd do with herself if she didn't go into work.

'No, it would not be best. We don't need any more incidents like the one earlier. I will keep you informed of every little detail.' Dorian paused. 'I enjoyed our evening, Elise. It is not often I encounter a woman of your rare intelligence. I can show myself out, you needn't go to the bother.' He gave her a short little bow. 'Until next time.'

Elise waited until she heard the front door shut and the sound of Evans shooting the bolt before she left the library and headed upstairs to bed. She undressed on her own and sat down to brush out her hair, replaying the events of the night in her head. The evening should have been a success. Dorian had reported to her. He'd asked her opinion. He'd come dressed the part. He had argued with her, but respectfully so and had acceded to her wishes. He hadn't blinked an eye when she'd told him the plans were hers.

What more could she have asked for? She doubted any other master builder would have been as gracious. His manners had been impeccable. He hadn't importuned her with his provocative remarks.

Elise halted the brush in mid-stroke. That was when she realised it: he hadn't kissed her. He had simply bowed and walked out the door, taking his secrets with him. She wasn't sure she liked this version of Dorian Rowland any better than she liked the other, which surprised her very much because she should have.

Chapter Seven

A walk was precisely what he needed to clear his head. Dorian pulled at his cravat, tugging it free with a sigh of relief. He'd played the gentleman tonight in high form, clothes, manners and all. It was a role he hadn't assumed for some time, but it was as stifling as ever, limiting what he could and could not say or do. But that was society's way—demanding manners until it made castrati of its men and vacuous dolls of its women. He understood entirely why Elise Sutton resisted. The road propriety laid out for her was unappealing, demanding she marry or fade into the background as a respectable spinster, living with her mother or brother.

Her resistance wasn't completely flagrant. She wasn't protesting in the streets or walking around in men's clothing or something equally as rebellious. She was trying to resist within acceptable confines. Dorian saw plainly what she was playing for. She was hoping society would accept her running her father's business, that she wouldn't have to choose, that she could live in a world of greys instead of blacks and whites. He wasn't convinced such a world would make her happy. Greys could be just as frustrating as the black-and-white boundaries that marked who was 'in' and who was 'out'. He knew, he'd tried it. Black and white suited him better and he suspected it would suit Elise better, too, if she could be made to see it. *Not* that it was his job to help her along that path. He gave himself a stern reminder that he was in this for the boat, nothing more.

Dorian crossed the road, looking carefully into the dark side streets before he did. Even Mayfair had its thugs after hours. He would catch a hackney soon for the rest of the journey back to the shipyard. Only a foolish man would tempt fate by walking through the docks at this time of night. He'd been foolish enough already tonight, sitting with Elise and letting the conversation wander afield from the business he'd come to discuss. They'd ended up in front of the fire and the next thing he knew she was asking questions about his family, about *him*: the two things he never discussed with anyone. Yet he'd discussed them, however briefly, with her.

At least he'd left before anything untoward had happened. That was one thing he'd done right, although it had been hard. Elise had looked positively beautiful, the firelight picking out the chestnut hues from the dark depths of her hair, the delicate sweep of her jaw in profile, the slender length of her neck shown to subtle perfection by a loose chignon at her nape. It would have been the work of moments to have her dark hair free and her lips plump from kisses. She'd proven on more than one occasion to be a willing participant in those kisses.

But tonight would have been about more than kissing. Fireplaces and cold evenings worked all nature of magic and the following mornings brought all nature of regrets. It wouldn't have stopped at kissing. His thrumming body attested to it still, after several bracing minutes in the cold night air. He'd heard the loneliness in her voice as she'd spoken of her father and he'd heard the loneliness in his own bitter response. Even if she didn't recognise it for what it was, he did. It was a deuce terrible feeling to know he'd been home for two months and no overture had been made to acknowledge his return.

Dorian hailed a hackney trolling the streets where a party was in progress, looking for a late-night fare. If he waited much longer, his options would dwindle to nothing. He jumped in, giving directions to the Blackwell Docks, and sat back.

The ride was accomplished in short order, a much shorter order than during the day. Without traffic filling the streets, the transition from West End to East End was far swifter. It wasn't until after he'd paid the driver and had stepped through the heavy gates that his senses went on alert.

Something was wrong. Dorian reached stealthily for the knife in his boot and stood still, letting his eyes adjust to the darkness. There was the sound of muffled motion to his right, the sound too heavy to be mistaken for a rat or stray cat. Besides, this shipyard was impeccable. There'd been no earlier signs of animal life.

He swung towards the sound and called out in a strong voice, 'Show yourself! You are trespassing on private property. Show yourself now or face charges from the law.'

They were on him then, stupidly both from the same side. Two burly forms with clubs of their own came at him out of the darkness, but he was ready for them and ready for a fight after the frustration of leaving Elise's with an uncomfortable hunger.

The first attacker swung his club. Dorian moved into him, grabbing his wrist and twisting hard, disarming him before bringing a knee up into his groin. The man fell heavily to the ground, groaning.

The second attacker was more cautious after seeing his comrade fall. He would need his knife for this one, Dorian reasoned, lifting the blade to catch the lantern light in hopes of scaring the second man into surrender. Knives had a special persuasive power all of their own and he had no real wish to carve the man up. The second attacker might be more cautious, but not necessarily more intelligent. He didn't take the surrender option. Instead, they circled each other while he waited for an opening.

'You're taking too long. Are you going to strike or not?' Dorian goaded him, flashing the blade in a fancy arc. Just the feint on his part was enough to send the other man back a step. Dorian feinted again, but provoked no aggressive response. At this rate they'd be here all night. The man's left side was unprotected. The third time, Dorian lunged and drew blood. The man dropped his club out of reflex to clutch his wounded arm.

Dorian was on him, blade to his throat. 'Who sent you? What do you want?' Even in the dim light, he could see the man was pale.

'Don't tell him!' the man's companion wheezed out between groans.

'If he doesn't tell me, I'll try you next,' Dorian growled. 'We'll see how well you do up against a blade.'

'I don't know exactly,' Dorian's man prevaricated. 'A cove with money. He said all we had to do was look around and report what we saw. We didn't come here to hurt anyone.'

Dorian pressed the blade harder. 'You came with clubs.'

'For our own protection.'

Dorian didn't believe that for a moment. 'What were you supposed to look for?' Had Halsey tracked him down already? The blade bit into the skin, drawing a tiny bead of blood, just enough to convince the man he meant business if he didn't get his answers.

'The b-b-boat,' the man managed.

Dorian eased the pressure as a token of goodwill and a sign that the man was now supposed to supply more details. He did. 'We were supposed to come and see if she was building a boat.'

That was not the answer he was looking for, but there

was no time to fully dissect what it meant right now. Dorian pressed again, his efforts redoubled. 'I'll ask one more time, who sent you?' It obviously wasn't Halsey, which meant he had absolutely no clue. It also meant he couldn't kill them. Halsey couldn't very well go to the law without incriminating himself. But whoever had sent these chaps would come looking for them if they didn't return and he might bring the watch with him. Unless Dorian got to the watch first.

Dorian backed his man to a post and reached for the twine, tying him thoroughly before turning his attention to the other man with the rest of the twine, trussing him up like a stuck pig. 'If you won't tell me, perhaps you'll tell the watch.' Dorian shoved his knife back in his boot with a grin. 'I've used about twelve different knots on those ropes, so I expect you to be here when I get back.'

That made them nervous. He thought it might. 'Um, maybe we should tell him, Bert,' said the one tied to the post.

'Don't use my name!' the other one hissed.

Dorian stopped at the gate and pulled his knife back out. 'I think your name is the least of your worries right now.' He fingered the blade. 'I can be reasonable. If you tell me who sent you, I won't call the watch.' Dorian shifted his eyes from man to man. 'But we'll do it my way. I don't want any lies. So I'll come to each of you and ask you to whisper a name in my ear and a description. That name had better be the same from both of you or I'll get the watch, no second chances. I can't imagine the man who sent you would be all that thrilled to come and bail you out. He might just ignore you and leave you to rot in order to save his own hide,' Dorian reminded them.

He strode over to the man at the post. 'You first.' The name the man whispered caught Dorian entirely off guard. He knew this name. It was not a good name to know. It made men like Halsey look like saints. '*He* definitely would have left you to rot.' Dorian masked his surprise and moved on to the other. 'All right, Bert, it's up to you. Give me a name that matches your friend's over there and you are free to go.' Dorian almost hoped Bert would give another name. It would be worth the hassle to call the watch and stay up all night sorting this out if the culprit was anyone other.

But Bert whispered two disappointing words, 'Damien Tyne', and Dorian's heart sank. The encounter mopped up quickly after that. He untied them and marched them at knifepoint to the gates, Bert being heavily assisted by his comrade, and he locked the gates behind them. Not that locked gates would stop Damien Tyne.

Dorian went into his shed and stripped out of his clothing, carefully packing it away in his trunk. He was going to need those clothes more often than he thought. Tomorrow he'd have to pay another call on Elise Sutton. She had to know what had transpired here tonight. Dorian lay down on the cot, hands folded above his head. He didn't expect to sleep, not right away. Tonight would be a long one and tomorrow even longer.

Damien Tyne had made a fortune in the Mediterranean with several unethical business ventures. He was ruthless and thorough, not exactly the enemy anyone wanted to have. The question was: whose enemy was he? Had he sent those men tonight because he'd learned Dorian was back? There was definitely enough bad blood between them from their Gibraltar days to warrant such an action, or had Damien sent those men because of Elise?

Dorian suspected it was the latter. The man had said they'd been sent to see if *she* was building a boat. That didn't make him feel better. He'd far rather have Damien Tyne after him than Elise. If Tyne was after him, he'd have answers. He'd understand perfectly what the situation was. If Tyne was after Elise, he was starting at ground zero.

What business did a reprobate like Tyne have with Elise, or, more probably, with Sir Richard Sutton? Why would Tyne care if Elise was attempting to build a yacht? Dorian could come up with some plausible suppositions, but even so they seemed extreme for Elise's world, which brought Dorian back to the same conclusion that had been lurking in his mind since Bert had confirmed the name: Elise was in danger.

Dorian shifted on the cot, stretching his back. This conclusion suggested several things: his presence at the shipyard doubled her peril. Tyne would be overjoyed if

he thought he could get the two of them in a single effort. Second, that he wasn't the only the one with secrets. Beautiful Elise Sutton wasn't as open a book as
he'd been led to believe.

It was just his luck. He should have known better.
When something looked too good to be true, it usually
was, Elise Sutton notwithstanding. Most men would
walk away and see to their own safety. But he'd never
counted himself among their number. Dorian smiled
in the darkness. Tomorrow he'd ferret out Elise's secrets, right after he got a dog or maybe two. Miss Sutton was in danger and she'd just dragged him into it
along with her. Of course, that made her all the more
interesting, too.

'I do say, Miss Sutton, you are a most interesting font
of knowledge.' Charles stood back a step to let her pre-
cede him through the door of her town house. They'd
just returned from a drive in the park, taking advantage
of a rare fine day in early spring.

'I'm not as interesting as all that.' Elise laughed off
the compliment. 'I think you're being polite.' They'd
been talking of wind and sails. Rather, she'd been talking and Charles had been listening. It had been disappointing to discover that even though Charles's father
had been one of her father's investors, the interest in
boating stopped there. Charles like the social aspect of
the yachting season, but didn't care much for the en-

gineering. In fact, he'd known nothing at all about the differences in ketch or cutter riggings.

'You make it easy to listen,' Charles offered gallantly with a smile.

'Will you stay for tea?' Elise asked, removing her bonnet, only to be met with a discreet cough from Evans, who waited to take her things. 'Is something wrong, Evans?' She couldn't imagine what it could be. Evans never interrupted. But even the littlest things could be a crisis in his eyes. Perhaps Mary the cook had burnt the scones, or there weren't enough tea cakes. It would be her own fault. She'd been encouraging Mary to scale back her food preparation now that there was only one person in the house to feed. Well, two, counting the meals sent down to Dorian.

'Miss Sutton, you have a caller waiting,' Evans said neutrally.

'More specifically, *I* am waiting.' Low, masculine tones drew Elise's eyes to the doorway of the drawing room. Dorian stood there, leaning negligently against the door frame, but his eyes belied his informality. There was tension behind them and displeasure. 'I've been waiting over an hour.'

He was scolding *her*! He'd barged in unannounced and made himself comfortable in her home and then accused her of being unavailable to him. His audacity knew no limits. Elise drew herself up and squared her shoulders. 'Then you should make an appointment.'

'I wasn't aware I needed one.'

Charles was looking decidedly uncomfortable at the interchange. 'Lord Rowland, I had heard you were back. Welcome home.' But there was no welcome in Charles's voice. She heard the coldness, the implication that Lord Rowland was not appropriate company for her. She heard the scold, too, over her disobedience. He'd asked her to dismiss Rowland and she hadn't. 'Miss Sutton, might I have a word with you in private before I go? Lord Rowland, if you'll excuse us?'

Charles's face was red with emotion when they stepped into the small music room off the main hall. 'Will you allow me to stay? Or perhaps you will allow me to escort him from the premises? You cannot be alone with the bounder!'

Poor Charles, she doubted he'd have any success removing Dorian even if she wanted him to. She'd seen Dorian take on a bully much larger than Charles. Such an action would only serve to embarrass Charles. 'I appreciate the offer, but I assure you it is unnecessary. Lord Rowland has news of the shipyard, nothing more.'

Charles's faced turned even redder. 'There is another issue, Miss Sutton—*Elise*, if I may? We've been friends for a long time. I feel it is my duty to bring this to your attention. Your conduct is not all it should be. It hurts me to say it and I know this is a difficult time for you. Your family has abandoned you, but you cannot abandon convention. You cannot continue to live alone in this house and you certainly cannot entertain men without a chaperon!'

He warmed to his subject, his ardour for the topic not in doubt. 'Elise, you should not have invited even me in for tea. But to have one man invited in and to have another man waiting for you, it is most unseemly. If anyone were to find out, it could be disastrous. We are fortunate town is still deserted and the Season isn't under way yet.' He paused to gather his breath after his last rush of words. 'Let me send someone to you. My aunt, perhaps?' He looked at her expectantly. 'I know you are alone. But you don't need to be.'

'Thank you, Charles. I will think about it.' She hoped she sounded sincere. She had no wish to hurt his feelings. He was doing what he thought best. But frankly, she was mortified by his outburst. Was he really as prissy as all that? She had not noticed that vein had run so deep before. Of course she'd never stepped so far out of line before, either. There'd been no need for him to preach. Really, that was the only word for it. There was being concerned about propriety and then there was *concerned*. Charles was of the latter and she had no tolerance for that. She was a grown woman of twenty-three. She was more than capable of looking after herself.

He gave her a stiff bow, hat in hand, his demeanour slightly colder than when he'd arrived. 'Good day, Miss Sutton.'

'Are you happy now?' Elise faced Dorian once the door was shut on Charles's departing back. 'You've managed to anger one of my dear friends and make me look quite the strumpet.' Whatever *détente* they'd experienced last night over tea and a fire had been nothing more than a mirage. Except for the clothes, there was very little of that gentleman about Dorian today.

'He'd like to be more than a friend,' Dorian scoffed. 'Is that the sort you prefer? No wonder you'd never been kissed. I can't imagine he knows the first thing of how to go about it.'

'My preferences are none of your business.' Elise felt her face heating up as she swept past him into the drawing room. She was not having this conversation where the servants could hear whatever outlandish remark might come out of his mouth.

'You might think differently about what is my business or not after you hear what I have to say.' Dorian eased the doors to a half-shut position, allowing them some privacy.

'I do not like the look on your face or the tone of your voice,' Elise replied.

'I assure you, you will like even less what I have come to say.' Dorian gestured to the sofa and settled into the matching chair across from her. 'Now that we're comfortable, why don't you tell me how you've come to know Damien Tyne?'

Chapter Eight

'I don't know him at all,' Elise didn't even hesitate to answer. The name was nothing to her.

'Did your father?'

Elise shook her head. 'No. I kept all the orders and accounts. If we'd had any business with him, I would have known.'

Dorian looked doubtful and she felt the need to protest her point. 'I would have known,' Elise insisted, wanting to wipe that sceptical look off his oh-so-sure face.

'Unless your father had private dealings with him.'

'Is "private" your way of suggesting "secret"?' Elise bristled at the connotations wrapped in Dorian's implication that all was not as it seemed. 'My father was not that sort of man.'

Dorian remained unfazed by her challenge. 'I'm not insinuating he was. But Tyne is exactly the sort. Most of his dealings are not public.' He leaned back in the chair, assuming a pose of relaxed confidence, so certain he had the upper hand, so certain he knew more than she did about her own business's dealings, and the assumption galled. 'Let's assume for the moment that you are correct and you or your father had no knowledge of Tyne. Explain, then, why he sent two men to your shipyard last night.'

'What?' Elise's earlier fears that something had happened surged to the fore. 'The boat? Is it all right?' She didn't know what she'd do if the boat was ruined. There was no question of starting over. Until this moment she'd not fully realised how much she was counting on that yacht. It had come to hold all her dreams, her future, her *everything*.

'The yacht is fine.' Dorian gave a wry smile. 'I'm fine, too, thanks for the asking.'

'Of course you are.' Elise covered her impolite manners hastily. It wasn't well done of her to think of the boat first. She'd just been so shocked. 'Otherwise, you wouldn't be sitting here.' She was rambling now, still trying to digest the implications of *armed* men coming to her shipyard. Dorian's comment clearly indicated it hadn't been a social call or even a business call. 'If you'd been hurt, I'd have been outraged,' she protested.

Dorian laughed. 'Your concern is touching and almost believable. Maybe next time you should flutter your eyelashes and look a bit pale when you say that. Fortunately, I was more than a match enough for the two of them, no need to worry.'

'Perhaps that's why I wasn't,' Elise replied smartly.

Whatever sympathy she'd been mustering on Dorian's behalf fled at the teasing. The man who'd pressed a knife to an employee's throat for a simple infraction was more than able to handle two night-time thugs. She could also easily imagine that such men were not as foreign to him as they were to her. It had not escaped her, in all the shock of Dorian's revelations, that he was worried because *he* knew this Damien Tyne.

Elise folded her hands in her lap and looked Dorian squarely in the eye. 'Let us reverse our roles for a moment. I cannot answer your question, but it seems you can answer mine. Why don't *you* tell *me* how you know Damien Tyne?'

She noted the tight line of Dorian's mouth as he answered, 'He's a man you don't want to know.'

'Some say that about you,' Elise challenged, recalling Charles's reaction when she'd told him. 'I'm afraid I'll need to know more than that before I can decide what is to be done.' She was tired of men deciding who she should or shouldn't know. For a moment, she thought Dorian would refuse, but he had none of Charles's qualms.

'He's a gun runner. I came across him in the Mediterranean.'

Elise schooled her features to give nothing away. She'd been prepared for unpleasant news and Dorian was trying to shock her. Still, this was *quite* unpleasant. 'How do you know this?'

Dorian shrugged noncommittally. 'I was in a position to know, that is all. Tyne is a man with no code, no loyalties, and now he's come looking for you.'

'Or for you.' She would not let shock overrule her sensibilities and reason. 'I had no such trouble until you came along. Forgive me for saying it, Mr Rowland, but this Damien Tyne seems more like your sort.'

Such words would get a rise out of any man she'd ever known. But he merely sat there, an infuriating grin on his face as he nodded, carrying on some secret discussion in his mind she was not privy to.

'I liked it better when you called me Dorian,' he drawled. His blue eyes held hers in a most disconcerting fashion reminiscent of spontaneous kisses and the promise of illicit pleasures. 'For your information, Tyne *is* more my sort, but he definitely came looking for you. The men last night said explicitly they'd been sent to see what was going on at the shipyard.' He paused, his tone softer when he spoke again. 'If it makes you feel better, I'd hoped it might have been me, too.'

That caught her off guard. It reminded her briefly of the man she'd glimpsed last night in front of the fire, who had for a short period of time seemed almost like a gentleman. Best not to be swayed by the clothes, she scolded herself. Beneath these layers lay the man who swaggered around in low-slung culottes. Still, Elise couldn't help but be touched that this man she barely knew had wanted to take her place.

His hand reached out across the short distance between them and covered hers where they lay in her

A Lady Dares

lap, his eyes serious. 'I might suggest you start thinking about the identity of the rat who would have tipped
Tyne off about the boat.'

'I've told no one,' Elise answered truthfully. She'd
held her tongue on the one opportunity she'd been
tempted to tell Charles.

'Then who did you tell about me? Anyone besides
Charles?'

'No.' There'd been no one else to tell. It was a rather
sad realisation. With her brother gone back to university, there'd been no one else to discuss her days with.
The house was as empty as her social calendar, not
that her acquaintances would have approved of such
conversation. The only one of her friends who might,
Mercedes Lockhart, was miles away in Brighton and
newly married.

'Well, there you go. Charles is your rat.' Dorian released her hand and sat back with smug satisfaction at
a mystery so easily solved. 'It's not a huge leap of logic
to assume you've hired a foreman because there's actual work to do.'

No, it wasn't. She couldn't argue with that and
Charles's father had been an investor. He'd known there
was a yacht left uncompleted. Even the obtuse Charles
could put two and two together. 'I can't imagine Charles
would be acquainted with a man like Tyne.' Elise rose
and walked to the window, looking down into the street.

'And yet, I'm here. I'm sure there are those who'd
argue it isn't likely for a gently bred young lady like

yourself to know a man like me. If you could know me, what's to stop Charles from knowing a man like Tyne?'

Elise turned from the window. 'I find it doubtful. Charles is so very proper, as he demonstrated today, so very conscious of his social standing. It makes little sense that he would run to a man such as the one you've described and give him that information. And for what reason? Charles doesn't want to hurt me.' They hadn't even begun to address motives for Tyne's sudden interest in the shipyard.

Dorian gave one of his disbelieving shrugs. 'Perhaps it's more of a question of who does Charles know who might know someone such as Tyne?'

Elise blew out a breath. His cynicism made her head swim. She just wanted to build her boat and here he was spinning conspiracies. 'All we know for certain is that two unsavoury individuals sent by another unsavoury individual came to the shipyard last night and suddenly you have Charles selling secrets to gun runners.'

'If a duke's son can work for the daughter of a knight, anything is possible. The yachting world has always made for strange bedfellows. Just ask the Royal Thames Yacht Club—they were nothing more than a group of citizens with boats until Cumberland came along.'

She couldn't entirely discredit him. Just like horse racing, yacht racing had its own culture and underbelly. Races were contested all the time over foul play, sliced rigging and dashed hulls. What would she do if Dorian was right and this was just the tip of some sordid effort to claim her father's boat? The boat itself had been meant to be revolutionary. What if Tyne had heard about it and wanted the boat for himself for whatever reason? She had to stop those thoughts. Now she was sounding like Dorian. The emptiness of her world must be hitting her hard today.

Elise sighed. 'It must be very exhausting living in your world full of informants and dangers lurking around every corner.'

'I prefer to think of it as exciting.' He was up and moving, crossing the room towards her, his eyes hot and sincere all at once as if he could read the myriad emotions surging through her: the anger, the frustration, the loneliness and the fear that for once she might not be equal to the task, that all it would take would be more than she had.

Elise liked to think it wasn't clear who moved first, but in her honest moments she was certain it was her. There was such a small distance between her and Dorian, it had been the merest of motions to turn into his arms, to find her head resting on the strong expanse of his chest, breathing in the clean soapy scent of him, no masking colognes for this one. His arms had welcomed her, folded around her, held her close. When was the last time someone had held her thus?

'All I wanted to do was build my father's boat,' she whispered, fighting back the sob that threatened in her throat.

His voice was muffled against her hair. 'And we will.'

* * *

Dorian felt an utter fraud in those moments. He would protect her from Tyne, but who would protect her from him? He'd taken this position knowing if he could manage this boat for himself he would. Yet here she was, in his arms, looking to him for protection, for answers. How desperate she must be! She was not the type to seek those things from another, a sure sign of how draining these past months had been on her mental resources. He had stepped into the breach at a most convenient time for his own enterprises, but now that he was here, there were other emotions at work.

He'd seen the forces arrayed so covertly against her: Tyne and his underworld, Charles and his virtuous pomposity, attempting to bring her back into the bland fold of society. The Charles Bradfords of the world were plentiful and they would make her choose between themselves and the boat. That stirred something else in him—jealousy? Surely not. Protectiveness? Perhaps, although it seemed irrational on short acquaintance. But he'd travelled this path of hers, too, once upon a time. He'd faced similar choices long ago, albeit for different, less-noble reasons.

He smiled over her shoulder into space. When he'd jumped into her carriage, he'd been looking for an escape. He'd not thought to find a kindred spirit—not that she'd believe any such thing. She thought him a scoundrel. The idea they had anything in common would be ludicrous to her. But he knew better.

Dorian's arms tightened about her. He didn't want to give this vibrant, intelligent woman over to the cold fish of the aristocracy that would have no use for her skills. Ah, he was being covetous. Being protective was one thing; a decent man was always protective of those in his purvey even if that man was something of a pirate. Being covetous was another, more worrisome, thing altogether. Covetous implied a level of wanting. Dorian tested the statement in his mind. Did he want Elise Sutton beyond a short physical liaison? If so, how had that occurred? At what point had he begun to think with something other than his libido? For his own welfare, the answers to those questions deserved exploration in the near future.

All he knew for certain right now was that he did not want to give her to the likes of Charles Bradford, who would never be man enough for her. Would she know that? For all her own strength, did she know what she needed? He couldn't free her, only she could do that, but he *could* open the door and see what happened, starting tonight. Out of the window, dusk was falling on a crisp, clear night.

'Come on, let's go.'

She looked up, green eyes quizzical. 'Go where?'

He smiled, unwilling to give up his secret. 'Just out. You'll see. You need to get out of the house and away from your troubles.'

'Should I change?'

'Put on something warm and grab a cloak. I want

to get a few things from your kitchen. You still owe me a meal for today.' Dorian released her with a wink. 'Trust me.'

She laughed at that. 'Do you think that's wise?'

Dorian grinned. It felt good to make her smile. 'Maybe not wise, but it's bound to be fun.'

Chapter Nine

'We're not going to the shipyards?' Elise pulled her cloak tighter around her shoulders and stared about the dark pier, a quiet reminder that she'd gone out into the night with a man she barely knew and with no idea of their destination.

'I told you, no work.' Dorian waved down a wherry man. 'The Vauxhall Stairs,' he called.

'Vauxhall?' Elise questioned, taking his hand and stepping aboard. 'It's March.'

'So?' Dorian grinned.

'So? You do know Vauxhall is closed. It's not open until June.' She hated to ruin his plans, but he'd been gone—perhaps he'd forgotten.

'I know.' He gave her a lazy smile, his hand warm at her back as he guided her to the railing of the wherry for the short trip across the Thames. He leaned close, making her acutely aware of his proximity. 'It makes it more fun. We shall have the place to ourselves and no one shall be the wiser.'

It took Elise a moment to digest his meaning. 'We're going to break into Vauxhall?'

The wherry bumped against the wharf, signalling their arrival. Dorian leapt on to the pier, slinging a haversack over his shoulder. 'In answer to your question, simply yes.'

This would be the perfect time to turn back, her conscience prodded. *Before* it was too late. This was the height of insanity. He had her lying to her butler about her whereabouts and breaking into pleasure gardens.

'Well? Are you coming, Elise?' He turned towards her, hand outstretched, blue eyes dancing with mischief. 'Don't tell me you've got cold feet now? If you're worried about being seen, I've provided you with the perfect outing. No one will even know we're here.'

'This is outrageous!' she scolded. He really meant to do it, really meant to break into the closed pleasure gardens.

'Outrageous? Well, you should know. You're the woman who is building a boat.' Dorian laughed and she was helpless to resist. His enthusiasm was infectious. Her feet moved of their own accord, her hand slipping into his with astonishing ease, even knowing this was poorly done of her. He had taken advantage of her on more than one occasion. She should have dismissed him from the start. But he was still here, still tempting her towards yet another indiscretion, this one larger than the first.

Earlier, she could have taken comfort that she had no

other choice. She couldn't dismiss him. Who would finish her boat if not him? But that logic's usefulness was long past now. Sneaking into Vauxhall had absolutely nothing to do with finishing her boat and she could take no refuge in the idea that she was forced to endure his company. Tonight she'd turned to him quite voluntarily for reasons she'd care not to explore too closely.

At the entrance, she knew a moment's reprieve. The gates were locked against them, strong sturdy iron bars. Dorian's lark would end here. But Dorian merely turned aside and followed the high hedgerow that hid the garden wall. 'Ah, here it is.' He stopped and parted the greenery, revealing a door in the wall. Dorian held up a slim tool from his pocket and waggled his eyebrows playfully before inserting it into the keyhole. 'Watch this, my dear.' Within moments he had the door open. He motioned her through with a gallant gesture. 'After you, my lady.'

Dorian shut the door behind them and reached for a lantern to light. 'This is technically a crime.' Elise tried one last time for sense.

'It's only a crime if we get caught.' Dorian struck a match and the lantern flared to life, casting its light on the deserted garden paths. She'd been here before with her parents on a few occasions. Then, the place had been thronged with people. Tonight, the gardens were less festive, but far more intimate without the noise of the crowds. Or it might be the company. Elise expected anywhere would be more intimate with Dorian. He could turn the most mundane of settings into something remarkable, as demonstrated by what had occurred in her offices on two occasions.

'Shall we take in the sights?' Dorian was all exaggerated gallantry, offering her his free arm, the other one burdened with his sack and the lantern. 'May I draw your attention to the statue of Handel?' He held the lantern high, illuminating the sculpture of Handel in his bathrobe and slippers. Elise laughed and let him talk while he guided her through the Grand South Walk. There were no other signs of life except for the squirrels in the bushes and she started to relax. Perhaps Dorian was right and scandal only became a crime if one was caught. This evening could be a moment out of time, something no one else ever had to know about.

'I must apologise, we have no fireworks tonight or gaslight display.' Dorian toured her past the rows of supper boxes to the open tables in front of the orchestra. 'But perhaps I can interest you in a little picnic?' He set down the sack and began unpacking.

'This is what you were doing while I got my cloak?' Elise watched in amazement as he produced a square of white linen and spread it on the table before settling the lantern in the centre.

'There, we'll have candlelight for ambience.' He grinned impishly and continued pulling out items: a loaf of bread, a wheel of cheese, slices of ham. 'Not nearly as thin as Vauxhall's famed ham, but your Mary cuts it well.' There were plates and glasses, knives and napkins and, miracle of miracles, a bottle of wine. The bag seemed seriously depleted once the feast was laid out.

'This is incredible,' Elise breathed, taking a seat. She couldn't believe she was doing this; sitting down to a picnic in deserted Vauxhall with this rather extraordinary, if not eccentric, man. It begged the question. 'Why are you doing this?'

Dorian pulled the cork from the bottle and poured her a glass. 'Why not?' He raised his own glass, blue eyes mesmerising. 'You're an intriguing woman, Elise Sutton, and I like intriguing things.'

'Those are bold words.' Never had a man spoken so frankly to her.

'As bold as the woman herself,' Dorian said in low tones. 'To you, Elise, and your latest undertaking.' He drank to her, the words sending a delightful shiver down her spine. He made her sound so sophisticated in her unconventionality. She'd not thought of herself that way.

Elise reached for a slice of bread and cheese. 'I don't see my yacht as an act of audacity. It is simply an extension of who I am. Boats are what I do. You make too much of it.'

'Perhaps you make too little of it,' Dorian replied. 'It's not every woman who knows as much about yachts as you do. May I ask what sparked your interest in the first place?'

Elise smiled. 'I've been drawing designs forever.' She'd meant to keep the answer concise, but Dorian nodded and cocked his head in interest, his eyes resting on her, intent in her story. Before she knew it, one story became two and soon she was telling him how she'd gone to work with her father when she was a little girl, how she'd sit at the drafting desk by the window and draw, how her father would put her on his shoulders and walk about the yard with her, telling her the names of all the parts of a ship. How, later, she'd begun keeping his books to free up more time for him to conduct business, how he'd started consulting her on the builds and then the drawings. She told him how her mother had scolded that this was no pastime for a young girl, but that hadn't stopped her or her father. It had become the pattern of their days. Now he was gone and she knew nothing else.

'Perhaps that's why I'm so determined to see this ship finished. I don't know what else I'd do. Even now, having been banned from the shipyard...' she looked up and gave him a pointed stare '...I don't know how to fill my days.'

'Having you there is difficult. These are not your father's men. Surely you understand this?' Dorian answered. 'But they were all I could find, given the circumstances.'

Elise nodded. She did understand, she just didn't like it, especially now with the threat of an interloper stalking the shipyard. She wanted to be there. Elise looked about the table. The wine was drunk, the food eaten. She'd talked far longer than she'd planned, exposed more of herself than she'd meant to. 'I'm sorry, I didn't mean to talk through the whole meal.'

'I didn't mind,' Dorian drawled. 'You're interesting.'

Charles had said the same thing that afternoon. It was what gentlemen said to ladies, to be polite. But Dorian made it sound as if he meant it and the thought warmed her unexpectedly. She shouldn't care what this rogue of a lord's son thought of her or her family. His opinion carried no weight, he was a social outcast by his own admission. Yet, here at their purloined supper table, the words meant the world.

Dorian might have been right. He might be starting to grow on her after all, a thought that both thrilled and dismayed her. He was merely passing through her life. One day in the very near future, as soon as he had his money, he would move on, taking his smile and his seductive brand of flirtation with him. But for the present, it did make a girl think about the possibilities that existed until then.

Dorian gathered up their plates and glasses, stuffing them back into his sack. 'Come walk with me, there are still some unexplored areas. We haven't taken in the Rural Downs yet.' He guided them towards a path that led away from the Grove. 'We should see Milton's statue at least before we go.'

'What about you? How did you get interested in ships if your family was disposed towards horses?' Elise asked, hoping he'd be more forthcoming than he had been.

'As I told you, at first I just wanted to be different. I was looking for a way to spite my father and yachting seemed perfect. After a while, though, I was genuinely interested.' He paused. 'A boat is freedom. I could go anywhere and everywhere. I could see parts of the world others only dreamed of.'

'And so you did. Is that why you went to the Mediterranean?' The Mediterranean sounded positively exotic to her, so far away although she knew British interests extended far beyond the south of Europe.

She could *feel* his smile in the darkness. 'Ah, Elise, the Mediterranean is a fascinating place with Europe on one side, Africa on the other and Istanbul somewhere in the middle, a gateway to the Far East and China and all that lies beyond. There are potentates and pirates, beaches and deserts and mysteries beyond imagining.'

She was in his thrall, hanging on each picture his words painted. 'Tell me more. Tell me about the sea.' They'd arrived at Milton's statue, a lead rendition of the author, but she was far more interested in the man beside her.

'It's warm, Elise. A man can bathe in it off the coast of Spain. Can you imagine such a thing? Swimming naked in the ocean with dolphins for playmates?' His eyes danced. He was deliberately being naughty. One did not talk of such things in polite company.

'Have you really swum with dolphins?' She suspected he was teasing her. She didn't dare ask about the naked part. She was certain he had.

'Yes, once in Gibraltar. I will never forget it. They're friendly creatures.'

'I envy you your adventures,' Elise said softly. The intimacy of the evening and the sweet blur of the wine were starting to conspire. They'd been down this path before. If she was smart, she'd suggest they leave before any damage was done, damage she'd regret once the wine and loneliness wore off.

'You could have adventures, too. You could feel the Mediterranean wash across your feet; you could bury your toes in the sand of its beaches.' His voice caressed her as assuredly as the hand at her neck. 'Do you ever think of it? Of sailing away in one of your creations?'

'A fantasy only,' Elise confessed. The practicalities eluded her. A woman alone was at risk even if she could sail a yacht on her own. But she could hardly think of that with Dorian so near, so charming, so seductive. She should not let him touch her. Any touch at all seemed to ignite her.

'You need a partner,' Dorian murmured, his mouth at her ear, his teeth nipping gently at her lobe.

A wicked thought came to her. She needed him, this pirate in gentleman's clothing who talked of far-off places and laughed at propriety, who didn't care a whit for any of the things that occupied the hours of Charles's days, who could wield a knife and take on intruders. He would be the perfect partner. She would be safe with him.

That was definitely the moonlight and wine talking!

Vauxhall's vaunted reputation for indiscretions among its many arbours was not unearned. There was magic here aplenty if she was ready to cast aside the hard-learned lessons of her dalliance with Robert Graves and the vow she'd made to never *need* a man. However, she'd been clear with herself that needing was not the same as wanting. Wanting was voluntary, needing was a necessity. All right, just as long as she understood her own rules, she could *want* Dorian Rowland.

'You smell like the lemons in the south of Italy,' Dorian whispered between the kisses he placed along the column of her throat. She should stop him, but all she did instead was arch her neck, inviting his lips, his caresses. His hands cupped her face, his mouth taking hers in long drinking kisses that nearly made her weep. She *was* weeping—deep at her core she was hot and damp, desire gathering firm and insistent at the private juncture between her legs, demanding to be assuaged.

She knew precisely what she felt and she knew what she wanted—one night, just one night, out of time. Dorian would be the perfect lover. He wouldn't raise her expectations with false promises to be dashed later because this time there would be none. This time there would be only pleasure. She was older, wiser, and this time when she played with desire she knew exactly what she was doing.

Dorian knew, too. His hands were at her skirts, drawing them up, finding the slit in her undergarments that gave him access to the weeping centre of her, the wet heat that would not be quenched. She gasped in desperate frustration, urging him to hurry. Dorian's hand was on her even as his mouth claimed hers once more, his every touch riveting her body's attention. His fingers searched unerringly, intimately, for the little nub hidden in her folds. He rubbed gently, tantalisingly, drawing his thumb across the tiny, sensitive surface again and again until she thought she'd scream from the delight of it. Very soon everything would be resolved, her body knew it as she arched against his hand, her cries a mingling of sobs.

'Let go, Elise. Let go for me.' Dorian's voice was ragged at her ear, his own breathing coming in pants as he stroked her, his own body rigid against hers. It was all the coaxing she needed. Elise arched one last time and shattered, her world an expanding kaleidoscope of sensations, her body shaking, her knees quivering. She remained upright due only to the strength of Dorian's arms and the old oak at her back. Dorian's eyes glittered dark and dangerous in their desire, watching her explode.

'I think there is no more beautiful sight than a woman achieving her pleasure.' He leaned an arm against the oak, his hair falling in his face as he bracketed her with his body. He was hoarse, proof that the moment had not moved her alone.

'And a man? He is beautiful in pleasure, too?' It had not escaped her that he had yet to find his own release.

His muscles were taut against the lines of his clothes, the tension of his own need obvious.

Dorian smiled wickedly, encouragingly. 'You should judge for yourself. After all, beauty is in the eye of the beholder.'

The moonlight had made her reckless. She reached for him, cupping him between his legs as he had her. He was hard against her touch, so very long, so very rigid, a potent force beneath his trousers. 'Or the hand, as the case may be.'

Chapter Ten

Dorian flicked open his trousers in a deft movement. 'Then by all means, my lady.' Her hand closed around him, firm and decisive, sliding to the root of him. Dorian sucked in his breath, letting her learn him. The firmness of her grasp was a sign of her confidence if not also her knowledge. There was wide-eyed appreciation in her gaze even as she recognised the power she held in those moments. She was newly come to such intimacies, but not without imagination.

She stroked up, finding the wet, tender tip of him, a smile lighting her face at the discovery. She stroked downwards and then up again, establishing a rhythm that fired his blood. Her hand was cool and welcome on his heated flesh. He would not last long at this rate, nor did he want to. The promise of exquisite relief waited just beyond the moment. Dorian reached back and dug his hands into the bark of the tree, pumping hard into her hand, uttering a harsh groan as release took him.

Elise was exultant. 'What are you smiling at?' Dorian teased.

'I'm smiling because I was right. A man *is* beautiful in his pleasure.'

'I don't think anyone has ever called me beautiful before,' Dorian drawled with a nonchalance he didn't feel. He kissed her then, drawing her close against him so she couldn't see his face, couldn't see how the comment affected him. He felt the first stirrings of new arousal. There was more he'd like to do with her, this bold princess of his, but not tonight, although his body was willing.

He was no stranger to seduction. He'd seduced women before: married women, widowed women, flirtatious débutantes, the touched and the untouched. He had few boundaries when it came to sex. What boundaries he did have, Elise was provoking. His earlier thoughts about coveting and protecting were threatening to resurface at a most vulnerable time—right after intimacy when he was open to susceptibilities. 'We need to get back,' he murmured against her hair.

The walk to the hidden door was quiet, but not awkward. They'd strolled slowly, his arm about her waist, keeping her close. He had no doubt her mind was as full as his was at present. Their spontaneous outing had been illuminating, although probably for different reasons. Dorian found it was easier, less troublesome to his conscience, to think about her thoughts than his. He was not convinced this was her first encounter with raw passion—perhaps with the depth of pleasure the encounter had wrung from her, but not the nature of the encounter itself. Still, first encounter or not, he could guess what was racing through her mind: what had she done? Was there shock or shame over her own audacity? Was she pleased at the discovery of such pleasure? Emboldened by it even? Or did she think herself the wanton for having enjoyed it? And she *had* enjoyed it, Dorian knew she had. Most of all, she was likely wondering what it meant. Anything? Nothing? Everything?

That was the place at which his thoughts intersected with hers and it was where he'd made his first mistake. By his own rules, he shouldn't have allowed it to happen—not yet, not without an agreement. Up until now, all of his seductions occurred *after* some explicit or implicit plan had been established, interest signalled and accepted by both parties.

With that signalling came an understanding. What would proceed would be a seduction in which he would gladly take the lead, but to which there would be an end. There would be nothing beyond. If and when both parties concurred on those negotiations, *then* such things as what had transpired tonight would take place, but not before.

Tonight had got the plan backwards. And he'd set himself up for it. He'd gone to her house to inform Elise of the break-in. He should have left it at that. He should not have allowed himself to be moved by the stoic sight of her bearing yet more bad news on those slender shoulders. He should not have been moved by the way she'd turned into him: *I just wanted to build my father's boat.* And he *never* should have said the words that had followed: *we will.* If Elise Sutton was walking beside him right now thinking they were in this together, that she could trust him, that he would stand beside her through whatever might come, it was his fault.

As if to confirm it, Elise spoke softly. 'When I first met you, I didn't like you very much.'

'And now?' They'd reached the hidden door and he held it open for her.

She smiled up at him as she passed. 'And now I like you a bit more. Are we becoming friends, Dorian Rowland?'

'Friends? No, never that.' Dorian chuckled. Whatever it was he wanted from Elise Sutton, he wanted far more than friendship. He waved down a late-night wherry man.

'Then what?' Elise asked once they were on board, watching the Westminster stairs come into view.

'Something else,' Dorian answered cryptically, wrapping his arms about her, hoping his touch would be answer enough until he could work out a better one. Although the answer, when he found it, might not please her. But tonight was not the time to tell her that women relied on him for sex, nothing more. Anything beyond momentary pleasure was not his to give. He'd not proven reliable in that regard in the past and he had no reason to believe it would be any different this time. He was coming to believe his father might be right. Singular devotion simply wasn't in him. And that's what Elise Sutton would expect from a man. It's what she had a *right* to expect.

He saw her safely home, part of him worried Tyne might try to personalise his attacks. It had occurred to him that Tyne would seek retaliation for the discomfort of his two henchmen and that Elise would be a natural target.

'Will the boat be all right?' she asked in the darkness of the carriage as it drew to a stop in front of the town house. Dorian chuckled. Her mind had moved on from the pleasures of the evening to what had brought them together in the first place. Or perhaps it was her way of restoring balance to what had become a deeply personal evening with an unlikely partner.

'I took on a guard dog today and alerted the watch, although I put more faith in the dog.' Dorian chuckled. 'He's a big brindle hound and *he* can't be bought.' Dorian was fairly certain Damien Tyne would see to the watch soon enough and there'd be little protection from that quarter once Tyne's machine was in motion.

Dorian opened the door and pulled down the steps. Playing the gentleman had come easy to him this evening. It was a bit of a surprise to see how easily it'd come back to him. 'Goodnight, Elise.'

'Goodnight, Dorian. Thank you for the evening.' She smiled politely at him as if she'd not pleasured him just an hour before, or screamed her own pleasure to the skies a quarter of an hour before that. When she wanted, Elise Sutton could be a cool customer. But he knew better. She wasn't cool in the least. An arousal started at just the thought of all her heat, all her passion hidden behind the calm exterior with which she met the world.

'The hull is nearly timbered, then we'll caulk,' Dorian said in hopes of subduing his arousal before it became troublesome. 'I will contact you when it's finished. Shouldn't be more than a few days.'

Disappointment clouded her eyes. Disappointment over not seeing him tomorrow or disappointment in not being invited to the shipyard? With Elise it could be either or both. 'You will contact me if there's trouble before that?'

'Yes, most certainly.' He gave her a short bow. 'Goodnight.'

Disappointment? Relief? Elise wasn't sure what she should feel. She tried to sort through those feelings while she got ready for bed. She'd dismissed her maid as soon as she could. Whatever those feelings were, she wanted to sift through them alone.

Her maid and Evans had waited up for her, concerned that she'd been working late. She felt terrible for the deception. They'd been worried and she'd been out having fun. Of course, they would have worried more if they'd known the truth. What she'd done tonight had been scandalous. Breaking into Vauxhall had been a minor scandal compared to what else had transpired.

Even alone in the dark of her room, she blushed at the memory. But not from shame. What had occurred between her and Dorian had been intimate and wondrous. She had never guessed such pleasure existed. Would it happen again? *Could* she let it happen again?

The right answer was no. She should not risk it. Dorian was clearly no stranger to such circumstances. But it would change the nature of their relationship. Perhaps it already had. He was building her ship. She was in charge. What if he sought to use seduction as a means to usurp her authority or to place himself in the role of an equal partner?

Elise bit her lip, thinking of all the mistakes she'd made over the evening. She had turned to him in the drawing room, seeking comfort from the disastrous news. She'd allowed him to be in charge of their adventure—an entirely *delinquent* adventure. In short, she'd allowed herself to be weak for a few hours only, but even those few hours could have been potentially damaging. He would finish the boat and he would leave. And she would what? Be alone? In the dark, Elise strengthened her resolve. She needed to begin as she meant to go on, by herself. Anything else was too risky and right now she had too much at stake for any more risks other than the ones she was already taking.

Besides, her practical self reminded her, Dorian Rowland was a poor risk to take. He was fun and clever and he loved ships as she did. He'd had exciting adventures galore. In short, he represented a life she envied. But he was also dangerous; a social enigma with a clouded past that most likely involved exile from his family. What he had said about Damien Tyne had been most revealing. *I was in a position to know.*

It spoke volumes. Dorian Rowland had captained the *Queen Maeve*, was called the Scourge of Gibraltar and fraternised with gun runners. He might not have a golden earring dangling from his ear lobe or a tattoo on his cheek, but he was nothing more than a pirate himself, a most delicious and dangerous discovery indeed.

Chapter Eleven

'We've been discovered and so soon in the game. Your men were not as reliable as hoped,' Maxwell said bluntly, knowing full well that few men dared to speak to Damien Tyne with such arch boldness. In the privacy of his own study, he could say whatever he damned well pleased. It was part of the reason he'd insisted they meet here instead of the coffee house. The other reason was that one discovery was all he wanted to risk.

Tyne's single slip had changed the nature of the game. If he wanted his hands on that property and Sutton's last yacht by April, things would have to progress faster and more covertly than planned. For his part, Maxwell didn't want Rowland or anyone connecting him with Tyne while play was in motion. He wouldn't admit it to Tyne, but he was anxious. He couldn't afford for this gambit to get too messy. He was the legitimate face of their questionable business. He had to stay as clean as Tyne was dirty.

Across from him in the other chair, Tyne didn't appear the least perturbed by the latest developments. He gave his brandy an indolent swirl. 'It was unfortunate Rowland chose that moment to return.'

'What was *unfortunate,*' Maxwell said with emphasis, 'was that *two* men were overpowered by one. Two men, I might add, who specialise in violent living. They should have been more than enough for Rowland.'

Tyne shrugged. 'Our Miss Sutton is building a boat and Rowland is helping her. Don't belabour it. In the end we got what we went for.'

'Yes, and at a great price,' Maxwell groused, unable to be as glib.

Tyne leaned forwards, clearly undaunted by the scolding. Then again, he didn't have an identity to protect. Anyone who knew Damien Tyne knew exactly what he was. 'Maybe this can work to our benefit. Rowland will have told her. She knows it's me. That should scare her, perhaps enough for you to make an offer she'll listen to.'

'She rebuffed the investors when they first offered to buy her out.' Hart had been a quiet, invisible party to that negotiation. He'd been shocked when the lucrative offer had been turned down, even more shocked when the investors had offered it a second time after threatening to force a refund of their monies if she didn't sell. She'd refused and she'd paid their threat.

'She wasn't scared then. She was in the throes of mourning and wrapped up in sentimentality. Such emotions can make a person brave and stupid,' Tyne said silkily. 'Now, she's had months of realities. Now, she's alone, her funds are depleted and she knows with definite certainty there's no white knight riding to her rescue. She's far more desperate than she was earlier and she's about to be more so.' Tyne gave an evil smile that raised even the hairs on the back of Maxwell's neck.

'What have you done?' Maxwell asked cautiously. He was just as ruthless as Tyne, but far more subtle. Tyne didn't appreciate finesse.

'Don't worry, nothing much. There's a disgruntled worker at the shipyard who doesn't like our Mr Rowland. It seems Mr Rowland put a knife to his throat for looking at the lady wrong, which is interesting enough in itself. Seems Mr Rowland has developed a fascination for the Sutton girl.' Tyne sighed dramatically. 'The man would have left, but I'm paying him to stay. He will be useful not only for information, but for the odd bit of sabotage when the time comes. If I were you, I'd get my bid ready within the week.'

It had been a week since their outing to Vauxhall and Elise suspected she'd have gone round the bend before the morning was out if the note from Dorian hadn't arrived. She might still go crazy from the excitement the note had stirred in her. The boat was done! Well, not precisely *done*. The hull was timbered and caulked. There was still plenty to do, but this was an enormous step forwards.

Elise glanced at the mantel clock in the sitting room,

the note clutched in her hand. Dorian would be here within the hour. There was just enough time to change. She rang for her maid and headed upstairs.

It was ridiculous to be so giddy over the prospect of Dorian's call and the subsequent journey out of the house, but she could understand it. In the past week she'd written countless letters, cleaned the attics and still had plenty of time left over for her thoughts. She'd thought about everything and anything in the interminable days since Vauxhall.

Never had she felt at such loose ends while she waited for news. By her efforts she'd become a prisoner in her own home. She was on her own for the first time in her life, had more freedom than ever and yet the very aloneness constrained her. Oh, heavens, just listen to her! She hated sounding like Charles. Worse, she hated *acting* like Charles. She could almost hear Dorian's mocking laugh in her head, chiding her for prudish notions. In fact, she'd been chiding herself over such behaviour this week. This was *not* who she was.

This week, she'd come to recognise that her father's death had left her in no man's land. She couldn't go out and socialise and yet she didn't want to stay home alone, hidden away. Young daughters weren't required to wear black, but she was too old to be considered in that category. Even her clothes were in fashion limbo, she thought, staring at the muted lavender and grey gowns. They weren't strictly appropriate for this phase of her mourning, but it was all the concession she was willing to make. Luckily, she looked fair enough in those shades. But she looked *better* in deep, rich jewel tones. With that erroneous thought, the ideas that had chased each other around her mind all week began to coalesce into one momentous decision.

'Perhaps this one, miss?' Her maid, Anna, held out a lavender gown trimmed in a thin black-velvet ribbon. Standing in front of her subdued gowns, everything changed. It wasn't just the dresses, although they'd certainly been the straw that broke the camel's back.

'No, Anna.' Elise drew herself up with squared shoulders. 'Bring me my other gowns. I am done with these. Have them packed up after I've gone today.' It had occurred to her during her dreary week that she owed the rules nothing. She'd already broken so many others. What had obedience to rigid strictures ever got her? Her best moments had come from breaking the rules: working with her father, designing racing yachts. If she meant to see her boat succeed, she could not let herself become marginalised.

Anna looked at her as if she'd grown two heads, or maybe four, and her skin had turned green. 'Miss?'

Elise stood her ground. 'Bring my other gowns. I want the green carriage ensemble with the black frogging on the jacket.'

The ensemble was wrinkled from storage and it took a bit of time to press it into decency but it was worth it. Elise smoothed the snug jacket over her hips. The outfit was perfect. People couldn't truly complain. There was a touch of black trim to lend respectability and the dark green was hardly garish or the classic lines ostentatious. Anna had recovered from shock and twisted her hair up neatly beneath a jaunty little hat that sat cocked on her head, more ornament than actual 'hat'.

Elise reached out a hand and took Anna's in appreciation of her efforts. 'Thank you. I'm not sure I can explain it, but I wasn't myself in those other dresses and there are things that need doing for which I most definitely need to be me.' There was a scratch at the door, a footman informing them of Lord Rowland's arrival.

Anna nodded. 'Truth is, we'll all be glad, miss. It's no good, you shutting yourself up in the house. It's not right, no matter what the rules are. Young ladies should be out in society.'

'I couldn't agree more. But there are bound to be people who will take issue with that sentiment,' Elise cautioned with one final look in the mirror. Her decision had been about more than putting on a dress. The dress was merely a public announcement. If people only speculated she'd set aside mourning by continuing about her business, her lack of mourning dress would take the guesswork out of it. Charles would have an apoplexy, and Dorian? Well, she would see what he'd do in just moments. Her heart was hammering as she took to the stairs.

She saw him first. He was in the hall looking at a painting, a minor work of Turner's, a nautical theme that had impressed her father. Today Dorian had chosen buff trousers and blue jacket along with high boots. His thick blond hair was once again pulled back at his neck into a luxurious tail.

He turned at the sound of her half-boots on the stairs, his blue eyes registering his surprise, the smile on his mouth suggesting he was enjoying it. 'If I'd known timbering the boat would get this sort of response, I'd have finished it earlier. What brought this on?'

Elise smiled and raised her head a notch higher. 'I have decided to be scandalous.'

Dorian's grin widened. 'You look enchanting.' He bowed over her hand. 'Scandal becomes you.'

'If you must know, it's probably your fault. I lay all blame at your feet.'

Dorian tucked her hand through the bend of his arm. 'I am glad to be of service, most glad.' An all-too-familiar tremble shot through her at his words, at his touch, at the mischief dancing in his eyes as he teased and flirted. It wasn't the man who raised such a flutter in her, she told herself resolutely, taking her seat in the carriage. It was the freedom he represented that explained her intense reaction to him. That was what she craved, not the man himself. Any interest in the man sprang from knowing he was not part of the rules. He was something else altogether.

Elise had nearly convinced herself of this line of logic by the time they reached the shipyard. She stepped down and let the familiar smells wash over her: scents of fresh timber, the strong smell of tar. Had she only been gone a week? It felt an eon and yet the sights and the smells were not strangers, not faded memories from another time. They were the scents of the present and of *home*. She belonged here. Elise shot Dorian a sideways glance. He'd have a fight on his hands if he tried to ban her again.

The men had known she was coming. Dorian had prepared them. Threatened them was more like it. Every one of them stood at taut attention like a staff receiving their lord, work clothes clean, eyes respectfully averted. Mostly. The man Dorian had drawn a knife against wasn't quite obedient. His eyes kept straying although his body held rigid.

'You told them,' she said in low tones after they'd passed the line of employees.

'Yes. I expect order on land or sea from my men,' Dorian said simply. 'No one is required to work here. They all had a chance to leave.' His hand was firm at her back, guiding her towards the form of the yacht.

'There it is, Elise. Your hull.' There was no mistaking the pride in his tone as he presented it, or the seductive tone in his voice as his tongue ran over her name.

Her hull. The beginning manifestations of her dream come to life. Tears threatened, but she held them back. There'd been too many tears lately. There would not be tears now, she silently vowed.

'It's beautiful,' Elise managed. She bent under the prow, running a hand along the smooth side. 'It's just as

I envisioned it.' Long, lean and low in the water, every ounce designed for efficiency, every angle destined to drink the wind and ride the waters. 'How much more time do you think?'

'Two weeks, assuming all goes well.' Dorian was watching her face and smiling softly as if he could read her mind—which would be a bit embarrassing because her first thought was that this meant two more weeks of Dorian.

What she said out loud was, 'The middle of April, in time for the Royal Yacht Club's opening trip.' She knew the club's calendar as well as she knew her own. Her father's life had revolved around the club and yachting season. The racing matches would begin soon afterwards. She'd been part of the boating trip since she was fourteen. She wasn't going to miss it this year.

Suddenly she brought her head up, her reveries interrupted by a smell, a smell inappropriate for the surroundings. At the same moment, a howl went up from the corner of the shipyard. Dorian's dog, the identity registered briefly with her as she shot a look at Dorian. 'Do you smell that?'

'Smoke.' Dorian's eyes were alert, quartering the yard. She followed his lead and scanned, looking for signs of that smoke or, worse, flame. Fire was anathema to shipyards. Whole forests of lumber could be lost and coal-based tar burnt nastily and thoroughly, spreading fire of its own when ignited. Elise didn't even want to think about what it did when it exploded. Her eyes went immediately to the barrels of tar lined along the perimeter.

'There!' She pointed to the beginnings of the flames a mere ten feet from the barrels. With all the other scents of the yard, the smoke had had plenty of time to gain momentum before they'd noticed it. 'Dorian, if it explodes...'

She—*they*—would lose everything. Dorian was off at a run, shedding his coat, before her sentence was finished. If the tar exploded, lives would be endangered along with the shipyard. 'Water!' he shouted orders. 'Form a bucket brigade!'

Fortunately, water was in good supply. Two huge barrels expressly for firefighting stood at the ready. But he could see flames travelling towards the tar as if guided there by a fuse. Dorian placed himself at the head of the line and threw the first bucket. If there was to be an explosion, he'd bear the brunt of it. He reached for a second bucket, positioning himself between the flames and the tar. 'Faster!' The water was slowing down the flames, but not dousing them. It wasn't until the third bucket that he realised who handed them to him. Elise. She should have been ushered to safety by now or had the good sense to seek safety on her own.

'Elise! Get out of here,' he shouted. 'There's no guarantee we can stop the flames.'

For an answer, she thrust a bucket into his hands. 'We'll stop them. Now, come on.' Water sloshed on her green habit and her hair had come loose with the exertion of passing buckets heavy with water. She looked intent and wild, and really quite scandalous. That would please her. He'd tell her as much *after* he'd finished shouting at her.

Ten minutes later, the fire was out, the remains nothing more than a smoky smoulder. The damage was thankfully minimal; a perimeter fence had been scorched where the fire had started, ostensibly the product of kerosene-soaked rags left out in the open and a carelessly dropped match.

'How did this happen?' Elise stood beside him, surveying what used to be the pile of rags. Her jacket was off and the white blouse she wore underneath was spotted with soot. She'd worked hard next to him. Her efforts and bravery were admirable. 'One minute we were talking about the club's opening trip and the next the yard was on fire.'

Dorian bent to the ground, his hands digging through the ashy debris. The flames had run straight and true to their destination. He'd thought it the work of a fuse when he'd fought the fire. Now, as his hands ran across the tough, warm cording beneath the ash, he was certain. He held up the line. 'Here's your answer.' He lifted it and followed its trail, tightly hidden away against the fence. They were lucky they hadn't lost the fence. 'It's a fuse.'

Elise's face paled. 'Fuses aren't lit by accident.'

'No,' Dorian offered tersely. 'They are not.' He studied it for a moment. 'It's a miner's fuse, the kind used in Cornwall for opening rock walls,' he said quietly, letting her digest the implications. If it could open rock walls, it could easily have destroyed everything in the yard. *And everyone.* Dorian gauged its length. The fuse was relatively long. If someone had truly wanted to blow up anything, they'd have set a shorter fuse, one he couldn't have reached in time.

He took Elise's arm. 'Why don't we go up to the office and discuss this latest occurrence? We were lucky this time because someone wanted us to be.'

Chapter Twelve

The office had changed in the week of her absence. It bore an indelible sense of *him*. Papers and drawings lay on the work table. His tools were here, too, hanging from a belt on the coat tree. Resentment flared. This was her space. It was full of her father, of the time they'd shared together. The thought of another claiming the space sat poorly with her, even if that person was Dorian. *Especially* if that person was Dorian. How was she supposed to forget him if his presence lingered?

'I'm coming back to work, starting tomorrow,' Elise blurted out. She hadn't meant to begin the conversation that way, but memories and resentment had got the best of her in the aftershock of the fire. She would protect what was hers.

'I won't hear of it,' Dorian growled. 'You shouldn't have been here today. I was wrong to bring you here. It put you in danger.'

'You didn't know there'd be a fire.' Elise dismissed the comment impatiently. His logic was ridiculous.

'Not a fire specifically, but we knew trouble was brewing. Tyne wouldn't have risked a break-in and nothing more.' Dorian paced the length of the office, agitated. 'He was waiting and watching for the right moment.' The man had given them a week to grow confident.

'Fuses take premeditation.' Elise followed him with her eyes. He was like a great tawny cat, restless in a cage. His broad shoulders were taut beneath the ruined linen of his shirt. His body fairly vibrated with the angry energy of him. How could anything hurt her with this lion on guard?

Dorian nodded, pausing in his pacing long enough to swear. 'Damn that man. Tyne has someone watching from the inside, someone who would know when the hull was done. That someone would be ready to put a damper on the festivities and would have advance knowledge of that timeline, plenty of time to plan.'

Elise recalled the man with wandering eyes. 'The man who doesn't like you, perhaps? His gaze kept drifting.' Now that she thought of it, the man's gaze had kept going to the tar casks.

In response, Dorian opened the top drawer of her father's desk and pulled out the longest knife she'd ever seen. 'Stay here, I'll be back.'

'Dorian, no!' Elise put herself between him and the door. 'You can't go around threatening everyone with a knife.'

'It's not a knife, it's a machete and I'm not threatening "everyone", just him,' Dorian corrected, his eyes flashing with angry determination. 'Bent needs to learn he can't go around sabotaging shipyards in a language he understands.'

Elise wasn't sure if the 'he' in that sentence denoted the worker or the elusive, villainous Damien Tyne, but she was pretty sure the language in question was 'knife'. She stood her ground, arms crossed over her chest.

'This is my shipyard and I say this type of behaviour will not be tolerated. I'm not moving.'

'You will move, Elise, or I will move you.' Dorian put the blade between his teeth, looking utterly piratical, and took a step towards her. She didn't doubt he'd do it. She decided to move. The last thing she needed was to appear the fool and that was exactly what she'd look like trussed over his shoulder.

He gave her a short nod as he passed. 'Thank you. Now, stay put.'

Dorian wasn't gone long, but he was none the happier when he returned, his knife looking suspiciously clean. 'Our culprit has fled,' he groused, throwing the knife back in the drawer.

'We usually kept paper and ink in that drawer,' Elise said pointedly.

Dorian glared and continued, 'In doing so, he has declared his guilt, but I'm sure there's more he could have told us. Primarily, what purpose the fire was to serve.

Fire is risky. If I hadn't acted quickly, much could have been lost and that would have defeated Tyne's purpose.'

'If he's after the boat, burning it makes little sense.' A bit of hope took her. 'This is good, then. The boat is safe. He won't harm it. The fire was nothing more than a warning, hence the long fuse.' There, logic had triumphed over the emotions of the moment to render a rational answer to their riddle of the fire.

Dorian allowed her a moment's peace before he pierced her with a hard blue stare. 'But you're not.' He closed the distance between them, reminding her of his complete maleness and strength with his nearness 'Have you thought of that? I'm safe for a while. If he wants the boat finished, he's got to keep me alive a few weeks longer at least. But you...' Dorian drew a long finger down the trail of her jaw and shook his head '...you are expendable, my love.'

The words brought a chill to her, but she shrugged them off. 'Kill me over a boat design? Over a yacht? A life for a boat? That's preposterous, Dorian. People don't trade lives over wood and sails. That's far too extreme.' But even as she said it, she doubted the strength of her conviction. She was remembering what Dorian had told her previously. Tyne was a gun runner, a man with no scruples.

'Of course they do, Princess. Sometimes they do it for something even less tangible, something they can't hold in their hands: speed. The history of nautical advancement, after all, has been centered on the acquisition of speed.' Dorian gave a harsh chuckle. 'If you don't believe me, consider your yacht club's races. Grown men ramming other boats' hulls in a race to slow and disable, slicing sails all for the sake of speed. And that's just to win a paltry silver cup. Think what men will do when wars and kingships are on the line.'

'Thankfully, just a "paltry cup" is on the line then,' Elise replied tartly. 'I appreciate your insight, but I think the concern is exaggerated.' He needed to understand she would not be frightened easily.

Something flared in his eyes. 'Then appreciate this, Elise.' Dorian took her mouth in a bruising kiss, dancing her the short distance to the wall. Her back rammed up against its hard surface. This was harsh and punishing, nothing like the hot exploration of Vauxhall. Elise shoved at him, pushing with both her hands against his chest.

'Stop it, Dorian. You've made your point.'

'Have I?' Dorian stepped back, fury still etched on the planes of his face. 'I stopped. Don't think for a moment Tyne will stop until he has what he wants, and he won't let up simply because you've asked. You're a clever woman, Elise. Don't let stubbornness blind you to the realities. This world you've stepped into is dangerous and you are new come to it.'

Elise summoned her confidence. She was a bit shaken; she wasn't foolish enough not to be. Still, she didn't want Dorian to see how exposed she felt. Danger was in motion, but she'd meet it as best she could without letting it rule her life. 'My father survived it and so shall I.'

Dorian's brows went up. 'Did he? As I recall, he's dead as a result of a freak boating accident.'

That was outside of enough. He was just being peevish now and those were cruel words. 'What are you insinuating?' Elise narrowed her eyes. It was just craziness, nothing more. He was angry with her; he didn't mean anything by it. But her brain sped up anyway, unearthing the thoughts she had tried so hard to stifle. Dorian couldn't possibly know how close to home the comment had struck, how many nights she'd lain awake, thinking the same thing. Only for her, it wasn't an angry shot in the dark.

'What do you think I'm suggesting?' His words were slow and measured, the anger going out of him. His face echoed the query, his brows drawn in question, his blue eyes sharp.

Elise shook her head. 'Nothing. It was merely your choice of words.' She was reading too much into a sharp rejoinder to an argument and words chosen in the heat of the moment.

'I disagree.' Dorian took up residence in a chair and settled in as if he didn't mean to budge. 'I think there's something you're not telling me.'

She said nothing. What she thought was almost too horrible to say out loud. But Dorian was far more stubborn and persistent than she'd given him credit for.

His voice was low and private, seductive almost.

'Tell me about that day, Elise. What happened? What do you know?'

'I know very little.' She studied her hands. The lack of detail regarding her father's death seemed like a great crime to her when it had occurred. Surely someone should know exactly what had happened. 'They were out in open waters. They'd wanted to try the new steam engine in rougher sailing than the Thames. The engine exploded. That's all. It was at sea, there was no one around.'

'They? Your father wasn't alone?' Dorian pressed.

'No, he was with a friend. The yacht was his and he'd wanted my father to test it.' She shook her head, anticipating Dorian's next question. 'There were no survivors. They were both lost. The only reason we know anything at all about the accident is because a nearby cargo ship saw the explosion and lowered a boat to investigate. A Captain Brandon was kind enough to pick up the bodies.'

'What else did he say?'

'There was nothing more to say. He said the yacht was in shambles, just pieces of wood really, by the time they arrived. It gave every indication of having exploded from the inside.'

'Steam engines blow up.' Dorian laced his fingers across the flat of his abdomen and stretched out his legs, giving the appearance of a man who had no intention of leaving his chair in the near future.

'Not my father's.' Elise bit her lip. She wished she

hadn't spoken so hastily. She saw too late that that had been Dorian's plan. He'd meant to bait her with a statement she was loath to accept.

'It wasn't your father's boat.'

'My father would never have taken a boat out into open waters if he was not familiar with it,' Elise answered sharply. She drew a breath. 'I'm sorry. My mother says it's been hard for me to accept that a man with my father's skill would have been victim to an accident caused by his own ineptitude when he was an expert.'

Dorian did leave his chair then. He crossed the room to her and knelt before her, taking her hands. 'But you disagree?'

'Maybe it's just easier to disagree. Maybe thinking foul play was involved offers me the reasons I'm looking for to justify such a tragedy.' Elise sighed. 'There's been a lot of drama today.'

She said it as a way to excuse the conversation and move on, but Dorian seized the words as an opening. 'Exactly, Elise. There has been drama today—a fire. After a break-in. A break-in after an unlikely death. Perhaps your suspicions are not so far-fetched. Have you asked yourself the necessary questions? Who would have wanted to see your father removed? What could they have gained that would have required a death to achieve it? There's been a lot of drama in your life the last six months, all of it centered on letting go of this shipyard. Do you not feel it's more than coincidence?'

Elise pulled her hands free. She thought more clearly when he wasn't touching her. 'I think drama, as you put it, over the shipyard is a natural consequence of settling my father's affairs.'

'But we know Tyne is after the yacht at least. Why not the yard, too? I assure you he is definitely the sort to use extreme measures if there's enough on the line,' Dorian argued softly.

'Don't look at me like that,' Elise answered.

'Like what?' A little smile played on his lips.

Like I want to melt into your arms, lay every trouble at your feet and forget every silly vow I've ever taken about swearing off the need for a man. 'Like you could solve my problems for me. I don't want that. I don't *need* that. I can solve my own problems.' Moments like this made her doubt it, though, made her want to find the easy road, and that was so very dangerous. Even if she did a need a man, Dorian wasn't precisely stable with his wandering ways and questionable lifestyle. He lived in her shed, for heaven's sake. But it was so easy to forget that in moments like this. He'd certainly been reliable today, acting swiftly enough to save the shipyard.

'We're getting away from the issue.' Dorian rose from his crouch. 'I understand how wild your thoughts must have seemed earlier. You had no idea who an enemy might have been. But now you do. You may not know the reasons, but you do know that Damien Tyne—a confirmed villain, I might add—has arranged a break-in and most likely was the mastermind behind the fire today. It is not beyond the scope of reason that he started this game with your father's death. That's something you could not have considered until recently. It may be useful now with your new information to revisit your suspicions.'

'I don't know, Dorian. It seems useless to pursue it. There's nothing left of the boat. What remained has sunk to the bottom of the ocean. We'll never really know what happened.' She was right. Her thoughts and the conclusions they led to were too terrible to have mentioned. Thoughts became much more real when spoken aloud to someone.

'You're right. We'll never know,' Dorian echoed, his eyes on her. 'That's awfully convenient, isn't it?'

'Awfully.' It was positively horrific to think her father had been murdered—that was the only word for it if any of their suspicions bore merit—for a fast yacht and a shipyard.

Dorian reached for his coat on the coat tree, his voice quiet. The mood in the office was solemn, a far more sombre atmosphere than the more volatile one in which they'd arrived. 'I think we've had enough excitement for one day. I'll see you home.'

The gentleman was back, the mask of politeness and manners in place as surely as the return of his coat over those broad shoulders.

'I'm still coming back to work,' Elise said once they had settled in the carriage.

'All right,' he said quietly.

'All right?' Elise fired back, but there was little heat in it. 'I thought you were determined that I wouldn't?' After the disclosures this afternoon, she'd expected him to resist even more vehemently than before.

Dorian grinned, his first smile in an hour, and tucked his hands behind his head. 'I changed my mind, that's all. You should be pleased. You've got what you wanted.'

But he'd got what he wanted, too, and that's what had her suspicions on alert. He'd only capitulated because he'd seen a benefit in it. He laughed. 'What's the matter, Elise? Can't stand winning? Not everything has to be a fight.'

'But some things should be.'

'Before you go into battle, just remember I'm on your side.' Dorian winked. 'I don't get paid if that boat isn't finished.'

His humour was a startling reminder of yet another reality. That's all this was to him, of course. A job. She was part of the job, something she'd been apt to forget on occasion. The word *we* had slipped into her vocabulary with alarming ease and stealthy regularity. When she thought of the yacht club's seasonal trip, she pictured them going together. When she thought of the upcoming races it was with Dorian at the helm of the new yacht, although they'd not spoken of it. These were especially dangerous fantasies and all because he'd kissed her and shown her pleasure beyond imagining. And, oh, how she wanted to feel that pleasure again! But that was setting herself up for disappointment because it could never be more than a fleeting satisfaction. She knew better and she had the experience to prove it.

The carriage rocked to a stop in front of her town house. Elise wished her thoughts would do the same. 'Do you still feel like being scandalous?' Dorian asked, handing her down.

She smiled. Her comment seemed hours ago in another lifetime devoid of mysterious fires and machete-wielding foremen. But her devotion to the claim hadn't diminished. If anything, circumstances had conspired to make her embrace that decision even more. 'Absolutely.'

'Then how about dinner with me tonight? I know a decent restaurant you'll enjoy. We should celebrate the yacht even if today wasn't perfect.' There he went again, acting more than the employee, more than the gentleman. This was the devastating rake who knew perfectly well the scandal he provoked by asking her to dine out and did it anyway.

She should say no. There might be more than a dinner on his mind. Their last dinner together had certainly led to more than dessert. 'You may call for me at seven.'

She was very aware she'd said yes for all the reasons she should have said no. He had her spinning; there was no doubt about it. He was a gentleman, a rogue, a pirate all rolled into one enticing package. She wondered which one would pick her up tonight?

Picking Elise up at seven was something of an illusion. *She'd* sent the carriage for him at half past six and now it would make the return journey to her town house. Usually, it irked him to be so reliant on a woman's hospitality. It made him feel like a kept man. But tonight, Dorian was happy to let the illusion lay. He needed all the reasons he could come up with to keep her near him. Dorian flicked a speck of dust from his green jacket and settled back against the squabs.

Tyne would come after her. Elise's inability to believe it would not prevent it from happening. She was a rock through a town house window away from finding out he was right. He'd relented on her return to the shipyard because it served his purpose. He could continue to work on the yacht and keep an eye on her. Tyne would be hard pressed to get to her if she was at the office. Tyne would have to go through him first and, for now, Tyne was loath to do that.

Having her at the shipyard had *nothing* to do with actually wanting her there. She was bossy and dictatorial. She'd try to poke her nose into everything just when he had a system established. Dorian laughed out loud in the empty carriage. He could tell himself all he wanted that these precautions were for the sake of protecting the boat. This boat would be his way of getting back at Tyne for the *Queen Maeve*. But that wasn't the whole truth. Elise Sutton had got under his skin in a most novel and intriguing way.

They'd quarrelled today after the fire and much that he'd meant to say had gone unsaid. The quarrel had sidetracked his intent. He hadn't scolded her for staying. In retrospect, it was for the best. He'd been furious she'd tried to fight the fire, to put herself in harm's deliberate way like that. He'd been furious because he'd been frightened for her, *by* her. She was fighting for her dream. She was strong in the face of adversity. He didn't want to like her, but he did. She didn't deserve any of the things that were happening and she didn't deserve him.

If he did care for her, what could come of it? She wasn't his usual sort of woman. If she knew the things he'd done, if she knew he wasn't much better than Tyne, she'd have nothing more to do with him. Her brother, William, hadn't known the half of it when he'd made his acquaintance. William thought he was the usual sort of rake, a gentleman who'd had an adventure or two. Young William would be furious, but Elise would feel betrayed.

She would be right to feel that way. He'd probably frightened away Charles, her very decent suitor who could have been brought up to scratch if she'd followed the rules. But Elise had opted for scandal instead of obscurity. His fault, too. He'd awakened her passions, her hopes, and when those crashed he'd be far away, in Gibraltar with a new ship beneath him, starting over.

That was the plan at least. There were holes in it, such as where he was going to come up with a new ship if he couldn't romance the yacht out from under her or convince her to give it to him. He'd convinced a pasha's daughter to give him the secret password to her father's arsenal once. He'd stolen the arms and resold them to the pasha's enemy. Surely he could coax a little yacht out of Elise Sutton. But there was the fact that he liked her. He hadn't much cared for the pasha's daughter. He was back to that again—liking was a damnable thing.

He was starting to have crazy thoughts—what would Elise think of Gibraltar? Recently, he'd started imagining her at his place in the hills overlooking the beach, taking her down the winding stairs to the beach at sunset, letting the water lap against their bare toes, making love in the sand. She could build her boats. Would that be enough for her? Enough to convince her to tie her fate to the Scourge of Gibraltar, a smuggler *extraordinaire* in his own right? Right now, it was simple enough to dream. There was no need to expose realities. They were together for a few short weeks; there was no need for details between them. But if he wanted more, he'd have to tell her all that he was.

At the town house, Elise made him wait, leaving him plenty of time to cool his heels in the drawing room studying the art. Her father had a decent nautical collection full of windswept seas and tilting boats in addition to the Turner in the hall. Skirts rustled at the door and he turned, his breath hitching at the sight of her.

Tonight, she'd chosen a gown of deep red with black velvet and jet beads for trim. It moved and shimmered with her in the light. The ruby pendant at her throat glowed against the pale backdrop of her skin, her dark hair the perfect foil. Dorian took her hand and kissed it. 'You look like an Italian *signorina*, which suits my plans all the better.'

She looked up at him from beneath her lashes, a most coy gesture. 'It sounds as if you mean to seduce me.'

His groin tightened in reflex. Nights were much more exciting with her than their days: less sparring, more passion.

'Perhaps I do,' Dorian replied. 'We'll see how the evening goes. Have you ever had Italian food?'

Chapter Thirteen

Italian food. Yet another thing she'd never done, and most certainly, she'd never done it *this* way—dining out in Soho. Elise took Dorian's hand and stepped down from the carriage into the crowded *mélange* of the neighbourhood.

It was hard to believe they were still in the West End of London. The Soho area had a cosmopolitan feel to it that was entirely foreign to the stiff English uniformity of Mayfair's wealthy citizens. London's rich had forsaken Soho almost fifty years ago, leaving it to the immigrants who would make a home for themselves away from home. As they walked, the languages of Europe swirled around them. Elise laughed up at Dorian at one point, 'There's so much French being spoken here, I feel like we're in Paris!'

'We're to be Italian tonight, remember?' Dorian grinned. 'But perhaps we can be French the next time we come.'

The next time. Her heart gave an irrational trip of excitement. There was a wealth of promise and commitment in those words he tossed off so casually. Did he mean for there to be other nights like this one? And what did *that* mean? She knew what it didn't mean. He *wasn't* courting her. Dorian Rowland wasn't the courting type. Yet, he was investing time in her, time that went beyond an employee's obligation. It made her wonder what he wanted and what she'd give in return.

'Ah, here we are.' Dorian ushered her towards a little restaurant with three arched windows with a sign reading 'Giovanni's.' The immigrant population of Soho had taken good advantage of the growing penchant for dining out and opened eateries showcasing the foods of their native homes. Giovanni's was no exception: an Italian trattoria lodged between a French bistro and a German delicatessen.

Elise stepped inside and was immediately wrapped in the enticing smells of tomato and basil, garlic and fresh baked bread. A dozen tables draped in white cloths with candles in red jars to mute the light filled the room, all of them occupied with patrons and enormous bowls of pasta. Elise closed her eyes and breathed deeply, taking a mental picture complete with scents. She felt adventurous and decadent in her red dress and she wanted to remember this moment, being here in this exotic neighbourhood with this exciting man beside her. Moments like this, experiences like this, had been rare in her life. Her world had been far smaller than she'd realised. 'It smells divine. What is it?'

'Spaghetti bolognese,' Dorian whispered at her ear. 'Giovanni makes it on Wednesdays and Sundays. It is his special dish.'

The kitchen door swung open and an enormous black-haired man swathed in a great white apron burst through, arms outstretched. There was only a moment's warning before he embraced Dorian, kissing him soundly on both cheeks. *'Buona sera, mi amico.'* More loudly, he called out, *'Che Capitano Dorian!'*

'It is good to see you, Giovanni.'

'You have brought a pretty *signorina*,' Giovanni said in broken English, turning his attention her direction.

'Allow me to introduce Miss Elise Sutton. Her father has the yachtworks over at the Blackwell Docks.'

'It is my pleasure,' he effused. 'Come, take the table in the window, Capitano Dorian.' He led the way towards the one empty table in the little establishment.

'The best table, Giovanni?' Dorian teased. 'A beautiful woman is always good for business, *si*?'

'Ah, you wound me, *capitano*.' Giovanni put a hand over his heart. 'I would seat you at the best table always, even if you came alone.' He cast a quick look over his shoulder towards the kitchen. 'I'll send Luciano with a little bread and a little vino. But for me, I have to go back to work. There is always business, no?'

'Do not worry.' Dorian smiled in assurance. 'I will be here a while. There will be time to catch up later, my friend.'

'How do you know these people?' Elise asked once Giovanni had left.

'I know them from my adventures in Naples,' Dorian said evasively, conveniently saved from disclosing more by Luciano's timely arrival with fresh bread, olive oil and wine.

'Is this a *taurasi* of your uncle's?' Dorian sniffed the wine while Luciano beamed.

'Of course, *capitano*. Only the best for you.' Luciano poured two glasses after Dorian gave it his approval.

'A *taurasi* is a red wine native to Naples,' Dorian explained to her. 'Giovanni's brother has a vineyard there in the hills above the city. Every region has its wine. Tuscany has its *chianti*, but Naples has its *taurasi*.' Dorian lifted his glass to Luciano. 'Send my compliments to your uncle.'

Luciano inclined his head. 'I will. He will never forget how you saved them.' He looked at Elise. 'Do you know what he did for my uncle? There was a poor harvest one year and money was short. We had no way to get our wine to market to make back our money. No captain would take our casks with only a promise of future payment. But Capitano Dorian took the casks and he got the best price we've ever had. He saved us. My uncle would have lost everything. For that, his money is no good here. We will feed Capitano Dorian for life as long as he is in England and not haring off on dangerous—'

'That's quite enough, Luciano.' Dorian held up a hand good-humouredly. 'Miss Sutton will get the wrong impression. I am sure you have other patrons to wait on.' He sent Luciano on his way, but Elise wouldn't let it go, especially not after that piece of insight. Assisting a vintner didn't seem like the usual activity for the Scourge of Gibraltar, but he'd been a long way from Gibraltar. Such a piece of information made her hungry for more.

'You're not getting off that easily.' Elise fixed him with a sharp look. 'I believe we were discussing how you know this family before Luciano arrived. What were you doing in Naples in the first place? Italy is a long way from Gibraltar.' It must be quite a story, she reasoned, to have earned a gratitude which spanned Europe. She was intrigued, too. She'd not known his interests, whatever they were, extended so far east.

Dorian shook his head. 'I doubt there's anything about those adventures you actually want to hear, Elise. Try the bread.' Dorian dipped a slice into the olive oil dribbled on a plate and held it up to her lips. 'Now, try the wine,' he coached.

Elise drank, acutely aware of Dorian's eyes on her as she swallowed. 'You will tell me nothing?' she said, meeting his gaze.

'Tonight is about the future, Elise.' A small, private smile flitted on his lips. He raised his glass. 'I would offer a toast. To the boat, Elise. May this be the first of many nights we toast its victories and milestones.'

Elise touched her glass to his, momentarily overcome with emotion. He was intoxicating like this—wine, candlelight and words that spoke the very thoughts of her own mind.

She drank to the toast and set her glass down. He'd adroitly shoved aside the personal in lieu of business, a reminder that perhaps he had bandied about his earlier words with carelessness. 'Since we have a better idea of when we'll be done, I can start contacting potential buyers. I have a list of my father's clients who may be interested. We can use the opening trip as a chance for them to join us on board.' In her mind, she was already planning that event. They would need cheese and wine and cold meats, maybe even champagne. Planning the event and writing the letters would take considerable time. She had her father's lists. But the idea of selling the yacht left an empty pit in her stomach. This was silliness. Selling the yacht was her plan, the *key* to her plan. She couldn't get sentimental now. Warm hands closed about hers, stilling her thoughts.

'Stop, Elise. Your mind is going a thousand miles an hour.' Dorian gave a soft laugh. 'It's a bit soon to think of selling the yacht. We should name it first.'

'Heavens, no! That will only make it worse.' Elise cringed. 'It's like naming a cow you have to slaughter for beef.'

'That's a very colourful way to look at it.' Dorian chuckled. Then he sobered and cocked his head to one side, studying her with those mesmerising blue eyes of his. 'Why sell it, Elise? Why not keep it? People can still purchase yachts built like it from you.'

He really could read minds. She took a sip of her wine to cover her agitation. 'Selling the yacht is part of the plan. You know it is. I need to sell the boat to raise money to make other boats and to get the word out that we are back in business.'

Dorian gave her an assessing nod. 'That may be. I think it's too soon to tell yet. There might be other options.' He slid the last of the delicious bread in her direction.

'What other options?' Elise sopped up the remaining olive oil with the slice, trying not to let her curiosity give away her interest. Could she save the boat? It would be an ideal solution and he made it sound easy. She'd learned to be wary of easy, though. There must be a catch.

Dorian shook his head. 'Not tonight, Elise. Tonight is about pleasure first and right now we have pasta to enjoy.' He gestured towards Luciano, who was bearing an enormous bowl of spaghetti with the bolognese sauce on top. Another man followed behind with a plate of Neapolitan meatballs.

'We'll never eat all of this.' Elise laughed, watching Luciano set down the bowl with effort.

'You'll never know until you try.' Dorian winked and dug in, undaunted by the size of the serving.

As they ate, he told her of Italy, the food loosening his memories and the wine his tongue, although Elise understood implicitly these stories were carefully vetted. Still, if it was all he would share of himself, she'd take it. He told her of foods and wines and cheeses, and lazy afternoons spent in hillside villas, of evenings roaming the seaside towns. 'More English will discover Italy in the near future, mark my words. But for now, it remains blissfully unanglicised.'

'*I* want to discover it,' Elise said. She meant it. The stories had transfixed her, as had the man telling them. She'd love to have listened to more, but the restaurant was emptying of patrons and still they lingered over the pasta.

Dorian nudged the last meatball in her direction. 'Yours.'

'I can't eat another bite.' Elise put a hand to her stomach.

'You'll have to eat dessert. Giovanni will be offended and his tiramisu is extraordinary. And you haven't tried the *vin santo* yet.'

Elise feigned a groan. 'I won't fit into any of my dresses.'

Dorian leaned across the table with a wicked smile. 'That's easily solved. We'll keep you out of them.'

Her blood boiled at such a thought—of Dorian slipping the gown from her shoulders, his hands on her bare skin as the silk slid to the floor. The wine, Dorian—perhaps both had made her a wanton. She wanted nothing more than what he described, she realised with shocking clarity.

'What? Nothing to say to that, *mio cuore*?' Dorian said in low tones.

'No.' She smiled. 'Absolutely nothing.'

Despite her protests, dessert was served. Luciano brought *vin santo*, a sweet wine.

'Are you trying to get me drunk?' Elise sipped from her tiny glass.

'I did promise to seduce you.'

'You said you'd think about it,' Elise teased.

'And I have. I've been thinking about it all night.' Dorian's eyes had darkened. She'd seen that look before. Her stomach did a little flip. As if on cue, Luciano appeared, violin in hand, and began to play a slow adagio, one of Vivaldi's.

Elise shot Dorian an accusatory glance. 'I feel immensely outgunned.'

Dorian shrugged. 'What can I say? The Italians are people of great passion. When they see a man with a beautiful woman, they naturally assume it is love. Will you dance with me, *mio cuore*? I wouldn't want to waste the music.'

He rose and held out his hand. She had to take it. It would be the height of insult to deny the great captain in his own territory. She could only imagine what Giovanni would do. Slowly, Elise stood, half-fearful the wine had affected her legs but there was no need for such worry. Her legs held.

Dorian drew her to him. His hand was at her back, his other hand holding hers, her own hand resting at his shoulder, but this was to be no typical waltz. He held her far closer than she'd ever been held in any ballroom.

Their thighs met, her breasts brushed the front of his jacket. Dorian began to move them. They swayed more than danced, turning in a small square instead of motions that took up an entire floor.

'Is this really a dance?' Elise murmured. But she had no complaints. It felt wonderful to be held in his arms, to be so close to another. She could smell the faint vanilla of his cologne, the cedar sachets that had protected his clothes in a chest. He was starting to smell familiar. She would forever associate these smells with Dorian Rowland. 'It seems more like an excuse to be together.'

Dorian's warm chuckle was near her ear. 'So it does. A pretty good excuse, wouldn't you agree? I like holding you, Elise.' There was no mistaking the low tones of want in his voice, or the hard thrust of his erection against her leg. She could have him, could have the pleasure again if she would accept the veiled invitation.

There needn't be any complications. Dorian wasn't the sort to deal in complications. He lived in the moment; he was offering her the same opportunity. After months of looking beyond the moment, it seemed like heaven. She'd promised herself not to make the same foolish mistakes she'd made over Robert. She was being true to that promise. What simmered between her and Dorian wasn't anything like it at all.

'Elise?' The sound of her name, low and seductive, sent a *frisson* of desire down her spine so strong she nearly trembled. 'Do you want me?'

She licked her lips. 'Yes.'

Chapter Fourteen

Elise settled herself in the carriage, her body thrumming with a delicious anticipation, her eyes on Dorian. The whole night had been leading to this. Perhaps they'd been leading to this since the first day when his body had pressed against hers in the street.

Every touch, every look, every illicit kiss, the wicked delight at Vauxhall, now served in retrospect as a prelude, arousing her curiosity until there was no other choice but to satisfy it about one question above all others: what would it be like to be with a man such as Dorian Rowland? A man who was not constrained by society or its expectations, a man who lived outside the rules? Now, miracle of all miracles, he was willing to answer that very question and she was going to let him.

Why not? There'd been no one beyond Robert Graves who'd grabbed her attentions in the nearly six years she'd been out. Her choices were limited to the staid likes of Charles Bradford and his ilk. If that were to be her lot, why not seize this chance to see what lay beyond such offerings? If there weren't any offers from the Charles Bradfords of the world, then her logic held doubly so. And, by heaven, she was going to enjoy her one night, no matter what society said. This brash, handsome man was about to be hers. For a little while at least. Dorian Rowland would never truly belong to anyone. He was too reckless, too wild, to be tamed and claimed. Perhaps she'd start with his cravat, pulling it slowly from his neck. At Vauxhall they'd been rushed by the overwhelming energy of their passion and more than partially clothed. Tonight there would be no hurry. Tonight there'd be no clothes. She was wet already, just thinking of it.

'You're staring.' Dorian's voice was husky, his eyes burning.

'I was thinking about undressing you,' she confessed, her bold words only somewhat surprising her. She'd always been forthright in other aspects of her life—why not in this aspect, too? The unknown had not stopped her before from experimenting with copper fastenings below the waterline on a boat. Tonight should be no different. She was simply trading waterlines for belt lines.

'Ah, very good.' Dorian stretched his legs across the carriage and leaned back, utterly relaxed. 'We are of the same mind, then. I had you down to your chemise. How far did you get with me?'

'Your cravat.' It hardly sounded decadent now.

'We'll have to do better than that, unless of course you planned to tie me up with it before you undressed the rest of me.' The husky gravel of his voice acted like a friction on her body, caressing it from a distance. Her nipples hardened, her core wept. It would take the merest of touches, she was certain, and she would shatter as she had in the pleasure gardens.

'Would you like that, Elise? Would you like to have me at your service, naked and bound, existing only to pleasure you? Some women, bold women like you, enjoy such games. There is no shame in it. Others like games of possession where they can be the one who is controlled. Would you like to be my captive, Elise? Shall I come to you some time as your master and bend you to my will? I like games, Elise, and I would like playing them with you.'

She bit her lip to keep from crying out. Such games did appeal to the boldness within her. Her blood was hot from the images conjured by his words. Surely she would explode now. It was all she could do not to tear her clothes off in the carriage, waiting for the decency of her bedroom be damned. She didn't want to be decent, she wanted to be ravished.

Dorian was beside her in a fluid movement she almost missed, his hand gently cupping the curve of her jaw, a delicate kiss on her lips at odds with the rather indelicate discussion. 'Trust me, you don't want our first time to be a jolting carriage, no matter how fine the squabs. It won't be much longer now, *mio cuore*. We're nearly there. How shall I come to you?'

She knew what he meant. There was still the issue

of logistics. Evans would have waited up and her maid, Anna, too. There was no question of Dorian marching up the stairs to her room or even stepping foot inside the house. She might have chosen to live scandalously, but that did not mean she could choose that for her staff. 'Use the garden gate in the back,' she whispered, trying to clear her mind of Dorian's decadent images long enough to formulate a plan. 'It will give me time to send away my maid. But how to get in?' She was having difficulty forming any rational thought.

'Don't worry, I shall be inventive.' Dorian chuckled.

'And shall I?' Elise asked. For all her bold willingness, she wasn't sure what her approach should be. They'd talked of undressing each other, but perhaps he'd prefer she already be naked, waiting for him.

The carriage drew to a halt. Dorian kissed her again, a private kiss full of promise. 'Do nothing but wait for me, *mio cuore*.'

The door opened and Dorian jumped out first, the gentleman once more as he handed her down. 'Elise,' he said quietly at her ear as she passed, a little reminder that he only looked like a gentleman. 'Don't worry. I know exactly what you want.'

Dorian eased open the garden gate. He'd told the coachman he wanted to walk and, after a decent interval to give the man enough time to make it back to the mews, Dorian had begun his own approach.

He did know what Elise wanted. She wanted the

wedding night. She might be open to the more wicked games they could play, but she didn't want them tonight simply for that reason. They were so obviously games and while they were arousing and carried their genre of lusty satisfaction, they were not *romantic*. The fantasy she wanted was more oblique. The lines between fiction and reality could blur. She could pretend for a while all was genuine. And it might be.

Dorian searched the garden for something to use as an improvised ladder: trellises, vines, even a real ladder left by an errant gardener. He wasn't set on *having* to use an improvised ladder. He was happy enough to climb a real one. Improvised ladders were highly overrated in Gothic romances. A light flared in a window. Good. Her room was at the back of the house and, glory of all glories, it had a small Juliet balcony that arched out with enough room to accommodate a single person looking out into the garden. She'd forgotten to mention that bit of luck.

Such an omission of details was hardly surprising given her state when she'd left the carriage. She wasn't alone. He'd forgotten to ask such an elementary question. This wasn't the first woman's house he'd stolen into. But if she'd been aroused to the point of shattering—and she was, he could see it in her eyes when the carriage lamp had caught them, her pupils had been dilated wide—then he was as hard as timber.

Dorian's eyes lit on the shadowy outline of a wall trellis. He could climb it and pull himself up on the balcony. He crossed the garden and gripped the lower rungs, pausing before he made the ascent, the words *and it might be* haunting him. Elise wanted him, that much was true. He didn't doubt she knew her own mind on that issue. He *did* doubt if she understood the reasons for it. Tonight, she believed she wanted him to satisfy some physical curiosity. He could give her the night *and* the satisfaction, but heaven help her if she changed her mind in the morning. He understood, even if she did not, all else that had gone before had been extended foreplay, leading them to this consummation. *Consummation.* That, too, was a wedding-night word and one his body was all too eager to engage in. Well, he could certainly engage. He would make this good for her. Tonight he would be her bridegroom. The bottom line was, he wanted Elise Sutton and he'd deal with the morning when it came. With that in mind, Dorian began to climb.

The trellis held, although there was a questionable moment or two when he reached the top. There was a bit of irony in that; the higher one climbed, the weaker the trellises seemed to get. But he didn't want to contemplate such irony when he was hanging twenty feet above a rock-hard garden not completely thawed from winter. A fall would be unpleasant at this juncture, although it would undoubtedly dampen his libido.

Dorian reached over his head and grasped the iron railings of the balcony. With a strength born of years at sea hauling cargo and nets, he levered himself up until he could hoist himself over the railing. He took a moment to catch his breath before knocking softly on the French doors. He pushed the doors open and laughed at her quickly stifled gasp. She'd been startled. 'Who else were you expecting?'

'No one, of course. I just didn't expect...' Her words fell off and she made a little gesture with her hand to fill in the gap. Words were useless to describe the sight of Dorian Rowland standing in *her* bedroom, stripping out of his coat and making himself at home.

'You actually came.' Elise gave voice to the little fear that had niggled at her in the interim since she left the carriage. Would he change his mind? 'You climbed the trellis for me.' She was amazed he'd done it. That trellis was *old*. He could have broken his neck.

'How did you expect me to get up here?' Dorian moved towards her, taking her in his arms, his touch raising delightful prickles of sensation on her skin. 'Don't tell me there's an easier way. The rung at the top of the trellis is about to go.' Not all that different from him, if the bulge in his trousers was anything to judge by. It would be unseemly to mention she'd noticed such a thing, but it was comforting to know she wasn't in this alone.

'I will tell the gardener to have it fixed immediately.'

'The gardener can wait, but I can't, not any longer,' Dorian growled, sealing her mouth with his. In that kiss, he became the sum of her world. She could taste him, smell him, feel him. His hands were in her hair, searching for the pins that held her coiffure. He released her dark waves one by one until they cascaded over her shoulders, his fingers combing through them while he kissed her face, her throat, the place at the base of her neck where her pulse beat, a veritable drummer beating out the rhythm of her passion.

'I promised to undress you, Elise,' he murmured, moving to her back, hands swiftly undoing the tiny buttons marching down her spine. A button popped and he blew out a frustrated breath. 'This gown would drive a bridegroom insane, Elise.' He nipped at her ear, the last button finally free. His hands skimmed her shoulders, warm and confident as they pushed the material down until it slithered past her hips and to the floor.

'Turn around, Elise, let me look at you.' She turned and he took her hands, drawing her arms away from her body, a gesture that made her feel deliciously exposed. His breath hitched at the sight of her and she took pleasure in the effect. She was not without her own power here.

He turned them towards the long mirror in the corner of her room and positioned her in front of him, his voice low and naughty as his hands cupped her breasts through the linen of her chemise. 'Look at yourself, Elise. See how the lamplight outlines the curves of your breasts, see how they fill my hands, see how the dark press of your nipples strain against the fabric when I touch them?'

And she did see. The sight of the woman in the mirror

in the early throes of passion was wanton and intoxicating, made even more powerful by the presence of the man behind her, coatless, his hair loose, his hands upon her, his eyes on the shadowy silhouette of her mons. 'You're a veritable Venus,' Dorian whispered huskily. 'Let me worship.'

He turned her and went to his knees, sculpting her with his hands on his way down, pressing a kiss to her navel through the linen of her chemise. Her own breath hitched as he neared her mons and then she exhaled with a tiny moan of disappointment when he passed over it. 'Later,' he vowed.

'Toes next. Now, my lady, you must sit for this next part.' He nudged her towards the bed and she went willingly. 'I'll need a moment to gather my supplies.' He rose and fetched the basin and ewer from her washstand, snatching up a small vial of lavender at the last moment.

'What are you doing?' She'd followed him with her eyes, watching every movement.

'Trust me. You'll like this and I haven't been wrong so far.' Dorian grinned. He knelt at her feet, taking her foot in his hand. 'Stockings next, I think.' He looked up at her, watching her breath catch as his hands disappeared beneath her pantalettes. He found the ribbons that held the stockings by touch, her skin warm against his hands. He rolled the silk down slowly, caressing the slim shape of her calf on first one leg, then the other until her feet were bare to him.

He pulled the stopper from the lavender vial, letting

the scent fill the room as he poured a few drops into the basin. 'Breathe deeply, Elise.' He mirrored the action with a deep breath of his own. He bathed her feet, massaging and tugging at her toes by turn. 'A woman's foot is so much more graceful than a man's and usually much better kept. Did you know the Turkish physicians believe massaging the feet opens up our body's channels for experiencing pleasure?' He gave a gentle pull. 'Especially the big toe. What do you think, Elise?'

Think? He expected her to think at a time like this? She was breathless when she answered. 'I think they were right,' she managed. His eyes darkened. Her response pleased him. She was starting to understand; her arousal was his arousal and right now he was on fire, the slim shape of her foot sliding through his hands, slick with lavender water, was an intoxicating metaphor for what his body would do with hers shortly.

'They say sucking helps, too.' His voice was nothing more than a husky rasp. He took her toe into his mouth, stroking it with his tongue until she went rigid with her want.

'Dorian, please.'

'Not yet, I promised to undress you. We are not completely there. But this will help. Raise your arms.'

Dorian pulled the chemise up over her head. Never had undressing felt so licentious, so erotic, her breasts freed at last to his full gaze. He gently pushed her back on to the bed and slid the pantalettes over her hips, his own member making its presence known where he bumped her thigh, a reminder that she wasn't the only one in need of undressing. His trousers had to go. Her hands went to his waistband, but he stalled them, covering them with his own. 'Wait. Tonight, let me.'

She turned her head to follow him as he rose, offering the simple instruction, 'Stay just like that, Elise, I want to watch you watch me.'

How could she not watch him? She was helpless to do anything else. He was mesmerising, stripping himself with fluid grace. His cravat, his shirt fell to the floor followed by his boots and finally, oh, finally his trousers, which had housed that most tantalising bulge all evening, were off. She'd thought him glorious at Vauxhall, but it was nothing compared to him fully revealed.

Elise reached for him, instinctively wanting to touch, to cup. 'Come to me, Dorian.' And he did, levering himself over her, his mouth trailing kisses between her breasts to the wet juncture between her thighs. He kissed her there inside the private folds and she burnt. Vauxhall had not been a one-time fantasy. Tonight proved the pleasure could happen again. She arched against him in invitation.

'Open your legs for me, Elise, cradle me, *mio cuore*.'

His eyes burnt with coal-like intensity, holding her gaze as he slid between her thighs. The intimacy of their bodies threatened to overwhelm her. There was a wild, primal beauty in lying like this with a man, with *him*. He'd worshipped her tonight: with wine, with food, with dance, with his touch and his kiss. He'd coaxed her body to a fevered pitch as she had coaxed his and now those fevers were about to be joined in one conflagration.

Dorian took her mouth in a hard kiss just as he positioned himself at her entrance and thrust, a deep penetrating motion. She gasped into his mouth feeling the pleasure of a man sliding home. He picked up his rhythm, her hips matching him of their own accord, the pleasure returning like a flower opening to the sun.

Elise closed her legs around him, holding him close, unwilling to let him slip away until she claimed her release. His name became a hoarse litany on her lips until speech became an impossibility. Words were replaced by sounds and still they soared into that sun and finally, at long last, when all thought had become obliterated, she burst into the radiance of that sun aware only of Dorian beside her, joining her in the piercing brilliance of the moment.

Chapter Fifteen

Three simultaneous thoughts crowded Elise's waking moments the next morning. The first was that Dorian was gone. She didn't have to open her eyes and look around to know. She could *feel* the absence of him, which was a good thing because her second thought was that it hurt too much to do anything else like open her eyes. *So* he had been trying to get her drunk her last night. She'd been right and now she had proof. Her head ached, it hurt to open her eyes, her tongue felt thick and there was a dreadful taste in her mouth.

It was impossible to even imagine doing anything about those conditions since all solutions required sitting up—a monumental feat at present. The third thought was that it was unusually bright in her room. Against her better judgement, she did hazard one open eye to see the cause of it. Better judgement had been right. That was a bad idea. Even opening one eye hurt. But she had her answer: sunlight. Not that she was opposed to sunlight. Normally, she'd have been thrilled to wake up to a sunny morning in early spring. Goodness knew they were rare enough. But it was unfortunate the London weather gods had decided *this* morning had to be one of them. Unfortunate, too, that Dorian had left the doors to her little balcony open and now the sun streamed through. However, it did bring a smile to her lips to picture Dorian climbing down from her balcony.

The trellis rung! He'd mentioned it wasn't stable last night. A moment's worry crossed her mind. Elise tried to push it away. If he'd fallen, she would have heard him. Right? She wouldn't have heard a thing, not in her current state. She should go check and see if he was lying in her garden, if only she could move.

Elise risked another peep, this time at the white porcelain clock on her bedside table, and groaned. She was going to have to find a way to move. It was after ten o'clock. The morning was more than half over. She was late for the office and there was so much to do. By the time she got to the shipyards it would be noon.

Elise gave herself fifteen more minutes of recovery before ringing for Anna. She congratulated herself on being upright when Anna arrived, bearing a tray of hot chocolate and a morning pastry. Elise thought her stomach might be able to tolerate that much. She could use the need to get to the shipyard to circumvent the breakfast that would be laid out for her downstairs. The merest thought of eggs and ham was enough to turn her stomach just now.

Anna made cheery chatter as she bustled around the room, laying out clothes. The chatter did nothing for Elise's head. At one point, Anna stooped to pick up the red dress from the floor and shake it out. Elise tried not to look overly interested in the process.

'You should have called me, miss. I would have come back up to help you undress. And look, there's a button missing. I don't know how you got out of this by yourself with all the buttons down the back. We're probably lucky you didn't lose more than one.'

'It was late. I didn't want to wake you,' Elise mumbled into her cup of hot chocolate. She could feel her face blush, her mind a riot of memories as to how that dress had come off and what had followed afterwards. It was the one thing she'd avoided thinking about so far this morning. 'I want to wear the blue gown today.' Elise attempted to focus her mind on something else. She wasn't ready to contemplate the previous evening and she certainly wasn't going to do it under Anna's watchful eye.

Anna gave her a quizzical look. 'Are you all right, miss? You look a little heated.'

'My room got a bit warm last night.' That was an understatement. 'I opened the doors,' Elise offered hastily. Perhaps Anna would believe that also explained the absence of a nightgown. 'I've got to hurry now, though. I slept too late and I've got things to take care of down at the shipyard.'

If there was anything Anna disliked, it was a rushed

toilette, and the mention of such a possibility did the trick, taking Anna's mind off any other awkward questions. Elise was feeling more herself by the time Anna finished. She looked slightly pale but, other than that, any telltale signs of her night of sin and dissipation were not in evidence.

Navigating the stairs and the short journey to the carriage proved it. Everyone greeted her as they did every morning. No one thought it odd that she eschewed breakfast, which she sometimes did, although not often. Her coachman helped her into the carriage and set off for the docks as usual.

It was something of a surprise to Elise that she didn't look different, nor did she feel different except for the headache and a bit of soreness between her legs. Such a momentous occasion should mark her in a more obvious way. But no one around her seemed to notice. For everyone else, it was another ordinary day. But it wasn't for her. Today was the first day after she'd slept with Dorian Rowland, the Scourge of Gibraltar. To her mind, this event posed a great divide: the time before and the time that would come. Nothing would ever be the same again.

Elise sank back against the squabs of the seat. What had she done? Her rationales last night had seemed solid enough, justifiable enough. This morning they seemed flimsy. Even if she lacked a logical understanding of the evening, she had enjoyed Dorian's seduction. Quite a lot. Perhaps that was what bothered her most. She *didn't* regret it. In fact, she thought she might even like it to happen again, and that was very naughty of her indeed. Of course, next time, they'd have to be more careful. They couldn't leave dresses around for Anna to find and she couldn't forget to put on a nightgown.

Elise stopped her thoughts right there. *Next time.* There wasn't supposed to be a next time and here she was planning it. She remembered very clearly one of her rationales was based on this being a one-time experience meant to satisfy curiosity. Only now there were other appetites begging to be fed. Next times were complicated. Next times implied a relationship which was absolutely not what she wanted with Dorian Rowland. *What* do *you want with him?* came the question.

I want him to build my boat, Elise answered staunchly in her mind. But her conscience wasn't appeased with a half-truth. *And?* it prompted.

And maybe I want to use him for sex. Then she added hastily to her conscience, *There's nothing wrong with that. It's not as if anyone will know and it's not as if he'll mind.* There, that should satisfy.

How wicked she'd become in such a very short time. It was only yesterday she'd decided to embrace scandal and cast off her lavender gowns. Now, here she was recovering from a hangover and contemplating taking a lover on a more permanent basis. Of course, it was all Dorian's fault. No one knew how to be wicked better than him. All she'd done was change her gowns. Dorian had done the rest.

* * *

He was still doing it, too, Elise noticed once she was settled in the office. She'd glanced out the window and spotted him immediately in the yard, swaggering around in his culottes, chest bare, tools dangling from a belt slung at his hips, blond hair pulled back with a thong. She went hot at the sight of all that masculine beauty. There was a private, heady knowledge in knowing it had been hers last night, every intimate inch of it. Oh, yes, she was definitely using him for sex. It was a most liberating thought until her bloody conscience piped up again. *If you're using him for sex, what's he using you for?*

Sex. The answer came easily and obviously to her. A man such as Dorian liked sex, even needed sex. But what if sex *wasn't* the end for him, but the means? The means to what? There was nothing she had that he could possibly want. He technically outranked her if he cared to claim it. His family was richer than hers, again if he wished to claim the connection, while her shipyard teetered on bankruptcy. He wasn't looking to marry. There was absolutely nothing she had that he didn't also have. She was overthinking it. Perhaps sex was all it was for him, too. But she couldn't get one thought out of her head—*what if it's not?* What if last night had been calculated for something more than a romp in her sheets?

Which was why, in spite of her favourable thoughts about what had transpired the previous night, the first words out of her mouth when he came up to the office were, 'Did you get me drunk on purpose, knowing full well it would make me late to work?'

Dorian stopped in the doorway, his customary grin on his lips. 'Feeling a little tap hackled, are we?' Damn him for not showing a single side effect and he'd drunk twice as much as she. With a tan like his, he wasn't even pale. It wasn't fair.

'Well, did you?'

Dorian took off his tool belt and hung it on the coat rack. 'No. I'm sorry you're feeling poorly, though. Get some coffee in you and the worst will pass. I can send a runner over to a nearby tavern and get something if you like.'

Elise shook her head. She hated coffee. 'No. My headache's nearly gone. I had hot chocolate this morning.'

'Good, then we can proceed with business. I came up because we need to talk about...'

Elise drew a breath. *Last night.* Of course he'd want to talk about it. They would need ground rules. They would need to be clear on expectations or the lack of them before this could happen again.

'The rigging.'

Elise blinked twice. *The rigging?* He wasn't going to talk about last night? She couldn't decide what was worse. Actually talking about last night or not talking about it at all. Not talking about it treated the incident as if it hadn't happened.

'Yes, the rigging,' Dorian repeated. 'I need to get the mast cut. Have you decided to go with cutter or ketch?'

'I think cutter.' Elise quickly redirected her thoughts from pleasure to business. 'I've been thinking since our earlier discussion...' *since the night you came to my house and we drank tea by the fire* '...that cutter rigging gives us the option for installing an inner forestay, which would be useful if someone was looking to sail the boat in both river currents or in the heavier weather of open water.'

'But ketch rigging is more minimalist. If there was an accident, the ketch rigging can go forwards with only the mizzen and headsail functional,' Dorian argued.

'My ships don't have accidents,' Elise countered. 'I don't build ships assuming they'll be destroyed. I build ships designed to win races first, limp home under their own power second. If you build for defeat, that's exactly what you'll get.'

Dorian smiled at her. 'Bravo, well said. Then the cutter rigging it is.' The compliment warmed her inexplicably. 'Now, is there something else you wanted to discuss?' His blue eyes were dancing and she had the distinct impression she was being teased.

'No. What gave you that idea?' Elise leaned back in the desk chair, steepling her hands and deciding to play along.

'You seemed startled that I'd come up to discuss rigging. Perhaps you anticipated us talking about something else?' Dorian crossed the room, skirting the desk and circling her chair.

'Such as?'

'Such as last night or tonight or tomorrow night?' Dorian's voice was low and private, caressing her as assuredly as a touch.

'I thought you might want to discuss the rules of our association since they seem to have changed overnight, literally.' Elise thought her reply was quite sophisticated, worldly even.

Dorian chuckled. '*You* thought *I* might want to discuss such things? Or is it you who needs to discuss it with me? I don't need rules, Elise. They ruin the spontaneity. For instance, if we had rules, I might not be able to do this.' He bent and nipped at her ear lobe, eliciting a gasp of startled delight. 'Or this.' His tongue flicked along the shell of her ear, tickling, teasing in its circuitous path.

It was positively wicked. She needed another word in her vocabulary. With Dorian, wicked was the new normal. He proved it by sliding to his knees in front her.

'Dorian, what are you doing?' Elise gave an undignified yelp at the feel of his hands running up her legs. 'Someone could walk in.'

'And see you sitting behind the desk? Fancy that. I'm sure no one *sits* behind their desk at work.' His thumbs were at the apex of her thighs, one on each side of her mound, stroking, teasing. 'They won't see me. The desk blocks all view of anyone who might be underneath it.

Of course, they might think it odd you find ledgers so very exciting.' His head had joined his hands beneath her skirts, up her legs. He blew against her. 'It's up to you, Elise. What will an intruder see? A woman engrossed in her work or her pleasure?'

She'd always thought of herself as a person of good self-discipline, but the moment Dorian's tongue flicked along the furrow of her mons, she was lost. There was no doubt anyone who happened into the office would see a woman claiming her pleasure. Dorian's tongue moved up to lick across her pearl, teasing every last sensation from the little nub until Elise was entirely lost, her hands gripping the arms of the chair, her bottom sliding down ever further in the seat as Dorian conjured up a pleasure so intense she was helpless against it. Perhaps it was the risk of discovery; perhaps it was the host of physical sensations assailing her all at once. The arms of the chair were no help.

Her hands slid into Dorian's hair, anchoring and urging, her hands saying what she could not, words having escaped her abilities. *Hurry, hurry, take me there to the place where I will shatter.* There was fierceness now in his seduction. Dorian's breath came rapid between her legs, his own body trembling. His hands cupped her buttocks, sandwiching her between his hands and his mouth most intimately, and then it came, wresting from her a cry of elation while Dorian's head slumped against her thigh in satisfaction.

'Pleasure,' Elise breathed. 'They would see pleasure,

but not much else considering how far I've slid in the chair.' Dorian chuckled contentedly, the rumble of his laughter muffled against her leg.

'Why are you doing this, Dorian?' She idly combed through his hair with her fingers, savouring the quietness of the moments that followed such an intense climax.

'Doing what?' Dorian murmured.

'Seducing me. Don't deny it.' She wished there was a cot in the office. She was feeling rather drowsy.

'I wasn't aware you were opposed to it.'

'I'm not. I just want to know why.'

Dorian lifted his head. 'I slept with you, Elise, because you're a desirable woman and, if my actions haven't made it clear, I'd like to do so again in the very near future.' A grin took his face. 'And you? Why are you seducing me?'

Elise smiled and gave him a taste of his own. 'If my actions haven't made it clear, I am using you for sex.'

Chapter Sixteen

What was he doing? Dorian checked his cravat one last time in the little cracked mirror he'd hung over his improvised washstand of two stacked crates. A white ewer and tin basin stood atop the structure, the ewer sporting a hairline fracture of its own running down the side. It wasn't enough to make the pitcher leak, but it was enough to claim a matched set—cracked ewer, cracked mirror, he liked to joke.

He could add himself to the set these days. He was cracked in the head the way he was mooning after Elise Sutton. He was Dorian Rowland, he didn't chase after any skirt. *They* chased after him. But here he was, digging out one of his three good outfits from his trunk, tying a cravat and haring off for supper with Elise.

Dissatisfied with his knot, Dorian yanked on his cravat and tried again. He never should have started calling her that. He should have stuck to Princess. He could hardly fault himself for pushing for first names. Any master of seduction knew using a first name early and often was a key component in convincing a woman of his genuine interest. Well, he'd certainly succeeded there. He'd seduced her and himself in the process.

What had started out as a game to position himself for the boat was rapidly turning into something more. He liked the haughty princess. He liked teasing her with his outrageous comments; liked coaxing her ever so subtly to push the boundaries of convention, and goodness knew he liked what they'd done today in the office. Her pleasure had been contagious and he'd been caught up in it as well.

Dorian grimaced at the reflection of his cravat. It wasn't perfect, but it would have to do. It had been a long time since he'd cared about the state of his cravat and even longer since he'd had a valet to tie it for him. While he'd been in the Mediterranean, he'd lived aboard his ship and done for himself, careful not to put himself above his men. This was just one more reminder that he had to caution himself when it came to Elise Sutton.

She had him caring about things that hadn't mattered, *wanting* things that hadn't mattered for quite a while. Three outfits were plenty. He'd gone months at a time without even needing *one* of them. But this evening when he'd gone to dress, part of him wished there was at least a different waistcoat to put on, one she hadn't seen before. He'd worn each of his outfits already: the one to call at her house that evening they'd drunk tea, the other when he'd called the afternoon he'd sent Charles Bradford on his way and the last to dinner at Giovanni's. Going to Giovanni's had been risky. Giovanni knew about him, could have spilled the entire sordid truth to Elise. Giovanni wouldn't have meant any harm. To Giovanni, he was a hero. But Elise would not see the heroics in the things he'd done. Why should she when his own father certainly did not?

Remember the plan, Dorian told himself, shutting the door to the shed behind him and whistling for Drago, who was turning out to be quite the guard dog. He was to convince Elise not to sell the boat. Then he was to convince Elise to sell or give the boat to him on generous terms. He'd pay her for it, he just didn't have the money upfront, something she could relate to.

Dorian stopped in the yard to rub Drago's head and stare up at the boat. It was really coming along. It would be every bit as magnificent as he'd imagined, perfect for running cargos in the Mediterranean, legal or otherwise. Of course, there was more money in 'otherwise'.

'Stay, guard the boat,' he told Drago. The yacht had to be completed for his plans to move forwards. If the boat were destroyed, his seduction would have been for naught. Well, not for naught, he'd rather enjoyed it. It wasn't as if it had been unpleasant work, or work at all, which was the problem. Genuinely liking Elise hadn't been part of the plan, but it was now. Although, she might not like him if he kept her waiting. She'd invited him to dinner and he was running late. The carriage had probably been outside already for a good ten minutes.

Dorian secured the gate and settled into the carriage.

He felt in his coat pocket to assure himself it was still there, a small gift for Elise. He might be the Scourge of Gibraltar, but he had enough breeding to know a man didn't show up for dinner empty-handed. Manners seduced just as surely as kisses.

His previous visits had been different. He'd been strictly an employee then, reporting on business. The gift was small, something from his travels, but it was all he had to offer. He was currently not a rich man, although once he could have dazzled her with silks and spices and jewels beyond compare. *And arms. Don't forget the arms.* A gun wasn't exactly an appropriate hostess gift. Then he remembered the pistol she'd wielded the first day they met. It had been bulky and unwieldy in her hands, too heavy for her. Maybe Elise *would* like a gun, a lady's pistol perhaps with a pearled handle, one that could fit in a reticule.

A lamp glowing through the lace curtains welcomed him when he alighted. Everything was as it should be, a quiet town house preparing for a quiet evening. No one could argue anything improper, Dorian thought as he climbed the stairs. There were other carriages in the street, taking people to evening entertainments. Not nearly as many carriages as there would be in a few weeks when the Season started. Then, this quiet square would be thronged. A man sat across the street, reading a newspaper on a bench near the key park.

If he hadn't been so absorbed in the mental exercise

of picking out a gun for Elise, he might have noted how odd it was to be reading the newspaper on a park bench this time of night when the light was fading. As it was, Dorian didn't think much of it, his thoughts occupied with other things.

Elise was waiting for him in the drawing room, looking particularly lovely in a gown of deep turquoise, her hair drawn up high on her head with a few tendrils left to curl temptingly at her neck.

'Dorian, welcome.' She came to him with outstretched hands, the greeting warm and yet formal, just the right tone to strike in front of the servants, he thought, taking those hands and bending in to kiss her cheek, the kind of greeting close friends or family relations might exchange. What a hostess she would make, sitting at the head of some nobleman's table— or his table in the Gibraltar villa. What was he thinking? He couldn't ask her to sit at his table. He'd seduced her, but he couldn't keep her. It wasn't in the plan. This sudden change of feeling wasn't in the plan, either, and he didn't quite understand where it had come from, only that it was here. Elise Sutton had definitely become more than a physical interest.

Her eyes were alight with excitement. He knew instantly she had news, *good* news. 'Something has happened since I saw you this afternoon,' Dorian remarked. It must have been good because she was definitely recovered from any lingering effects of her hangover.

'Yes, and there's just enough time to tell you before

dinner.' Elise went over to the console table against the wall and opened a drawer, taking out a paper. 'No machetes. My drawers aren't nearly as exciting as yours.'

Dorian grinned. 'Your drawers were plenty exciting this afternoon, as I recall.'

'And here I thought you were going to be on your best behaviour.' Elise handed him the paper, but not before the slightest hint of a blush stained her cheeks.

'What's the fun in that?' Dorian took the paper and scanned it, noting the seal of the Royal Thames Yacht Club at the top and the signature of the club president, Commodore William Harrison. 'You have membership? *You?*' He hadn't wanted to bring the subject up with her before, but if she meant to keep racing with them, she'd need membership with her father gone.

'I do.' She looked so pleased with herself, so lovely and smug he didn't want to bring her down. Yet it was so extraordinary and unlikely that they'd award membership to a female.

'How did you do it, Elise?'

'I simply signed my brother's name to the application and wrote a letter asking that the membership which my father had held be continued.'

Dorian smiled. His princess was inventive. 'Was there a reason William couldn't do it himself?'

'He's away at Oxford, it would take too much time to bother him.' She turned away to put the letter back in the drawer, but he sensed she was far more uncomfortable with that answer than she had been sharing her deception.

Dorian went to her, his hands at her arms. 'Tell me, Elise, will William be surprised to hear he's now a member of the Royal Yacht Club?'

'It hardly matters. The membership is paid and the deed is done. There's nothing William can do except cause unnecessary awkwardness.' She turned to face him, her arms twining about his neck, lips parted in invitation. 'I have champagne chilling with dinner to celebrate.'

'Then we shall celebrate.' But Dorian recognised her efforts for what they were—a distraction, a very lovely one, a very inviting one. She could not have made it plainer that she didn't want to talk about her brother. Interesting. He'd been under the impression they were close. But in his experience, one did not look gift horses in the mouth, one kissed them, except when stiff butlers might walk in at any moment to announce dinner. He'd wait and hope for better things when those butlers weren't around.

Fortunately, the butler and footmen made themselves scarce after laying the meal. Elise had arranged for the meal to be served *en famille* and had kept the fare simple: a roast, baby potatoes and carrots and fresh bread along with the promised champagne and a tray of cheeses and fruit at the ready, waiting on the sideboard for dessert.

The table had been thoughtfully prepared, too: two

chairs situated close to one another, two single candles
in silver holders instead of a massive, imposing cande-
labra. It was a daringly intimate setting. It made Dorian
wonder if perhaps tonight she meant to seduce him. A
most arousing thought indeed.

'I told the servants we didn't need to stand on ceremony tonight,' Elise explained, delightfully flustered
for a moment.

'That's all right,' Dorian whispered huskily at her ear,
his hand light but proprietary at her back as he ushered
her to her seat. 'It's much more fun to sit on it.'

What a terribly bold comment. Elise wished she had
some witty comeback but she came up with nothing
but a pointed look that said she understood the naughty
nuances. As far as she was concerned, he could sit on
it, lay on it, jump on it, she didn't care which as long as
they didn't talk about William.

Evans poured champagne before retreating with the
rest of the staff. Elise took a sip to cover her nerves.
Ice-cold champagne was her absolute favourite, one
of the few things she'd enjoyed about her Seasons in
London. Dorian had guessed correctly that William
would not approve. Her brother wasn't opposed to the
yacht club, he just wouldn't see the need for it, not when
he felt they should be closing the shipyard and moving on.

But Dorian wasn't as compelled to leave the subject
alone. 'How is William doing with his studies?'

'He's doing fine. He loves it.' There'd only been the two letters since he'd left, but she justified their scarcity knowing he was busy. 'He doesn't have much time to write once he's immersed in his studies.'

Dorian laughed. 'Oxford must have changed since my time. Are you sure it's his studies he's "immersed" in and not some pretty tavern wench?'

Elise fixed him with a disapproving stare. She might be at odds with William over the shipyard, but he was her brother. 'I am sure. Not everyone goes to Oxford to carouse.' Still, she was a little surprised he'd gone to Oxford at all. He didn't seem the university type. Libraries and lecture halls seemed far too confining for the likes of Dorian Rowland.

'Everyone gets the education they need at Oxford, books or otherwise,' Dorian put in. 'There's no question of that.'

Elise leaned forwards. 'What kind of education did you get, Dorian?'

'Otherwise.' Dorian winked and she laughed. 'And it's served me well in my line of work.'

'Which is?'

'Building ships, sailing ships,' Dorian answered easily between bites of the meat.

'That's all? Just building and sailing ships? That's hardly scandalous.' It wasn't nearly scandalous enough to be so completely cast out of society. The candlelight was doing fabulous things to his hair, burnishing and shadowing all those golden hues.

'It is if you're the son of the Duke of Ashdon. Dukes' sons don't deal in trade or carpentry,' Dorian answered calmly.

'But you were a captain of your own ship. Surely that's enough to garner respectability and it's not as if you are the heir. Your father should have been glad you had turned your hand to something.' Elise wasn't going to let go of this chance to learn more about the socially exiled Dorian Rowland.

'Is reconciliation really so out of the question?' she asked softly. Her family had been everything to her and she missed it dreadfully now that it had fallen apart, everyone scattered to their own corners, living their own lives.

Dorian drained his glass. 'Yes. And we'll leave it at that. This is supposed to be a celebration.' He refilled their glasses. 'To the Royal Thames Yacht Club and the hopes of next season.'

And to the hopes they wouldn't mind too terribly much once they realised William had no intention of showing up at any of the races, Elise added silently. She was through the first hurdle. She had the membership. It was time for the second. She drew a deep breath. 'There's something else I hope we can celebrate tonight as well.'

Dorian's eyes glittered wickedly with indecent thoughts that made her shiver with anticipation. 'I am sure there is.'

Best to come straight out with it. 'I want you to captain the yacht on the opening trip.' She'd made her decision once word had come of her membership application.

'Elise, do you know what you're asking?' Something clouded the glitter of his gaze.

'Yes, I am asking you to stay beyond your contract. We'd agreed you could go once the boat was done, but now I need you to stay. It's not for much longer than originally planned,' Elise argued gently. She really did need him to stay. It made sense. He knew the boat, every last timber of it. He'd be the only one to have taken it for a trial. He had no pending engagements to be elsewhere that she knew of. He'd mentioned nothing other than the need to pay back Halsey for the confiscated cargo.

'Elise, it's more than that.' Dorian shook his head, looking distinctly uncomfortable for the first time in their acquaintance. 'You're asking me to enter into society. Society and I parted ways a long time ago.'

'Perhaps it's time to re-enter,' she answered staunchly. 'What do you have to lose? If they've already rejected you for good, then nothing changes. But if they were willing to give you another chance, opportunities might open up.' She felt a bit dishonest here. She was hoping those opportunities might be with her shipyard. Perhaps he could be persuaded to stay on as master builder.

He reached for her hands, covering them with his grip, warm and firm. 'Elise, I'm not worried for me. I don't care what they think of me now or ever. I've made my choices. I am worried for you. Don't you see what association with me could do to you? All your plans will be for naught.'

'People know you're here already.' Something tugged at her heart to hear him speak so disparagingly of himself. 'Charles knows, and who knows who else knows by now that you're working at the shipyard?'

'A select group of yachters probably do know,' Dorian agreed. 'That's not the same as the whole of society knowing. It's also not the same as flaunting it in their faces. The yachting community might tolerate me being around behind the scenes, but to put me up on your deck in the role of captain would be to rub their noses in it. You need someone who will be good for business.'

Elise cocked her head to one side, considering. '*You* will be good for business. I am banking on you and all your notoriety, Dorian, and of course a fast ship pays for all. No one will care if you'd stolen the Crown Jewels when the boat is as fine as ours.' She'd known it would be a hard sell. She shouldn't be surprised that he was proving so resistant. She *was* surprised she felt so very desperate inside when she'd had his measure all along.

Elise eyed the remaining champagne, just a bit in the bottle, but enough for what she intended. 'It seems like you could do with a little more persuading. Let's see what we can do about that.'

She knelt before him, hands at the fastenings of his trousers, pleased to note that he was rising for her already, his manhood roused at her first touch. Pleased, too, that he understood this was a game of sorts. She wanted to do this for him. It was as arousing to her to touch him, to take him like this, as it was for him to be taken. This was no literal act of whoring herself to get what she wanted.

Elise opened his trousers and took him in her hand, feeling the pulsing heat of him. 'You are so big.'

Dorian chuckled, sliding down in his chair to better position himself for her. 'That's what every man wants to hear, Princess.'

'I doubt every man is as well endowed,' Elise said coyly, starting to move her hand up and down his shaft, smoothing the bead of moisture from his tip over the entirety of his length. She reached for the bottle of champagne and glanced up naughtily at him while she poured the remnants over his length.

'That's a bit cold.' Dorian jumped a bit at the contact. She felt a moment's guilt.

'I know, but my mouth isn't.' She closed her lips over the head of his shaft, taking in the salt of him and the dry sweetness of the champagne all at once. It was a heady ambrosia made all the more delicious when mixed with Dorian's moans of approval. She worked him with her mouth, sucking and licking until she was sure all his reservations had deserted him.

He was pulsing and tense, she could feel the muscles of his thighs quivering with the effort to hold back, his hands clenching the sides of his chair, his back arching his body up to her. That's when everything shattered.

Literally shattered.

Her head flew up from between Dorian's legs and Dorian exploded from the chair with lightning speed. He raced towards the drawing room. She was steps behind, skittering to a stop at the sight of broken glass on the floor and flames from the destroyed lamp racing up the heavy curtains.

Oh, lord, her house was on fire.

Chapter Seventeen

Elise grabbed a vase, the first item she laid eyes on with any water in it, and doused the curtains with a splash, petals and all, to little effect. Dorian seized a section of the curtains that hadn't caught fire and yanked hard, bringing down the *portières* with a crash. 'Watch your skirts!'

Elise backed away just in time to avoid catching fire herself while Dorian smothered the flames with great stomps from his boots. The room filled with her staff, alerted to trouble by the commotion and already carrying buckets. Dorian shouted orders and the flames began to diminish. They were gaining on it. Five minutes later, they conquered it. She wasn't going to lose the house, but what a mess!

There was a jagged hole in the broken window, glass shards scattered on the floor and the curtains obviously beyond repair. Smoke and flames had damaged the hard woods where the curtains had landed. Dorian's decision had likely saved the house. If the flames had gone up the curtains to the ceiling, nothing could have stopped the fire from spreading. Smoke and water stained the furniture.

Elise began to make mental notes. Furniture could be cleaned and repaired, she'd need new curtains, and a carpenter to repair the floor and she'd need a new window. That would be the first priority. She could imagine what the house looked like from the street.

The neighbours! An involuntary gasp escaped her and she covered her mouth with her hand as if to try to hold it in. What must they think? With a shattered front window, there was no disguising the disaster. 'There will be no hiding this,' Elise mused out loud. Her eyes met Dorian's across the room where he stood by the broken window. 'Is there a crowd? Is it very bad?' she asked, hoping for the best.

Dorian's response confirmed the worst. 'Shall I get rid of them for you?' He didn't wait for an answer. He strode to the door and stepped outside. She could hear his commanding tones carrying down to the street. 'We're all fine here, just a rock that was kicked up by a passing carriage. You can go about your evenings. Thank you for your concern.'

'They're gone.' Dorian smiled when he returned inside, looking all the more handsome for the mess he sported. His hair was loose, his shirt mostly untucked from the waistband of his trousers—that was her fault, not the fire's.

Elise couldn't decide what would cause the worst

scandal tomorrow: the fire or the fact that her neighbours would know without equivocation a man had been with her in the town house when it had occurred. Sensible neighbours would be thankful she hadn't been alone. Without Dorian, the house and perhaps theirs would have been lost. But Mayfair neighbours weren't sensible. They'd see only the breach of protocol in Dorian's presence instead of the luck.

'Elise, you're pale. Come with me. Evans can handle things from here for tonight. Mary will send a tea tray.' Dorian took her arm and she let him lead her away to a small sitting room at the back of the house. Now that the crisis had passed, she was starting to shake. A mixture of fear and anger swept through her. She was more than glad to turn the situation over to Dorian for the moment. She let him take the tea tray from Mary. She let him put a warm tea cup in her hands while she tried to formulate a coherent thought.

'Why would someone do this?' she said at last, the heat of the tea cup rallying her senses.

'You know who and you know why,' Dorian chided gently, fixing his own cup. 'What happened tonight is a terrible thing, but you can hardly be surprised. We've been waiting for the other shoe to fall since Tyne's thugs visited the shipyard, since the fuse was lit to ignite the tar barrels. Now it has.'

He paused and Elise waited for him to say the rest. 'I told you the day of the fuse fire we were lucky. The intent had been to scare us, not really to ignite the barrels. Tonight was about more than scaring us. Tyne is getting desperate. He wants this situation resolved soon.'

'I won't give him my boat. It would be fairly hard to anyway since he hasn't made an offer and technically I don't know it's him behind all this madness.'

'He agrees with you,' Dorian said solemnly. 'At this point he knows you won't give over the boat, not as long as you live. If you were dead, it might be an easier matter. There'd be no one left who cared what became of the boat.'

She looked up from her cup. 'No one except you.' It was true. William would gladly be rid of it and her mother had already washed her hands of it.

'There would be me. I'd rather it didn't come down to that, though.' Dorian took her hand. 'I want to go after Tyne. I want to confront him and put an end to this.'

Elise shook her head. She knew what he meant. 'I won't sanction murder over a boat, Dorian.'

'Think of it as self-defence. As long as he lives, you are not safe.'

'As long as I have something he wants, I'm not safe,' Elise amended. 'As soon as I sell the boat, I'm no longer of interest to him.' It would be imperative now to go forwards with plans to sell the yacht. The brief fantasy Dorian had invoked over wine and pasta of keeping the boat would come to an end out of vital necessity. There could no longer be consideration of any other plan.

'Don't be a fool, Elise. Tyne can live on revenge alone. Don't think for a moment he'll forgive you for thwarting him. It may not be as easy as you think to sell the yacht. Yachtsmen and sailors are a superstitious lot. If Tyne were to spread rumours about the boat, buyers would be thin on the ground.'

'Are you saying it's hopeless?' Elise challenged. 'I'm damned if I do and damned if I don't? I didn't take you for a fatalist, Dorian.'

She made to rise, but Dorian pulled her down. 'Not a fatalist, Elise, a realist. You don't know him like I do.'

'I would if you'd just tell me,' Elise snapped. Anger had overcome her fear. How had her life become so complicated that she was in her mother's drawing room, alone with a man and discussing the murder of another man who wanted her boat as if it were a casual item on a meeting agenda? 'You tell me nothing of yourself, nothing of our apparent common enemy and you expect me to take all my direction blindly from you. That has never been my way and it won't ever be my way no matter how good in bed you are.'

A horrid thought struck her. She rose, shaking off Dorian's hand. 'Is that what all this seduction has been about? Gaining my blind compliance? I suppose next you'll be offering to take the boat off my hands as a favour to lead Tyne away from me while satisfying some hidden agenda of yours!'

'You dare to talk about agendas and using people?' Dorian rose, too, eyes flashing. She'd pushed him too far in her own anger. 'I'm not the one who only an hour ago was using all of her seductive prowess to convince me to captain her boat. If anyone has been underhanded, it has been you! You're the one who has applied for yacht club membership by forging your brother's signature on the application. I've never been other than what I seem.' He held his arms wide in a gesture of transparency. 'What you see is what you get with me, Princess.'

'I did what I had to do,' Elise fired back. Dorian's eyes were blue coals of rage. He hadn't missed the implication that perhaps he'd been used along the way. Well, let him infer what he liked.

'Are you always that free with your favours, then?'

But not that. How could Dorian think such a thing? How could he *say* it? Her hand came up of its own volition, slapping him hard across the face, the sound of it a loud and unmistakable clap of skin on skin. 'Get out. I don't want to see you until the yacht is done. For both of our sakes, I hope you can finish ahead of schedule.'

'I can finish, Princess,' Dorian said with nasty innuendo. 'I will expect to be paid for my services.' Looking straight past her, he strode out of the room, shoulders square, head up as if he had nothing to be ashamed of.

And maybe he didn't except for those last words. Elise sank to the sofa, her heart hammering with the emotion of the quarrel. How had things become unravelled so fast? She hadn't meant to pick a fight with him. But the dam had burst and all the doubt had come rushing out, probably because the dam hadn't been well built in the first place. Perhaps this was what happened when one slept with a man one didn't really know and then tried to convince oneself the feelings were genuine. The truth was he'd been very blatant about not wanting to discuss his past. He'd been just as blatant about that as he'd been about not wanting to discuss their one night. What had he said? *No rules?* It couldn't get much clearer than that.

Tears started to burn in her eyes. She covered her face with her hands. She'd been so very foolish! It wasn't just sleeping with Dorian that had been foolish. It was everything else: thinking that what they'd done would mean something; that she could outwit the villainous Damien Tyne; that she could build this boat and salvage the business. All she had to show for her efforts was a broken window, a fire-damaged town house and a madman after her. And what had she done? She'd sent away the one man who could help her find her way out of this mess. Oh, *foolish* didn't begin to cover it.

She needed to apologise. But she'd be damned if she was going to chase after Dorian Rowland in the dark to do it. She didn't have much left after tonight, but she had her pride.

Dorian stopped at the corner. He leaned against the lamp post, catching his breath. He should walk back in there and apologise. He'd said rough words to her, words a decent man didn't say to a decent woman. It was further proof he wasn't a decent man. But dammit, a man had his pride if nothing else. She'd accused him of seducing her for ulterior purposes. *She's not far from the truth and you know it*. But it wasn't like that, not when it had come down to it. He'd slept with her because he'd wanted to, because he'd desired her. He still desired her.

Tonight was supposed to have ended differently. The necklace in his pocket was a sad reminder of those intentions. It still could, if he'd just go back. And what? Beg? Grovel? Elise had been angry. He'd seen her temper on full display, her wit sharp, her tongue cutting. Maybe it was better this way. Yes, it was *definitely* better this way.

Dorian began to walk. First down one street, then another, and another until he was too far away to conveniently turn back, his mind rolling out all the reasons he was right to have left. He would not beg. He could apologise for his words, but not his choices, and that would not be enough for Elise. He could say he was sorry for his secrets, but he would not tell them. She would truly despise him if she knew the things he'd done. The motives behind them would not be enough to clear him in her conscience.

What was the point anyway? Confessing all to Elise wouldn't solve anything. It wouldn't protect her from Tyne, it wouldn't change the nature of their relationship—which was temporary. He couldn't keep a woman like Elise. She'd wanted to talk about their relationship this afternoon. That should have scared him. His gut usually twisted at the mere mention. Talking about relationships meant admitting to having them—the very first step on a slippery slope to commitment. But this afternoon, the familiar twist hadn't been there. Still, he'd diverted the discussion because he could offer her none of the reassurances women looked for.

What he could do, though, was make enquiries about Tyne, help her resolve the doubts about her father's death and he could finish her boat. Then he could give her up. He could walk away as if she were just another woman he'd slept with. Only she wasn't. The realisation was so strong, struck so deeply, Dorian had to stop walking and steady himself. How had that happened? She had him dressing up and climbing unstable trellises. She had him thinking about captaining her yacht and re-entering society, something he'd sworn never to do, and all for a pretty face. Oh, no, she wasn't just a pretty face. That was how it had happened. He'd fallen for her intelligence, her passion, her boldness. The reasons hardly mattered. What did was that he'd *fallen*

'*Get a grip on yourself, Rowland,*' he muttered under his breath. '*Build the boat and walk away. She's just a woman you can't have.*' But that didn't solve anything because he never walked away from a challenge.

Heaven help him. He wanted Elise Sutton. He might even love her.

Heaven help her when he was finished with her. He wanted Elise Sutton with a vengeance. Damien Tyne paced the small, crude office he kept on the Wapping docks. It was not nearly as nice as Blackwell and the East India set-up or as well located. He and Maxwell had guessed poorly and invested unwisely, while Richard Sutton had done the opposite. Sutton had leased the more-expensive site at Blackwell while he and Maxwell Hart had bet on the cut-through to be built between Limehouse and Wapping, joining the docks directly to the Pool of London. The cut had never materialised, although it had been talked about a great deal over the last twenty years.

It only fed his vengeance to know Rowland was doing more than building the boat. His man had reported Rowland's presence at the town house after hours on several occasions, the latest being four nights ago. Rowland had come for dinner, all dressed up and riding in the Sutton carriage.

Rowland's ability to land in the most lucrative of beds never ceased to amaze him. He'd taken Rowland's ship, effectively running Rowland out of business for the nasty turn of events over the incident with the pasha. It should have broken Rowland. Without a ship, Rowland couldn't run his cargos and he'd be too dangerous to be hired by another. No decent businessman would risk his ship being hunted down simply because Rowland was at the helm. Even with all that against him, Rowland had thrived. The lucky bastard was now privy to the elite innovations of Richard Sutton's last yacht, bedding the lovely Elise and living the good life without expending a pound of his own money.

Tyne pulled out his pocket watch and flipped it open. It was nearly eleven in the morning. Miss Sutton should be receiving Maxwell's offer right about now. Perhaps after the fire four nights ago, the tide would begin to turn in his favour. Elise should be frightened. This game was serious and, without meaning to, Dorian would have helped it along. If he cared a whit for Elise Sutton, he would have cautioned her that this was for real. That he, Tyne, would stop at nothing. What would she think about Maxwell's offer? Would she look at it with relief or with suspicion?

He could picture her slitting open the envelope, her green eyes scanning the letter, the pulse at the base of her neck leaping in surprise, shock or excitement. He could picture her doing other things, too. Unfortunately, she'd been doing those things with Dorian Rowland. But very soon, she would be doing those things with him, for him and he would have his revenge on them both at last.

Chapter Eighteen

Elise studied the sheaf of documents in her hand, unsure what to make of them. They contained an offer for the shipyard, now of all times. Charles stood at the French doors leading out to the rose garden, patiently letting her peruse the paperwork. He'd been the harbinger of this latest development, arriving with the papers shortly after eleven that morning and turned out in his daytime best.

She had not seen him since the day Dorian had all but driven him out, but Charles didn't seem to hold that against her. He was the epitome of concern, exclaiming over the fire damage and worried for her safety. He said he'd been away on some business for his father in Southampton. She hoped that was the truth. She didn't want Dorian to have alienated him. She might not be head-over-heels in love with Charles Bradford, but her friends were few and far between these days. It made her question the offer all the more. Should she view it with suspicion or serendipity? Beyond the sitting room she'd taken over as her office at the back of the house, repairs continued on the town house—repairs that strained her budget. This offer would solve that financial need and more.

Elise's eyes returned to the final number at the bottom of the last page. With that kind of money, she could easily pay Dorian and his crew for their work on the yacht and walk away with a sum that would keep her and her family comfortably. For her part, she would not need to worry about relying on her mother or brother for funds. She could continue to live in the style to which she'd been raised and maintain her independence.

To do what? What would she use that independence for? Without a shipyard, there'd be no point in designing yachts that would never be built. She knew what her brother would say and her mother, too.

'It's a good deal, Elise. It's more money than the investors offered to pay.' Charles turned from the doors, ready to engage in persuasive conversation.

'Is that what you are to convince me of?' Elise gave him a thin smile. She understood the role Charles was sent to play. He was the messenger, chosen carefully to use his leverage as her friend to bring back an affirmative decision to this business man, Maxwell Hart.

'Anyone would tell you the same,' Charles replied. 'I'm not here to mislead you, but to help you if you have questions and to offer my opinion if you ask for it.'

That was a more pliable, gentler side of Charles, Elise noted. Usually, he was very rigid with his black-and-white views on life. Her own smile softened in answer. 'I appreciate that, Charles. I do have questions. Who is Maxwell Hart and how do you know him? I don't recall him from my father's associations.'

'My father knows him through some shipping arrangements. He's wealthy. As an importer, Hart knows the value in the shipyard's position. He has a warehouse and a boat works over in Wapping, but he's looking to move to a better location and your location is the best there is, as you well know.'

Charles fiddled with a porcelain figurine on the fireplace mantel. 'Personally, I think he's given up hope that a cut-through will ever be built at Wapping.'

Elise could understand that. The cut-through had never materialised and the difference between the more tedious waterways at Wapping and the efficiencies of the East and West India docks with their modern developments was quite marked. 'The offer seems straightforward,' Elise began, unwilling to share everything that had occurred lately, 'but it comes at a most interesting time.'

Interesting was a delicate way of putting things. It came at a time when a dangerous man was attempting to damage the yard and steal her boat. It would be all too easy to sell out and pass Damien Tyne on to the new owner. But selling out came with a price, too. She suspected the offer was so high because of the yacht. The documents clearly stated the yacht was to remain with the yard.

'It seems to me that it comes at a most opportune time,' Charles corrected. He made a gesture towards the door. It stood half-open, not entirely blocking out the sounds of repairs being done in the front room. 'You've had a run of bad luck these last months, Elise. The tide could be starting to turn in your favour.'

'That's just it, Charles. Perhaps this seems too perfect, too suspicious.'

Charles looked affronted. 'Are you implying Maxwell Hart is attempting to force you out through coercion? Do you really think a man willing to pay such a sum would resort to throwing rocks through your windows or lighting the very shipyard he wants on fire?' He shook his head. 'I don't see the logic.'

Put that way, she didn't see the logic, either. Charles was right. It made no sense to think this man would ruin the property he wanted to acquire. It made even less sense when she knew, as Charles did not, that Damien Tyne was behind the attacks. Unless Dorian had been wrong all along about Tyne and about Tyne's motives.

It had occurred to her in the days since her quarrel with Dorian that she'd accepted his explanations at face value. Perhaps he'd lied about the thugs' reasons for breaking into the shipyard. Perhaps they hadn't been there looking at her yacht, but had come for him. She'd mentioned as much the night he'd first told her of the break-in.

'It's a difficult decision to walk away from all I know and everything my father worked for,' Elise said slowly, trying to articulate the hollowness that filled her at the thought. She didn't expect Charles to understand.

Charles took the seat across from her, an earnest look on his face. 'Think of it this way, Elise. You can walk away now and make a *lot* of money, or you can wait until the last moment and be politely forced out when the shipyard can no longer sustain itself. If so, you'll end up with nothing except for the yacht and that's *if* you can find a buyer in time. Hart is willing to pay you for the shipyard, the boat and the contents of the shipyard if you walk away now.' Charles loved numbers. His whole face lit up when he talked about projected profits.

There was sense in that. The offer was tempting. She saw the profit in it. It was why she hadn't immediately discarded the option. Her dream of building her father's last boat and selling it had been financially motivated. She'd hoped to use the money to keep the boat works open for herself. If she sold to Hart, she wouldn't *need* the company to support herself.

Then Dorian had come along and filled her head with the idea of keeping the boat at a time when she'd been susceptible to such a concept. After seeing the hull completed, it was harder to imagine letting someone else take the boat. But Dorian had filled her head with a lot of other unworthy notions, too, and in the end it hadn't got her anything but heartache and disappointment. Charles had real numbers and results to support his position.

'You may tell Mr Hart that I will think about it.' Elise

clenched her hands in her lap, willing herself to speak the words before she could change her mind. 'I will let him know in a couple of days.'

Charles nodded neutrally. 'He will be pleased to know you are considering it. May I give you something else to consider? Perhaps something of a more personal nature? It cannot have escaped your notice, my dear Elise, that I have held you in great esteem for some time now and that esteem has grown into affection.'

Oh, lord, he was going to propose. Elise felt her stomach tighten into a ball. He was outlining his prospects which, she thought cynically, would look a lot better once he calculated in her profit from the shipyard. 'I had wanted to wait a decent interval, Elise, but I think now is the better time,' Charles went on. 'After all this to-do with Rowland and the shipyard, I think the sooner we can marry the better.'

In other words, she needed a husband to bring her into line. Elise bristled at the very idea she couldn't manage her own life, not that she'd done a great job of it to date. But she could hear the lifeline Charles was throwing her in the proposal. She knew she had to consider this offer as carefully as the one that had come from Maxwell Hart. Marriage to Charles was her last chance to claim respectability. This was society's way of letting her know they would not hesitate setting her aside if she continued down this current path of independence and the flaunting of convention.

Elise looked down at her hands, clenched to white-

ness in her lap. 'I am honoured, Charles, and yet surprised by the suddenness of your offer. It bears thinking
about and I must ask you to give me some time to do
that thinking. It would not be fair to you otherwise.'

He looked more disappointed over this pronounce-
ment than the one she'd given him over Hart's offer.
'What would not be fair, Elise, is to leave you at the
mercy of that bounder, Rowland. He is a bad influence.'
A bit of anger fired in Charles's eyes. 'In the absence of
any female companionship at the moment, or any family members to guide you, I fear he's convinced you
to court scandal by leaving off your mourning and by
continuing your efforts at the shipyard. He has clouded
your good judgement; perhaps he has even turned your
head. But you are smarter than that.'

Was she? Elise thought Charles might be wrong
there. She saw him to the door personally, effusing her
thanks for his visit and going through the motions of
farewell, but most of her mind was focused on Dorian.
It had been difficult to sit through the interview with
Charles and not wonder what Dorian would have made
of it all. What would Dorian think of Hart's offer?
What would Dorian think of Charles's proposal and the
exigencies behind it?

Elise shut the door behind Charles and pressed her
forehead to the cool wood. She hadn't seen Dorian since
the night of the fire. Good lord, it had been only four
days! She was acting as if it were months. She'd not
meant for even four days to pass, but the hiring of work-

men and overseeing repairs had kept her here when she'd wanted to be at the shipyard. There'd been no chance to apologise and she hadn't wanted to do it in a note. She doubted what she needed to say could be said accurately in writing anyway.

Elise drew a breath. There was no time like the present. She would take Dorian's lunch down personally and then they would talk.

Elise came to an abrupt halt inside the shipyard. She shielded her eyes against the bright sky and looked up. It was amazing what four days could do. The mast, the rigging, was all complete. Men climbed the boat, hanging sails, and at the top of it all was Dorian, in culottes, open shirt and shoes, swinging from the lines with the ease of a trapeze artist. She'd only seen circus performers with that kind of grace. Watching him now, seeing her yacht so near completion, was enough to make her want to forgive him on the spot. Really, it was enough to make her want to beg his forgiveness.

She had to be cautious with such emotions. He'd built her boat, that was all. She had to be careful the accomplishment didn't unduly outshine their differences. She'd had doubts about him once again just this morning and those doubts were justified. And there were harsh accusations between them, proof they didn't know each other as well as they should. Just because he'd finished her yacht, didn't mean he was off the hook.

She caught his eye and waved up at him, pointing to

the hamper at her side, and then enjoyed the sight of him shimmying down a rope to the boat deck. He sauntered towards her, his culottes low on his hips, his hair loose. She should be used to the sight of him by now. She'd seen him naked, for heaven's sake. But her heart did a somersault anyway at the blatant sensuality on display.

'I brought lunch. I hoped we could talk. There are things that need to be said.' They weren't the most elegant words. She hoped they'd be enough. She bit her lip, waiting for his response. Was he still angry? She'd accused him of trying to steal her boat. Would his answer be something flippant and crude? She'd not realised until now how much she wanted, needed, to talk with him.

She knew a moment's relief when Dorian nodded and called over to a tall young man working at the helm, 'Johnny, I've got business to take care of, you're in charge.' He looked at her. 'Will I need my shirt for this?'

'Unless you want to talk in the office? I have the carriage. I thought we might drive out towards Greenwich.'

'Give me a moment to change.'

Dorian returned quickly, dressed in trousers, boots, shirt, the appropriate coats and an expression far too serious for her liking. He picked up the hamper. 'Shall we?'

The formality of his tone hurt. It made it difficult to find her tongue, to start the conversation she'd come to have. But she didn't want to start it in the carriage.

She wanted to start it at lunch, on the grass on the bluff overlooking the river with the whole afternoon spread out before them. For now, she opted for small talk. 'The yacht's nearly done.' She started with something positive.

Dorian gave a thin smile so different from his usual grin. 'It is done. We just need to name it and take it for a trial.'

A month ago those words would have filled her with elation. Today, her first reaction was sadness. Dorian's job was complete. He would be free to leave.

'It's a good thing. The yacht club's trip is next week.' Elise offered a smile. Good lord, this conversation was stilted. She wanted their former easiness back, she wanted his shocking bluntness back. She wanted it all back. Had their quarrel really ruined everything? How could she not have realised what was at stake? If she had, Elise doubted she'd have chosen to rip it apart with callous words.

Dorian stretched his long legs, his gaze lingering on her face. 'Is this how you want our discussion to go? Short factual sentences or are you hoping for something more?'

There was a hint of his old seduction in those words and her hopes rose. She was tempted to play with those words and come up with a witty response, but it was too soon. She had made her move by coming down here. He needed to make the next one.

He did. 'As for me, I am hoping for something more.'

He paused and she held her breath. 'It does me good to see you, Elise. I regretted our parting the moment I left.'

'I should not have let you go like that.' Elise felt relief course through her. They were dancing towards reconciliation with their careful words.

'I should have come back. I thought about it. I stood at the lamplight on the corner for a long time, thinking about just that.'

'I meant to come sooner, but I couldn't get away.'

'How are repairs going?'

'Good—noisy, but good. They'll be done soon.' She waved the subject away. She didn't want to talk about repairs. 'This…' she made a gesture between them with her hand '…doesn't mean we don't have to talk about what happened.' She didn't want him to think an implied apology on both their parts was enough. Rapprochement was only one of the reasons she'd come down here.

Dorian's answer was quiet and sincere. 'I know.'

By the saints, it was good to see her! He wasn't relishing the upcoming conversation, but he was relishing this moment. She'd come. He'd begun to fear she wouldn't. He'd thrown himself and his men into work on the yacht, keeping long hours to get it done. It had become a personal labour for him. This would be his gift to her. He would make her the most beautiful of racing boats, the fastest and the sleekest. Whatever he couldn't say to her, couldn't give to her, he could pour into the boat.

By tacit agreement, they waited until they were settled on the bluff, the picnic spread out before them while they watched the boat traffic on the water. He waited for Elise to start. He would let her lead the conversation. Would she start with business or pleasure?

'I received an offer for the yacht and the shipyard today. Charles brought it just this morning. It was not from Damien Tyne.' Business and pleasure mixed, then. He knew what she implied.

She was watching him for signs of surprise or something else. He kept his features neutral. 'You think I lied about Tyne.' It was not a question.

Her answer was just as careful. 'I think I was surprised the offer wasn't from him after all the trouble he's put us through.' *Hypothetically.* The word hung unspoken between them. She wasn't sure any more that he'd told her the truth. The doubt stung.

'Who did the offer come from?' Dorian ventured. Damien Tyne didn't necessarily have to offer directly, all the better to protect his involvement.

'Maxwell Hart. I'm not familiar with him, but Charles's father knows of him. He has a boat works in Wapping.'

Dorian felt as if he'd been punched in the gut: clarity at last. 'That gives Charles and me something in common,' he said drily. 'It just so happens that I know Maxwell Hart, too.' Hart. Of course. Tyne had worked with Hart before. *Boat works* was a rather liberal term for what Hart had in Wapping. He had a warehouse that stored goods of a questionable nature. The boat-works portion was where he outfitted ships for dangerous adventures before sending them south with Tyne.

Dorian watched Elise swallow, disappointment shadowing her face. 'You *were* thinking of selling,' Dorian said in soft amazement.

'Thinking only,' Elise said quickly. 'Nothing has been decided.' She plucked at a grass stem. 'It was just an idea. I wanted to talk to you first.' It was an implicit statement of trust and absolutely the best thing she could have said to him. She didn't completely doubt him. Normally, he wouldn't care what anyone thought, but when it came to Elise, everything was different. He cared very much. She was looking at him, those green eyes demanding an answer when all he wanted to do was roll her under him and bury himself in her until they both forgot all the difficulties and impossibilities that lay between them.

'Is it really a bad idea? Hart wants the yacht, too, that's why the price is so high.'

Dorian set aside his baser urges. 'Yes, it's a bad idea.'

'Are you going to tell me why?' She threw down the ultimate gauntlet. This had always been the sticking point between them. It was what she'd wanted from the start—to know him, to know what he knew. She still wanted it. It had been at the heart of their recent quarrel.

Dorian lay back on the grass, his head propped against a boulder. 'I'll tell you, Elise, although you might regret it. You'd better open that bottle of wine in the hamper. It's a long story.' When it was over, she might not be the only one regretting it. Yet this was the only way forwards, painful as it might be. What better way to prove to her he was sorry for the other night than to tell her about Hart and Tyne? Of course, the opposite was also true. What better way to lose her for good? He couldn't tell her about Hart and Tyne without telling her about himself.

Chapter Nineteen

'Tyne and Hart were the ones who took the *Queen Maeve* and scuttled her before my eyes. I watched her burn.' He'd watched more than a ship burn that night. He'd watched his livelihood, his dreams, everything go up in smoke, down with the ship. It didn't matter which cliché one used, in the end there still was nothing left.

'Why?' Elise was looking at him with something akin to pity in her eyes. He didn't want her sympathy. She'd lose it soon enough when she heard the rest. There were plenty of people who thought he'd got what he'd deserved and it wasn't as if he hadn't known the risks.

'I crossed them.' Just as Elise was crossing them now with her refusal to sell the yacht. 'I've told you before that Tyne was an arms dealer. He did the dirty work, the meetings with the pashas and chieftains, he made the actual deliveries. But Hart was the supplier. Hart never leaves England. He sets up the shipments, finds the arms—good solid British arms or sometimes

French—and he sends them to Tyne. That's what he's got up at his warehouse in Wapping.'

'Then what's Tyne doing here? Shouldn't he be sailing his ship somewhere?' Elise's mind was running ahead of the story.

Dorian drew a breath. 'He doesn't have one at present because I sunk it in revenge for the *Queen*.' If there was a touch of manly pride in his tone, so be it. He might have been bound and helpless the night the *Queen* burnt, but he did not let anyone harm what was his without retribution.

Elise's expression grew masked. 'What happened? We seem to have skipped over the part about why you crossed them.'

This was the harder part to tell, the part where he wouldn't seem so heroic. Perhaps he'd look no better to her than Tyne and Hart. 'Arms are a lucrative and arguably legal market in the Mediterranean. I saw a chance to make money and I took it. It's not just Turkey where there's military unrest. There's Egypt, too, and Greece and amongst the desert chieftains along the north of Africa in Algiers and Morocco—parts of Spain, too.' He gave a grimace. 'Not everyone is happy with the return of the Spanish monarch, and for whatever else the French liked or didn't like about Napoleon, he's made them greedy. They see the profit of colonies close to home. Algiers and Morocco are just across the sea and the French are drooling already at the thought. The British will never tolerate simply handing those ports to the French so we've moved inland, thinking to rally the sheikhs to our cause, convincing them the French will take their independence.'

Dorian shrugged. 'It's a lie, of course. It will be some time before anyone actually threatens the independence of the nomad sheikhs.'

'You've seen them?'

'Yes, I had to journey inland quite a way to make my deliveries. But that's not the point. The point is, I sold arms, too. Mostly, I operated out of Gibraltar and made small runs to Algiers. But as time went on and my reputation for quality arms grew, I began to see the allure of moving further east.'

Elise nodded, the pieces coming together. 'That's how you crossed them. You became too big, too successful, and then you infringed on their territory.'

Dorian pushed a hand through his hair. 'Exactly. There were warnings—a little accident here and there meant to encourage my leaving. I retaliated by being bigger and bolder.' He told her of the pasha's daughter and stealing the arsenal in order to sell it to his rival. 'Of course, the best part to me was that the arsenal had been supplied by Tyne.' It had seemed symbolic at the time. Tyne had been furious.

'Tyne offered to buy the *Queen*, several times. But I was too proud. I couldn't sell her. I had built her. I'd paid for her with my own money saved from my runs. She was the one thing I had that truly belonged to me.'

His eyes were on the sky, but his thoughts were much further away.

'One night, Tyne came after me. He seized or killed most of my crew. We did try to resist, but we were outnumbered. I suffered a blow to the head and when I recovered consciousness, I found myself bound to a tree on a bluff overlooking the harbour. I had a perfect view to watch my ship burn.'

Elise fiddled with the grass, twisting the blades into little wreaths. 'Why didn't Tyne kill you? That would have solved his problems.'

'Dead men can't be broken and Tyne does like to break a man. Besides, I think he worried about repercussions in England. My father likes to pretend I don't exist, but if anything did happen to me my father might suddenly get paternal again. Tyne didn't want to risk it.' Dorian sighed. There was more to tell, but perhaps this was enough for now. Perhaps she'd spare him and puzzle the rest out.

'You do see why I've told you all this?' Dorian rolled to his side and propped himself up on one elbow. 'You are crossing him now. He's issued his warnings and yet you do not relent. He's behind Hart's offer. The offer is your last chance. Tyne will come for your boat, and maybe even for you.' There was no maybe about it; he just couldn't bring himself to say the words.

The thought was enough to make him shiver. For all her boldness, Elise was no match for Tyne. 'He most certainly will come for me, though.' On his own, Dorian could handle Tyne. But Elise complicated things. She could be used against him, making her doubly valuable to Tyne.

'Then it's good I'm alone.' Elise looked up at him with a forced smile. 'With my mother and William away from London it will be harder for him to reach them.'

She was starting to understand. Dorian reached up his free hand to push a strand of hair out of her face. 'You're not alone, Elise.' She had him for whatever that was worth. He definitely came with disadvantages. He was a magnet for Tyne. He'd cost Tyne his ship and an expensive cargo of Russian guns for the Turks, a deal that had taken over a year to put together. But he could defend her. 'I'm here.'

'For how long?' The question was ruthless. In one simple question she'd united the business and pleasure sides of their relationship, linking them irrevocably together once more.

'For as long as it takes, Elise.' It was the best answer, the most honest answer he could give. He would not leave her open to Tyne's treachery, but neither could he articulate anything permanent about their relationship. Nor could he articulate anything temporary. He wondered if she'd thought of that.

'And then?' Elise pushed on, seeing only the temporary nature of his answer. 'Where will you go after this?'

'It will depend.' Dorian shrugged. 'It's not a priority right now and it won't be a priority until Tyne is dealt with and you're safe.' He wanted to kiss her, wanted her to stop thinking about the future and start thinking about right now.

A coy smile hinted at her lips. 'What is a priority, Dorian Rowland?'

'You.' He was hungry for her. He had to know she'd let him protect her, that his disclosures hadn't driven her off.

'Right here? Out in the open?' The prospect of something so risky spoke to her. Her pupils widened, her pulse quickened.

'Yes.' Dorian kissed her neck, his free hand in her hair, drawing her, urging her close to him. They had all afternoon. He would take this nice and slow.

'No.' He felt her body tense in resistance, a mirror to her words.

'No?'

She gave a rueful smile. 'Apparently there's one woman in the world who can resist Dorian Rowland.' She looked down, away from his face. 'I'm sorry, I can't.'

Dorian blew out a breath. 'Is it because of the things I said that night? I had no right. They were unconscionable and they were untrue.' He'd regretted those harsh words the moment he'd spoke them.

'No. We were both angry.'

'Then what? Don't you trust me, Elise?' The words sounded ridiculous coming from him after all he'd told her. He'd run arms, he'd stolen arms, he'd destroyed another man's ship in retribution. Why *should* she trust him?

Elise scooted away from him and stood, surely a bad sign. Most of what he wanted to do on a picnic blanket required sitting down at least.

'I trust you to protect me against Tyne.' But not from himself. He thought he understood. He rose, too, prepared to persuade her otherwise. Her next words stalled him full force. 'Dorian, there's something else. Charles came with two offers today. The other was a proposal. Charles has asked me to marry him.'

And she was considering it. He wanted to shout, 'No, you're mine!' but he had no idea what that meant—did it mean *he* wanted to marry her, or merely that he wanted to sail away with her and make love on sandy beaches until they tired of one another? How could he promise anything to her?

Dorian schooled his features into bland neutrality and cocked an eyebrow. 'Are congratulations in order? Have you accepted him?' Surely his instincts weren't wrong. She couldn't have, not when she'd been his not so very long ago.

Her own features mimicked his in their neutrality, some of the earlier stiffness returning to their conversation. 'No, I have not. I just thought you should know.' *I will not be sleeping with you or kissing you, putting my mouth on you, or anything else until the situation with Charles is resolved.*

Dorian studied her face, watching for some telltale give-away. '*Will* you accept?'

'I don't know,' Elise answered slowly. 'It will depend on what happens with the shipyard, I suppose.' There was a flicker of hope in her eyes that suggested it depended on more than the shipyard, that it might depend on him.

'We haven't done very well today.' Elise gave a little laugh. 'I still don't know whether or not to take the offer. Either of them.'

Dorian laughed. At least she wasn't going to run home and accept Charles's proposal. He still had a chance if he wanted to take it. 'We might be doing better than you think.'

She shot him a dubious look. 'I would hardly call inviting all-out war with an arms dealer doing "better than we think".'

'If you sell, it's more than understandable.' He would hate that decision, though, and she would come to hate it, too. It would haunt him all his days to see that yacht in Tyne's filthy hands, but if it kept Elise safe, he would live with it. 'If you choose to resist, I'll protect you to the best of my abilities. Either way, I can't make that decision for you, Elise...' he gave a wicked smile and leaned in close to her '...but I can do this.' His hand cupped the sweep of her jaw, just before he kissed her.

He tasted the sweetness of her, the strawberries and wine mingled on her lips, he felt the small straight ridges of her teeth where his tongue ran over them. Most of all, he felt compliance, ever so briefly, before she remembered her resolve, but it was there. And that meant there was hope indeed.

'I told you, I can't,' Elise protested softly.

'But I can. Charles didn't propose to me.' Dorian kissed her again just to prove his point.

Elise stood at the launch gate of the shipyard. In her hand was the rope cord that would send the bottle of champagne sailing into the side of the yacht. Excitement and trepidation coursed through her in equal parts. The breeze off the water toyed with her hat and she reached a hand up to steady it. The wind was good. In spite of overcast skies, conditions for the test sail couldn't be better.

The momentous day was finally here. She was well past the point of no return and had been for much longer than she'd realised. Since the beginning there had been no question of selling the yard, or even of selling the boat, even if she was only now coming to realise it. She understood it now, though, standing on the launch site while the sun rose with Dorian beside her. This boat *belonged* to her, it was a product of her plans, her designs, her efforts.

Yet for all the pride she felt in the moment, there was a loneliness, too. Past launch days had been huge festive events, her father a great showman. The launch gate had been crowded with invited guests. Other yachts of invited celebrants had been moored in the river to join the sailing, and a select few would be aboard the prized vessel. There'd been food and champagne and a rousing speech from her father. Even the members of the royal family were present on occasion.

Today there was no such pomp. Today there were only a handful of people: herself and Dorian and enough crew to get the boat launched. She'd named the yacht *Sutton's Hope* and Dorian had made her hold up a lantern last night so he could see well enough to paint the name along the prow. The paint had dried just in time.

'This is it, Elise, give the rope a good yank.' Dorian came to stand beside her, the last of the preparations done. Dorian, *not* Charles, was here with her, came the reminder. Dorian had helped her realise this moment, a moment Charles had not been in favour of from the start. Charles had scoffed at her ambitions. Dorian had embraced them. That should count for something.

Dorian was dressed in buff breeches and a thick sweater against the early morning chill. He looked well rested in spite of the late night. Elise knew she did not. She'd hardly slept with her mind so occupied with the yacht launch, the contretemps of Damien Tyne and Charles's proposal. She'd spent most of the night weighing Charles against Dorian, although her practical side didn't know why. It wasn't as if she had to choose. Charles had asked for her hand, Dorian had asked for nothing.

'Elise, the rope,' Dorian prompted again with a smile. She let go and watched the bottle give a satisfying smash against the side. Her father would have loved to have been here. She'd not dared to write to William or her mother with an update. William didn't know yet that he'd signed on for a membership with the yacht club.

Elise helped Dorian and the other two crew members get the yacht under way in the river, but she was eager to stand at the railing and feel the wind in her face and feel the roll of the boat beneath her. She was nervous, too. Would the great experiment with the buoyancy bags compensate for the narrowness through the centre of the boat? It would be absolutely tragic if, after all this, the design simply didn't work.

For the trial, they'd planned to sail down the Thames to Gravesend. The route was the standard below-the-bridge racing course used by the yacht club. It would be a good chance to see how the sails tacked in the wind. Already she could feel the cutter rigging picking up the breeze. The boat *felt* fast. She could hear Dorian calling out instructions. She didn't remember the point at which everything fell silent on board, only that Dorian had come up behind her and boldly wrapped his arms about her, his body warm and comforting.

'She's doing magnificently,' Dorian reported. 'The cutter rigging was exactly the right way to go. The new cut on the sails has made an enormous difference with the windage.'

Elise smiled. 'That's precisely what I wanted to hear.'

'The *Hope* is fast, Elise.' Dorian's voice was at her ear, low and intimate. She should dissuade him from such liberties. It wasn't fair to Charles or to Dorian or to her. If she meant to accept Charles, it was the height of cruelty to tempt herself like this. She didn't need to compare kisses to know Charles did not rouse her, *could not* rouse her, like Dorian did. There would be none of the pleasure, none of the fire she felt with Dorian. But there would be honour and Charles would respect her. No, that would be misleading to think so. What kind of respect? Respect only if she acceded to his wishes. He would never countenance something like today.

'How fast?' She was fishing for compliments now.

'Fast enough to outrun them all.' Dorian blew in her ear. 'Don't tell me you haven't thought about it.' She'd thought about it all last night in the long dark hours: about keeping the yacht, about rejecting Charles, about sailing away from London. Let Tyne and Hart have the shipyard if she could have Dorian. Fanciful notions all. If Dorian was right about Tyne and Hart, her ethical conscience wouldn't allow conceding to such blackguards.

'Thought about what?' She breathed in the wind-tinged scent of him, a man out of doors and in his element.

'About keeping the yacht and racing it on your own.'

'Oh, that.' So not about keeping him, then. What would he say if she said she'd thought of sailing away with him?

'You could pay the workers from prize money.'

'That's a big risk. What if we didn't win?' She had

no cash reserves to pay those wages. She was worried enough about paying them in the very near future. She had no buyer. She'd have to sell off furnishings if one didn't materialise soon.

'We'd win, Elise. She's a champion in the water.' Dorian sounded confident. It made her want to believe in so many impossible things.

'There's a regatta right after the opening trip, with a four-hundred-pound purse and a silver cup, sponsored by the royal family. They're calling it the Saxe-Coburg Cup in Albert's honour.'

'You are surprisingly well informed for someone who shuns polite society.' Elise gave him a suspicious smile. This was the perfect opportunity to bind him to her just a little longer if she dared. 'To do such a thing, I'd need you at the helm. Would you do it?' They'd not finished that discussion the night of the fire and he'd been reticent. She turned in his embrace, her arms about his neck, Charles forgotten for the moment. It was hard to remember much of anything when she was with Dorian.

Dorian swallowed hard, his jaw clenching. 'If it's what you want, I'll do it.' She didn't pretend to understand all the reasons why he was so reticent to associate with society, but she knew the decision cost him mightily.

Elise beamed and rose up on her tiptoes to kiss him full on the mouth. 'Can we sail the yacht ourselves?' she asked softly, her mouth inches from his.

'We could manage.' He gave her a teasing wink.

'You're not the only one who can innovate. I borrowed some mechanics from ketch rigging and adapted them to your cutter rigging to make the yacht more efficient for a small crew.'

'I am suitably impressed. Put the crew aside at Gravesend with fare to get home and I'll give you a proper thank you.'

Dorian grinned. 'And Charles? Does this mean you've refused his offer?'

Elise nodded, more solemn now. 'I don't think I ever could have accepted him, not when I really thought about it.' There was more to it than that, but for now she was interested in kissing Dorian with the wind in her hair and her decisions made. There would still be a fight ahead of her. She didn't believe for a moment simply making decisions solved her problems. She would continue to persevere. Maybe there was a miracle out there for her where she could keep the shipyard, keep the boat and maybe, just maybe, she'd find a way to keep Dorian without needing him too much.

'She's a beauty.' Damien Tyne handed off the binoculars to Maxwell Hart. 'Just look at her.'

'That's my fiancée you're talking about,' Charles said tersely, raising his own binoculars to his eyes, his horse shifting under him on the bluff as they watched *Sutton's Hope* pass in the sunrise.

'I meant the boat, but the comment suits either way,' Tyne teased meanly. 'I don't know if I'd use the binoculars if I were you. You might not like what you see. It appears Rowland shares our assessment of the latter.' He elbowed Hart and the two of them laughed.

Charles grimaced, his anger rising as he stared through the eye piece, watching Dorian come up behind Elise and wrap her in his arms. 'How dare he!' Charles spluttered. No gentleman behaved so boldly with a woman.

'How dare *she*?' Tyne inserted with a sideways glance in his direction. 'It doesn't look to me like she's overly upset. In fact, they look quite cosy, quite comfortable with one another as if…'

'Don't even say it,' Charles ground out. He'd thought the same thing. They looked much too easy together for this to have been the first time. The way Rowland was whispering in her ear, the way she turned in his arms, laughing up at him, confirmed those jealous suspicions. Rage boiled through Charles. 'I'd like to see him dead.'

Tyne laughed. 'That can be arranged, my young friend. That most *definitely* can be arranged.'

'Not yet,' Hart cut in sharply in a tone that made Charles think Tyne wasn't truly joking. 'There's still a chance she might accept the offer and then any nasty conclusions to our business with her can be avoided.'

'Always the optimist, aren't you, Maxwell?' Tyne shook his head. Charles looked between the two. When he was with them, he always felt as if there was another game going on between them that he and the others weren't privy to; that somehow this was about more than a simple business venture to build fast boats.

'I can't afford not to be. I have to live here after you leave to soak up the rays of the Mediterranean,' Hart reminded Tyne. 'Raising the ire of the Duke of Ashdon might not bother you, but it will make business on this end deuced difficult for the rest of us. It won't matter if we have the yard and a fast boat once Ashdon gets done.' That was more like it. Charles understood that sort of rationale. Hart knew what was good for business.

Tyne groused and scuffed the toe of his boot through the dirt. 'When's the opening trip?'

'Five days, why?' Hart asked.

'Let's give her until then. If she's not responded to the offer affirmatively by the opening trip, I get to work my magic.'

Charles felt a shiver. He didn't mind Tyne and Hart carving up Rowland between them, but now they were dragging Elise in, too. 'Now see here, Tyne, my father and I won't stand for seeing Elise hurt.'

Tyne gave a cold smile, his gaze fixed on the boat growing smaller in the distance. 'She'll come out of it all right if she's smart. So will you, Bradford.' Tyne turned and fixed him with a stare. 'Don't get any ideas about betraying us at this late date. She's not the only one who needs to play this smart.' He paused for a moment. 'Are we agreed then, Maxwell? Opening trip?'

Maxwell Hart gave a nearly imperceptible nod, the line of his jaw set grim and tense. 'Opening trip it is.'

Chapter Twenty

'I've put the crew off. I gave them money for fare back and a pint or two.' Dorian came up behind Elise and wrapped her in his arms, enjoying the feel of her as she sank into his body. This was one of his favourite positions with her—his arms about her, the two of them at the rail of a boat. They had stood this way, too, the night they'd gone to Vauxhall.

'We have the boat to ourselves,' he murmured in her ear. She turned and put her arms about his neck, her eyes dancing with life, her cheeks flushed from the wind. She looked utterly alive in his arms. There would be seduction today. Their bodies were primed for it with the thrill of the morning sail. The privacy of the cove he had anchored them in ensured it. But he was going to have to decide very soon what to do about her. Their time together *would* end. After the opening trip there was nothing to hold him here except the personal. Would she ask him to stay? Would he be willing to pay the price staying demanded? Or would she come with him if he asked? Could he make her happy in Gibraltar? That was a fantasy that had taken up far too much of his nights lately—sailing away with Elise and finding the happy ever after.

'I do not like the look in your eyes one bit.' Elise laughed up at him, but he feared she'd seen too much. Perhaps she understood, too, that this affair could not go on indefinitely without reaching a resolution. It was time to redirect. 'Come eat, Elise. I've got our picnic laid out.'

She'd been lost in thought when he'd returned. He'd left her at the rail with those thoughts and taken time to spread the blanket on the deck and lay out the picnic: cheese and bread, apples and, best of all, champagne. Elise loved champagne, loved to do wicked things with it.

'You've been busy.' Elise sat and tucked her skirts around her. He joined her, pulling off his boots. The sun had broken through the clouds and the blanket was warm. The boat bobbed gently beneath them. For the moment, everything was perfect.

'My father would have loved today,' Elise said softly, as unwilling as he to disrupt the peace around them. He'd guessed she'd been thinking of her father. How could she not on such an important day? Whether she knew it or not, Elise Sutton had an enormous capacity for love. He suspected, however, it was a capacity she guarded carefully.

'*Sutton's Hope* would have made him proud.' Dorian

popped the cork on the bottle and poured out two glasses. 'You would have made him proud.' He handed her a glass. 'Shall we have a toast? To Richard Sutton, to his vision and to his daughter.'

Elise blushed, her eyes watering a little at the tribute. He was glad she understood he was sincere. 'Thank you.' She touched her glass to his. 'How about a toast to the builder? To Dorian Rowland, a most extraordinary man.' Her eyes met his, and he let their gaze hold, a feat more difficult than he would have thought. Of all the things they'd said to one another over the past weeks, these toasts might have been the boldest.

These words were the closest they'd come to any verbal expression of their feelings. They'd done things together: rash things, intimate things, dangerous things. But never once had they spoken of how each made the other feel, as if saying the words signified a commitment neither were prepared to make.

'People say things like this when they believe someone is leaving, perhaps never to be seen again. It's one of the reasons I hate farewells.' Dorian set down his glass and reached for the wheel of cheese. 'Do you think I am leaving, Elise?' He passed her a chunk of cheese and slice of bread. He'd not planned to address their future today, but perhaps now was the right time after all.

Elise took the slice of cheese and bread from him, gathering her thoughts. Her answer, when she made it, would be careful. 'I think your business obligations to me are nearly over. If you stay, it will be out of something more. Staying will require some decisions.'

'We are dancing around it again.' Dorian gave a wry smile. 'It was one thing to use me for sex before the Season, but once everyone comes to town you'll need something more substantial. Is that it?'

He watched her swallow the champagne hastily to keep from choking on it. The bolder turn of the conversation had caught her off guard. 'Yes, something like that. Sex is fine for now, but eventually it has to mean something.' She stared into her glass, watching the bubbles disappearing. 'I'm afraid that's my fatal flaw, Dorian. You should know it before it's too late. Sex has to mean something to me. It can't just be for fun, not always. If we were to continue, eventually, I fear I would expect from you more than you might be prepared to give.'

How could he answer that for her when he wasn't sure he could answer it for himself? What was he willing to give? It was easier to know that answer if she'd come away with him. But what if the only way to have her was to stay? Her shipyard was here, everything she wanted was here. Would she leave it all for him? Would it be fair to expect that from her when he wasn't sure he could give it in return? But that wasn't all she was asking him with the revelation.

She was telling him something else, too—that *this* had happened before. He'd known, of course, he wasn't her first lover. There'd been someone else who'd tempted her and failed her. She'd expected love where there'd been none. A spurt of anger went through him, anger directed at the nameless man who'd teased her so carelessly. Dorian's thumb was under her chin, tipping her face up, forcing their gazes to meet when she would have preferred to have avoided it. 'Is that what happened the last time?'

'Yes.' She met his gaze evenly. There was defiance in her tone. 'I was more emotionally invested. He was more physically invested. At the time, I didn't understand the difference until it was too late.'

'Do you think that will happen here? That you are invested, but I am not?'

She gave him a wry smile. 'It would be too easy to love you, Dorian, even though I know what kind of man you are. On occasion, I suspect I'm already halfway there. After all, I've turned down a perfectly good suitor for you on my own volition.' Then she shook her head, 'But, no, Dorian. I don't think it could happen here. I'm smarter and wiser and you've made no secret about your intentions and that makes all the difference.'

Leave it to Elise to mingle compliments with a scold, but he was moved all the same. What would he do with that affection should she let it loose? Could he be trusted with it? Dorian rocked back on his heels and cut more bread while his mind reeled. She loved him. He wanted to celebrate that, wanted to jump up and down with the thrill of that knowledge. But the last part held him back, the part about intentions. He sensed the crux of the story lay there. 'Why don't you tell me about secret intentions? We're well fortified if this is a long story.'

'There's not much to tell. I was eighteen. I was in the throes of my first Season. My father's social circle extended to the lower rungs of the peerage and we had the royal patronage by then. It enabled me to garner the attention of a different kind of gentleman, the sons of barons, which meant there were titles to go with the estates. Before, the most I could have expected were the attentions of nice gentry farmers with lands and a comfortable income. I became infatuated with a Mr Robert Graves, heir to a baronetcy in Devonshire. He was dashing, a little wild, but it appeared he liked me, too. Before I knew it, we were dancing together every night, he was driving me in the park and we were sneaking out to the gardens for kisses.'

'Kisses?' Dorian waggled his eyebrows, pretending shock. A little levity was not amiss. She was starting to relax.

'Well, considerably more than kisses. We became intimately involved. I had no qualms over it. I was certain he had marriage in mind and we wouldn't have been the first couple to anticipate matrimony. He talked about plans and I assumed those plans were for us.'

Dorian's anger flared. 'Who were they for?' He'd like to wring the bounder's neck.

'For his fourth cousin, Miss Mary Southmore,' Elise said quietly. 'What hurt most was the way he broke it to me. He said he had never harboured any intentions of marrying me. I was a craftsman's daughter when all was said and done. My family built boats. I never should have believed anything more could come of it.'

'I'm truly sorry.' It explained much about Elise, about the guard she kept on her feelings, not willing to reveal too much.

'Fortunately, what I felt for him wasn't real love and I learned from that mistake.' Elise gave a sad smile.

'Not every man sees the world as Robert Graves does,' Dorian put in softly. He stretched out on his side, drawing her to him, wanting to show her there was honour in him yet, that he could be trusted to deal honestly with her.

'No, but a good lesson all the same.' She snuggled down beside him, their faces close.

He pushed a strand of hair back out of her face. 'We both know I'm not Robert Graves, Elise, not in temperament or in practice.'

'I know,' she whispered, her breath catching as he moved against her ever so slightly, enough to close the gap between their bodies and to make his arousal known. Her hand slipped between them, finding the length of him. Lord, he loved the feel of her hand on him.

'Now there's something else we both know, Elise. I'm dying to make love to you.'

She smiled. 'I thought you'd never ask.'

He leaned over, raising himself above her, hands braced on either side. She was beautiful beneath him, her hair falling down about her shoulders, her green eyes looking up at him full of desire, a desire for *him* that was nearly overwhelming. Her hands were at the waistband of his trousers, unfastening, freeing. He managed her skirts and undergarments with a hand, his mouth trailing kisses down her throat, need rising with each touch. The wanting of her consumed him.

'God, how I want you, Elise. You don't know, you just don't know.' He was mumbling incoherent phrases against her throat, his breathing ragged. He moved, positioning himself. He was sliding home into the depths of her and nothing had ever felt this right. She was locked about him, holding him, rocking with him in his rhythm as he slid and thrust, pushing them towards the release he desperately wanted and never wanted; how he'd love to stay like this with her forever! In these moments there was no threat from Tyne, no social dilemmas to unravel regarding their future. There was only the knowledge that he was made for this moment and she was made for him and that was all that mattered, until it shattered into a million shards of pleasure, peace and perfection.

In the aftermath of that release, one question intruded: what would he be willing to do to have such a moment again? Could he stay for her? For this?

He'd stayed for her! Today, Dorian would be at the helm of the boat and at her side. He would stand with her on one of the most important days of her life: the day she showed the world Elise Sutton could build a yacht.

That one thought raced through Elise as she made her way through the streets leading to the docks. It was the opening trip and the streets were crowded with people anticipating the start of the yacht season. Spectators gathered along the waterfront to see the boats, sails hoisted, preparing to set out. Elise understood their excitement. She felt it, too. After a long bleak winter, there was an undeniable thrill at seeing the Commodore's pennant flying from his yacht at Blackwell as it had in seasons past, a sign that while some things change, not all things change.

She let the excitement of the opening trip fill the pit in her stomach. Even if there was just the opening trip to worry about, she'd still have had butterflies. It was her first official outing since her father's death. There would be those who would look askance at such behaviour.

But there was so much more. There'd been an ugly scene with Charles the day before. She had officially rejected his suit and he'd shown himself to be a poor loser. There was Tyne and Hart to worry about. She couldn't keep them dangling much longer, but to refuse them outright put her in harm's way. Then there was Dorian and the host of feelings and dilemmas he raised.

He was here for now, but for how much longer? Had they really reached any sort of consensus on the boat in spite of their disclosures and torrid lovemaking? Charles had not been wrong when he'd accused her of being infatuated with Dorian. She was and quite possibly more. Charles had insinuated Dorian had put her up to this nonsense with the yacht, but Elise knew better. She'd have ended up here, flaunting convention, with or without Dorian. Dorian simply made it easier. With Dorian, she had an ally.

Dorian was waiting for her beside the yacht, a welcome sight in the press of people. He was dressed in the new outfit she'd had sent over: spotless white trousers and a navy-blue jacket. He looked like the other captains, only *more*—more alive, more vibrant.

'Miss Sutton, your yacht awaits.' Dorian handed her up with grave formality that she might have believed if it hadn't been for the familiar twinkle of mischief in his eye. 'Several people have been eyeing the boat.'

'Jealous, were they?' Elise laughed, forcing herself to relax. She'd worked hard for this day. She *wanted* to enjoy it. Ladies passed by on the arms of gentlemen, many of them casting coy glances in Dorian's direction. 'I wonder if it was the yacht everyone was looking at?' she teased Dorian.

'Probably not,' he admitted honestly, taking his place at the helm. 'You'd better be prepared for scandal by dinner.'

Scandal would be better than some of the other options she'd mentally braced for. Elise went to stand at the railing and looked out over the river at all the boats assembled. She recognised several of them; the *Lady Louisa*, the *Brilliant*, the *Phantom*. All of them had been her father's competitors and friends over the years. She waved to a few acquaintances on boats nearby. Some of them waved back.

Well, Charles had warned her. Dorian had warned her. She'd built a boat, she'd forgone mourning and she'd hired a scandalous captain. What should she have expected? Still, it was one thing to anticipate being snubbed—it was another to actually have it happen. It was rather eye-opening to realise that she would be the larger source of scandal than Dorian.

A fast boat will pay for all. Elise repeated her sustaining mantra. They would see what *Sutton's Hope* could do and they'd cease to care about anything else. She'd come to the conclusion that she could build other boats like the *Hope* without selling it. In theory, it was a conclusion that gave her the best of both worlds. Of course, she had to impress them today and then she'd have to impress them on the race course. Rather, Dorian would have to impress them.

She needn't have worried on that account. Dorian knew exactly what to do. The opening trip was technically non-competitive, but that didn't stop people from jockeying for position behind the Commodore's yacht or from showing off. Dorian made the most of the *Hope*'s sleek manoeuvrability, deftly coming up on the Commodore's starboard side for prime positioning. A few captains, less concerned about issues of social status and more concerned with appreciating good sailing, shouted back good-natured comments.

Most of the captains had been hired for the event

as they would be for the races. Few owners captained their own yachts any more, having learned from experience that a well-built yacht wasn't always enough to win. One needed a talented captain, too.

The Commodore came to the railing of his yacht and called over, 'That's a fine-looking yacht, Miss Sutton. Is that one of your father's?'

'The last one, sir, and the only one of its kind!' Elise called back proudly over the wind.

'She's a gem. I look forward to seeing her race.'

One down. Elise hid a triumphant smile. At least they weren't going to kick her out of the yacht club. Without membership, she wasn't eligible for the regattas.

The opening sail took them past Erith and Rosherville, all the way to Gravesend where rooms had been spoken for at Water's Hotel. There would be dinner and dancing to celebrate the opening of the season. Some people would drive home in prearranged carriages. A few, like Dorian and Elise, would sail back although it would be dark.

Dorian was dazzling at dinner, all manners and polish. He charmed the ladies with flirtatious banter and compliments. He impressed the men with his knowledge of ships and the state of English presence in the Mediterranean. Surely, *this* Dorian Rowland could be received back into society.

Chapter Twenty-One

The thought hit her hard. Was that what she wanted? Dorian to stay in London and take up his mantle as a duke's son? She supposed so. She'd certainly thought of Dorian staying. She'd not spent much time dwelling on the details of it. Surely, the latter would be part of it. Elise wasn't the only one who thought so, either. The ladies' retiring room was full of the same conversation. There wasn't a woman there who didn't want to talk about Dorian.

'I thought I'd faint when he sat down beside me at dinner.'

'He's so handsome!'

'Oohh, those blue eyes seemed to look right through me.'

'What I wouldn't give for my husband to look at me like he did.' That was just the matrons. The daughters were equally as giddy.

'Mama says he's not received!' one girl whispered behind her painted fan.

'I think that makes him even more delicious,' another said, trying to be wicked.

'He's still a lord. He's the Duke of Ashdon's son,' another added practically. 'His wife would still be a lady.'

On it went. Elise would have laughed at their nonsense if it hadn't so closely mirrored her own thoughts. Part of her wished Dorian was always like this, the perfect fairy-tale rogue who turned out to be a gentleman in the end. The other part of her knew better than to want that or to believe it. Dorian wasn't going to magically become a prince. He wasn't exactly a pirate, either, but somewhere in between, and that would not be good enough for London society.

Elise wondered what the ladies would think if they could see him in his culottes, his chest bare, a knife between his teeth or up against the throat of an unruly worker. The silly girls in the retiring room had no idea what Dorian could do to them, their minds limited to a chaste kiss stolen in a dimly lit garden. But she knew and it was beyond any of their imaginings. Worse, she didn't want to think of anyone else being the recipient of such decadent efforts.

Elise left the retiring room as soon as she could, unable to stand any more talk of Dorian. A few women cast unfavourable looks her way as she passed. She didn't need to hear what they said to know the content of the conversation that would take place shortly. She'd heard similar snatches throughout the evening. The gentlemen had been polite at dinner, asking her questions about *Sutton's Hope*, but the women had been less so.

'It's shameful how soon she left off mourning.'

'I hear she's attempting to run her father's business.'

'To show up here with Lord Rowland, of all people! Doesn't she know better?'

To which one catty woman responded, *'She knows better, I'd wager my pin money on it.'* The woman might as well have called her a blatant hussy. It was patently unfair that Dorian, who was a real scoundrel, had shown up after years of absenteeism and been an object of acceptable curiosity while she hadn't done more than try to make her own way in the world and was shunned for it.

'Smile, Elise. People are watching. You look as if you want to flay someone alive.' Dorian materialised at her side the moment the orchestra struck up. 'The retiring room all you'd hoped it would be?'

'Stop it. It was awful. Everyone in there was talking about you,' Elise groused. Smiling was the last thing she felt like doing.

'If you don't like the conversation, my advice is don't spend so much time in the ladies' room.' Dorian laughed. 'Now, come and dance with me and let's give them something to really talk about.'

'You were waiting for me?' Elise felt her spirits lift as she took his hand and let him lead her out to the dance floor for the opening waltz.

He gave her a naughty half-grin. 'There's no one else here worth waiting for.'

'That will come as a disappointment to many of the ladies present.' Elise put her hand on his shoulder, wanting to read more into his words than she safely should. He'd made her no promises save to defend her against Tyne should it be necessary. 'Don't you want to know what the ladies were saying?'

Dorian shook his head. 'Not really. I can guess and it won't happen. I'll never turn decent. They can all let go of that fantasy right now.'

Elise smiled, but she understood the warning was there for her, too, just in case she needed the reminder—and she did. She'd been toying with the premise of a decent Lord Dorian Rowland off and on all day. 'I like you just the way you are.' Although the liking made things more complicated. 'I wish society would say the same thing about me.' She gave a little pout as they turned at the top of the ballroom. Dorian was a masterful dancer. 'Today hasn't gone well in that regard.'

Dorian smiled, but didn't deny it. 'You knew there was a chance of that. Still, today was not an entire loss. People are impressed with the boat, as we'd hoped.' Dorian swung her in a tight turn to avoid the other dancers, his grip firm on her waist, possessive.

We. How she loved the sound of that! Elise smiled up at him. 'Impressed enough to order from me?' If she meant to avoid selling the shipyard, she had to have orders and soon. There'd been no sign of Tyne and her boat had shown well, but Tyne and Hart couldn't be fobbed off forever. 'A decision must still be made about Hart's offer.' After her reception today, her earlier resolve was wavering. Maybe she should take the money and ethics be damned.

'Really? I thought you'd made your mind up.' Dorian raised an eyebrow in disapproving challenge.

'I keep prevaricating. The day of the trial run, I was certain I could keep the yard and the boat. But I don't know if I'm willing to risk so much. If I turn them down, I am engaging in war.'

'And your principles? You know what those men are, Elise. You would take their money and give them a prime location from which to carry out their activities?'

She gave him a sharp, serious look. 'I've never heard you talk like that. You've run arms, too. You can't turn hypocrite.'

'Not like them.' Dorian's tone was equally harsh. 'Those men are nefarious. I don't care if Charles Bradford and his father have decided to consort with them. The Bradfords and their ilk can't make men like Tyne decent. I'd rather you didn't do any amount of business with them.'

'Then you'd better hope I find buyers for the boat design because it's all I've got left to support myself with.'

'You can't build boats without a shipyard,' Dorian shot back. 'I guess that settles it. You couldn't possibly sell right now. Where would you build your boats if you did?' He was right. She hated when he was right.

'This is hardly the place to talk about business,' Elise snapped. He was dancing her breathless with his grace and speed. She could barely think, let alone contemplate the options laid before her.

'Or the night,' Dorian whispered seductively at her ear. 'We had a beautiful day on the water, a delicious dinner, and I have a fascinating woman in my arms.' She felt his hand at her back pull her closer to him. 'Why don't we go back to the yacht, drink champagne and make love? I've wanted to get you out of this dress since I saw you in it. Come with me, Elise.' His eyes were hot as he said the words. She'd follow him anywhere in that moment, so potent was his gaze, the touch of his hand at her back. If only he'd ask her to go somewhere else besides the boat and bed.

It was cold on the river when they returned. Elise shivered as she lit the lanterns. A fog had formed in their absence and the sail home would be slow.

'Elise,' Dorian called out, working the sails. 'Go below to the cabin and stay warm. Open some champagne and I'll be down shortly. But don't, under any circumstances, take off that dress. I want to do that.'

Elise climbed down the ladder to the cabin, her mind on the lovemaking to come. Maybe tonight, she'd finish what she'd started with the champagne the night of the fire. Between her distraction and the darkness, it didn't register until too late that she wasn't alone. Someone was in the cabin! She could make out the vague form of a man.

She summoned a scream, but it never came. A rough arm seized her from behind, dragging her against a barrel-chested form, a hand clamped across her mouth. A match flared to life across the cabin, illuminating the form of a man, this one with dark satanic eyebrows and black eyes. He calmly lit the lamp and crossed his legs, sliding a sharp-looking knife out of a sheath.

'Please, Miss Sutton, have a seat. I don't believe we've been formally introduced. I'm Damien Tyne.' He fingered the knife. 'I believe we have unfinished business.'

Real fear came to Elise for the first time since the whole duel for the shipyard had begun. The man before her was evil personified, from the devilish wing of his dark brow to his sinister eyes. She knew instinctively he was a man who gave no quarter. She had not truly guessed the depths of such malevolence.

The fear fuelled her. She fought her captor, kicking and twisting in his grip, but she was no match for the burly giant. He wrested her into a chair and shoved a gag in her mouth in spite of her best efforts to stop him. Tyne tossed him a length of rope and fright coiled in her belly at the thought of being entirely helpless against the knife, at being unable to warn Dorian.

Tyne gave her an oily smile. 'We can't have you running off until our business is concluded. How long do you think it will be before Rowland joins us? I do so look forward to meeting him again.'

Elise strained her ears. She could hear Dorian's footsteps overhead. She could hear him call out her name, wondering what was taking her so long to retrieve the champagne. She struggled against her bonds, desperate to warn him, to tell him not to come down.

'Elise! Whatever are you doing?' His voice was closer now, his feet nearing the ladder. She willed him to stop, to use some sixth sense to know danger waited below.

'Ah, good,' Tyne muttered. 'It won't be long. Your lover and I go back quite a ways, Miss Sutton. Perhaps he's told you?' His eyes slid in Bart's direction. 'Get ready.'

Elise watched in horror as Bart positioned himself behind the doorway with a club. Dorian's boots appeared first. He had a fraction of a second to take in Tyne's appearance, his hand reached instinctively for the knife in his boot but he couldn't retrieve it before Bart's club met with his skull. The thud of wood on a skull sickened her. Elise felt her stomach churn. She watched Dorian collapse unconscious. She was on her own. It would be up to her to save them both.

Chapter Twenty-Two

Why in blazes did his head hurt? Dorian groaned against the pain. There was bound to be a lump. He attempted to raise an arm to test the side of his forehead and found he couldn't. In his befuddled state it took a moment to realise why. He was bound at the wrists and ankles. What was going on? This was not Elise's doing.

He pushed his fuzzy mind past the throbbing to gather his thoughts. Elise had gone down for champagne. He'd come to check on her and then? Tyne! He remembered that awful last moment of consciousness. Tyne sitting on the cabin bench, looking smug, fingering his bloody, ever-present knife, and Elise bound to the chair, eyes wide with terror. He'd bent for his own knife, but too late. He'd been set upon from behind.

The reality of the situation hit him with full force. Tyne had Elise. Dorian had no idea how long he'd been out. How much time had Tyne had? What had he done to her? Dorian willed himself not to panic. He was alive and for the moment that was all that mattered.

He couldn't save Elise if he was dead. Tyne must have crept on board the yacht while they'd been at dinner. Dorian sorely wished he'd hunted the man down in spite of Elise's objections.

He forced his eyes shut against the great temptation to take in his circumstances. To open them too early would be careless and dangerous. Once he indicated he was conscious, the next level of the game would be engaged. He needed to be ready. There was light, he could feel it on his face. He could also feel hardness beneath him. The bastard had left him on the floor, probably right where he'd fallen. He could also feel stillness. The boat wasn't moving. Had Tyne pulled into shore somewhere? That seemed unlikely and it would indicate he'd been unconscious for some time. Tyne wouldn't risk pulling to shore so close to Gravesend where another of the yachting party might notice them. Dorian thought it was more likely they'd dropped anchor. Tyne would want the isolation of the water for whatever he had planned.

Dorian opened his eyes, his vision focusing on the bench. Tyne was there, all right, one leg negligently crossed over the other and drinking champagne. *His* champagne. Dorian knew a surge of anger, but none so great as the surge that took him at the sight of Elise, still bound to the chair. Her gag had been removed. There was no reason for it, Dorian supposed, now that he could no longer be warned.

'Ah, you're awake,' Tyne said in tones of false conviviality. 'We were wondering when you were going to join us.' He held up his glass of champagne. 'I am anticipating a celebration. Miss Sutton and I are about to reach a business agreement, aren't we, my dear?'

'Don't sign anything, Elise,' Dorian ground out, levering himself up into a sitting position against the wall.

'Not even to save you, Rowland? I think you might change your mind on that,' Tyne said silkily. He nodded to someone on the periphery of Dorian's vision. 'Bart, you know what to do.'

A hulk of a man approached, armed with Dorian's own blade. Dorian recognised him as one of the men from the break-in. 'Time for a little revenge, Rowland. Shall I start with your face or your hands, or maybe with something a little more dear? I seem to recall I owe you for a kick in the groin.' He jerked the knife in the direction of Dorian's testicles. Dorian drew up his legs. If the man got any closer, he could get one good kick in and it would hurt. Bart seemed to understand it wasn't going to be easy. Across the cabin, Elise choked on a scream.

'So you do care for him a bit. I was beginning to wonder, although you two looked cosy a few days ago during the trial run.' Dorian felt Tyne's gaze on him. 'I like to watch, you see.' A cold finger of anger ran down Dorian's spine. Tyne had spied on them. How much had the man seen? Tyne's gaze returned to Elise. 'Do you know why I like to watch, Miss Sutton?' He trailed a finger down Elise's jaw. Dorian's insides clenched.

'I like to watch because it's all I can do any more,

thanks to Rowland. He gave me an injury that has subdued my abilities to perform as a man should.'

'Was that before or after you burnt his ship?' Elise retorted. Dorian mentally applauded her bravado, but she had no true idea what she was up against. Tyne's evil knew no limits.

Tyne laughed. 'It was after, my little spitfire. As I said, it has *subdued* my abilities, it hasn't rendered them entirely useless and you seem to have a salubrious effect on them, my dear. Perhaps in a while we'll see just how salubrious.'

Elise did pale at that. 'I'll sign the deal if you let us go.'

'No!' Dorian yelled, keeping an eye on Bart. Bart's next move would bring a fight. He might be bound, but he was not helpless.

'Can I do him now, Boss?' Bart called out.

'No, I've changed my mind. It might be more fun to watch these two argue since they're at cross purposes. She wants to ink the deal and he doesn't.' Tyne finished his champagne and poured another glass. 'Bart, go up on deck and see how we're doing. The three of us are going to talk for a while.'

Dorian knew what was coming next. Tyne's favourite weapon aside from his knife was mind games. 'Don't believe anything he says, Elise.'

'Don't believe anything *he* says, Elise,' Tyne interjected. 'You're a pretty girl and a smart one to run your father's business. Have you thought about why Rowland doesn't want you to sign the deal? It's very simple. You're worth more to him with the shipyard. What are you without that? What could you possibly have that would appeal to a man like Rowland?' Tyne picked his nails with the knife. 'He's nothing more than a pirate. Has he told you? He ran arms.'

'Yes, I know all about it, Mr Tyne,' Elise snapped with impressive fortitude. Some of her colour was returning now that there was just the one knife between them.

'And you hold with that occupation? He encourages warfare, Miss Sutton. If there's no war, there's no business. He doesn't care for national loyalties. He'll sell guns to the French to use against the English if there's enough money in it.'

That wasn't how it had happened. Dorian gritted his teeth, struggling with his bonds. He was almost there. He could feel the ropes starting to slip. If he could just get his hands free, the playing field would be a bit more equal.

'I understand you do the same,' Elise replied coolly.

'I might. What do you care about what I do? You're not in love with me.' Tyne grinned cruelly. 'He would drag you down with him, turn your shipyard into a clearing house for weapons. He's seduced you into ignoring reason.' Tyne chuckled. 'What else has he told you? Has he filled your head with visions of sandy beaches and the Mediterranean? Has he convinced you to keep the yacht, spinning tales of racing it for prize money maybe?'

Good lord, Dorian groaned. The man had eyes everywhere. But what came out of his mouth next was by far the most damning. 'Make no mistake, Rowland wants this yacht. This boat is fast. He'd be unstoppable in it and he's willing to make love to you to get it.' He paused. 'I see the thought has crossed your mind, Miss Sutton. Why is Rowland so willing to invest his time in this project? You've wondered.'

'These are *his* plans, Elise,' Dorian argued, horrified to watch her eyes dart to him with the old doubts rising in their depths. Hot words from their old quarrel flooded back to him. She'd accused him of what Tyne accused him of now. But there was clarity, too. Tyne and Hart's plans were clear now. They wanted the better location to expand their own arms business. Tyne wanted to take the yacht back to the Mediterranean where he could continue to sell weapons to those who would fight the Empire while Hart arranged suppliers from here.

Dorian gave a final tug, his hands slipping free. He would wait for his moment. Tyne rose and leaned over Elise, his blade slipping through the ropes. 'Miss Sutton, if you'd come up on deck with me? You have five minutes to make your decision. If you choose not to sell, we'll have no choice but to fire the yard. If you choose not to relinquish this yacht to me, we'll have no choice but to fire the yacht as well. A pity, really, since you'll be on board. It's an incredible craft. Your father knew

it. But like him, you'll be able to go down with the ship.'
Tyne winked to Dorian as he shoved Elise up the ladder. 'You can go down with the ship, too, Rowland.'

You first, you conniving bastard, Dorian thought,
reaching to undo the ropes at his ankles the moment
he was alone. *You first.*

Elise stood at the railing, shivering from cold, from
fear, her thoughts racing in a thousand directions. Tyne
and Bart flanked her on either side. She knew where
they were. They were across from the shipyard. She
could see the pier dimly. She'd been foolish to think
any decision she could make would matter. She could
no more save herself than Dorian could. She was just
tied with a different type of cord. Tyne would not hesitate to kill her or Dorian. Tyne had killed her father,
demonstrating he'd go to any length. Dorian had been
right in that regard and therein lay her one last hope.

'I think you're bluffing,' she said with quiet authority.

'I beg your pardon?' Her words caught Tyne off
guard as she'd meant them to.

'You're bluffing,' Elise repeated. 'You won't fire the
yard. You've worked too hard for it.' Even as she said the
words, she knew he wasn't. In the distance, she could
hear Dorian's dog barking. Someone was there, waiting for the signal.

'I won't let Rowland have it. If I can't have it, neither
of us will have it,' Tyne answered with an unconcerned

shrug. 'You should believe me. The same goes for you and the yacht, in case you're wondering.'

'What guarantees do I have you'll let us both go if I sign?' Elise replied smoothly. Dorian's cynicism had rubbed off on her. For the moment she was glad of it. She stared across the dark water, gauging the distance. Could she swim for it? The distance was not great, but the waters were choppy and cold. Her skirts would be heavy within moments and it would mean leaving Dorian to his own luck. Even if she made it, there'd be an enemy to deal with once she came ashore. Whoever waited in the yard was not her friend.

'Two minutes, Miss Sutton. Bart, prepare the signal.'

'Is this the deal you made my father?' Elise asked as Bart moved away. If she meant to jump, she'd need to do it now while there was just one of them.

'No, he never saw me coming. It was easy enough to fix the steam valves. I didn't trust him. If he suspected anything, he might have left a letter or a clue behind and alerted you.' Tyne chuckled. 'I've been most generous with you. It was Hart's idea. He thought two deaths in the family would be suspect. *He* felt things would follow a natural course of events without violent intervention, but you exceeded our expectations and our time limit. You've had all the time in the world, Miss Sutton, and now your time is up.'

'You're wrong, Tyne. Your time is up,' came the unmistakable rough tones of an angry Dorian Rowland.

Elise turned, instinctively moving away from Tyne,

but not fast enough. Tyne grabbed her about the waist and hauled her to him, blade pressed to her throat. She stifled a gasp, not wanting to distract Dorian with her fear.

'I see we're of a like mind.' Tyne sneered at Dorian. 'You've got my Bart and I've got your girl.'

Dorian shoved Bart aside, his corpse already limp. She hadn't realised. 'Bart's dead and you'll be joining him shortly.' There would be no signal to the shipyard. The boat works was safe, that was something at least. 'Put her aside, Tyne. It's always been about you and me. Let us settle this once and for all.' Dorian held his arms open in a 'come-on' gesture, tempting Tyne to battle.

'Better yet, fight me for her,' Tyne growled. 'Maybe you'll live long enough with my knife in your gut to watch me have her. It will be the last thing you see before you die.' He released her then, shoving her into Dorian, hard. Dorian stumbled from the sudden impact, caught off balance. Tyne took advantage, leaping towards Dorian as Dorian pushed her aside to safety. The gesture cost him. Tyne's blade sliced into Dorian's arm. Even in the dark she could see the blood seeping from the gash.

Dorian switched the blade to his other hand. 'Come on, are cheap tricks all you have?'

'Better than you, Rowland, you've only got one good arm now.' Tyne laughed.

'It's all I'll need.' Dorian advanced, creating a graceful, lethal dance about Tyne in a tight circle that left little margin for error.

Determined to make herself useful, Elise crawled to Bart's form, frantically searching in the dark for what she wanted. Her hand closed over the metal of a pistol butt and she knew a moment's relief, then a moment's terror. She had a weapon and the weapon was empty. Still, there might be a chance to use it. She willed herself to watch and to wait.

But watching was hard. Dorian struggled. Blood flowed from his arm. He couldn't toy with Tyne for long and Tyne knew it, too. Elise saw Tyne's plan instantly. All he had to do was wait Dorian out. Dorian's strength would fail unless he struck soon. And he did. Dorian made a swift lunge, catching Tyne in the shoulder. Blood spurted. She covered her mouth with a hand to keep in a scream, the only thought she had was *good, the playing field is equal now.* Dorian staggered, his back to the rail, clutching his shoulder. The effort had cost him.

Tyne advanced clumsily, giving no quarter. This was her chance if she meant to take it. She couldn't stand there and watch Dorian die. What had Dorian told her once about his death? Ah, she had it. Elise stepped forwards, pistol raised as she called out, 'Do you think the murder of a duke's son will go unpunished, Tyne? Kill Rowland and the Duke of Ashdon will bring down a retribution so swift and sinister you'll wish you'd died.'

Out of the corner of her eye, she saw Dorian edge towards her, leaving Tyne alone at the railing.

The words had the desired effect. But she didn't want Tyne to have too long to think about them, lest he decide she was bluffing. She held the gun steady. 'This has to end, Tyne. Neither of you is in any shape to fight.'

Tyne's breathing was ragged. Even in the dark, he was pale. 'What do you propose?' His eyes slid to the waters. She knew what he was thinking: did he have the strength for a getaway? Could he reach the water before she fired?

'A race. My yacht against a yacht of your choosing. Winner takes all. A duel on the Thames. My second will call on Maxwell Hart tomorrow.'

'Done,' Tyne growled and then he was gone in a surprisingly fluid moment over the rail. She heard the splash of him hitting the water and she lowered the gun to her side, weary. She slid to the deck, her legs turning to jelly now that it was over.

'What have you done?' Dorian half-staggered, half-crawled to her side.

'Saved your life.' She thought he'd be a bit more relieved. Frankly, he sounded ungrateful.

'You've risked the boat, Elise.' Dorian lay on his back, catching his breath.

'I had to do something. You weren't having much luck,' she said briskly. She fumbled with his shirt, dragging it off him. Her first thought was to stop the bleeding.

'How docs it look?' Dorian tried to peer down at the gash.

'It could be worse.' Elise fought back bile to look at the damage. It was bloody, but the gash was not as deep as it might have been. 'It hasn't hit bone,' she assured him.

'It hurts like hell,' Dorian groaned.

'I'm sure it does, but you'll live.' It wasn't said glibly. A few minutes ago she hadn't been so sure either of them would.

'You could have shot him.' Dorian groaned as she wiped at the blood.

'I could have, but that requires bullets. I only had a boat.'

Dorian tried to sit up. 'God, Elise. You faced him with an unloaded gun? What were you thinking?' Dorian bent his head to hers. He was warm and sweaty and he smelled of life.

She put her hand against his cheek. 'I was thinking I loved you, silly man.' She didn't give him a chance to respond. 'Let's get you on your feet and down below where I can take care of you properly.'

It was cumbersome work getting him below, but she managed. The yacht was stocked with staples for the day voyage. There was alcohol for cleaning the wound and fresh bandages for any incidental injuries. Once below, Elise made quick work of bandaging.

'How's your head?' Elise said, tying off the bandage.

'Still reeling.' Colour had returned to Dorian's face. That had to be a good sign.

Elise reach up, fingers in his hair to search out the damage from Bart's club. Bart had certainly got the worse end of that deal. But Dorian's hands closed over hers and drew them away. 'I'm not reeling from the bump. Sit down, Elise.'

'What is it? Are you sick? Feeling nauseous?' Elise asked anxiously, searching his face for a sign.

Dorian shook his head. 'It's not from any injury. It's from you.' His hands tightened over hers. 'It's not every day a man hears "I love you". It's not every day a woman risks the thing she holds most dear for him, either.'

Elise flushed. 'Well, it's done. Now we have a race to win.' She paused, the enormity of what she'd done sinking in. 'We will win, won't we? You said the yacht was fast, that it was unstoppable. Is it true?'

Dorian gave a half-smile. 'I guess we're going to find out.'

Elise nodded. There was going to be a lot of 'finding out' in the next few days. She loved Dorian Rowland. She'd confessed as much tonight. But how far would she go for that love? How much of what Tyne had said tonight was true? Could she live with a man who had no national loyalties? Most of all, would that man even ask her to? Had she risked it all for a man who couldn't love her back once again?

Chapter Twenty-Three

'You've been up a while, Dorian. I missed you.' Elise joined him at the rail where he stood watching the morning come alive. Sunrise was his favourite time of day, a luxury he'd seldom been able to afford himself. They'd stayed on board last night, trying out the new bed. There'd been no question of trying to dock the boat in the dark with the fog and him sporting only one good arm, even though they were just across the water from the shipyard.

Elise had wrapped a blanket about her shift and her hair hung loose and dark about her. His groin tightened. Sunrise was his favourite time of day for other reasons, too. There wasn't anything quite like making love in the morning. It got the day off to the right start. She stood beside him in silence, taking in the quiet of early morning with him. If only life were this simple, waking aboard a boat each day with her. Neither of them spoke. He knew both their minds were full, although he doubted her mind contained the erotic thoughts plaguing his.

He passed her the cup of coffee he held in his good hand. She smiled as she took it. Perhaps that was a good sign she wasn't angry. She'd told him she loved him and he'd not given the requisite response last night. Or maybe it was a bad sign? Maybe she'd rethought that confession and no longer cared? 'What happens now, Dorian?' she asked in the stillness.

He looked at her, taking in her chemise and the blanket. He let a wicked grin play across his mouth. 'I take you back to bed and make good on my promises from last night before we were so rudely interrupted.' A man had to try, after all.

She smiled in spite of the shake of her head. 'We can't keep going to bed instead of resolving our issues, as delightful as the option is.'

Dorian leaned on the railing, looking out over the water. 'What's on your mind, Elise?' It would be one of two things: him or Damien Tyne.

'There are some things Tyne said last night,' Elise began hesitantly. 'He sells arms to anyone who will buy, even the French. He sells them good English guns to shoot English soldiers. Do you?' she asked in a tight whisper. 'Are you of the same mind? Was he right about that?' She was watching him, holding her breath. That had to bode well. She hadn't given up on him. She wasn't regretting her efforts last night, but she was deciding. He knew that much. Elise was a businesswoman.

She would be weighing what she could live with and what she could live without.

'I've run arms in the past. I've told you as much. There's good money in it and in my youth the thrill was quite extraordinary,' Dorian admitted. 'But never, Elise, never did I sell to the French or to anyone knowing beforehand that those arms would be used against England.' The discrepancy hadn't been enough for his family. Would it be enough for her?

'What do you run these days?' She still hadn't looked away.

'Expensive items others aren't willing to risk. It's hard to explain, Elise. These days it's about speed. Britain might have tamed the Mediterranean, but people will pay well to get their items to market faster than anyone else. There's still danger. There are those who will pay to stop goods from reaching markets in order to enhance their own profits. It's simple supply-and-demand economics.' Dorian shrugged. 'We have an expression in the Mediterranean. If the sea belongs to no one, it belongs to everyone.'

Elise nodded. 'That phrase has been bandied about Britain quite regularly in the last decade. My father even used it in his own conversations with investors.' She gave a little laugh. 'I think it might be the Navy's secret motto.' Elise paused. 'I'm starting to see why Giovanni was so grateful to you; why it was so important you took his wine to market.'

Now it was his turn for questions. 'Why do you care, Elise, if I ran arms to enemies or not?'

'Because I have to know how much loving you will cost me and whether or not I can pay that price, just in case you might love me, too,' she said softly.

He should have said the words last night. But even now with a second chance before him, he couldn't say them. 'Don't you know the answer to that already?' He'd like to take her below and show her.

'I'm not sure I do.'

'I can't change for you, Elise, if that's what you're thinking.' He might as well get it out in the open. If she thought he'd reconcile with his family and stay living in London, she'd be severely disappointed. She had to know that already. 'My family believes I am a traitor. As for myself, I have no wish to rejoin society's fold. I have no desire to stay in London *ever*. I was only here because I had a cargo to deliver and I'll be leaving as soon as I can arrange a ship back.'

'I wouldn't dream of asking you to change. I thought I'd made that clear.' Elise looked away, but not before he sighted tears in her eyes. She'd known his answer and had still been disappointed by it. Had he somehow misread what she was fishing for? Was there something else she wanted from him?

Elise straightened her shoulders. 'Well, we have a race to win. I imagine we both have business to take care of before then. How's your arm?'

'It will be fine.' Dorian threw out the rest of his coffee into the river. 'I'll get us ashore.' So much for a morning tumble. So much for a second chance. Maybe it was better this way. What good could saying 'I love you' do if he couldn't be there for her? An impossible relationship would hurt all the more when he sailed away after the race. He really couldn't stay any longer.

'I'll see that you have your money, Dorian. Will you be able to pay the workers for me? I will need a day or two to get the funds.' She halted. 'Seeing as how the boat isn't going to sell, I'll need to speak to someone about our art collection. It should bring enough to cover expenses.'

'I can make those arrangements.' If they were in Gibraltar he could have given her the money. But he had no funds here. Here, he was a veritable pauper. It was better this way, he repeated to himself. Gibraltar beckoned. In Gibraltar, he was a king and he was free. He turned from the rail to watch Elise walk back to the cabin, her hips swaying beneath the blanket, her hair gently buffeted by the breeze. Something new inside him, something that had just begun to live since he'd met her, was starting to die. And he knew, *just knew*, it would never be resurrected if he didn't save it now. It couldn't end like this.

There was only one thing he could think of to say. 'Come with me, Elise. Come to Gibraltar.' The words were out of his mouth before he could think. She turned. His world stopped. *Let her answer be yes.* He closed his eyes and waited for Elise Sutton to seal his fate.

* * *

Say yes. Her fate hung in the balance. Conventional wisdom would have her reject the proposal out of hand, but the realities of the past months suggested otherwise. She didn't belong here. Yesterday had made that clear. She could build the fastest ship the world had seen and it wouldn't be enough. At the beginning of this adventure it had seemed straightforward: build a ship and everyone would respect her. She would pick up where her father had left off.

But yesterday's outing had proved otherwise. She would not be allowed to. There was no place for her here. Society had spoken. Richard Sutton's daughter would not be permitted to build her boats here. The race with Tyne would be the final scandal. After that, any bid for respectability would be over. Still, she wouldn't go with Dorian simply because there was no place here for her. There was her heart to consider as well.

'Say yes, Elise.' Dorian held her gaze intently. She could not be swayed by that gaze.

'Say yes to what, Dorian?' She took a step towards him. Women couldn't go haring off to foreign ports with men without certain guarantees, guarantees she didn't think he could give.

'Say yes to building your yachts in Gibraltar. We can sail them up to England for those who want them and there's a market down there from the Spanish, the French—everyone, really. People need boats for business, for pleasure. And no one would care about the silly things. Think how grand it would be, Elise—you and me, bashing about the Mediterranean, building yachts, racing yachts, the sandy beaches, even the dolphins. I have the most beautiful house in the hills.'

She gave a little laugh. He could make her laugh at the most inopportune times. 'I'd been warned you might try that line of reasoning.' She'd moved within arm's reach of him, her body unable to resist what her mind felt compelled to argue against.

'It's a good line. Is it enough, Elise, to convince you to be my wife and live in Paradise forever? I love you. I should have told you last night.'

In that moment, she knew what she wanted and it stood before her, even though accepting it broke every rule left to her. Elise Sutton threw caution to the winds. 'Yes, it's enough.' She twined her arms about his neck and kissed him hard on the mouth. Why not? What had the rules ever got her?

'Does everyone understand the rules?' Commodore Harrison stood on a bunting-draped dais above the crowd assembled for the race. In the days before the race, rumour of the event had spread throughout fashionable London. Elise shaded her eyes against the sun and looked up at the dais. 'The race shall begin here at Blackwell and shall end at the Thames Tavern. The course shall pass Erith, Rosherville, Gravesend and Lower Hope Point. There shall be no foul play, no cutting across the other's bow or the like. This is to be a fair match, gentlemen.'

Across from *Sutton's Hope*, *Phantasm*, Tyne's personal yacht, bobbed black and sleek on the water. The breeze was good today, and both boats' sails billowed eagerly. Elise looked away, trying not to concentrate on the fine lines of Tyne's boat. Dorian stood at the helm of *Sutton's Hope* with Drago beside him. He radiated confidence and her own confidence soared. Dorian would not fail them.

Them! Her heart beat a little faster at the prospect. They'd win this race and then they'd go to Gibraltar and start their life. The future lay just past today. Dorian's eyes met hers. His hair was down, his eyes glowing with fierce competitiveness. He was dressed for the sea today in his culottes and bare feet, his shirt open at the chest, his shoulders bare of any coat. He'd not wanted to be confined by any concession to fashion today. He'd need all his strength at the wheel. For a moment he looked past her and mouthed the words 'My father.'

Elise turned to catch sight of the Duke of Ashdon's coach along the side of the river, in line with so many other carriages ready to follow the progress of the twenty-mile race. She smiled at Dorian. 'Better not let him down then.'

'Gentlemen, at the ready!' the Commodore shouted out and the crowd stilled. The flag was dropped and they were under way.

The water was smooth in the early going and the

Hope made the most of the wind. The *Phantasm* sailed beside them, easily keeping pace, the crowd on the river banks cheering them on. Plenty of money would pass hands today. But by Gravesend the weather began to change. The sun of the morning gave way to clouds. The cheering crowds thinned out, daunted by the mounting winds and greying skies. By Lower Hope Point, a full storm was engaged.

Sutton's Hope began to rock. Elise prayed the narrow frame and the buoyancy bags would hold. The last portion of the race was upon them. *Phantasm* began to make its move, slicing closer to the *Hope* in the water. Now that witnesses had thinned to almost nil, Tyne was taking more chances.

'Take the wheel, Elise!' Dorian yelled over the wind. 'We need to reef the mainsail, we need a flatter entry point for the wind or we'll flip.'

Elise took the wheel, feeling the yacht buck beneath her, the wheel fighting her to stay on course. The last thing they needed was to drift too close to shore and chance the rocks. She shot a quick glance at the *Phantasm*. It was pulling ahead and Tyne was refusing to reef his sail, taking a gamble with the wind. Above her, Dorian was in the rigging, working the sails—first the Cunningham to move the draught point. He managed with confidence, unfazed by the height and the wind, but she'd relax when he was safely back on deck.

She felt the results of reefing immediately. The wheel stabilised, the boat no longer pulling against her, but the *Phantasm* was moving ahead. 'Reefing has cost us some speed,' she said over the wind when Dorian claimed the wheel.

'Not for long. The wind will start to work against him,' Dorian said confidently. 'By the time he is forced to reef, it will be too late. It's always easier to bring in the sail before the storm hits in full than during.

'It's time to make our move, Elise.' They'd charted this course in the days before the race. The race would be won in the last miles. They'd take advantage of the *Hope*'s low hull and the *Phantasm*'s confidence.

Dorian drew up slightly behind the *Phantasm*, using the other boat as a shield against the wind to regain speed. Tyne waved an angry fist their direction. 'Stop draughting, Rowland!'

Dorian shouted back, 'You should have reefed your sails when you had the chance!' When the yachts were even, Dorian swung back out into the centre of the river, using every trick he knew to harness the wind and gain an edge. He needed a slight edge to dominate the river. The plan was to block out the river through serpentines and swerves so the *Phantasm* could not pass them in the curves at the end of the course.

'Go, Dorian! Now,' Elise shouted, surveying the course from her post at the prow of the ship. This was critical. If they could manage this manoeuvre, they'd have the race.

Tyne realised his mistake too late. In an effort to hold position, Tyne swerved into the *Hope*. If Dorian veered, he would give up his position on the river. If he didn't, they would likely collide unless they simply weren't there when Tyne's boat arrived. They needed more speed.

'Elise! The wheel!' Dorian was at the ropes, adjusting the sails with swift, sure movements, the wind in his wet hair, his shirt plastered to his chest. He looked primal in those moments, a man against all. He looked triumphant in the next as the *Hope* shot past the *Phantasm*'s intended strike point.

The Thames Tavern point came into view through the rain, the last spot before the Thames gave out into the open ocean. A few carriages waited on shore. Elise thought she could see the Commodore and the flag. The *Phantasm* was close, though. She could see the crew. She imagined she could hear Tyne cursing over the wind. But it didn't matter, they were almost there. Then they were, sailing past the flag, victorious and whole. They had won!

She turned to throw her arms about Dorian in celebration and screamed. She couldn't believe it. Tyne was breaking the rules! The *Phantasm* had turned too sharply and was aimed at the stern of the *Hope*. At these close quarters there would be no escaping. 'Dorian, no! Don't slow the boat! Full speed!'

Dorian let the sail fill, they shot past the Commodore, the *Phantasm* close behind. A new race was engaged, a race with no rules and the open sea ahead of them. Dorian was grim at the wheel, the sails were open in spite of the dangers. There was no margin for caution now. He was desperate for speed, calling on all his expertise to marshal the wind to his advantage.

'Grab hold of something, Elise, we're going to tack hard to starboard!' It was all the warning she had before the boat lurched, waves rising grey and menacing as the yacht took to its side.

Dorian tacked again and again, creating a zig-zag pattern through the water, each pass drawing them closer to land. 'Isn't it dangerous to get so near shore?' she shouted.

'That's the plan! We want to lure them in and turn sharp enough to avoid the rocks while they get stuck on them.'

In a flash of insight, Elise understood. 'But we could wreck!'

'Not if your design holds. She's tacking beautifully, Elise.'

But the rocks neared and Elise paled. Dorian had nerves of steel, but she did not.

'Does Tyne guess?' It looked like the *Phantasm* was keeping up fine.

'Oh, he guesses.' Dorian smiled. 'But he thinks he's smart enough to avoid it.'

Dorian tacked, once more, twice more. The *Phantasm* neared. She could see Tyne's dark eyes, they were that close. Tyne drew a gun. At this angle, with their side exposed, Tyne would not miss. 'Dorian!' she cried out. Dorian turned, but not fast enough. The shot fired. She threw herself at Dorian, knocking him aside. They went down, sliding across the tilting deck. The bullet whistled overhead, the boat was listing, waves rose, slopping the deck. Dorian scrambled to the wheel, struggling to right the yacht. Balance was slowly restored.

Elise scrambled upright, sopping and wet. 'Look!' Behind them the *Phantasm* had run aground, the yacht caught up on the rocks. 'He'll be arrested.'

'I don't know about that.' Dorian breathed heavily, his clothes dripping.

'I do. Your father's there. That's his carriage, isn't it?' Elise pointed in the distance at the entourage on the coastal road converging on the grounded yacht. 'He followed us the whole time.'

Dorian laughed. 'Well, I'll be.' Then he sobered. 'We're well past the finish line. Shall we go back and claim your prize?'

Elise wrapped her arms about his waist. 'Why go back? The ocean is right there. Seems like we should just keep going. We meant to anyway in a few days.'

Dorian's blue eyes looked down at her. 'Do you mean it? What about all your things?'

Elise smiled up at him. 'Everything I need is right here.' And it was. She reached up and kissed him. Her practical side couldn't resist asking, 'You do have the five hundred pounds from your last job though, right?'

Dorian laughed. 'Tucked away in my wife's reticule.'

His wife. She liked the sound of that. It was almost

true. She'd be his wife in truth just as soon as they reached Gibraltar. 'Good, it's right where it belongs then.'

'And you are right where you belong, in my arms.'

Two weeks later, Elise stood on the beach in Gibraltar, her hands clasped firmly in Dorian's grip, the gauzy white fabric of her dress fluttering against her legs. Her feet were bare, her toes curled into the warm sand while she listened to the vows that would bind her to Dorian Rowland for life. They were pronounced man and wife as the sun sank over the sea as if on cue. There could be no more perfect wedding in the history of the world, even if this one was attended by more waves than witnesses. Her heart was full.

Dorian bent to kiss her. 'You have succeeded in living most scandalously, Mrs Rowland.'

'I have succeeded in living well,' she replied. Life had become infinitely simpler the moment she'd stepped on to *Sutton's Hope* with nothing more than Dorian's trunk and the money in her reticule. 'Thanks to you.' She meant it. With Dorian, because of Dorian, she was who she was meant to be.

Dorian drew her away from the priest, taking her to the water's edge and letting it lap their toes. 'Is it all you'd hoped?'

'You're all I hoped,' Elise answered honestly. Dorian was something of a modern pirate, racing the tides and merchants to market for the best prices. There were definitely those who were jealous of his success. But he was also something of a king here in this part of the world, she'd discovered. People came to him, asking for favours, asking for help. And he gave it. Some of those people were farmers like Giovanni's relatives; some were diplomats looking for ways to broker alliances through goods and trade. Wherever Dorian went, life would always be exciting and it would always be fast—she'd see to the last part.

'I think this turned out pretty well, Mrs Rowland,' Dorian said as the last rays of light disappeared on the horizon. 'You needed to be lost and I needed to be found.' It was true. She'd had to lose everything to find the one thing that mattered. Now that she'd found him, she'd never let him go.

'Our wedding night awaits,' Dorian whispered naughtily. 'Shall we?' He gestured towards the stairs leading up the cliff to the Spanish-style villa.

Elise smiled. She was about to be royally screwed. Funny how her adventures kept coming back to that same point. This time quite literally and with the emphasis on the screwed.

* * * * *

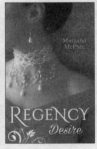

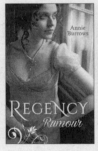

MILLS & BOON®

The Regency Collection – Part 2

Join the London ton for a Regency
season in part 2 of our collection!

Order yours at **www.millsandboon.co.uk/regency2**